But he had scarcely given utterance to the words, when a terrific flash of lightning caught the tree, near to which he was, and split it to the root, striking him at the same time.

THE

MAID OF THE VILLAGE;

OR,

THE FARMER'S DAUGHTER.

BY

MRS. KENTISH.

LONDON:

PUBLISHED BY E. LLOYD, AT THE OFFICE OF THE "ILLUSTRATED EDITIONS OF STANDARD WORKS," 12, SALISBURY SQUARE, FLEET STREET.

1847.

THE MAID OF THE VILLAGE.

CHAPTER I.

" These two, a maiden and a youth, were there
  Gazing—the one on all that was beneath,
  Fair as herself, but the boy gazed on her ;
  And both were young.————————"

I ask no pledge to make me blest,
  In gazing when alone ;
Nor one memorial for a breast,
  Whose thoughts are all thine own.—BYRON.

THEODORE had resolved to pursue his way to Oxford, by easy journeys on horse-back, in the early part of the morning and in the cool of declining day, and to remain one night on the road.

It was a delightful evening at the close of July, when they stopped at the principal inn of a pleasant hamlet, about eighty miles from the Park, and, having taken refreshment, he sauntered out to enjoy the beauty of the evening

Attracted by the surrounding scenery, he wandered a considerable distance, until a winding path led him through a shady lane to a beautiful valley. On one side he beheld extended plains covered with flocks, on the other hills crowned with richly-laden orchards, and fields yellow with the golden treasures of autumn.

The breeze came laden with fragrance, and a sentiment of indescribable luxury stole over Theodore's senses. "How true," said he, "are Shelly's remarks, that

> ' Our simple life wants little, and true taste
> Hires not the pale drudge Luxury, to waste
> The scene it would adorn———————'

Oh, that my future hours might glide away amidst these delightful recesses."

Here a clustering village, with the spire of its church, appearing from amongst the foliage of embowering elm and beech trees, there a variety of cottages from amidst the gardens, gave animation to the scene.

But one of these rustic habitations peculiarly attracted Theodore's attention, and he took the path that wound around it. Its green latticed windows were half concealed by the intermingled branches of the honeysuckle and the jasmine, the exuberant tendrils of the vine encircled its rustic porch, and formed a striking contrast with its white front, whilst several vases of flowers, tastefully arranged, adorned its windows.

"It is impossible," said Theodore, "that any but a mind of superior cast can have planned this sweet retreat, and the exquisite garden surrounding it." A few snow lambs gambolled over the emerald verdure of the little hill that arose behind a clear rivulet led its crystal waters through the valley that wound below.

Theodore was pursuing his path, when a female voice enchained him to the spot, whilst in a strain of native melody she sang the following air :

> Oh, sweet Contentment, come and smile
>   Upon my rustic cell !
> In vain ambition shall beguile,
> Or Fortune's lure or Pleasure's wile,
>   With thee alone I'll dwell.
> A rural altar here I'll raise,
>   Thy constant votary be ;
> My lyre shall warble forth thy praise,
> To thee I'll tune my rustic lays,
>   Oh, come and dwell with me.

The voice ceased, but it had sunk deeply into Theodore's soul. Was it enchantment? What expression—what silvery sweetness of tone! He sought for an aperture in the surrounding foliage—he found one, and looking anxiously through it, he beheld a form—a countenance of which features and complexion formed the least charm.

"This then," whispered Theodore, "is the presiding goddess of this delightful scene!" He scarcely dared breathe, as his eye followed her sylphide form. Here she stooped to pluck a withered leaf from a favourite myrtle—there she entwined the wandering branches of the clematis around the mountain ash. At length, over powered by the warmth of the evening, she threw off the straw hat that had hitherto shaded her features, and her exuberant ringlets fell on a neck, white as the clustering lilies that grew beside her path. She raised her hand to throw them aside,—every action was replete with native elegance, her form that of a wood-nymph, her cheek the exquisite tint of the newly-blown rose.

"So lovely a casket," said Theodore, "must contain a gem of equal lustre!"

"Adela, Adela!" exclaimed a female voice from the window, "your father is coming, love."

The interesting cottager hastily replaced her hat; with the step of a sylph she ran to the garden gate, leaned anxiously over it, and looked to the valley below. A graceful figure, in the habit of a peasant, crossed the opposite corn-field. Adela was by his side in a moment : she tenderly embraced him, placed her lovely hand within his arm, and they slowly ascended the path that led to the cottage. They entered, the gate closed, and Theodore remained entranced in a vision of loveliness that appeared too exquisite for reality.

Could there be a sweeter picture of filial tenderness and parental love? The voice that warned her of her father's approach, the smile of pleasure that irradiated that bewitching countenance—her haste to welcome him; everything assimilated with the cottage, and the scenery around it; everything bespoke its inhabitants elegant, amiable, and united by the purest affections that can embellish human nature, uncorrupted by the vices, follies, and dissipations of the busy world.

Awakened to a sentiment entirely new, an hour had elapsed before Theodore (anxious that some fortunate chance might produce the re-appearance of this lovely vision) had moved from the position in which he stood when the door closed. And he might still have remained, his arms folded, and his eyes fixed on the cottage, but for a heavy shower. Roused at length from his reverie, he beheld a light at the window, which he supposed to be her chamber, and a white hand closing the casement, and drawing the muslin curtain, which shut out his ardent gaze : he then pursued his reluctant way back to the inn.

Ralph had ordered supper at half-past ten, that his master might retire early, so as to obtain sufficient repose to proceed on their journey in the cool of the morning. He stood watching his return from the window. Eleven o'clock struck—then half-past. When the pelting shower commenced, he could no longer restrain his anxiety, but taking an umbrella, and throwing his master's cloak over his arm, he sallied forth in the direction which he saw him take when he left the inn.

But Theodore in his musings had struck into another road, which brought him back by a different path. After a long search, and numerous inquiries of the several villagers chance had thrown in his way, he returned, and found his master seated by the open window, lost in a profound reverie.

"Won't you change, sir?" said the anxious fellow.

"*Never!* It is impossible," replied Theodore. Ralph smiled. It was, indeed, an odd reply.

"I suppose your honour is joking with me," replied Ralph, "but your clothes are wet, and I have got out your dressing-gown and slippers."

Theodore had been for a moment the inhabitant of another sphere; but Ralph's observation brought him back, and with his usual suavity he approved the arrangement, and urged the kind-hearted lad to take the same precaution; who, delighted to see his cheerfulness restored, stationed himself behind his master's chair, while he took his evening's repast.

Theodore retired to his pillow, but not to sleep. The Village Maid, in the elegant seclusion of her father's cottage, her soul-beaming beauty—her innocence—her unaffected tenderness for her father—were yet before her eyes. Every action, every circumstance of those few delightful moments passed again in succession before his imagination ; and if at the approach of morning, sleep came over his eyelids, it was only in his dreams again to "hang enraptured o'er her song."

Ralph was among the first who were on foot in the inn. He got every requisite arrangement in forwardness. His master's breakfast, with every little delicacy the hamlet could produce, was laid by the assiduity of the landlady beside the window that looked into the garden. Eight, nine, and ten o'clock struck, but no bell summoned his attendance. No sound !

Ralph crept softly to the chamber, and unclosed the door. The noise, though gentle, awakened Theodore, and he replied with his usual kindness to Ralph's inquiries,—

"It is a fine day; everything is ready, sir. Will you continue your journey after breakfast?"

"Why, I don't know, Ralph, I have a headache ; and I fear the day will be too far advanced by the time breakfast is over."

"It seems as though it would be a very warm day, sir ; and, may be, the sun will make your head worse."

"Well! we will pursue our route in the evening."

Theodore breakfasted, and had just dressed, when the sky became clouded.

"We shall have a thunderstorm," said Ralph.

Theodore sighed ; his thoughts were in the cottage on the brink of the valley.

The day continued wet ; and notwithstanding his impatience and irritability, he was obliged to defer his anxious wishes. He, however, determined once again to enjoy the felicity for which alone his journey had been delayed, even at the sacrifice of another day from his studies.

"Would your honour please to have a newspaper, or a book to amuse you, this dull morning ?" said the landlady of the inn, on entering with three neatly-bound volumes on a waiter ; for she had resolved no one should attend the young gentleman but herself. "And will you please, sir, to accept a rose or two out of the garden?"

Theodore received the flowers with his accustomed condescension, and selecting one out of the books, he sought to wile away what he trusted would be only a shower.

In about an hour he closed the book, threw up the window and looked anxiously out. The rain still continued to fall amidst the lilac-trees and rose-bushes that decorated the garden.

Dinner was ordered ; four o'clock arrived, still the sun's golden lustre remained eclipsed by a heavy opaque mantle of dusky clouds.

"Fate really seems resolved that I shall not see my lovely girl to-day," murmured Theodore, "the rain is coming down in torrents !"

Dinner concluded ; Ralph placed the wine and fruit on the table.

"This will be a clearing shower, sir," said he, "it is too violent to last."

In another hour, Ralph entered again. "The rain has passed off beautifully, sir—will you leave this evening, or take another night's rest, that you may get quite rid of the cold you caught yesterday evening ?"

"I have not absolutely determined," replied Theodore ; "the sun is breaking out delightfully—return this volume to our good landlady, I will see what effect a cup of coffee will have on my head. I will then take a short walk—and when I return I shall perhaps feel more decided."

The past rain had rendered every scene yet more delightful than on the preceding evening. Again the woodland choristers mingled their lay of love with the breeze, that came laden with freshness and fragrance. Many a sparkling gem trembled in the bell of the lily, and the bosom of the newly-blown moss-roses, that grew around Adela's cottage window.

Theodore watched every casement. His eye rested on the arbour. It glanced with eager haste down the shady avenue and unsheltered walks of the interesting retreat ; but not a shadow of its lovely inhabitant! He heard from the conversation of two farmers, that the greater part of the neighbours were absent at a fair in the vicinity. How vexatious, that such an opportunity should pass, without the exquisite enjoyment of uninterruptedly gazing on her! At the sound of a foot his heart palpitated, the rustling of a leaf filled him with emotion.

Adela at length appeared at a distance ; her mother leaned on her arm ; she carried a small wicker basket of Spanish workmanship.

"What exquisite loveliness! She indeed," whispered Theodore, "needs not the foreign aid of ornament. In her russet gown and simple straw hat, Adela is irresistible."

Concealed behind the arbour that formed an angle of the flower-garden, he saw her ascend from the valley ; he listened to her voice. She had been on an angel's errand, ministering to the wants of a neighbouring villager, suffering under sickness and affliction. Oh, that he could speak to her—could gain one glance of recognition.

They entered the cottage. The mother sat down to her needlework, and Adela spread their evening's repast, whilst her father took a book from a small library opposite the window, and read to them in a sonorous voice, and in a style that evinced a superior education, occasionally pausing, to infix the moral of the tale more impressively on the mind of his daughter, by appropriate observations.

Oh! with what regret did Theodore observe the conclusion of their repast—how breathlessly listen to their evening devotions! With what sorrow did he see the windows and the door closed for the night! and the excluding muslin again drawn by that fair hand across the window of that sacred shrine of innocence and peace.

And wouldst thou, Theodore, disturb that peace? Wouldst thou chase that innocence?—Heaven forbid!—what then is thy purpose? Thy father is avaricious, proud, and ambitious. Adela a simple village maiden, her only dower her artless beauty; her only wealth, her parents' love, and the halcyon of peace of her own guileless bosom.

Theodore felt irritable and uncomfortable; he had in fact no fixed purpose; he scarcely knew what he wished, but he felt that he could climb rocks, and traverse burning deserts one-half of his existence, if the other half were to be recompensed by listening to her voice and gazing on her smile.

Theodore tore himself from the fascination that hung about even the inanimate objects around that magic abode. He returned to the inn, complained of indisposition, awakened many doubts and anxieties in the heart of his faithful Ralph, declined supping, and retired to a sleepless pillow.

When alone, he ventured thus to question his heart:—

"Why this perturbation, this irresolution? Was Adela the only lovely female on the earth? Are there not many women of fortune, amidst the circles of his uncle's and his father's friends, highly educated and remarkable for beauty? Alas! would they bear the comparison? Oh nature! thou art indeed pre-eminent!" sighed Theodore; and he resolved, since he could no longer with prudence delay his return to Oxford, to visit the oak that spread its shadow over Adela's bower, at the dawn of day, and inscribe on its bark an indelible proof of his love and his despair. But who is this young enthusiast? We will revert to a scene of his early infancy—a period when the chords of an infant heart first responded to the touch of sorrow, and that will lead us gradually to the present moment.

CHAPTER II.

A serious, subtle, wild, yet gentle being,
Graceful without design.—SHELLEY.

"And where are you going with those flowers, Theodore?" said Mr. Villars, as the blue eyes, shining through their tears, were raised to his countenance.

The question startled him—the memory of a thousand little scenes of maternal tenderness had rendered him unconscious of his father's approach, until his hand was placed on that beautiful shoulder, which appeared yet more exquisitely fair in contrast with his mourning robe.

"Where are you going with those flowers, my boy?"

"To the grave of mamma!"

"My poor child!—but this only keeps up an affliction that will do you harm, and will not bring your mother back to you!"

Theodore's hand sank on his bosom—his infantine anguish found utterance in sobs that were almost hysterical, and his tears fell amongst the flowers his hand had gathered. One, enshrined in the bosom of a newly-blown rose, sparkled so beautiful—a tribute of filial regret, that it might almost have won the pure spirit from its heavenly sphere back to this sublunary scene of sorrow and vicissitude.

And what might not have been expected from this dawn of virtuous sensibility—had not an erroneous severity at one period, and a misplaced indulgence at another, perverted a nature which had awakened the fondest hopes of his lamented mother. But that gentle bosom was now cold, and the little Theodore deprived of her tender admonitions.

Louisa Warthington, under the care of the most enlightened of parents, had attained her seventeenth year, blooming as the children of Flora, that shed their fragrance around on that sweet month that hailed her entrance on this varied scene. Death then deprived her of a father, and the vicissitudes which had previously removed them from a mansion to a cottage, on the estate belonging to Villars Park—now weighed yet more heavily upon them.

Fate seemed relentless in her pursuit of this family—for the same month that deprived them of an adored husband and fond father, not only destroyed the little income produced by his recent exertions, but also, by the failure of their banker, the little wreck of their former affluence,—carefully set aside as the resource of age.

Edward Villars saw the lovely mourner; he had been drawn by an almost magical attraction to a nature altogether the reverse of his own; for wealth had hitherto been the idol of his devotion—the love of wealth had checked the tear that started to his eye, as he hung over his father's bier. It had induced him to make proposals for the hand of one, of years sufficient to be his mother, whose nature was repulsive and her person uninteresting.

For the honour of humanity I trust there are few young hearts thus indurated. It is in the nature of youth to be alive to all the beauty of virtue—brave to heroism— replete with benevolence and generosity—the charms of nature should awaken in the youthful bosom a sentiment of enthusiasm elevating the soul to its Creator, with a pure and sincere adoration. Self-interest, avarice, cold-heartedness render youth a being out of nature, which must awaken our apprehension and even terror, for what a succession of years, with all their dark realities, may make him.

Villars had been in the habit of seeing Louisa, during occasional visits to the cottage, and (as their landlord) had always been received with politeness. He had offered to have any improvement made in the cottage or garden which Louisa's taste might suggest—merely to form an excuse for his visits. He was unconscious that even then he was binding himself irrecoverably in the chains of her attractions; but it was not until death had laid her lamented father in the dust that he had dared breathe, even to his own cold heart, the project of rendering their desolation the medium of her dishonour. But how little do such beings appreciate the power of that intellectual beauty which casts its halo around the form—the features it irradiates—" driving far off each thing of sin and guilt." Edward Villars rode over to the cottage, ruminating upon the wealthy alliance which would enable him, without incurring the self-reproach of imprudence and prodigality, to proffer the lonely orphan and her mother an income better suited to the sphere of life to which they had been accustomed.

He dismounted at some distance—gave his horse to his servant, and pursued his course along the flower-embroidered path that led to their dwelling; the door stood half open, but what a vision of beauty presented itself!

The lovely Louisa—her pale cheek streaming with tears—knelt at the feet of her widowed parent; her beautiful arms were thrown round her, whilst, with the tenderest accents of persuasive eloquence, she pointed to that future scene when their present trials would be rewarded by a re-union with their beloved, deplored one, amidst a scene of never-ending felicity!

Villars did not possess a mind alive to the pure spirit of real piety; but he had a powerful tincture of religious prejudice. He was neither guided by reason nor reflection, but preserved the unquestioned opinions inculcated by his father, who had received them hereditarily. But, however insensible to the sufferings of others, selfishness rendered him keenly alive to the fears of a future state of retribution, and it was with a sort of tremulous awe that he paused on the threshold. Her sentiments astonished him! Was this the being who could submit with cheerfulness to the severest deprivations whilst cheered by the consolation of a self-approving mind? She, whose lovely lips, repeating the benign precepts of her departed parent, pledged herself to devote her remaining days to virtue. Was it then this seraphic being whom he had selected as the victim of immorality? Impossible! the words died away on his lips; his voice faltered, and before the hour he had passed at the cottage had elapsed, he had positively arrived at the point of making her an honourable proffer of his heart and hand—receiving a promise from her mother of a decisive answer on the following week.

Louisa's heart had never awakened to any sentiment but that she had felt for her parents; the care, the agonising anxiety with which she hung over her father's pillow while hope remained, had passed away. He was now a pure spirit—"above he joys—beyond the cares of life," the inhabitant of a celestial abode! The sole object of absorbing interest was now her hapless, her declining, her widowed mother,—there every energy concentrated to cheer, to console her—the tear was dashed away—the rising sigh stifled, and a melancholy smile assumed as a veil to overwhelming regret;—with her she wished to live—with her to die—amidst their present cherished obscurity. But for her mother she trembled to reflect on the future —there nought awaited them but the severest destitution, and all that contumely

> " Which virtue sunk to poverty must meet
> From giddy passion and low-minded pride."

All the little domestic elegancies, the vestige of happier hours, had passed away one by one, to provide for their daily necessities ; they were deeply in arrears for rent, and the steward, conscious of his master's usual severity, had not been very measured in his terms, when he found it was still likely to remain unpaid. She ooked hopelessly around her—her mother's languid eye was turned to her—she gazed on that pallid countenance and wasted form ; they were irresistible ! The empire over self was gained, and in a month from that period, the lovely Louisa was mistress of the mansion at Villars Park, whither her mother, by previous stipulation, removed with her.

But it is not with a heart devoted to selfishness, mean, petulant, and proud, that a soul replete with sensibility can assimilate. Occasions were not wanting soon after their union to awaken the young and lovely bride to a sense of her situation ; her pallid cheek, her languid eye—spoke of her soul's despair—and the unkindness evinced to her beloved parent, during the last hours of her existence, rendered this impression indelible.

Louisa wept over her lamented mother's tomb—a long and severe illness followed ; but the sensibilities of a then joyous heart were directed into another channel. She became a mother, and while she clasped the baby form of her Theodore to her bosom, she felt—as the wanderer, who finds a spring amidst the desert. She felt that heart was still alive to bliss, and that she had yet a duty left to perform !

The gentle, the generous benefactress of all within the sphere of her influence, the return of the day on which she first arrived at the Park—was held as a little festival by the villagers. But, alas ! the sixth anniversary had scarcely been celebrated when she was laid in the tomb, and the little Theodore, then only five years of age, became alive to a sorrow which for many months refused all consolation.

Villars felt his loss ;—there was a want of comfort in every room in the spacious mansion. He loved his boy :—he did not like to hear his question (while he hung over her lifeless form), " when mamma would awake ?" or his bitter wailings when he found how lasting that slumber ! With Villars this impression was not lasting, nor did it require any very powerful effort to overcome it. He determined on taking this opportunity of passing a month at his town residence ; this purposed month was extended to six weeks ; at the end of which period, on his return, he could see her portrait, her accustomed chair, her silent harp,—yes ! even her lovely boy, without any further uneasy sensations arising in his heart.

With the infant Theodore it was far otherwise ; he would sit for hours together— his little arms folded on his breast, contemplating her picture. Every morning the fairest flowers were gathered to adorn her tomb—where tears of inconsolable sorrow—of the truest affection, were scattered to her memory.

Day succeeded day, until Theodore had attained his eleventh year. Left altogether to himself, unless at those hours when his father sought his society as a relaxation from the weight of his own ; his education would have been altogether neglected, but for the care of the housekeeper, who, fondly attached to her departed mistress,—highly educated, but reduced from a superior station—devoted every leisure hour to the cultivation of a mind, which formed, even at that period, a singular combination of beauty and eccentricity.

Impetuous and versatile, alternately joyous and serene, he would leave his young associates, in the midst of their diversions, to seek the solitude of the shadowy recesses which beautified the grounds surrounding the Park; gather lilies that grew on the borders of the lake; or listen to the sound of the leaves scattered in his path by the breath of autumn. Ralph, his faithful Ralph, a young villager, whose mother had been among the participators in his departed parent's benevolence, who had been received an infant orphan at the Park, and brought up with Theodore as his future attendant, was his constant companion. In gayer hours he would steer his young master's boat on the lake—engrave his name on the bark of the spreading oak which extended its branches above, sheltering them from the sun and the shower—gather him the earliest strawberries, or point out to him the many-tinted rainbow, that shone over the dewy mountain. When sad, he followed his steps in silence, mingled his tears unobtrusively, and in secret, and watched the first returning smile, as the night wanderer for the earliest dawn of day.

Theodore had made choice of a beautiful little spot of ground on the border of a stream. Assisted by Ralph, he carefully cultivated it; the most beautiful shrubs and plants, the acacia, the myrtle, the moss rose, the dahlia, a variety of heaths and geraniums mingled their brilliant tints and exquisite fragrance. During two entire months, every morning, they visited this favourite retreat; every evening it was watered from the stream.

Theodore had arisen earlier than usual; and, as Ralph had gone to the nearest town to purchase him some additional drawing utensils and new books, he sauntered down a path which was separated from an adjoining lane by a hedge of sweet-brier: something like a contention caught his ear, and through an aperture he perceived two lads, much his seniors, who had taken a beautiful linnet, which each resolved to possess:—a contest ensued, and the young barbarians would undoubtedly have destroyed their helpless little captive, had not Theodore leaped over the hedge—valorously overcome both his antagonists—and having then satisfied their united demands for the bird (which he had determined should not incur any farther danger from their violence), bore it off in triumph.

Theodore found its little wings had been closely clipped; his first purpose, therefore, of giving it its liberty (for bondage of any description was revolting to his feelings), was rendered impossible. On Ralph's return, therefore, a spacious cage was purchased, and Lillo (for this was to be his future name) suspended in his chamber, charmed and cheered him through many a morning and evening hour.

The garden was now neglected. Theodore was alternately employed in finishing some drawings, reading the new publications Ralph had brought him, and listening to Lillo's strain of melody. The weather was intensely hot; Ralph, absent on one of his young master's missions to his uncle, Sir John Villars, who resided many miles distant; and more than a week elapsed before he passed that way: at length his garden recurred to him—but what a change! the earth was parched and dry; his myrtles, his favourite flowers, were withered, and weeds had sprung up in the path where they had never before been suffered to intrude. A sentiment of sadness passed over his mind—he returned thoughtful and pensive; but Lillo warbled forth one of his favourite melodies,—and the garden, its weeds, and its withered flowers were forgotten.

And long might Lillo have retained his ascendancy, but that Ralph, on his return, brought a beautiful spaniel, as a present from Sir John to his nephew. Theodore was delighted; he had heard and read a thousand interesting tales of the sagacity of these faithful creatures. This was, indeed, a welcome present— an acquisition of the utmost importance. Walking or riding, Dash now became his constant companion; and the last amount his benevolent arrangements had left him (for Theodore's heard was " open as day to melting charity,") was expended in a silver collar, carefully lined with crimson velvet.

Theodore was so incessantly engaged by the sportive gambols of his new favourite, in playing with him on the lawn, washing his beautiful silken coat in the stream, and showing him to his young associates—that days elapsed before his imagination reverted to his once cherished favourite! In vain did the little captive warble his lay of pathetic complaint, shake his plumage, grate his little beak across the wires of his gilded prison;—Theodore heard him not—heeded him not; and it was not until the arrival of Sir John, who came to spend some days at the Park, and who, taking a great interest in all his nephew loved or regarded, inquired for his bird—that he ran to the cage.

Lillo, Lillo!—alas! Lillo heard him not; the little sufferer's sorrows were at an end. His feathers ruffled, his beak sunk upon his breast, his eye glazed,—he was no longer conscious of the voice, or the encouraging chirp of his master.

A sentiment of grief, of agony, stole over Theodore's heart, which now lent its keenest reproaches—was it for this, then, that he had protected and preserved him. Alas! better a momentary death than the lingering torture of such a fate as thine. He sighed as his warm tears trickled on the little lifeless form. Oh! that his remorse—his regret, could restore him! the wish was unavailing, and Theodore, silent and gloomy, sought his favourite solitude. Ralph vainly endeavoured to console him—in vain did Dash, putting his two fore-paws upon his knees, place his head upon them, and, with a whining sound, express his sympathy.

Theodore's heart was tenderness itself, and if, when by a momentary dereliction or unintentional forgetfulness, he at any time inflicted pain on others, he felt so deep a regret—what must have been his affliction when the seal of death had prevented all compensation?

But Theodore accompanied his uncle on his return to Beechwood, and change of scene, variety of amusement, and cheerful society, succeeded in banishing sadness from his youthful heart. Sir John had also so strongly urged the necessity of his nephew being put under the care of an intelligent tutor, that his father at length consented, and the period between eleven and eighteen, produced a most salutary improvement in a mind that only required the hand of culture.

In the year following, Sir John was so eloquent in favour of Theodore's being sent to college—that, much as Mr. Villars shuddered at the expense which must necessarily be incurred—not daring to disoblige his uncle, he consented. His heart also whispered him—that with a finished education, united to so graceful an exterior—his son might in a few years, aspire to the hand of one of the wealthiest heiresses in England.

And well might Theodore excite a father's ambition—there was a fascination in his countenance, totally independent of the elegance of his features; his eye beamed with intelligence, his dark brown hair waved over a forehead which might have served as a model for a sculptor, his form graceful as the Apollo of Belvidere, and his heart free as the breeze that blows over the mountains.

Such was Theodore Villars when he arrived at college—a brilliant degree of native talent, united to that assiduity which carries everything before it, in a few months secured him the esteem and approbation of every professor, whilst his gentlemanly deportment, frankness, and, above all, his generosity, drew around him crowds of summer friends.

Liberally supplied by his excellent uncle, Theodore acted as though his funds were inexhaustible; but the numerous parties of pleasure in which he had at intervals engaged, the tales of distress to which he had lent a favourable ear, and the sums he had lent on the promise of having them repaid the moment certain remittances arrived (which remittances by-the-by never came, or at least, were never acknowledged), soon convinced him to the contrary.

Theodore wrote to his father for a renewal of his funds—a most resentful reply brought disappointment, and that sort of embarrassment entirely new to him; week succeeded to week those who were indebted to him shunned him, those to whose pleasurable excursions he could no longer contribute neglected him, and those to whom he could no longer lend calumniated him. Disgusted with those around him, and vexed with his own thoughtlessness, Theodore resolved to pass the remainder of his time in the seclusion of his own apartments—to economise the trifling sum he had left, and to act more prudently when his new consent

arrived.   Amidst this change of sentiment one only individual retained his esteem ;
but he had been too sincere from his first arrival, to be a welcome associate.

There was also a tincture of pensiveness, almost amounting to melancholy, in
George Clifford—little consonant with the noisy mirth of the giddy and the gay
votaries of dissipation, who taking advantage of the liberality of an unsophisticated
heart, had borne him along in their vortex ;—he had also, in some degree
withdrawn the attentions he had evinced to Theodore, as a stranger ; because, as
his advice had been neglected, and almost regarded as resulting from an over-
strained fastidiousness, he disdained to intrude where his attentions had not been
appreciated.

The novelty of the scene had also worn considerably off, and Theodore's cheerfulness had almost abandoned him, when Ralph entered the room, and presented
him with a letter from his father.   Theodore started—the seal was black—he
hastily broke it, and read as follows :—

"My dear Boy,   Beechwood, July 18th.

"My uncle is no more—never mind, your sorrow will not bring him
back again ; he has left you an excellent property.   Return instantly—I enclose a
small sum, which may liquidate any debts you may have contracted."

Theodore lost no time in preparing to obey his father's summons.   He left
Oxford without delay, and arrived at the Park on the following evening.   His
father succeeded to the title and hereditary estates ; but the greater portion of the
personal property had been bequeathed to Theodore—Sir Edward being appointed
as trustee, until his son should attain the age of twenty-one.

To Sir Edward, it will be pretty evident, the consolation came with the event,
but it was not so with Theodore.   Grateful, affectionate, warm-hearted, gladly
would he have made any sacrifice, could he have prolonged the existence of his
venerable relative ; and he followed his remains to their last abode as a real
mourner !

The manner in which Theodore's return to Oxford led to his visit to the village
on the brink of the valley, we have already described.   Let us now return to the
inn where we left him in a feverish and perturbed repose.

CHAPTER III.

'Tis past revealing,
The bosom's first awakened feeling !
When the young heart from long repose
First wakes, then tremulously glows
With loves's sweet pangs—and raptured woes.—Bandit Chief.

At the earliest dawn of morning Theodore arose, and having taken a blank
leaf from his pocket-book, he wrote with his pencil the following stanzas :

Oh, were I but the fragrant flower,
That blossoms on her rustic bower ;
Then haply I might please her eye,
And on her snowy bosom lie ;
Or e'en that rivulet so clear,
My lovely maiden wanders near.
Or that sweet bird whose woodland song
Is warbled these rude wilds among ;
For she with tender sympathy
Lists to its plaintive melody ;
Whilst I—unknown, unheeded—sigh,
The slave of hopeless constancy.

He then left the inn, unperceived by Ralph, and pursued his way to the cottage ;
with his penknife he engraved the name of Adela on the oak on that side next the
garden, and placed his poetical tribute, neatly folded, in the midst of a bed of
violets just below.   He stood some moments leaning against the tree, his eyes

earnestly fixed on the window—the curtain was yet drawn, the smoke arose in curling wreaths from the surrounding cottages; he saw the neighbouring hinds winding their way towards the various scenes of their daily occupation—the milkmaid sung as she passed him with her pails, but all was silence, all tranquillity in that interesting abode.

"Sleep on," said he, "lovely innocent Adela! may the angel of peace shed her roses over thy pillow, and retain the tenderest sentiments of thy poor heart unawakened—until that future hhour, when I again shall seek these halcyon recesses—not altogether, perhaps, hopeless of obtaining thy smile!"

He retraced his steps, and arrived at the inn just in time to prevent Ralph going in search of him ; for breakfast was in readiness, and it was not without a certain degree of anxiety that he found his chamber deserted.

"Well, Ralph," said Theodore, as he placed himself at the table, Ithinkwe shall take advantage of this brilliant morning to pursue our route, but I have a little commission for you previously."

Ralph was delighted at all times to receive a commission of any description from his master ; it added to his self-importance, it seemed to apply a confidence in his capability, and he anxiously approached to receive his commands; whilst Theodore proceeded to give him, in the first instance, a description of the situation of the cottage, its garden, and grounds, and then expressed his wish, that he should obtain all the intelligence possible in the neighbourhood, relating to the beautiful Village Maid and her parents ; for it seemed utterly impossible so much elegance of manner, so much taste in arrangement, could proceed from positive rustics.

Ralph listened with eager attention to every particular, and, as he took the road to the village on the brink of the valley, a new light dawned on his mind.

"Oh, oh!" whispered he, "I fear master's illness and his want of rest, has been brought on more by his heart than his head !"

Ralph seemed to tread on hair—he never lost a moment in the execution of any plan of which Theodore was interested, so the breakfast-table had scarcely been cleared, when he entered, evidently exhilarated by the success of his mission.

"Well, Ralph! what intelligence of the inhabitants of the cottage?"

Why, sir, I went as your honour directed me, but as I've heard that a village alehouse, or a village barber's, is considered the best market for news, I stopped at the little inn on that side near the five-barred gate—I think the sign's the Plough."

"Never mind the sign," said Theodore, "have you obtained the intelligence I require?"

"Oh, yes, sir!" replied Ralph, "and there is the most beautiful young lady in the world in it ; but, if your honour will give me leave, I'll begin from the first."

Theodore assented with a smile, and Ralph proceeded.

"Well, I went into the Plough, sir, just for all the world as though I was a traveller, and after ordering a bason of bread-and-milk for breakfast, I sat down in the bar, for the good woman was very civil, and a nice-looking young body, too, sir.'

"Nice weather, sir ?" she said.

"Very pleasant indeed, ma'am," said I.

"The corn looks pretty fair, doesn't it?" says she.

"It looks particularly well in that field."

"Which field ?" says she.

So I got up, and going into the little parlour that goes out of the bar—for the window looks just across a meadow to the back of the cottage, on the edge of the valley—I pointed to the field at the side.

"Yes, and so does all in our neighbourhood," said she.

I then admired the cottage.

"If you admire the cottage," said she, "what would you say if you could see the owner's daughter ?"

"Why," I answered, "is there anything so very remarkable in her ?"

"Adela St. Clair! anything very remarkable," said she ; "I should think so ; why she is our Village Beauty—our queen of the May! many a heart she has set aching, I'll warrant ye."

" I should fancy," answered I (just you see, sir, to get all out of her I could), " I should fancy, she'd get a rich husband."

" And plenty she might have if she chose," replied she—" the excellent offers that girl has refused !—In my mind, her heart's so full of affection for her mother and her father, that it will never find a place for any one else."

I then asked who her parents were.

" Why," said she, " Mr. St. Clair is now the owner of that cottage, and he farms the land round it, that is, he is a small farmer ; what he has been nobody can exactly guess, but everybody suspects he has been some very great gentleman, there's such a difference between his manners and those of the other villagers ; and then he is so learned ! he knows such a many languages ! and then Mrs. St. Clair is such a lady, and a saint upon earth ! to see her when any of the neighbours are sick, carrying them medicine of her own making—nourishment, that they perhaps can't afford ! though themselves far from rich,—and their sweet child ! sacrificing her sleep, her rest, her amusement, everything, and watching over them like an angel, for she is as pretty, and I do believe as good a one too."

Theodore arose and went to the window to hide the emotion, of which he was ashamed.   Ralph continued.

" How long have they lived in these parts ?" says I,—" for I thought, sir, I'd find out every thing."

" Let's see," said she, " I think Adela St. Clair was just sixteen last May—the 23rd of May—she was just a year and one month old, when they came ; yes ! they have lived in that cottage fourteen years.   Mr. St. Clair built it himself ; they lived in that on the right, while this was getting ready, and moved into it on the 23rd, Miss Addy's birthday."

" By this time, sir, I had finished my breakfast," said Ralph, " and hastened forward to give your honour all the news I could gather.'"

Theodore had listened to the recital of his servant with intense interest !—not a sentence had escaped him—not a scene described, but he had in fancy witnessed ; his imagination had followed the lovely Adela in her benign missions of consolation and charity ; he had beheld her smile, that seraph smile of dimpled fascination, irradiating her humble yet happy home, her parents' sole remaining earthly blessing ! he beheld her—the ardently-sought for prize—the darling ambition of many a youthful heart ; (why should his throb with so painful a vibration ?) the unattainable treasure, as yet insensible to all ! a dawn of hope, a sentiment of bliss revived in his bosom ; but not daring to pursue the train of his own imaginative musings at that moment, he made an effort to rouse himself, and the next half hour beheld him passing the turnpike gate.

Scarcely dared he turn his eyes in the direction of that scene of enchantment ; but followed by Ralph, rode at full speed down the road that branched off from the path he had taken on that eventful evening.   A moment's pause and his resolution had abandoned him ; nothing but flight could avail him.   In vain did the fascinating languor of a first-awakened passion urge his stay—in vain did every breeze whisper Adela ! Theodore was for once victorious ; he acquired in this instance a perfect empire over himself, and on his arrival at the (to him) cheerless seat of science, he applied himself resolutely and unremittingly to his studies, resolving to compensate himself by an early visit to the cottage on the brink of the valley.   But by this time, a sufficient interest will be awakened in the cottager St. Clair, and his lovely daughter, to render a relation of their previous history not unacceptable.

CHAPTER IV.

——————— He had ceased
To live within himself; she was his life,—
The ocean to the river of his thoughts,
Which terminated all: upon a tone,
A touch of hers, his blood would ebb and flow,
And his cheek change tempestuously—his heart
Unknowing of its cause of agony.—BYRON.

AMBROSIO's first dawn of intelligence (for by this name we shall at present distinguish the hero of the following little narrative,) arose on a scene of wild luxuriance and beauty. His protectress, a Spanish peasant, found him, an infant alone and crying bitterly, in the forest that led to her cottage. She took him home, dressed him in the vestments of her own baby, who had died some months previously—felt consoled by his artless endearments, called him by his name, and cherished him as her own.

Growing in strength and beauty, the little Ambrosio wandered amidst the exquisite scenery of that delightful land; he loved to run races with Sabastiano—to catch the oranges he threw down from the trees that overshadowed their little garden—to collect the grapes he had gathered, place them in the basket,—and imagined he assisted him greatly in carrying them to the kind-hearted Madelina, who had always their evening's repast spread at the cottage-door,—where the cool breezes of the evening seemed yet more refreshing after the fervour of the noon-day sun.

It was on one of these occasions that Don Manuel de Mello, having taken shelter beneath their humble roof from a heavy storm of rain and thunder, saw the little Ambrosio—he took the artless prattler on his knee, and, pleased with his blue eyes, light brown ringlets, and fair complexion (a style of beauty so unusual in that clime), he asked him if he should like to go with him to his castle, where he would find two pretty little play-fellows, a large number of toys, and extensive grounds to run and ride in.

Ambrosio hung his head—he looked through his dark eye-lashes at his affectionate Madelina, who had related the manner in which she had found him.

"You will, of course, be loth to part with him," said Don Manuel, "but you cannot evince your tenderness for him more powerfully than by accepting the advantages I offer him. He is a sweet child; and as I have long wished for a companion for my Luiz, in the retirement of our castle, they shall be educated together. Well, well! I see the tear in your eye," continued he, turning to Madelina; "reflect on the proposition I have made,—I shall pass this way on my return, in the course of nine or ten days; and if you determine on resigning your little companion to my charge, where, whenever you choose to undertake the journey, you shall be welcome to visit him—why, he shall accompany me."

So saying, Don Manuel put a purse into Madelina's hand, and rode off, for the storm had subsided, and Sabastiano removed their evening's repast, while she put her little charge to bed

But Ambrosio could not sleep—his innocent heart was contending with mingled emotions of affectionate gratitude and ambition.

To live in a beautiful castle! to have a great deal of money—which, with him, had no other worth, than that it would enable him to buy his dear Sebastiano a hat and feathers—just like Don Manuel's; and to make his beloved Madelina as fine as any lady in Spain! To have play-fellows! which he had never had before in his existence! But to leave Madelina! to pass days—perhaps months, without seeing her—without receiving her morning's blessing—her evening's kiss of love! He wept himself to sleep, and his pillow was wet with tears.

Sabastiano and Madelina also passed the night in anxious cogitations. The boy was dear to them as light, or life.—"What, then! should this tenderness be a bar to his future welfare? Suppose we should die," continued Sebastiano, "we are poor—my exertions can scarcely procure a subsistence from day to day—what, then, would be his fate?—Why, we should have saved him only for a heavier destitution, at a period when he would be more alive to it."

Madelina could not fail to yield to her husband's better judgment; and after shedding tears of tender reluctance over the sleeping innocent, and after resolving and relapsing repeatedly, during the space allowed for decision—her triumph was at length so far complete, that when the appointed day arrived, and a splendid carriage drove up to the cottage door—Madelina received him from Sebastiano's arms—clasped him with fervour to her breast—breathed a prayer to the Virgin, and not daring to trust herself with another look, consigned him to the care of Don Manuel de Mello.

No welcome could possibly be warmer than that given by the young Luiz, on the arrival of the little stranger. All his toys, books, aviary, young orange plantation, and his purse, became a joint concern. "From this moment, they are as much yours as mine," said Luiz, and as soon as Ambrosio was attired in a complete suit of his friend's clothes, until others equally magnificent could be prepared for him, he took him all over the castle and its beautiful grounds.

Don Manuel gazed on the youthful pair as they emerged from a shrubbery—Luiz's hand on Ambrosio's snowy shoulder, the dark eye, brown complexion, dimpled cheek, and ebon ringlets of the one; the blue eye, roseate cheek and glossy light brown curls of the other. The contrast was truly beautiful! and equally sweet the harmony produced by the cheerfulness of Luiz, and the pensive turn evinced by Ambrosio, even at so early an age.

Donna Angelica, the mother of Don Luiz, and the infant Aurora, possessed all the *hauteur* and family pride of her ancestors; she was, however, a fond mother—her conduct as a wife replete with complaisant dignity; and although, in the first instance, her distant manner chilled the heart of the little Ambrosio, in contrast with the extreme tenderness of Madelina, in a few weeks she was won by his artless gentleness and intelligence; and loved him because he was dear to her children.

At fourteen, Luiz and Ambrosio (who was apparently about a year younger,) had rapidly advanced in every branch of education; and, having the advantage of mingling their studies with the young people of a neighbouring castle, who had travelled through England and France, and had brought an English tutor in their suite, they had acquired these languages, in addition, with considerable facility.

But the lovely Aurora. Ambrosio had been her playfellow—Ambrosio had been the first to guide her fairy footsteps over the flowery lawn—to take one little hand while Luiz held the other, and lead her where Flavio, their favourite lamb, his neck enwreathed with roses, and ornamented with ribbons, awaited his fairy mistress. Ambrosio had first placed her pretty fingers on the strings of the guitar—had taught her to mingle her sweet voice with his, in the melodies of her country.

Meanwhile, Sebastiano and Madelina had availed themselves, on various occasions, of Don Manuel's permission to visit Ambrosio, had received many instances of hospitality at the castle, and numberless presents from their young friend, whom Madelina prophesied would certainly steal Don Aurora's heart before they grew much older, for no one could merit so beautiful a creature but her young cavalier!

When Don Luiz had attained his eighteenth year, a grand entertainment was given, to which all the neighbouring nobility were invited. Don Antonio de Mello arrived from Madrid; and after the three days' splendid festivities were over, he invited Ambrosio to accompany him with Don Luiz, on his return. Don Luiz accepted his uncle's invitation. Ambrosio declined it. He had hitherto been the lovely Aurora's instructor in English, music and drawing :—her parents evinced so much interest in her advancement, expressed themselves so delighted with her daily improvement—how could he absent himself? Ambrosio knew not that another—a far more powerful motive urged his stay!

> " There was but one beloved face on earth,
>   And that was shining on him; he had looked
>   Upon it till it could not pass away;
>   He had no breath—no being, but in hers."

And with a magic sympathy the same sentiment seemed unconsciously to have pervaded each guileless bosom.

Many months, however, had not elapsed, after the departure of Luiz, before the anxiety of the mother began to awaken suspicion in the bosom of Don Manuel—she had observed his hand tremble when placing the rose he had gathered amidst her daughter's beautiful ringlets—that the rambles of Aurora with her young tutor, beneath the rays of the moon, had become longer and more frequent—that there was a peculiar pathos in his tone and expression, when accompanying her on her harp ; that on the preceding day at dinner, when Don Manuel mentioned the proposals that were made for the hand of his daughter, Ambrosio's agitation was extreme, his countenance became pale as marble, and the glass fell from his trembling hand. That on the day before their son's departure, when Ambrosio was thrown from his horse, although not seriously injured, Aurora had fainted ; that her accustomed vivacity had given place to a thoughtfulness unnatural at her years : —in short, she assured Don Manuel, that if Ambrosio and Aurora were not now irrevocably in love with each other, they certainly would be so, if the former was not instantly sent away, and their daughter's nuptials with Don Ramella instantly solemnized.

"But why should the youth be sent away?" said Don Manuel ; "he possesses an immensity of good sense ; I do not believe his affection for our daughter is any thing but that of a brother ; but, even if he had any other idea, our immediate preparation for her nuptials would soon banish them. She is a good girl, and we shall not have much trouble in persuading her to give her hand according to our choice."

" Persuading !" replied the lady, " persuading ! truly, Don Manuel, you astonish me ! when I was a girl, I never heard of such a word—my parents both thought and acted for me,—command was their word, and obedience my reply."

"Well, my love, but we must allow a little for a girl half spoiled by all of us, and a heart, which, according to your account, is more than half given away."

" Indeed, Don Manuel," replied the Lady Angelica, " I loved Ambrosio as a child, although I have always fancied he looked more like a native of England than Spain. But when I saw him grow up so handsome and so accomplished, I thought what would occur from your allowing him such free access to your daughter ; but I did not oppose your wish, because I knew if I proposed one line of conduct, it was ten thousand to one but you would have adopted the very reverse."

" Perhaps in this instance I may have been wrong, but if an attachment has—"

"Attachment !" interrupted Donna Angelica ; "who would for one moment suspect a young lady, morally brought up, the daughter of one of the first houses in Spain, with her grandmothers and aunts, to say nothing of my own correct example before her ; who would, I say, suspect her of taking the liberty of forming an attachment ?

"When my father commanded me to become a bride, I thought of nothing but the selection of the most splendid jewels and richest brocades. Love, indeed ! marry first and love afterwards was my mother's motto ; but the young ladies of this age have the imprudence to love first, marry next, and ultimately become miserable ! But, Don Manuel, when will Don Ramella arrive ?"

"At the commencement of the approaching week," was the reply ; and Donna Angelica went to her dressing-room, and sent for her daughter to prepare her for the splendid alliance arranging for her.

A fortnight elapsed, (an age to these impatient and despairing lovers) during which time the Lady Aurora was cautiously confined to her own apartments ; Ambrosio's departure determined on, and letters of introduction written for him to Don Manuel's agent—and several of the first houses in Cadiz.

At length the day fixed for his departure arrived. Ambrosio with unequal steps paced the shrubbery ; he reached the little wood which had so long been their favourite haunt, and approached the grotto which stood beside the fountain ; whence that sigh ? he entered—" propitious Heaven !" it was Aurora, and, bathed in tears, he clasped her to his bosom.

" So then, Aurora! our dream of felicity is past, and this perhaps will be the last hour which will enable me to assure thee, that however fate may divide us, my heart will remain irrevocably thine, the last sigh it breathes, for thy felicity!"

" Alas! how little did I imagine," replied the weeping Aurora, " that when my mother requested you would assist me in my studies—when she permitted you to read, to ride, to walk with me—to pass so many happy hours together—that ere a few years had elapsed, she would order you away, and command me to forget you! Did not my father, a few months after your arrival, place my hand within yours, and smile when you kissed my cheek? did he not say, Ambrosio, she is your little bride! you must acquire every useful information; you must become a wise man and a brave cavalier in order to become deserving of her? when my brother Luiz left us, did he not unite your hand with his; did he not say, Luiz and Ambrosio, still continue as ye have been, brothers! educated together, the expansion of your minds has given a yet stronger rivet to that friendship, which I delighted to observe as the charm of your infancy? My father has too well succeeded in teaching me to esteem you! alas! how will he unlearn me the lesson?—how teach me to forget?"

Ambrosio wept, and Aurora leaned in tears on his shoulder.

"Alas, my Aurora! why did not my first protectress leave me to perish? why did not my second my more than father abandon me to that obscurity, which would have prevented my heart from aspiring to a felicity denied it by fate? Then I should have been the inmate of a cottage, amidst the seclusion of a forest. I should have laboured with Sebastiano during the day, and contentment would have brought repose to my pillow! agonizing refinement! which has rendered me susceptible to the charms of an angel! cruel destiny! which bids me wander an exile from her presence!"

" Or, Ambrosio," replied the weeping girl (looking tenderly on him), " had I been a cottager's daughter, and our parents had permitted our union, what felicity! to have shared thy humble fate, to have spread thy rushy couch, to have prepared thy rustic repast, to have watched thy return when the setting sun gilded our native mountains."

" Aurora! beloved one, cease! I dare not indulge my imagination in the scene of delusive felicity you picture; I am an outcast; honour, gratitude, all demand my flight. That hand is destined to another! I will hence," (continued the frantic youth striking his forehead) " to be the witness of this sacrifice were madness! Go! adored, lamented one! forget me, forget the past; yet should Aurora, (at a time perhaps not far distant) pass a humble tomb—lowly as the fate of its tenant—should she hear from some passing stranger that Ambrosio (his hopes for ever clouded, his heart withered) reposes within, she will haply strew one flower, drop one tear, to hallow the sequestered spot!"

" Ambrosio, dearest Ambrosio, forbear," said the weeping girl, " I will seek my father's presence, on my knees I will implore him, I will send for my brother, he shall be our intercessor. Live, live for me! while you are absent, forget me not! Remember! my heart, bound to you by the most indissoluble ties of affection, rises above the weakness of my sex. Ambrosio! I will be thine, by the consent of my parent; or follow thee, and share thy obscurity."

Ambrosio clasped her to his heart, and rushed franticly from her.

Ambrosio's first point of destination was the cottage of the good Sebastiano: he was welcomed with all the warmth of that disinterested affection, the bonds of which are bound more closely in adversity. He told them his destination without disclosing the reason of it, passed the fervid hours of the day beneath their hospitable roof, entreated Madelina to go from time to time to the castle to obtain intelligence of Donna Aurora, gave the name of the firm to which they might address any letters for him, promising to see them as frequently as so long a distance would permit; insisting on Madelina's accepting a purse containing a sufficient sum to add considerably to their comfort, and departed.

" Alas!" said the affectionate creature while she watched the last wave of his plume, as his receding form disappeared from her tear-swollen eye, amidst the forest foliage, " beloved child! I fear there is much more upon that generous heart than he will acknowledge." Sebastiano shrugged his shoulders and hummed an air, to conceal his anxieties, and Madelina retired to her humble chamber to weep, and kiss the solitary vestment in which she had found him.

CHAPTER V.

Thy presence only 'tis can make me blest,
Heal my unquiet mind, and tune my soul.—OTWAY.

WHEN Ambrosio arrived at his destination, he found that the gentleman to whom he had been consigned had made an arrangement for him, which only awaited his own approbation, with an English merchant, with whom his native language, united with his knowledge of English and French, would be an important acquisition; and Ambrosio, little heeding how his sorrowing existence might pass, since his adored Aurora was no longer to be its companion, agreed to it; he was not, however, indifferent to the prospect of independence it gave him, because he should be enabled to improve the hitherto adverse fate of his dear Madelina and Sebastiano —he had always also felt a powerful prepossession in favour of the English, and accepted Mr. St. Clair's urgent invitation to make his house his home, with a feeling of satisfaction which he could not have experienced on entering any other dwelling.

Mr. St. Clair's years could not exceed fifty: the slight silvery tinge of his hair seemed more the work of sorrow than of time,—and the melancholy which his young guest could ill conceal, seemed to bind them, even after a few weeks' intercourse, in closer unison. They always conversed in English; and Mr. St. Clair was much pleased at the facility with which the young Spaniard spoke his language.

Their evenings were employed in reading and conversation; and he frequently seemed anxious to discover the circumstance which had occasioned his young companion's secret grief, which seemed like the " worm i' the bud," to feed on and overshadow the cheerfulness so natural to youth.

Ambrosio wrote to Don Manuel a letter, in which he dared not trust himself to speak of Aurora. He sent his grateful remembrances to Don Angelica, and the friends of his earlier years; and expressed his warm acknowledgments for that competent provision for the future, which must always be acceptable to an independent mind.

Mr. St. Clair possessed a beautiful villa, whither they usually retired in the latter part of the week, and returned on the commencement of the following. On one of these occasions, Mr. St. Clair had gone to visit a friend at a neighbouring villa :— he was not, however, at home; and not finding Ambrosio in the drawing-room on his return, he sought him in the pleasure-grounds,—he passed softly round a shady path, and perceived him languidly reclining on the banks of the fountain. The tears chased each other down his cheek, and he imprinted a thousand kisses on the miniature of a beautiful girl, which he hurried into his bosom the moment he found himself discovered.

"Do not let me disturb you, my dear young friend," said Mr. St. Clair, as Ambrosio arose, in confusion ; " some little affair of the heart, eh ?" continued he, placing his hand on Ambrosio's shoulder. "But, seriously—if I can be of any service in banishing this melancholy—if the intercession of a friend will avail, I am ready to be that friend—if the unequal distribution of fortune has thrown a barrier between you—my coffers may, perhaps, supply the deficiency."

"Alas! my generous benefactor," replied Ambrosio, with that confidence this liberal proffer could not fail to awaken, " mine is an irremediable affliction; accept, however, my sincerest acknowledgements for this kind sympathy in the fate of a friendless stranger."

"Neither a stranger, nor friendless, while I live," said Mr. St. Clair, "time weakens the poignancy of grief—be comforted; my history (and on an early opportunity you shall hear it) will assure you, that there is balm on the wings of time !"

But the moment arrived when Ambrosio's anxieties were all to be concentrated to one agonising point. A letter was put into his hands. It was in the ill-traced characters of Sebastiano!—few the words, but their effect ran like wild-fire through his veins:—

MY DEAR YOUNG MASTER,

" If you wish to see the Lady Aurora alive, come immediately to my cottage.
" SEBASTIANO."

Ambrosio fell at the feet of his kind friend: he put the letter into his hands,—briefly related every circumstance from the time of his first entrance into Don Manuel's family—described the imperceptible progress of his tenderness for Aurora, drew her picture from his bosom.

" Will you, dear sir, permit my absence for a short period? Oh! should she expire without my seeing her?"

" Undoubtedly, my dear fellow;" said Mr. St. Clair, warmly pressing his hand, " go—take one of my best horses, my trustiest servant shall accompany you.—Perhaps this may be a blessing from Heaven—perhaps she is even yet not lost to you! Go! I will not detain you one moment—but in joy or sorrow be this your home! Write as early as possible."

Having given every requisite order, he insisted on Ambrosio's taking some refreshment, and entrusting a purse to the servant to be delivered to his young friend on the road, he accompanied him to the portal—exhorted him to hope for the best, and the anxious lover, putting spurs to his horse, was out of sight in a moment.

Ambrosio and his attendant travelled all night and all day—only pausing to take refreshment on his account.

It was about sunset, when, leaving Joachim, at a cabaret, where he ordered him to put up the horses, and await his return, he wrapped himself up in his mantle, and flew to the forest. It was a dark, rainy evening—the sod hummed under his rapid footsteps, over which his light and fairy footsteps had so often sported in infancy.

How different now were his sensations! The soul-harrowing words, " if you wish to see the Lady Aurora alive!" hung like a mourning-veil over her lovely image in his heart. " Was it at Sebastiano's cottage he was to learn his fate, previously to his going forward to the castle?"

Alas! many a heavy hour might yet detain him from her,—and the arrow of death might have stricken its victim before his swiftest speed could bear him thither.

The cottage is in view—the light twinkles through the lattice. It is a late hour for a light there! He hears a heavy step—

" What ho! my young master ?"

" Sebastiano—my good Sebastiano—tell, tell me all—let me not expire with suspense !"

" Oh, I am glad you are come!" This was accompanied by a grasp of the hand. In a moment they have passed the threshold. Madelina meets—embraces him warmly in silence—puts her finger to her lip, and leads him mysteriously to the inner chamber. Merciful Heaven! who reclines on that couch? with trembling emotion he approaches,—it is his own, his adored Aurora!

But, in what a state does she meet his anxious eye? her cheek is flushed with fever—she sleeps; but the tears are stealing through those dark lashes, her beautiful lips breathe his name!

As though bending before the shrine of a divinity he kneels beside her, he presses her burning hand to his lips, his forehead, his bosom, his tears fall on her pillow ; in vain did Madelina entreat him to be calm. " A good friar," said she, " who resides in the neighbourhood, and who is deeply skilled in medicinal plants, has visited this beloved child; he left her at sunset, at which time she fell into a more tranquil sleep than she has enjoyed since her arrival here—there is hope-dearest Ambrosio; be calm, and await with us the hour of midnight. Come, take some refreshment; I will remain here until your return, we will then together watch the eventful change."

But nothing could induce Ambrosio to relinquish that dear hand or remove one moment from his sacred charge; he consented only to take a glass of water, and in breathless expectation awaited midnight.

All was yet doubt; all involved in mystery. How had this lovely creature escaped from the bondage assigned her? Had she come alone and unprotected so long a distance? Alas! she must fall a sacrifice to so much exertion, so heavy a weight of affliction! Would he had died in infancy! Would he had perished in the forest!

He gently drew aside the muslin curtain that Madelina had arranged to shield the light from her eyes. Was there a magic in the touch of love? Had the pure offering of a faithful heart ascended to the Creator? The fever gradually subsides, the hector colour fades from the cheek, it now wears the pale hue of ivory, but the beautiful lips wear a tranquil smile, the breath is more regular, the sleep more composed. The hour approaches! Madelina prepares the draught, and trims the lamp; she draws near the couch, and places her hand gently on the lovely bosom.

"Holy Virgin! receive the devotion of a grateful heart," said she, and knelt at the foot of the couch where Sebastiano had also humbled himself in heartfel supplication.

At length those languid eyes unclose.

"Where am I?"

"In safety, dear young lady, with those who would sacrifice their lives to protect you."

"Am I safe from Don Ramella?"

"Quite safe."

"I am better. Oh! I have had a lovely dream; I fancied Ambrosio had arrived; even now I feel the pressure of his hand on mine! I cannot be mistaken; it is different from every other."

This was too great a trial of Ambrosio's self-command. The curtain which had hitherto veiled the youthful lover from her sight was drawn aside, and she received and returned the pure, the holy embrace—the soul-breathing kiss of unutterable affection! Their tears mingled.

"Ambrosio, we will part no more."

"Never, never! With the blessing of the Creator, to-morrow's dawn shall unite us. But sleep, my beloved, peacefully sleep until morning."

The lovely girl took the draught prepared for her, and, her hand clasped in Ambrosio's, tranquilly composed herself upon her pillow. In a few minutes a refreshing slumber stole over her. Ambrosio now suffered himself to be persuaded to take a glass of wine and a biscuit, and closing the curtain carefully round the couch, stationed himself beside it.

At dawn of day Sebastiano was despatched by Madelina to the neighbouring convent, with two large candles to burn before the image of the Holy Virgin. The good father arrived, and was pleased at the effect of the medicine he had administered. "But this, and every other blessing, is the gift of the Supreme," said he, raising his eyes to heaven. He then gave his benediction to the sleeper. In a few minutes she awoke, and, although weak and languid, evidently much better. The breakfast was arranged in the little sitting-room that opened out of the alcove, and the cottage-window thrown open to let in the fragrant flower-scented breeze, which was rendered more delightfully fresh from the shower of the preceding night.

The good father sympathised sincerely in the renewed happiness of the young strangers; they all breakfasted together, and the lovely Aurora received a cup of coffee from the hands of her Ambrosio. It was considered requisite that the fair invalid should be kept perfectly tranquil, converse little, and not leave her chamber until evening; when she arose, and, leaning on Ambrosio's arm, enjoyed the freshness of the evening beneath the shadow of the cottage-door. On the next morning the Father Jerome united them, and gave them the nuptial benediction.

What a powerful effect has the presence, the smile, the nameless little attentions of a beloved one, on the heart of sensibility! A few days were sufficient to restore the lustre to Aurora's eye, the vermilion to her beautiful lips. Ambrosio sent for Felix, and despatched him with a letter to Mr. St. Clair, containing a hurried account of all that had passed. In a few days afterwards he received the following reply :—

"Bring your young bride, my dear boy, and hasten to a home that is ready to receive you. I am very far from disapproving the step you have taken, the Creator never designed that the felicity of two young hearts should be sacrificed at the shrine of Ambition. You say that the parents of your Aurora shrink from an union with any one whose blood is less noble than that which flows through the veins of their family. Absurdity! The only true nobility is that of the mind; worth and talent the only just claims to superiority.

"Present my best regards to the Lady Aurora. I have sent a carriage with a female attendant; travel slowly, otherwise fatigue may occasion a relapse. Adieu, and feel assured of a real and warm friend in   "EDMUND ST. CLAIR."

Ambrosio and his fair bride took a most affectionate leave of Madelina and Sebastiano, having liberally repaid their care, and in a few days they were the welcome inmates of the Villa del Rio, and seated beneath the shadow of a bower of acacia and jasmine, Mr. St. Clair performed his promise of relating his history.

CHAPTER VI.

'Tis like a dreamer waking
  From slumbers that are blest;
Fair visions have been hovering
  Around his place of rest.
The forms that smiled upon him
  Then vanish one by one;
In vain he would recal them,
  'Tis day, and they are gone.—BAYLY.

"My father, my dear young friends, had four sons, of whom I was the youngest; he was immensely rich, and spared no expense in our education. I, however, had placed my affections on a young lady, with whose uncle my father was engaged in a law-suit, relative to a piece of land that separated their estates. Our tenderness reached my father's ears, and both families forbade our union; we met, by my Eliza's desire, to take a last farewell; love became triumphant; a clandestine marriage was the consequence. Both her uncle and my father were inexorable; the latter, however, sent me the amount he had designed for me, which I instantly embarked in commerce, and, with my beloved Eliza, sailed for this delightful land.

"In a few years a tide of prosperity flowed in upon us, and our felicity was only embittered by the intelligence of the death of my father; and that he had carried his resentment so far, as to have excluded me entirely from his will. We were at that time so wealthy that this circumstance would not have excited a momentary regret, could I have been persuaded that my lamented parent had only breathed my name in kindness; but it was a proof of determined resentment, and could not fail to inspire the most painful sentiments. But my Eliza gave a boy, beautiful as a cherub. With what anxiety did I look forward to the forming of his character, upon the model of all I deemed good and great!

"'What bliss,' said my Eliza,—

' To pour the fresh instruction o'er the mind,
To breathe the enlivening spirit, and to fix
The generous purpose, in the glowing breast.'

"We seemed to live upon the sweet idea that he would live to be the sunshine of our meridian—the charm of our declining days!

"At that period we had a country residence, on the brders of a forest ; the boundaries of our grounds led to a winding valley, which communicated with its confines. Francisca, our Edmund's nurse frequently carried him to the lemon grove, adjoining the portal, because of the extensive shadow it yielded our little treasure to play beneath ; but she was ordered never to pass its precincts.

"On one fatal day, however, this command was disregarded. Francisca had taken him early to this sweet recess, that she might enjoy the breezes of early morning ; at the hour of breakfast, she did not return—we went to seek her—nowhere amidst the spacious grounds could she be found ; we, who could scarcely endure an hour in absence from the idol of our hearts, suffered bitterly at this delay —the first messenger came, he had found the garden gate open ; " perhaps, Senor," said he, " she has wandered a little beyond the grounds, and will return ;" my beloved Eliza was distracted with a thousand terrible apprehensions : I endeavoured to console her with the hope of their speedy return. The hour of dinner arrived— no Francisca ! messengers were despatched in different directions—alas ! should we then behold our loved baby no more ? His mother fell from one fainting fit into another : evening came—the wood, the roads, the distant forests, all were searched, alas ! in vain, and in speechless sorrow we gazed on each other ; when Francisca's veil, drenched in blood, her slipper, her rosary and ebon crucifix, were brought in by a Spanish peasant, who found them beside a deep ravine.

"My child !" exclaimed my poor distracted Eliza, " oh, my child ! he also is murdered, we shall never behold him more !"—she sunk into convulsions ; midnight beheld her a corpse.

Alas, wretched St. Clair ! a few hours before beheld thee a happy father—a husband unspeakably blest :—thy Eliza's lifeless form now lay beside thee, thy lovely boy had fallen beneath the ruffian grasp of the assassin, lured by the little valuables of gold and jewels, with which maternal love had delighted to adorn him.

" Silent, gloomy, poor, amidst abundance ! I implored Heaven to send death as a relief to my woes, and nothing but the pure spirit of religion could have preserved me from self-destruction.

"I left the care of my commercial concerns to a confidential clerk ; and, after my Eliza's remains were consigned to their last abode, I left my country mansion, and came hither—where years elapsed in a sorrow not to be consoled, before I could again return to the affairs of a world of which I was weary.

" A friend, however, suggested to me to make one effort more ; the infant's hat and white plumes were adorned with a cluster of brilliants, its sleeves looped with bands of the same ; strings of fine pearl adorned its neck and its arms, for his poor mother conceived nothing good enough for her boy! Perhaps, said my head clerk, even now the baby may have escaped ; Francisca may have met her death in trying to defend the child's jewels—nothing of his clothing has been found ; they may have carried him away—for who could have the heart to destroy such a baby ? Offer a large reward with the promise of pardon and secrecy ; and the very robber may be entrapped into restoring him. I followed his advice ; alas, unavailing care ! I even mentioned the mark on his shoulder."

Ambrosio's complexion had varied frequently during the latter part of this recital, his heart beat wildly when the forest was mentioned ; but the mark on the shoulder ! He uttered an exclamation of joy, fell at the feet of St. Clair, threw open his collar.

" Behold, dearest sir ! I also from my earliest remembrance have had this azure tinted mark on my shoulder ; the distance of time, and, above all, the forest bids me hope."

St. Clair arose in an agony of impatience, he tore aside his collar.

" It is—it is my Edmund !" " my father, my honoured father," was all they could utter, and the lovely Aurora mingled her tearful smiles with those of a parent and a husband.

Felix was despatched to bring Madelina and Sebastiano. Mrs. St. Clair for w shall now call Aurora by her newly-acquired name, wrote a few lines to the former to bring with her the only vestment in which her little protege was found.

They arrived : the name written in the smallest possible characters in idelible ink on the cambric, would have proved his identity, had any other proof been required. All was now happiness and festivity. Sebastiano and Madelina parted with their cottage—became the head of the household, and [invaluable friends of St. Clair and his children ; for to them they were indebted for this renovation of hopes, apparently sunk in the night of the tomb. They went together to visit the little chapel, where his mother's dear remains were laid, and on their return, Mr. St. Clair's heart felt more relieved, and more capable of receiving its present joy.

He then wrote to Don Manuel, to mention the singular conclusion of the mystery of his, Edmund's, birth, the union of their children, and expressed the warmest acknowledgments for the hospitality he had received beneath their roof—he also entered into so satisfactory an explanation relative to his son's worldly possessions, as he conceived would be perfectly acceptable to Aurora's parents, and concluded by inviting Don Manuel and Donna Angelica to the Villa del Rio.

The reply filled the young bride with the deepest affliction, which, however, ultimately found consolation in the tenderness of her Edmund, and affectionate care of their father.

That letter forbade her even more to enter a home she had so deeply disgraced and dishonoured!—her father denounced her as an alien to the faith of her ancestors by uniting her destiny with that of a heretic,—which, independently of other circumstances, the wealth of worlds could not compensate, or years of repentance atone. And to the epistle both parents subscribed their names.

CHAPTER VII.

The spider's most attenuated thread
Is cord, is cable, to man's tender tie
On earthly bliss ; it breaks at every breeze.'—Young.

Edmund St. Clair and his Aurora became the happy parents of two children within the space of the first three years that succeeded their union—nothing was wanting to complete the felicity of their domestic circle—conjugal, filial, parental tenderness ! hearts unsullied by their communion with a world, of which the brightest side alone had been presented to them,—for independnetly of the bigoty which has power to steel even the bosom of a mother ! their experience of the human heart had not been unfavourable ; with the wish to be extensively beneficial to the unfortunate, the means were not denied them ; and they beheld their little Edmund attain his twelfth, and Aurora her tenth year—all that the most anxious parents could wish them, beautiful in person, intelligent in mind, docile and affectionate— they seemed to promise a long duration of comfort to the hearts that so fondly cherished them ;—but, alas ! for the duration of sublunary bliss ! A malignant fever raged amongst the peasantry inhabiting the huts and cottages surrounding the Villa del Rio. The elder St. Clair, with the benignity of a Howard, visited and relieved them ; his grandchildren always ran to meet and welcome his return ; the consequence was, that in a short time the venerable grandshire and his two beloved ones, had contracted it ; and all fell a sacrifice to humanity within a few days of each other ! Mrs. St. Clair's maternal fondness had seemed to render her insensible to bodily pain—her incessant watchfulness, both daily and nightly, over the couch of her father and idolized children—her intense anxiety for their restoration—her fear for her husband, that rendered her insensible to every other consideration : but no sooner were they, with all her ardent hopes for them, consigned to the tomb, than she sunk into a state of apparent decline, which awakened all her husband's tenderness and solicitude. He had mourned over the innocent pledges of early affection—he had endured the loss of the best of parents —the father and the friend—was he also to lose his Aurora ?

"Spare me, once more, this beloved one," said he, fervently, " and I will be resigned to all other dispensations of fortune or of fate !"

Heaven heard his prayer—he saw in his beloved wife, in the course of six months again restored to his wishes; but on the same day that she took the first airing in the carriage, intelligence was brought him of the failure of a London house in which he had funds to the amount of £100,000. For some days he forbore to disclose this wreck of their prosperity:—at length, as her health generally improved, he cautiously informed her of it—and found, that instead of the necessity of consoling her, that her strength of mind, was not only capable of enduring, but even cheering the most painful vicissitudes.

If we have survived the loss of what is,—oh! how infinitely more valuable than wealth—assuredly we can reconcile ourselves to this deprivation. "We are spared to each other, my beloved," said she, " and as long as the bliss of mutual affection is left us, the shades of felicity are few between the hut and the palace."

St. Clair pressed her to a heart to which she had communicated the purest consolation. Sebastiano and Madelina had both fallen beneath the ravages of the fever, which had swept off the parent and their children. Mrs. St. Clair yet remained extremely weak; it was thought a change of air might produce beneficial effects—and he resolved on converting all the property he possessed into gold, and embarking in the first vessel which might sail for England, where his three uncles still resided. This, however, was not the motive of their destination. If the father held no communion with them in prosperity, still less would his son seek their society in a less prosperous hour. It was considered that a change of climate would renovate his Aurora—and in a few weeks they were on board, and bound to the land of his forefathers.

Possessed of a degree of talent seldom equalled, with a sublimity of idea, perhaps inspired by the grandeur and beauty of the first scenes that attracted his infantine attention—a poet by nature! misfortune had given his early propensities a more decided turn;—and he looked on mankind at once with the eye of a critic and a philosopher—he pitied their frailties, but he spared neither their vices nor their follies. As he mingled with society, the favourable impressions he had formed of human nature had vanished, and he found he could no longer judge of it by the unsullied, the beautiful picture his own generous heart presented—he daily encountered individuals—lauded by the public voice, from whose discrepancies and vices his soul recoiled : he beheld crime and cunning triumphant—honour and candour cast into the shade. Here were the many creating, with the magic hand of industry, luxuries for the worthless few, while their own families were famishing. These constructing palaces, equalling Eastern magnificence, without a hut to shelter themselves or their children from the " pelting of the pitiless storm." Here he beheld the mock-patriot, borne on the shoulders of the people to the accomplishment of the only point on which all his ardours were concentrated, his own self-interest! There thousands, linked like beasts of burthen, to the car of tyranny, the idiots of custom, and submissive only from an ignorance of their own power.

Replete with truth and energy, armed with the most poignant and well-directed satire, St. Clair's writings could not fail to acquire the merited wreath of fame, as one of the first political writers of the age.

But the tide of prosperity had rolled past him—the sun of prosperity was o'erclouded, and the realities of life arose in rapid and sombre succession, through the vista of approaching years. His literary pursuits, although productive of much honour, were so little beneficial, and the numerous highly talented works with which he had really benefited society, produced so trivial a compensation for time and talent, that in disgust he cast his pen aside, and resolved to devote his future hours to agricultural pursuits, in the seclusion of some delightful, though humble, rural solitude.

Again his Aurora presented him with a pledge of tenderness. A little girl, beautiful as a cherub; and as St. Clair clasped the mother and her infant at once to his bosom :—" Thou art born in adversity, my little Adela," said he, " but like a flowret in the desert, thy filial love, thy innocence, thy beauty, shall shed their mild lustre over our solitude! Sweet cherub! nobility of sentiment and purity of heart, thou wilt inherit from thy mother; be it mine to cultivate thy virtues and thy talents as they unfold! An enlightened mind is a world within itself, and if it render its possessor more keenly alive to the evils of life, it produces also the most valuable of resources, the purest spring of consolation amidst sorrow and adversity!"

" At this time, St. Clair had been in England two years. One delusive speculation had succeeded another. The hope Mrs. St. Clair had rested on the success which ought to have attended her husband's literary exertions, had entirely failed, and £250 was all that remained to them on the month following Mrs. St. Clair's confinement.

Disgusted with society, and unfit for communion with such a world, their united wishes pined for solitude—what charm had the world for them?

> " Its pomp, its pleasure, and its nonsense all,
> Who in each other clasp, whatever fair
> High fancy forms, or lavish hearts can with?
> Something than beauty dearer—should they look.
> Or on the mind, or mind-illumined face;
> Truth, goodness, honor, harmony and love,
> The richest bounty of indulgent heaven."

St. Clair, amidst his rambles, observed a beautiful piece of land on the brink of a valley. The situation was romantic in the extreme, and perfectly suited to their taste and love of seclusion. He made an offer for it, a meadow, a corn-field, a garden, an abundant orchard; but it would require time to build a residence, humble, yet adapted to comfort. He hired a cottage in the vicinity of his purchase, and they had been making every preparation for their departure on the following day; when, about eight o'clock, the servant brought up a card—" Mr. J. St Clair." St. Clair arose, went down stairs, invited the venerable stranger into the drawing-room, where Mrs. St. Clair was delightfully occupied in nursing her little darling. There was an extreme candour in his manner, and on mutual inquiry he proved to be Edmund St. Clair's uncle, who with his only remaining brother, resided at a family mansion about twenty miles from London; a work of his nephew's had fallen into his hands. Unconscious of possessing any other relative but the above-mentioned brother; yet proud to find such talent attached to his name he ordered his carriage without delay, arrived in Cumberland Place, and a few miuntes conversation placed their affinity beyond the shadow of a doubt.

" You knew of our existence from my departed brother," said he, " we could not be aware of yours—why have we not met before? You are the last branch of our family:—you should have written to apprise us of your arrival in England."

" Had not the loss of fortune preceded that arrival," replied St. Clair, " I should undoubtedly have done so, but not in the hour of adversity."

" Well, well," said the old gentleman, " whatever vicissitudes may have fallen to your share—such a head—such abilities as yours are the highest honour to a name! Our gardens are not so beautiful as those Mrs. St. Clair has been accustomed to in her native clime; but we have some charming tulips—you must come and see them, and bring the little blue-eyed maid here," continued he, taking the baby from the mother's arms, and kissing it fondly, " Will you come to-morrow?

" Not to-morrow ;" replied Mrs. St. Clair, " on some future occasion."

" Well, well, my dear, make it pleasing to yourself; but promise me you will come and spend a month or two with us; the change of air will be beneficial both to mother and child."

They both expressed their sense of his friendly anxiety for their society,—promised to avail themselves of their invitation at the earliest possible moment.

The elder St. Clair took a social cup of tea with them, and departed.

On the following morning, the servants were paid and discharged, the apartments resigned, and the little Adela consigned solely to the charge of maternal love, with the purpose of hiring a girl, only to assist in the domestic arrangements on their arrival at the cottage.

At about five miles' distant, they stopped at an inn. Mr. and Mrs. St. Clair changed their usual habiliments for those of peasants—which, however plain, could not conceal their graceful figures and native dignity of mien.

Mrs. St. Clair, although past the early bloom of youth, was still a truly beautiful woman—features irradiated by intellectual loveliness, changeless, because they are not dependent solely on those circumstances and seasons that are destructive to the tint of the rose and the lustre of the lily.

> "Can silent glens have charms for thee,
> The lowly cot and russet gown!"

said the still elegant St. Clair, as he folded the interesting matron to his heart—whilst, with tears of tenderness, she warmly returned his pressure. And far more

graceful did she appear, than when her neck was encircled with brilliants and the finest pearls enwreathed amidst her raven tresses.

St. Clair and his little family had now become the inmates of a hired cottage; and, during the year he occupied it, his own was perfectly constructed, beautified, and aired for their reception; and they entered it on the day on which their little Adela completed her first year.

As time passed imperceptibly, every hour seemed to add to her beauty; she sported amidst the lambs that cropped their verdant food on the flowery hill that sheltered their rural habitation; she gathered the lily, the hearts-ease, the first violet of the spring to adorn their rustic board; and, as she sprang forward to meet her beloved father, on his return, she appeared like the genius of innocence and peace, and her parents felt the bitterness of regret for their lamented lost ones mellowed by time into a sadly pleasing remembrance.

No. 4.

This was an entirely new sphere of action for St. Clair. His habits of elegant indolence must be subverted; he must be amongst the hinds employed about his little farm shortly after sunrise; and although only the director of their labours. he found it no sinecure. But invigorated health was his reward,—his rural repast received an additional relish, spread by the hand of conjugal affection, his little Adela shared it with him. He hastened to his humble home as the abode of real bliss, and in their evenings, which were devoted to reading and music, he felt compensated for the fatigues of the day.

As years advanced, they found their Adela all their fond hearts could anticipate

Nor as her lovely mind unclosed,
Faded each fond parent's tend'rest care,
To guard the gems, that there reposed,
Of truth and talent rare.

What bliss! in that pure soul's intelligence
To see their rest of life's repose commence;
Her filial fondness banishes every care—
Renews hope's smile—or gives back tear for tear.

St. Clair wrote to his uncle, mentioning his removal, and requesting his letters might be addressed to the post-house of the neighbouring town. He received a most affectionate reply. The elder St. Clair considered his nephew's disgust of the world premature, and blamed him for quitting that society they were both formed to embellish. He warmly renewed his invitation; but a spirit of independence stood in the way of the closer cultivation of this friendly feeling: and, after many letters having passed between them, their correspondence became less frequent.

Their farming speculation produced them the comforts of life; contentment shed its mild lustre over their retreat,—their Adela attained her fifteenth year, possessed of all the elegance a communion with the most select portion of polished society could have given her, with all the unsullied purity of the mountain snow, or her favourite lily of the vale. She spoke and read the Spanish, French, Portuguese, and Italian, with fluency. Her flowers, figures, and sketches from nature, were not only elegant adornments for their parlour, but they produced a very useful little income when sold at the neighbouring town,—for St. Clair's was the pencil of a master, and his entire soul was in the desire that his Adela might excel in whatever she might undertake.

The Spanish guitar was the only instrument left to Mrs. St. Clair on their removal to the cottage; but even in infancy she had taught her daughter to touch it with so exquisite a degree of sweetness as—to "take the prisoned sense, and lay it in Elysium." Her voice we have before described.

———

CHAPTER VIII.

He looks so innocent—so mild,
With joy we clasp the beauteous child;
His cherub lip we fondly kiss,
We love his sportive tenderness!
Nor dreams the fond deluded breast,
That he can rob the soul of rest;
The cheek where beauty blossom's fading,
The soul's content, its peace invading;
Yet shun, oh! shun, his witching wiles,
For poison lurks beneath his smiles.B—ANDIT CHIEF.

GEORGE CLIFFORD had observed a mixture of sadness and seriousness in Theodore since his return. He saw his sable attire, and attributing his seclusion to that desolation which the hand of death sometimes leaves on the hearts of the living, he had determined once more to seek his society, and proffer that consolation the stricken heart is best capable of bestowing.

Clifford had felt his regard irresistibly drawn towards Theodore from his first arrival,—he had watched over his safety with a jealous eye—he felt half angry when his cautions were slighted, and relieved of a certain degree of anxiety whan he heard of his young friend's return home, trusting that his departure would be likely to weaken, if not destroy those associations, which might tend to cast an evil influence over his future prospects; and meeting Theodore, he clasped his hand, condoled with him upon his loss, and warmly pressed him to return to his chambers and take tea with him.

"Come, my dear fellow," said he, "I have just received a basket of little delicacies from my mother, these are always welcome to us solitary beings who are deprived of the domestic comforts of home; they are more so when partaken by a friend. Come, I will take no denial; when I conceived your gaiety would lead you into danger, I cautioned you, I advised you; permit me now, dear Villars, by a relation of my own irremediable affliction, to lessen the weight of that melancholy which appears to press so heavily on your heart."

Theodore suffered Clifford to mistake the cause of his sadness; he returned the friendly pressure of his hand, accepted his invitation, and they proceeded to his apartments.

It had been whispered that Clifford had met with an early disappointment, and as everything relating to that sentiment that now pervaded his heart was peculiarly interesting, he anxiously awaited the performance of his promise, and, on the removal of the tea equipage, he thus commenced his narrative :—

My father had retired on a valuable property, possessing a considerable interest in several of the first houses in the Brazils, where my cousin was settled; he determined upon sending me thither, and, at seventeen, I embarked for that place, with letters of introduction to some of the most distinguished families in the city of Bahia. I shall say nothing relative to my voyage : we had a fair wind with few exceptions, during almost the whole of the way, neither did storms awaken our apprehensions, nor long-continued calms exhaust our patience ; we arrived after a passage of seven weeks.

Nothing can be more impressive than the beauty of the prospect, on first entering the bay of St. Salvador, and more particularly delightful is the impression in that lovely season of sun and flowers, December! the bright azure of their cloudless skies, the luxuriant foliage embowering the white-fronted buildings with their green verandas, interspersed with the vine and acacia, the country houses, the distant rocas of their fidalgos and our English merchants : churches and grey fronted convents appearing from amongst orange groves, cocoa nut and manga trees,—whilst, in the depth of distance, the eye is carried to the dark shadow of woods

> Where e'en the sun's pervading blaze
> Can scarcely dart his golden rays ;
> Whose echoes human voice ne'er broke,
> Nor answered to the woodman's stroke.

One boundless shade—one wild unravelled maze !—the friendly reception of the Brazilian families to whom I presented my introductory letters—the even romantic attention of the younger branches of those families ; their invitations to the rural festivals of the season, their presents of fruit, preserves, and flowers in little tasteful baskets, decorated with true love-knots of various coloured ribands, and placed on silver salvers, could not fail of pleasing a youthful imagination : everything was replete with romance, beauty, and novelty. On the Sunday evenings we usually went to the opera, for after having paid their devotions at their churches early in the morning, and, during the day, they devote their evenings to visiting and festivity. On Monday, we met universally at an entertainment at the English consul's ; the remaining evenings of the week were divided between the very few liberal English and the very many hospitable Brazilian families, who pressingly invited my cousin and myself to enjoy with them the festivities of the season.

My cousin had a beautiful roca or country seat, a little beyond Fort St. Pedro. After the hours devoted to business during the morning, at the office in the lower town, we generally proceeded thither on horseback to dine ; and our evenings were passed away in the interchange of visits amidst a circle, around which frankness, candour, and hospitality spread an indescribable charm.

At a neighbouring roca resided a lady, the widow of an officer, with her daughter and niece. Donna Leonora was a dark-complexioned, black-eyed girl of eighteen, with fine features and a commanding air. But her lovely cousin ! how can language do justice to that countenance ! the mild lustre of those hazel eyes, the exuberance of the glossy ringlets that fell on her beautifully-formed neck, the form of symmetry. She was two years younger than her cousin, and had been left an orphan, with a considerable fortune, to the care of her aunt. Already had her hand been sought by many, and this circumstance had excited a degree of envious animosity little favourable to her domestic comfort; and the heart of the gentle Zephyrina sought repose and consolation in the warm friendship of Donna Constantia d'Oliveira, the only daughter of a family of distinction.

The parents of this young lady had long been childless, and anxiously wished, amidst their splendour, that

> " One might be when they were not,
> To tell that they had been."

At the period when this void in the heart existed, a favourite slave produced them a little mulatto ; and, as it is the custom with the Brazilian ladies to fondle and caress their young slaves, the mulatto became hourly more the object of her lady's care and solicitude. A chain of the purest gold adorned her neck, and her sombre cheek, formed a singular contrast with the snowy muslin or rose-coloured silk that veiled the senora's bosom.

Senor Jozé objected to the lavishing so many marks of tenderness upon a slave, because it would, perhaps, be difficult at a future hour to regain a sufficient command over her, to fall readily into those habits of submission that might then be required over her.

" It will be time enough for that many years hence," said the lady ; " besides, as we have no children, why should we not bring up Loo-loo as our own ?"

Senor Jozé smiled, and trusted to his dear Carlotta's natural caprice and versatile nature to banish this absurd idea, even though it might give place to another, and yet another folly.

But in this the Senor Jozé was mistaken ; every hour added to Donna Carlotta's infatuation, the little Loo-loo (for that was her pet name) in her embroidered frock, was still permitted to enter the drawing-room, and receive all sorts of attentions from her illustrious guests, in compliment to their hostess, although they inwardly smiled at her folly.

Nor was the little Luiza devoid of sufficient aptness to discover her power, and to use every art to secure it ; and this was cultivated by her designing mother's constant admonitions. If her mistress dropped her handkerchief, she would not suffer any one but herself to take it up ;—if she required her fan, she flew like lightning to fetch it.

She would get up behind the Senora on the sofa, place a rose, or a bunch of pinks amidst her hair, kiss the faded ones, and carry them in her bosom.

" Affectionate creature !" exclaimed the Lady Carlotta, delightedly ; " yes, my sisters may laugh as they please, I will bring up Loo-loo as my own."

But Donna Carlotta did not reflect, or perhaps her mind was not so constructed as to enable her to discern that this semblance of devotedness was a well-studied part, in which she had been tutored by her wily mother ; who, herself a favourite, made use of her daughter's growing influence in the exercise of all the baleful passions of her soul; who employed her to listen to the unguarded conversation of the other slaves of the household, in falsely accusing and bringing to unmerited punishment, any one whose interests might have interfered with her own, or who might casually have offended her, for even in so narrow a sphere, cunning is some-times triumphant ; avarice, ambition, and revenge, exert their sway, and many had only been consigned to solitary confinement, and even endured corporeal punishment, through the tales that had transpired amidst the innocent prattle a

Loo-loo, whilst she sat at her mistress's feet at the hour of breakfast, or during her toilette.

But a very unpropitious termination was likely to be put to the brilliancy of the little mulatto's prospects. After an union of fifteen years, a beloved one appeared to succeed to Senor Jozé's immense possessions—and to add a charm to the splendour of the surrounding scene.

The favourite pouted, looked sullen, and her mother gloomy; though the latter had sufficient cunning to conceal her bitter feelings, and even to utter exclamations of joy, as she hung over the cradle of the little heiress.

But the infant Donna Constantia hourly improved, notwithstanding the evil machinations of the malignant Lina, and the sly pinches of Loo-loo, when she could steal unperceived to the cradle. The delight of her parents, a new interest was given to their existence, and as the flight of years of felicity unfolded the graces of her mind, no expense was spared in giving it every embellishment education can bestow.

At seventeen, amongst the crowd of candidates for her fair hand, the fortunate being of her heart's election was Don Luiz, the heir of an illustrious family, minister for the home department, and my cousin's intimate friend. She conceded to her lover's prayer, and every requisite preliminary having been arranged the morrow was to make her his for ever !

It was a brilliant moonlight evening,—we had rode over to Bom-fim to the country villa of the Oliveira family; the silvery lustre shone on the church that reared its gothic structure beyond the wood that skirted the green and flowery lawn; we arrived just as the dance was concluded, and the supper was arranged on the finest damask—spread on the grass. Vases of flowers, the most exquisite delicacies, fruits, preserves; the richest wines were in profusion. The sable attendants, in their splendid liveries—the female slaves, their necks and arms glittering with their heavy gold ornaments, waited around:—a band stationed in the surrounding shrubberies, played during the repast—the music paused at its conclusion; the clarionet, the guitar, and the flute were heard at a distance, mingled with the harmony of female voices : a band of Pastoras entered, two advanced, and kneeling at the feet of the bride elect, presented her with a silver basket containing flowers from the convent of Solidade.

One among the graceful throng glided round and imperceptibly presented me with two half-blown Persian roses, united by a silver ribbon. I kissed the fair hand, and placed its gift in my bosom. She tripped lightly away, the party partook of the refreshments, and departed.

We retired early, that we might be in attendance on the happy pair soon after day-break ; but the nosegay never occurred to me, until I had thrown off my coat and waistcoat, and put on my dressing-gown, when it fell.

" Is that the way you treat a fair lady's love present, George ?" said my cousin. I took it up, observed an embossed paper, neatly enclosed in the silver circlet that bound the roses together. With a glowing cheek I unclosed it, and read as follows, in elegant Portuguese :—

> In vain my companions reprove,
>   To solitude's shelter I fly—
> To the depths of the shadowy grove.
>   These tears that bedew the sad eye
> Are Love's ! his the sigh in his bosom that swells,
>   In my bosom's remotest recesses he dwells !
>
> Oh, why did I pluck yon fair rose,
>   Unheeding the thorn that it bore ;
> My nights are devoid of repose,
>   Morn rises in gladness no more ?
> A bramble 'midst garlands of flowers inwove,
>   " A serpent concealed in this treacherous love !"

" Whose stanzas can these be ?,"
" Donna Zephyrina's, no doubt," said my cousin ; " is it possible you did

discern Donna Zephyrina, through the disguise of the Pastora? or it might have been Donna Leonora, for they are the same size?"

"I neither heard her voice, nor saw her features," said I, "it was the action of a moment, and the light-footed damsel was amongst the group of her fair associates."

I scarcely dared hope these lines had been traced by Zephyrina's hand,—she was so retiring, so distant in her deportment. Yet, when last I had the felicity of obtaining her hand in the dance, she suffered me to retain the lovely captive. She leaned on my arm as we walked through the orange grove, and permitted me to entwine the flowering myrtle amongst her beautiful ringlets. "Oh, yes! it is Zephyrina," said I, and covering the little poetical billet with kisses, I placed it beneath my pillow.

"But, my dear Villars, it is late," said Clifford, "it is hardly fair I should engross the whole conversation—we will take some refreshment, and defer the conclusion of my narrative until to-morrow."

Theodore had listened intensely,—he expressed the warmest interest, and obtained Clifford's promise to be his guest on the morrow. He then retired to his chamber.

"Alas!" said he, "is love, then, thus ever mingled with sorrow? poor Clifford seems to have become it's hopeless victim. I have only heard the commencement of his narrative; but he says his sorrows are irremediable! Why was I led by irresistible fatality down that path? Previously to that hour I was calm and happy! I walked, conversed, danced, and sang with the sisters of my young friends, but my heart remained free as the linnet that flutters on the bough. Oh! Adela, Adela, there is no face, no form, no smile like thine! How can I possess thee? insuperable barriers arise between us!—shall, then, another possess her? shall that lovely shrine of all that is celestial be sacrificed to the sacrilegious presumption of some wealthy boor? there is insanity in the thought! he shall not live!" continued Theodore, rising.

"Heaven grant my master has not taken leave of his senses," whispered Ralph, sideling as imperceptibly as possible towards the door, and taking hold of the handle: "What have I done, sir? have I committed any fault? have I offended you in anything?"

This appeal was accompanied by a look so woe-begone, that it instantly recalled Theodore to himself; for, lost in the most irritating reveries, he had spoken the last sentence aloud.

"No, my poor fellow," said he, "it is not to you I allude—it was an imaginary being. But you merit my confidence. The fact is, I cannot—I feel I cannot live without St. Clair's lovely daughter! I must see her again, or I shall die!"

"And why can't your honour pay another visit to the village? It's not so far! though, if you could but stay a fortnight, it would be better, and a month—better still. There are so many spies about, and if it should come to Sir Edward's ears!"

"A month! it is impossible!"

"Well, well, sir,—then a fortnight, if you please."

"Be it so, my good fellow."

Ralph had, by this time, become better satisfied of his master's sanity, he felt not only his affection, but his vanity flattered by this consultation, and Theodore fell into a restless and dreamy slumber.

CHAPTER IX.

These lips are mute—these eyes are dry;
But in my heart and in my brain
Awake the pangs that pass not by,
The thought, that ne'er shall sleep again.—BYRON.

"MY dear Clifford," said Theodore, seeing traces of the deepest melancholy on his fine countenance, "do not distress yourself by a recurrence to past calamity; much as I feel interested in all that concerns you, I cannot desire the conclusion of your narrative, at the expense of your peace."

"It is past," replied Clifford, "my heart is relieved of its extreme load, and it now appears like a mournful dream, which mingles with a pleasing sadness in a heart which can never more respond to the touch of joy! He continued as follows :—

That bridal day arose—(the ladies Zephyrina and Leonora were the brides-maids; my cousin and myself the bridegroom's attendants;) the fair bride, and the chosen of her heart, approached the altar: young girls in white scattered flowers in her path. Donna Theodora, as a friend of Donna Carlotta's, was a principal guest, and on descending from our carriages, she took her daughter's hand, and presented it to me, whilst my adored Zephyrina became the companion of my cousin. Those who have felt how much importance a heart, newly awakened, attaches to the merest trifles, will easily conceive my vexation. I even felt my resentment rise against my cousin, until his smile of candour reproved me—it seemed to say "my heart is in England! I am not the arranger of these things, but I cannot reject the hand of a lady!"—And such a hand—oh, Villars! I would have resigned an empire, had it been mine, to have possessed it : to have been the friend, the brother—oh, transport! the husband of this lovely, this innocent orphan!

The day was passed in festivity ; a splendid ball was to close the evening. Donna Leonora contrived to be so near me, that, without appearing remarkable, she could present me her hand to lead her into the dining saloon;—one of the ministers had the felicity of conducting Zephyrina,—but she sat opposite to me, and I thought I read a congenial feeling in her eyes, a sentiment of sorrow and and almost dis-pleasure—yet that displeasure was flattering, did it not imply a jealous interest respecting me ? At any rate, thought I, I will engage her as my partner in the dance; and having requested my cousin, in English, to engage Donna Leonora in conversation, when the company arose from table, I was going towards the veranda, where my lovely girl was pensively gazing on the lake below.

It was Ave Maria! every voice was silenced in a moment—every eye turned to the setting sun ; nothing can equal the sublime, the impressive stillness, the silent devotion of those few minutes! It seems as though all nature, amidst the most animated scene of business or pleasure was suddenly struck motionless by the power of enchantment!—they pass ! the conversation, which was stopped in the middle, is continued ; the laugh, the jest, the song, is renewed; the wayfaring traveller pursues his path ; and I was hastening to my Zephyrina, when Donna Theodora started forward, and placing her hand on my arm, "have you seen my daughter waltz, Senor Clifford?" said she. I replied, I had not yet had that pleasure.

"Oh, then," she rejoined, "you have a luxury left to enjoy! You shall be her partner—do not look so uneasy ;—no one else shall have her hand during the first part of the evening, I assure you! "

I thought I should have gone wild with vexation. Zephyrina had caught the last words of earnest assurance—"No one shall have her hand during the first part of the evening, I assure you! " Why she would think I was soliciting her cousin's hand ; madness was in the thought! She looked reproachfully at me! I took advantage of my cousin's passing out, to follow him. The younger part of the company had adjourned to the ball-room, which was magnificently decorated ;

I crossed the lawn, and told my cousin of my disappointment. "Never mind," said he, "sprain your ancle!" I laughed at the conceit, but took the hint; and when the old lady came to tell me the waltzers had commenced, my apology, although she bitterly deplored the cause, was sufficient: but it destroyed my hope of dancing with Zephyrina. I entreated my cousin to engage her hand on the first possible moment; and, when she was inclined, to leave the ball-room, to bring her to the music saloon, where I would await them.

The bride was seated at the harp—Don Luiz "hung over, enamoured;" but, like a phantom, there again was Donna Leonora!—and judge of my astonishment and disappointment, when, in a rich and powerful strain of melody, she commenced the very stanzas that had been presented to me on the preceding evening. The meaning she threw into her tones—the glance she cast on me—I could not be deceived! It was not then Zephyrina's gift of love! the sighs devoted to Zephyrina alone, had been given to sentiments traced by the hand of another. But my cousin, with a countenance beaming with the interest he felt for us, entered; my sweet girl leaned on his arm—her eye appeared to seek some favoured individual amongst the crowd;—he placed her on the sofa, on the arm of which I was leaning —that voice of music breathed its sympathy for my imagined accident.

I blushed at the deception; for, although my pure devotion to her had occasioned it, yet I felt it rendered me unworthy of her.

"Do take a seat on the sofa, I really suffer to see you stand!"

"What would I not endure?" said I, accepting the place she offered me beside her. "What would I not endure to obtain Donna Zephyrina's sympathy?"

"It did not seem so, from the early part of the morning," said she.

"Dearest girl—mistrust appearances! How much have I suffered this day!"

"Hush: my cousin will see us, and my aunt is coming this way. I would not she should catch a syllable of what you have just said, for the universe!"

"I will obey you, my beloved one! in every thing I am your's devotedly and entirely—through life, in death. But, say you will meet me in the lemon grove, beyond the hill, to-morrow evening."

"Not to-morrow, that will be impossible."

"The next day then."

"I will,—if possible, I will. My aunt calls me, I must be gone, dear Clifford; remain where you are, I command you."

I returned her smile with impassioned meaning; for my heart was relieved of a load of anxiety. Again I breathed freely, again I felt the worth of an existence which I inwardly vowed to devote to her alone. My ardent gaze followed her, although I dared not approach her. The pale rose brightened on her cheek whenever her eye met mine; and although I did not sit beside her at supper, the language of the heart was interchanged in every glance. I led her to the carriage when the company separated, and hastily imprinting a kiss on her hand—whispered the day after to-morrow."

Returning to my chamber, I took the little paper from my bosom, tore it into twenty pieces, and scattered it to the evening gale. I retired to rest with more felicity than I had ever before experienced; the next day we dined with an English party at the Consul's.

On the following we were to meet the bride and bridegroom, with their party, at Donna Theodora's, previously to their departure for Rio. The entertainment was splendid—every heart was gaiety and gladness. But the lovely Zephyrina did not appear.

Donna Leonora was constantly beside me, and I dare not inquire of her cousin, lest I should awaken the jealous feeling I had observed emanate from the few minutes' conversation I had had with her on the day of her friend's nuptials."

At length the bride entered. From her conversation I gathered that her young riend had so severe a head-ache, that 'he was unable to join the party; and every hour of that day seemed to wear away on leaden pinions.

Professing an indispensable engagement for a few hours, after which I should eturn, I departed before the company adjourned to the ball-room; and, having given my horse to my servant, at some distance, received my cloak from him, wrapped it round me, drew my hat over my eyes, and returned by a secluded path. I concealed myself for some minutes in the shrubbery behind the ball-room; saw from its opening portals the Lady Leonora displaying her graceful figure and fine arms in the waltz; and, with a light foot and beating heart, descended the little hill, and cautiously entered the thick shadow of the lemon grove. There was balm on every breeze, as it bore on its wings the mingled hum of the varied insect tribe. Bright as an emerald was the turfy carpet of this sweet retreat, which only admitted the clear moon's rays through the interstices of its

exuberant foliage, while the fire-flies glittering like brilliants studded the myrtle and laurel enclosures.

I sounded my repeater—I impatiently paced the path. It was full half an hour after the appointed moment. Had she then been sporting with my feelings? —impossible!—perhaps she was, even then, suffering under increased indisposition!

A light foot was on the grass—a silvery veil floated on the breeze,—and in a moment my arm encircled all that my youthful imagination could conceive of female loveliness. A few minutes were requisite to calm our emotions. That

No. 5.*

gentle heart was unfolded to me;—incapable of resentment, she related to me a thousand instances of her aunt's and cousin's persecution. The lovely orphan wept on my bosom—I mingled tears of the tenderest, the purest sympathy with her, and then we interchanged vows of never-ending fidelity!

We resolved on concealing our mutual passion, until the period allotted for my residence in the Brazils should expire; when a secret union should make her irrevocably mine, and enable me to remove her far away from the malignity of her aunt and cousin.

CHAPTER X.

" The marriage feast and its solemnity
    Was turned to funeral pomp—the company,
    With heavy hearts and looks, broke up; nor they
    Who loved the dead went weeping on their way
    Alone, but sorrow mixed with sad surprise
    Loosened the springs of pity in all eyes,
    On which that form, whose fate they weep in vain,
    Will never, thought they, kindle smiles again."   SHELLEY.

LET us now return to the Mulatta. She had also started into womanhood; and although she had lost her mother, (who had been summoned by the hand of death to the long account of all her treacheries) she evinced herself sufficiently tutored to require no auxiliary in an undeviating system of cunning; and, so well adjusted were all her arrangements, that she still retained a most powerful influence over the heart of her mistress!

"My beloved Constantia," said Donna Carlotta, " amongst my parting gifts, (as one of the highest value is a faithful attendant) I give you Luiza."

" Dear mamma! why should you deprive yourself of her services?"

" Have I not others who can supply her place? Besides, who can dress your hair so exquisitely? yes, yes, you must have Luiza?

Luiza was called.

"Loo-loo, I am going to present you to your young lady as her peculiar attendant!"

The brow of Luiza was overshadowed with gloom.

" Why, Luiza," said Donna Constantia, " you appear averse to go with me?"

" What say you, Loo-loo?" inquired Donna Carlotta.

" That I would rather not, Senha," murmured Luiza sullenly.

"Upon my word, Luiza," said Donna Constantia playfully, "mamma has completely spoiled you; at all events, had you evinced a little complaisance, I would not have removed you from mamma, with whom you have hitherto possessed a degree of favour above those infinitely more deserving. As it is, I shall accept the offer made with such maternal consideration for my convenience; you shall however remain here until I come back from Rio, because I have promised to take Claudina amongst my attendants, and I trust, by the period of my return, you will have acquired a proper degree of reasonable submission."

Four months elapsed, during which the stolen interview, the unobserved glance, that expresses more than volumes, the billet secretly exchanged, repaid the restraint we had imposed upon ourselves; every hour improved my Zephyrina's exquisite beauty, and the confidence she reposed in my honour and fidelity, not only rendered her cousin's malignity powerless to ruffle the calm of that pure bosom, but renovated health renewed its native roses on her cheeks.

Four months had elapsed! and another festival was preparing for the reception of the beloved Constantia, and our valued friend Don Luiz her happy husband, who had just returned from Rio, where the young bride had been presented at court, and Don Luiz loaded with the most distinguished marks of his sovereign's favour.

The halls, the grand saloon, the drawing rooms, were again hung with the most exquisite flowers, mingled with draperies of blue and silver. The tables were covered with luxuries, the light foot of the dancer beat in unison with the music, which resounded through the wrought and gilded roofs of her father's mansion.

My Zephyrina's heart throbbed with the purest emotions of friendship, and joy for the return of her Constantia : all was satisfaction, hilarity, gladness !

A glass of orgeat was called for, for the Senhora Donna Constantia. It was brought with hurried speed by Luiza, who came attired in the silver muslin turban and diamond ear-rings, given by her young lady on her return.

Don Luiz took the glass from her : what hand but that of love should be cup-bearer to his lovely bride ?

Thirst produced by exercise gave exquisiteness to the draught. Half an hour elapsed, the music suddenly ceased ! the guests rushed in crowds to the verandah where the Lady Constantia reclined on a sofa writhing with torture.

Her husband, with agonized tenderness, supported her in his arms, my Zephyrina bathed in tears knelt beside her, her distracted parents sent for the nearest physician; he came, he inquired what she had taken ; the glass of orgeat instantly occurred to the unfortunate husband.

"This," said the physician, " is evidently the effects of poison ! where is the glass ?"

At this moment Luiza, who had continued behind Donna Carlotta's chair, rushed forward to a sideboard, her eyes glared with an unearthly brightness ! she seized the glass, and threw it over the verandah into the lake below.

"Such," continued Clifford, " such, my dear Villars, are life's vicissitudes ! Who shall smile secure in terrestrial felicity? the breath of the zephyr, the sparkle of the dewdrops, are not more transitory. Alas ! that the honey of such a fate should so soon be converted into bitterness, the song of joy into continued wailing, the bridal vestment into the habiliment of the tomb !"

All was gloom, the gloom of that despair which nothing can alleviate. The windows darkened ; nothing interrupted the deep silence but the deep groans and convulsive sobs of the hapless mourners, who, enclosed in the chamber of death, despairingly gazed on the marble features, as though it were to ask, " If this were indeed reality ?"

The mother franticly rent her hair,—the father rested his silvery head on the pillow of death, and implored Heaven that ere morning he might share her repose ! The disconsolate husband knelt beside her couch ; he pressed those pallid lips, that ivory hand, which was no longer conscious of his pressure.

The last pious duties were performed, the dark hair braided by the hand of my Zephyrina over that brow of snow, the dark eyelash rested on the pallid cheek, the beautiful bosom rose beneath its covering.

" Alas !" fond mother, said my weeping girl, " how few months have since elapsed thy hand placed the bridal rose amidst those luxuriant tresses, and adjusted the silvery veil in graceful folds over them !"

"Hapless father !" said I, " how lately didst thou present that hand to the now distracted and bereaved one, who received it as the highest treasure Heaven could bestow !"

The vision of felicity, my dear Villars, had passed ; she slept with her unborn infant, in that slumber, from whence neither accents of love or despair shall awaken her.

The confesser had taken his station beside the couch of the expiring Luiza. In the moment of despair, when ordered into solitary confinement, until the awful and mysterious events I have related could be investigated, she had taken from her bosom and swallowed the remaining portion of that poison, which she acknowledged to have administered to her mistress.

From that day, our valued friend, our generous-hearted Luiz, was never heard of; and Donna Carlotta and Senor Joze were interred in the family mausoleum with their lamented daughter, within a few weeks of each other !

My Zephyrina drooped like a lovely flower beneath the pressure of this early sorrow. She sought her only consolation in my tenderness, and our mutual affection became boundless ! Three years had rolled imperceptibly past us, the melancholy fate of our early friendship had left a tinge of sadness over their memory, and together we had scattered the sweetest treasures of every varying season to embellish their tomb. No news of Don Luiz! our unfortunate friend had doubtless rushed to an untimely fate. Donna Leonora had refused several proposals for her hand, had given some unequivocal testimonies of her wish to supplant her cousin in the estimation she however *only suspected* her of possessing; and the friendly feeling which, for Zephyrina's sake, I wished to preserve, no doubt led her to anticipate a more satisfactory termination. Donna Theodora had also been urged very frequently, by several young men of distinction, to exert her influence in their favour with her niece. This affectionate relative hinted, that it would be more pleasing to her that she should either enter the seclusion of a convent, or accept one of these advantageous offers, as her presence might prove prejudicial to her daughter's future establishment.

I wrote my father an account of our attachment; and not only received his permission to act according to the dictates of my heart, but a warm invitation to bring my lovely orphan home, and have our nuptials re-solemnized in England. Having consulted with my cousin, I determined to wait on Donna Charlotta, and make proposals at once for her niece.

"We will dine first," said he, "and order our horses early in the evening."

Agitated and anxious, yet wrapped in visions of approaching felicity, I consented. We dined, and were taking our wine in the verandah that looked down the road, when a crimson and gold cadeira, or chair, the attendants in splendid liveries, appeared at a distance. As it approached we observed a lady, waving her embroidered handkerchief to us.

"Who is that?" said I.

"Donna Theodora," replied my cousin; "you cannot, assuredly, mistake the livery; but people in love are like no one else!"

By this time the cadeira had arrived at the entrance of the avenue; and my cousin went into the hall to offer his hand to the lady, and conduct her into the drawing-room.

After taking a glass of wine, and conversing a few minutes jocularly with my cousin, she motioned to me with her fan to attend her into the verandah; and, with very little ceremony, made me an offer of Leonora's hand and fortune.

"Several offers of the highest importance have been rejected by us, Senor Clifford," said she, "for my daughter has long been attached to you, and she has so high a spirit, that I fear some fatal consequences would result from opposition to her inclinations. She has been a spoiled girl ever since her father's death; and, I suppose, must still continue to have her own way."

An earthquake could scarcely have thrown me into greater consternation at the moment. "Pardon me, madam," said I, "that I cannot avail myself of so flattering a preference! Your daughter's hand is too great a treasure for my possession; but there is another obstacle over which I have no control. My heart has been during the last three years devoted to your niece, the Lady Zephyrina."

I cannot describe the astonishment, disappointment, rage, evident in her altered countenance and varying complexion. She moved ceremoniously, made no reply, returned through the drawing-room, waved her hand to my cousin, who led her to her cadeira, and departed.

My cousin laughed heartily at my embarrassment. "Take her away from them at once;" said he, "were I you, I would not hesitate a moment. Let the English consul unite you; and, if that is not satisfactory to Donna Zephyrina, Father Murphy is a good-natured fellow—we will invite him to dinner, give him plenty of wine, and he will perform the ceremony again. You can then go into the country for a week or so, until the Iris is ready to sail; and at this time of year all will pass smoothly enough, until you lead your fair bride into your father's dwelling."

I thanked him for his advice, which appeared to me so excellent, that I resolved to adopt it.

"But you may order the horses back into the stable," said I, "for I will not venture to appear in Donna Leonora's presence this evening, at any rate."

"Do as you please, my dear fellow," said he, " I shall go, to keep the old lady in good humour, and flatter the young one, whilst you meet your little girl in the grove, behind the hill. I hope your rash candour will not have made her a prisoner."

My cousin went, and I eagerly watched the approach of evening, to glide to the lemon grove, according to our last night's assignation.

An hour passed in the most painful apprehensions : at length the trembling girl threw herself into my arms : her heart beat wildly against mine, and some minutes elapsed before she was sufficiently recovered to relate the following events :—

" When my aunt returned, dear Clifford, she took my cousin to her dressing-room ; and having made her acquainted with the ill success of her mission, a violent storm arose. Leonora fell into hysterics, and my aunt, sending for me, bitterly reproached me with having withdrawn your affection from my cousin ; and declared it her decided intention, as my guardian, to immure me within the walls of a convent, unless I instantly agreed to resign my hand to her disposal." ·

" Fly, then, with me—my Zephyrina ! permit me to become your lawful protector ; then no earthly power will dare divide us. Let this moment free you from the bondage imposed by malignity and tyranny !"

" To-night ?—alas ! it is impossible !"

" Say, then, you will to-morrow. Remember, my beloved, a few hours may place a barrier, awful as the grave, between us !"

She shuddered, and, leaning her tear-bedewed cheek on my shoulder, whispered,

" Be it so, dear Clifford ! but now I must away. My Creola waits in the avenue, to warn me of danger ; my aunt's spies are around. Oh, Clifford, adieu !"

" Till to-morrow only, dearest girl."

I clasped her, with frantic ardour, to my bosom, alas ! in a last embrace. The clapping of hands was heard, and in a few moments her light and fairy footsteps bore her from my view.

Alas ! dear Villars, how often has this embroidered handkerchief, which she dropped in her flight, been bathed in my tears !—through years of unabated, yet hopeless, fidelity, this aching bosom has been its daily—its nightly dwelling ! but let me conclude my melancholy recital. I returned home : my cousin, aware of the danger of a momentary delay, set out to arrange a retired roça for our] reception ; where, in perfect seclusion, we might await the sailing of the Iris.

He gave every requisite order which might add to my beloved girl's comfort or convenience ; and I retired to my chamber, with sensations of mingled hope and tumultuous anxiety.

At breakfast, the next morning, I saw my cousin's arm in a sling, and hastily inquired the cause. He laughed heartily at my alarm.

" A mere trifle, my dear fellow," said he, "only a graze ; and every thing, you know, should be welcome from the fair hand of a lady !"

" Merciful Heaven ! are you, then, wounded ?"

" If I had not, it is more than probable you would have been,—for it appears the favour was intended for you."

" For Heaven's sake, dear Edward, be explicit."

" The fact is this : on my return last night, or rather this morning—for it was twelve when we left old Silva's roça, and we must have been an hour galloping over here ; I dismounted at the stables, left the horses to the care of the groom ; and, wrapping my cloak around me, walked up the winding path that leads the wood. A rustling amongst the aloes and laurels attracted my attention, when a female form closely wrapped in a veil, started forward, and drawing a glittering dagger from her bosom, aimed it at mine ! It was the work of a moment :"—

" Receive, perfidious Clifford !" said she, " the reward of thy ingratitude !"

" Gently, gently ! fair damsel," said I, firmly securing her in my arms, whilst with a steady hand I disarmed her (for I had caught the point of her weapon in my arm, and thus diverted it from its destination). I carried her into the broad moon-light, and, removing her veil, beheld—the Senora Donna Leonora !"

"Jesu Christo!" exclaimed she.

"Nossa Senora!" said I.

"My dear Edward!" said I, interrupting him, "why did you not call me?"

"What, for such a trifle? On my return, I passed into your chamber, and finding you had, apparently, just dropped into a perturbed slumber, had my arm properly attended to by the Senora Antonina, who bitterly lamented it. Poor old soul! she imagined I had been attacked by a robber."

"I hope sincerely," said I, "the wound is not deep, Barbarian! demon in angel's form—what did she say for herself?"

Oh, tears, hysterics, and graceful attitudes of course! She lamented her mistake, for which I thanked her, in your name. Her large dark eyes streaming with tears, she threw herself at my feet, implored me to conceal what had passed—promised to implore the blessings and intercessions of all the saints in the calendar in my favour, if I would not betray her.

She insisted on tying her silver scarf round my arm, kissed it when she had done so, and entreated me to pardon an act of insanity, proceeding solely from your ingratitude and her own hopeless passion. I here took advantage of the moment, to give her a very moral lecture. I endeavoured to awaken her to the terrible state of mind in which she must have been, had she taken your life! I urged the injustice of presuming to arrogate a power over the affections of the heart, which are uncontrollable!—pointed out to her, that if anything disastrous should occur either to yourself or her cousin, we should know where to seek the aggressor:—led her to her mother's gate, and impressively reminded her that my secrecy to all, excepting yourself, would be inviolable, whilst her conduct might be such as to warrant it."

"And is it thus," said I, warmly pressing the hand of this invaluable friend, "your generous interest in the fate of two unfortunate lovers has been compensated?"

"Could anything have been more romantic?" replied he; "why, the scene was worth the risking something for."

"But life! and such a life! Come—I shall not be easy until you have had surgical advice."

A few minutes brought Dr. Dundas; and, having assured me of the absence of all danger, I insisted on my cousin remaining in quietude on the sofa, whilst I made my arrangements for my departure in the evening. A barque was to be ready at the foot of the flight of steps that led from our grounds, by half-past ten. Father Murphy was to dine with us,—perform the nuptial ceremony, and the venerable Antonina, with her daughter, were to accompany my lovely girl as her attendants.

I awaited evening with sensations of mingled hope and mistrust of the felicity apparently so clearly within my reach. The bliss which would have warmed my heart, was checked and chilled by the remembrance of her aunt's tyrannic nature, and her cousin's unfeminine violence. Nine o'clock came—half-past—I stood beside the fountain so often the witness of our vows. Ten sounded on the gale, alas! something must of occurred. Eleven!—was I then, no more to behold her? Distractedly I rushed forward,—I approached the portal of her aunt's residence. No lights were visible at the windows, no sound met my ears. An aged black of the roça was lying on the grass, in the moonlight. I knocked furiously at the door; for murder, treachery—everything terrific rushed at that moment on my imagination.

The first sleep of a black is almost as deep as death; nevertheless, the noise I made aroused him.

"What does your grace wish?"

"To see your lady."

"Pardon me, my lord—I am rather hard of hearing. Does my lord wish to see the family?"

"I do."

"Santissima Trinidada! didn't they all sail for Portugal, this morning, at day-break?"

"Impossible! not the Lady Zephyrina!"

"Yes, all, my lord. The Lady Zephyrina seemed terribly frightened at the sea; for they were obliged to secure her in the chair, to carry her down to the water-side, and she was taken on board in a fainting fit."

Raving-wild, distracted, I wandered through the night. I knew not whither I went or what I purposed. I paced the woods and fields; the dew of the morning dried as it fell on my parched lip and burning forehead; and the meridian sun was burning on my uncovered brow, when I was at length discovered by my cousin's English servant.

By some degree of finesse and much persuasion, he induced me to enter the cadeira, which accompanied him to convey me home. Assisted by the good Antonina, he put me to bed, darkened the windows, and when my cousin returned (for, notwithstanding the wound in his arm, he had been during the whole of the night in search of me) he found me a raving maniac.

Months elapsed without the smallest variation. My cousin was my constant companion. Our friend, the excellent Dundas, mingled the attentions of friendship with the care and skill of a first-rate medical attendant. Mr. Lathem, an English merchant, and his wife, a Brazilian lady, evinced all that anxiety to alleviate my affliction, of which the warm sympathy of benevolent hearts are alone capable, and no night elapsed that one of these real friends did not watch beside my bed alternately.

No ray of returning reason was apparent; my cousin had written to my father the melancholy termination of my prospect of felicity; cautiously avoiding to break the unwelcome news too suddenly, and directing his letter to the house of a friend, lest my anxious and affectionate mother should sert it: being perfectly aware that the warmth of that devoted, that maternal heart, was too great to admit of such a disclosure, without the most fatal consequences.

At length a gleam of reason returned,—the past appeared like a distracted dream. I wept bitterly, and my heart felt relieved. My cousin rejoiced in the fervour of his friendly heart, and our kind friends sought by every gentle attention to recal me to myself.

At this period, when my mind was balancing between reason and illusion, I cannot describe the consolation, the charm that our friend L.'s children yielded me. His little girl, mingling all the infantine graces of both nations, all the frank generosity of her father, with the minute and fascinating attentions, a Brazilian lady only knows how to offer, with their peculiar effect. She was my solace, my companion, my play-fellow—no morning arrived that Zara and Ricardo did not bring me a nosegay, a basket of fruit, a salver of ornamental preserves, or some little mark of their tenderness and regard. If I was cheerful and conversed with them, their eyes sparkled and their cheeks glowed with pleasure. If I was sad and gloomy, Zara would sing her sweetest songs, with the hope of charming me. Never shall I forget one morning that these sweet children came, as usual, from their mamma, Donna Maria, to inquire after my health; I was in one of those gloomy abstractions when I would have given worlds to weep, and could not. Zara fetched her guitar, she placed herself on an ottoman at my feet—and, raising her expressive eyes to my face, sang the following air:—

> Oh, when to cheer night's darksome skies,
> Thou see'st fair silver Cynthia rise;
> Cast, lov'd one, on her orb thine eyes,
> And think on me!
>
> And when from this thy fav'rite bower
> I gaze, at that same sacred hour;
> We shall by fancy's magic power
> United be!

It was Zephyrina's song! It was the last her voice of melody had breathed for her lost, her desolate Clifford. I wept like a child! the tears streamed from my eyes—and those of the little Zara fell with them.—She then dried them alternately with her handkerchief, and sending away her guitar, declared she would not touch it again until poor Mr. Clifford was quite recovered!

It was a lovely evening, about six months after the destruction of all my earthly happiness; no news of Donna Theodora and her family! no intelligence of the idol of my hopeless heart! We sat in the verandah, my cousin reading to me, whilst I reclined, weak and languid, on the sofa. A sailor passed the portal, looked anxiously round, and balancing himself from side to side—as doubtful whether he should retain his equilibrium—came up the pathway; he inquired if "one Mister Clifford" lived there; and being answered in the affirmative, he pulled up his trousers with an air of extreme satisfaction, and untying his silk handkerchief from his neck, and unrolling it—

"Here it is!" said he; "no one is more ready than Jack Hathaway, to risk life and limb in the sarvice of two unfort'nate lovyers! yes, and even if I'd a been on the pint of drownding, I'd a put that ere in a bottle, and a floated it off in safety!"

I eagerly seized the proffered treasure; it was in Zephyrina's hand! Unconscious of any other recollection, than that of her memory which formed the universe of my hopes, fears, and wishes, I pressed it alternately to my lips and my bosom; the poor fellow eyed me with the delighted sympathy of an honest heart; and my cousin ordered him into the kitchen that he might partake of whatever refreshments he chose :—

"This," continued Clifford, "this is the letter! these are the characters traced by that lovely hand! this is the silken ringlet that once adored her graceful head! If the tears with which it has been so repeatedly bedewed, have yet left its characters legible, I will read it you."

"To Clifford.

"Betrayed by my own attendants, sacrificed to my cousin's inordinate cruelty and revenge, my aunt's unnatural tyranny, perhaps even reproached by my lamented Clifford! where shall the desolate Zephyrina find repose but in the tomb? that last retreat where my beloved parents and my Constantia sleep in peace!

"Have I not from infancy seemed the outcast of Fate? My father died before I beheld the light of day, my mother was taken from me before 1 had ceased to draw my nourishment from her gentle bosom! my Constantia at a moment when I most required the gentle offices of friendship—oh! then, beloved, lamented Clifford! then I sheltered my heart in thy bosom! and many a vision of future years, of thy tenderness and fidelity, consoled me! with thee I could have passed a life of felicity amidst the solitude of the desert. Alas, fond dreamer! a living tomb is all that now is left thee! and even thy ashes shall mingle with those of strangers! Clifford! the rose has faded from my cheek, the lustre has left my eye! the ringlets you delighted in no longer wanton on the breeze—one only I have retained for thee! sometimes look on it, and remember our evenings of felicity when we met beside the fountain.

"Perhaps another, a happier,—but no! I cannot—I dare not pursue the thought,—it is ten thousand times worse than death to thy

"ZEPHYRINA."

Like an infant, I wept over these sacred, these melancholy mementos,—tears of unutterable tenderness, regret, despair! a thousand times did I press them to my burning forehead, my lips, my bosom. A thousand times pledge them the vow of eternal fidelity!

My cousin returned; he waited till my first emotions had subsided, to inform me that this billet had been carefully consigned to the sailor's care, by a friend of the portress of a convent in Lisbon, where the young nun who wrote it had taken the veil, a few days previously; but he had not inquired the name of the convent, he did not know where to find the individual, and therefore every attempt at transmitting any sort of reply would be useless.

She was then living! and we were as much divided as though the grave had closed between us! A pervading languor, a slow consuming fever stole over me. My poor father arrived; he pressed me, the shadow of my former self, to his parental heart; and as soon as my strength would permit, we returned to England. My beloved mother possesses a soul of the most exquisite sensibility—in her maternal bosom I reposed my afflictions; she was capable of entering into all my feelings, she mingled tears of the tenderest sympathy with mine! she could not bid me hope, but with a spirit of that pure and natural religion, which sheds its halo over her every action, she taught me to look beyond this sublunary sphere, for a reunion in a brighter realm of unvarying felicity! She reminded me that I

had yet duties to perform, that I possessed parents, "would my beloved George, said she, "bring that venerable head with sorrow to the grave?—this continued anguish must be resisted, or it will corrode the principles of life. On thine, thy mother's life depends—thy tomb will be hers! where, then, shall thy sister seek a protector? will her brother cast her, young, lovely, and innocent on a reckless world,—an orphan like his lamented Zephyrina?" I clasped this best of mothers, this tender friend to my bosom; my sister was kneeling beside me—her blue eyes were raised, streaming with tears, of imploring compassionate tenderness to mine, and from that moment I breathed a vow, to rouse myself from the lethargy of woe, which had hitherto overwhelmed me. For their peace I endeavoured to acquire a

No. 6.

sufficient degree of calmness to converse with them, to appear amused with my sister's drawings, to read whilst my mother worked, and my sister employed her pencil. Their united care restored me in the space of a year to a comparative degree of health, but the seclusion of my chamber, the solitude of my pillow, repaid in all its exquisite luxury the restraint of the day. I shunned society, I dreaded to see my sister take her harp, lest I should lose the empire I had begun to acquire over myself; and resolved upon having recourse to the abstruse study of the law, that, in preparing myself as a barrister, I might have less leisure for the soul-subduing memory of the past!

Theodore's warmest sympathy had been excited, and taking Clifford's hand, " Alas! my friend," said he, "why cannot I bid you hope? your Zephyrina is lost to you, and a heart like your's can never awaken to a second passion; for I judge of your feelings by my own: accept, then, the consolations of that friendship which I shall be proud to cherish and improve, through every vicissitude of our future lives! After another hour's conversation Clifford took his leave, and Theodore in his dreams beheld his Adela, alternately in the habiliments of the grave, and in the vestments of a nun.

CHAPTER XI.

" Then sit thou gently on my knee,
    And let thy bower my bosom be;
    Oh, Cupid, so thou pity me,
    I will not wish to part with thee."   LODGE.

" ADELA, love!" said Mrs. St. Clair, as she gently unclosed the cottage door to admit her daughter, "you must not go into the parlour at present."

" Why, dearest mamma?"

" Because an accident, which might indeed have been fatal, has occurred to a young gentleman, whose horse took fright at the turning out of a load of hay at Squire Inglewood's stables. His horse unfortunately threw him; by the blessing of Heaven your father was passing, and insisted on his returning with him, ours being the nearest habitation. He has been bled, and your father is now rubbing his arm with that excellent embrocation which I trust will prevent any evil consequences.

Adela looked terrified, and turned extremely pale.

" Your father has taken care to ascertain the extent of the injury," continued Mrs. St. Clair, " and he assures me it is not serious. The servant, who appeared extremely anxious about his master, has taken the horses to the neighbouring hamlet, and we have persuaded him to remain here tranquilly until evening; so let Lucy put on a chicken, some broth will be the most suitable nourishment to prevent fever."

Mrs. St. Clair went to the parlour to attend her guest, and Adela into their neat little kitchen, to give the requisite orders to their attendant Lucy; for it had already struck one, and their repast was usually spread at two.

But we will return to Theodore. St. Clair had recommended his young guest to remain on the sofa until the fervor of day had subsided; for a thousand conflicting emotions had flushed his cheek, and he had left him to the care of his Aurora, who, he assured him, was the " best nurse in the world."

" Here, then," said Theodore, " has favouring fortune cast me into the paradise of this envied abode! what would I not endure rather than lose so felicitous a fate?"

The green shades cast a refreshing shadow over the parlour, where every thing breathed the pure spirit of the youthful goddess, whose hand had almost entirely embellished it. It was two small square rooms, thrown into one by folding doors; towards the orchard it opened through a small gothic porch and painted glass door; the front, which looked into the flower garden by a gothic window, also of exquisitely painted glass, which was now thrown open, and shaded by the green Venetian blinds; plants in china flower pots, on little beautiful stands painted by Adela's hand, shells arranged amongst china vases of flowers, and a small book-case, containing a few books neatly bound and elegantly selected. Byron, Shelley, Chateaubriand's Genie de Christianisme, Volney's Ruins, the Corinna of Madame de Stael, Holstein, the Paul and Virginia of St. Pierre, were here mingled. A Spanish guitar and some music books.

The carpet was the work of Adela and her beloved mother, during their winter evenings; a truly exquisite specimen of work of that description, and consisted of wreaths of roses, lilies and laurel, on a stone-coloured ground, the hearth-rug of the same material and pattern, differently and appropriately arranged, the card racks, screens and chimney ornaments were the sculpture of Adela's penknife, embellished with flowers and landscapes, the work of her scissors. The greater part of the paintings that adorned the walls were Adela's also; the rest, namely Mrs. St. Clair's portrait shortly after their union,—Adela when an infant, scattering flowers over the tomb of his father and their departed babes, the forest, and Sebastiano's cottage on its confines were St. Clair's, and masterly productions.

But hark! a light foot is heard—the door gently opens; Adela enters! a tremor —an indescribable emotion, warns him of her approach! and Theodore, not daring to trust the power of language at such a moment, closes his eyes and seems to sleep.

Adela gently approaches; as one enchanted she gazes on his varying cheek, his beautiful forehead, the fine dark brown hair that gracefully shaded without concealing it. With a newly-awakened sentiment of mingled pain and pleasure, she gazed on every feature, as if she would have carried away his portrait in her heart. Neither form nor face at all in their semblance had hitherto appeared to her, unless in the visions of ethereal bliss, that sometimes visited her dreams! A fragrant sigh is breathed on his cheek. It is too much for Theodore's philosophy to withstand,—his eyes unclose, but she has fled! and Mrs. St. Clair enters to inquire respecting her young patient.

The dinner hour arrived,—St. Clair returned, Adela hears his voice conversing with her father. She is requested to arrange the table before the sofa, where their guest yet reclines.

She enters—St. Clair introduces his daughter—their eyes meet,—both blush— both tremble; and Adela again leaves the room, and remains absent, until she accompanies her mother to share their simple, yet elegant, repast.

The conversation, during dinner, was such as to excite the esteem of St. Clair for the superior understanding and correct moral feeling of his guest; whilst Theodore's admiration for the courtly manners of his kind entertainers; the exquisite beauty of their daughter, and the mystery that shed its charm around them, hourly increased.

What singular vicissitudes could have placed such a family amidst this scene of seclusion? The more he conjectured the farther he seemed to diverge from probability. But his present situation was too seducing, it seemed too much the work of magic, not to be enjoyed in its fullest extent. "If it is a dream," said Theodore, "oh, may I never awake from it!"

The wine was Mrs. St. Clair's making, from the grapes of their own little vineyard, the fruit gathered by Adela's hand.

"I will concede you another half hour," said Mrs. St. Clair: "but, at the end of that time, I must interdict all conversation. Mr. Villars must submit to a Spanish custom, and take his siesta for a couple of hours, for I can observe that he has exerted himself too much already, and until your father returns, my child, place your table by the window, and finish the group of flowers you commenced this morning.

"You see, Mrs. St. Clair is very absolute," said St. Clair, offering his hand to his visitor; "but, as her commands are universally the dictates of reason, we all submit to her gentle sway."

Mrs. St Clair followed him out of the room, to give directions to the servant; and Adela and Theodore remained together. Singular perversity of the human heart! Theodore, who only a few hours previously would have given the universe, had it been at his disposal, to have obtained such a moment of felicity, was perfectly overwhelmed. He remained silent, agitated, confused! Some minutes elapsed before Adela dared look towards the sofa—and when she did, his eyes were again closed as in slumber. Her hand trembled, her heart beat with an unusual palpitation. She mixed the carmine for her roses with the green she had prepared for the leaves—blushed at her own stupidity, and hurried the group of flowers she had spoiled into her portfolio, that her mother might not see it.

She arose to look at their sleeping guest;—a sigh burst from his bosom!—hers echoed it. Was he then unhappy? so young, so elegant, alas! perhaps the injury inflicted by his fall had been greater than his fortitude would acknowledge!

Are there, then, Adela, no sighs but those of anguish?

Theodore still kept his eyes closed, that he might recover his self-possession. Already was he in imagination at her feet—the avowal on his lips.

Was this, then, to be the reward of her parents' hospitality? was it thus, then, he should deprive himself of their confidence?—her innocence would be terrified, her purity outraged by his rashness!

"Are you easier?" said Adela, seeing his eyes unclose.

"Much easier!" replied Theodore, taking her hand, as she stood beside him.

"How happy you make me!" said she.

Theodore pressed his lovely captive to his lips, while she gently endeavoured to withdraw.

"Can I feel less than the highest degree of felicity when Miss St. Clair honours a stranger by an expression of so much benignity?"

Adela blushed, turned over the sketches in her portfolio, and as her mother entered, she left the parlour. She sighed over the remembrance of the pathos the stranger had thrown into his graceful acknowledgments. She arranged her hair, placed a half-blown rose amidst its exuberant braids, and placed the tea or the table, ready for her father's return.

But by what Arabian-night adventure did Theodore fall into the situation he so ardently desired? for we suppose the bruised shoulder to be like Clifford's sprained ankle—merely a finesse, and employed upon the principle, or rather want of principle—"that deception is allowable in love, as in war." I am entirely of an opposite opinion, whatever may be the apology. Duplicity is always dishonourable, and frequently destructive of the cause it seeks to favour. We must not do evil that good may proceed from it, but strictly adhere to the beauty of sincerity.

Theodore, however, did not, in this instance, merit censure; he had faithfully kept his promise relative to the precribed fortnight; but, on the day of its completion, he was on the road, and about eleven on the following, the singular chance, coincidence, or whatever it may be deemed, occurred. A load of hay was actually laid down at the door of a stable, belonging to one of St. Clair's neighbours, at the very moment Theodore turned the winding path from the valley—intent upon nothing but enjoying one glance at the cottage as he passed the opposite angle of the lane leading to the inn, (his proposed introduction having been arranged for the evening, as a traveller who had lost his way) when his horse took fright, pranced, reared, and threw him; at the instant St. Clair arrived at the spot, offered his assistance, and insisted on his returning with him to the cottage, where Ralph remained with him until assured that the accident was not serious, and feeling satisfied that his master was in the best hands in the world,—he took the two horses to the stables of the inn, from whence he sallied twice during the afternoon, to inquire respecting that health his honest heart valued a thousand times more than his own.

But let us return to the cottage parlour, where Adela gracefully presided at the tea-table. St. Clair was pleased to find that his young friend had benefitted by repose, sufficiently to take an animated part in the conversation; and even with one arm disabled, he would have insisted on assisting Miss St. Clair; but her mother would not allow him to do so. His acknowledgments were those of the heart, and found their way to the esteem of St. Clair. A course of years is not requisite to form a friendship where sentiments correspond and minds assimilate; and I have seen the tenderest amities subsist, where esteem and veneration on the one hand, and affectionate interest on the other, have formed the only bond between the spring and autumn of life !

Theodore spoke with enthusiastic admiration of the scenery around.

" You hear possess," said he, " all the elegance a correct taste can create, united to the luxuriant beauty of nature in her most attractive form. Nothing is left to desire in so delightful a retreat—all is felicity, comfort, repose !"

" It is, indeed," replied St. Clair, " a welcome repose,—and we will not draw aside the curtain which veils the sorrow, vicissitude, and disappointment which giuded the pilgrim's steps to the shrine of nature and of peace.

" When I first purchased this land, it was all uncultivated, and wild as the manners of its surrounding inhabitants. The neighbouring cottagers were idle, illiterate, rude ! They appeared to possess no other motive for benefitting or assisting each other than that of selfishness, induced too freqently by a fate devoid of comfort. It is said, ' riches harden the heart.' That were unpardonable ; poverty and destitution must inevitably do so. Here we behold the worthless revelling in luxury, and daily expending in folly a sufficient amount to support a thousand families, who shrink from the wintry blast, without a shelter, or perhaps a covering sufficient to keep out its inclemency ;—destitute of hope, without bread for their children. Can we wonder that they are reckless and negligent of the softer sympathies of life, which, if nurtured, would only render them more keenly alive to their deprivations ! Render a people happy and you render them virtuous ; as far as our contracted power would allow, we have endeavoured to do so, and our reward has been ten-fold ! In erecting this humble habitation, I had some employment for almost all the indigent part of the little community around. I selected those who had fewest resources, as labourers in my grounds. The example of neatness, arrangement, and regularity spread rapidly amongst them, and the hours when I did not require their aid, were devoted to the improving their own huts, and cultivating their own gardens, so that, where previously weeds, useless bushes, or, at best, a few cabbages and potatoes were visible,—a variety of vegetables not only furnish their own tables, but produce a moderate amount when carried by their children to the next market. The vine's clustering tendrils, creep over the freshly-whitened front of their cottages,—the fruit-trees yield their autumnal store—which, when sold, add also to the comforts of the winter. I did not tell them, " industry is the parent of competence." I proved it to them by example ; and encouragement and profit sweeten their labour. In distributing employment equally, instead of dividing their interests, I combined them ; and where discord and envy previously reigned, peace, unanimity, and social feeling alone are observable.

" Two evenings during the week Mrs. St. Clair devoted to the instruction of the young girls of our village, whilst I attended to the improvements of the lads. A kind of approbatory word—a smile from Mrs. St. Clair was considered a valued reward for their application. In sickness, Mrs. St. Clair visited them ; in sorrow we endeavoured to pour the balm of consolation ; when this sublunary scene could promise no more, we pointed to a brigher sphere ! We gained their confidence by entering into their feelings ; and assimilating our interests with their's, we have given, by cultivation, to rusticity a touch of polished life, which yields its greatest charm, and thus have secured to ourselves a degree of devotedness and friendship, which would perhaps be vainly sought amidst a more splendid scene.

" Two of the young girls, in a few years, became sufficiently informed to take the charge of education off Mrs. St. Clair's hands, and they now instruct the infant part of the community, at a little school-house on the opposite verge of the valley. It is divided into two rooms ; and an elderly man, whose life commenced with more favourable prospects, attends to the boys, at a moderate compensation, whilst we monthly superintend their improvement."

" You are, indeed, a benign philanthropist," said Theodore, "your's is the empire of the heart, and shall remain unshaken, when that of the despot and the tyrant shall totter, and be levelled with the dust."

St. Clair clapsed his hand. He could appreciate the enthusiasm of a young and unsophisticated heart.   Mrs. St. Clair's dark eyes expressed the interest she felt, and a tear stole down the cheek of their Adela.

Theodore noticed a painting that hung over the chimney-piece.   The scenery, the superb mansion of white stone, appearing amongst the most brilliant foliage, rendered the dark shadow of the woods and forests in distant perspective, more impressively beautiful.   A fair and lovely girl was pourtrayed in one of the verandas taking a bird from the hand of her brother, an equally beautiful boy, to give it its liberty.

The resemblence to Adela was striking.   "Miss St. Clair, in infancy, is it not?" said Theodore.

"No, sir," replied St. Clair, "'tis the resemblance of her departed sister.   The Villa del Rio was the mansion of her father and grandfather; but Adela is the child of adversity—no prospects dawned upon her birth beyond those she now enjoys."

St. Clair's voice faltered,—Adela placed her hand on his arm—she raised her expressive eyes to his—

"And what felicity could the universe yield to me, my dear papa?" said she, "beyond your tenderness and affection, and that of my beloved mamma?"

"Have you not, my Edmund, repeatedly allowed," said Mrs. St. Clair, "that the mind is its own place, and may form itself a paradise or a desert.   Let us say nothing about the brambles that have intervened amidst our united path—they have not been unmingled with roses, and if we could forget the regretted aliena-tion of some, the loss of our parent and those beloved ones, we shall never cease to lament, what could be wanting to our present felicity?"

St. Clair smiled benignly his assent and presented his daughter with the guitar.

"Yes, love," said Mrs. St. Clair, "our conversation has been too much tinctured with pensiveness for the amusement of our guest.   A song will produce a pleasing variation."

Adela took the guitar, and with unaffected sweetness sung the following air:—

See our meads adorned with flowers,
Pleasure decks our rural bowers;
Love and mirth and joy be ours,
　　　Youth will quickly fly!

Shepherds gay, and maidens fair,
Love shall be our only care,
Love unmixed with pale despair,
　　　Blest with constancy!

Hearts to virtue's dictates true,
True to love and honour too;
What have we with care to do?
　　　Strew the path with flowers!

Let our native vales resound
With the lute, the viol's sound,
Sweet content, with roses crown'd,
　　　Guards our rural bowers!

Adela's voice ceased, and with an indescribable grace she received the tribute of heart-felt admiration which Theodore's eyes, more than his lips, paid her; and at his entreaty sung several others, in a style which might have charmed the most critical ear.   At length St. Clair threw open the glass door, and Theodore accompanied him in a saunter through the orchard, and round by a rustic gate which led into the flower-garden.   "This is more particularly Adela's domain," said St. Clair, "here her taste is permitted to predominate.   The child of nature —her very thoughts poetry—she instinctively rejects everything like the studied guise of art, so that we may almost say—

' Nature here
Wantons as in her prime, and plays at will
Her virgin fancies."

All was, indeed, simplicity and taste—from the honey suckle that entwined with the vine shaded the window,—to the rustic temple, around which the clematis wandered, and the acacia, jasmine, and rose paid their tribute of fragrance.

On their return they found a table arranged before the cottage door, and an evening's repast of strawberries and cream, custards, fresh eggs, newly churned butter and home-made bread, with wine of Mrs. St. Clair's making, was arranged on a cloth, that equalled Adela's favourite lilies in whiteness, and decorated with flowers—nothing could equal the enchantment of the scene—the distant prospect, the mingled song of the woodland choristers, the perfume of flowers, the sun's declining rays gilding the stream that led its rippling waters through the valley, Adela's presence, her artless smile, her voice of melody.

Powerful and overwhelming sentiment of first-awakened tenderness! why are thy earliest moments mingled with pensiveness, thy most expressive language sighs and tears?

The hour of departure arrived, Mr. and Mrs. St. Clair received the warm pressure of their young friend's hand, and warmly invited him to return on the morrow.

Mrs. St. Clair urged the danger of his pursuing his journey in his present state, and St. Clair repeated his request that whilst he remained an invalid, their cottage might be considered his daily home.

At this moment Ralph appeared at the gate, and Theodore with an expressive glance at Adela, to whom he could scarcely trust his voice to say adieu—departed.

For Adela—she had never heard the word farewell with so much regret before,—she watched his receding form, she listened to his last footstep as it died away in distance,—she then reluctantly re-entered the cottage, pressed her beloved parents to her artless bosom with an increased fervor, that seemed to arise from a self-reproachful consciousness that for the first time in her existence, another was dividing its sentiments with them; and, retiring to her pillow, she wept in the fulness of her heart. She wept herself to sleep! and even then did the image of the interesting, the elegant stranger haunt her imagination. Byron says—

> "————Dreams speak,
> Like sybils of the future."

Adela's mind wandered in the wood, on the verge of the valley, the stranger youth sat beside her on a flower-embroidered bank, the blue unclouded azure of the firmament above them was reflected by the stream at their feet; the stranger plucked a rose, he placed it in her bosom, he breathed the vow of inviolable fidelity! suddenly the scene shifted, the breath of autumn had scattered the path with yellow and fallen foliage: she called her companion, he answered not; she looked for the rose he had placed in her bosom, but its fragrance and beauty were no more, and nothing but its thorny stem remained.

She awoke trembling and agitated, breathed a prayer, and again slept:—she now stood in a beautiful temple—the stranger youth beside her: soft music floated on the air, a venerable figure presided at the altar, which was crowned with flowers.

Her hand was clasped in his; already was the vow on those love-breathing lips, when suddenly the brilliant azure of the skies became o'erclouded, the tempest arose, the thunder rolled, the lightning flashed, the temple shook to its foundation! their hands severed, terrific figures intervened, a deep and awful gulph is between them! and the darkness of night veils the terrible cavern from her view: —the scene again changes! the melancholy hue of twilight gleams over the desolated and ruined scene, uprooted trees are scattered round, the temple is in ruins—and where it once stood, arise two turf-covered graves.

She awakes—her pillow is wet with her tears.

Sweet Adela! where is now that balmy repose that was wont to shed its forgetfulness over thy rustic couch? Thy very prayers, the innocent effusions of thy pure heart are troubled; even amidst thy fervent supplications for thy parents, his image intervenes, and thy morning orisons waft a prayer to the throne of mercy for his recovery!

Lucy had twice tapped at her door, and with an eye somewhat less brilliant and a cheek less vivid, she descended to make her morning arrangements.

CHAPTER XII.

"And what unto them is the world beside
With all its change of time and tide?
Its living things, its earth and sky
Are nothing to their mind and eye.
And heedless as the dead are they
Of aught around, above, beneath;
As if all else had passed away,
They only for each other breathe."   BYRON.

THEODORE had returned, elate with hope and happiness, and delighted with the sport of favouring fortune, for such he deemed his accident.

Ralph never beheld him so cheerful before, and he continued to converse gaily with him until the honest fellow, fearing the varied circumstances of the day, united with the event that had marked its commencement, would produce an excitement, little favourable to the prospects he appeared even now to enjoy in anticipation, at length succeeded in persuading his master to retire to rest.

But Theodore could not sleep, one interrupted vision of felicity raised its fairy castle before him during the whole of the night, her glance of modest yet tender expression, her gentle interest in his comfort and recovery, her faltering farewell; morning arrived, he was neither sleepy nor weary; but his cheek was flushed, and his rapid pulse denoted a considerable degree of fever.

Contrary to Ralph's advice however he had arisen,   had just dressed when Mr. St. Clair was announced.

"Come, Mr. Villars," said he, "we have waited breakfast for you half an hour: Mrs. St. Clair felt apprehensive you were suffering from the effects of yesterday. But you are in a fever! you ought not indeed to have left us last night."

Theodore politely apologized, expressed his warm acknowledgments for the hospitality already received, and inquired relative to the health of the ladies.

"They shall answer for themselves," replied St. Clair, "come, we will return by a shady path, and place you again under the care of my little physician."

Theodore smiled, and having given Ralph instructions to employ his time according to his own inclinations, he took St. Clair's arm and departed.

Mrs. St. Clair insisted on preparing a chamber for him, that no care might be wanting to facilitate his recovery, and Theodore became a willing and delighted inmate at the cottage until his recovery might be effected.

It is said, and with very great truth, that a week passed in domestic intercourse beneath the same roof, developes the character, and creates a firmer bond of ntimacy than years of casual association. And this was verified in Theodore's visit to the cottage.

His candour and liberality of sentiment, his deference to St. Clair, his gentlemanly attentions to Mrs. St. Clair, his sincere gratitude for her almost maternal care, had long won their hearts, and as day succeeded day, his unassuming talent and congeniality of mind, rendered his presence almost necessary to the comfort of the litle circle.

For Adela! *she* regarded him with all the tremulous fervour of a first-awakened tenderness; with her the sportiveness of infancy had deepened into the more pensive cast of early womanhood. Idolized by her parents, her life had been hitherto as an unruffled stream, on whose pure bosom, the clear azure of sunny skies alone had been reflected; and whilst he sat beside her in the arbour, wandered with her amidst their sequested solitudes, read to her, or mingled his voice of rich and exquisite melody with hers, she unfolded her pure bosom's inmost recesses to an impression too capable of directing her future destiny.

Theodore lived but in her smile, his world was in her presence, she was the idol of his waking, the dream of his sleeping hour: the past to him was as nothing! the future formed no part of his consideration, for all the ardour, the energy of his soul was centered in the delirium of the present moment.

A month had elapsed before Ralph had dared venture to remind his master that prudence demanded his return. Not a thought of separation had yet glanced over his day-dream of bliss. He sighed, and acknowledged its painful necessity ; but when he wandered with Adela by moonlight, in the wood that led to the valley, he whispered his hope, that in absence, he might sometimes be recalled to her memory.

Adela's heart throbbed with a new and painful emotion.

"And has the seene, which Mr. Villars so lately termed the witness of his happiest hours, already lost its charm ?"

"Oh, Adela ! banish that appellation of coldness !—call me, Theodore, your
No. 7.

riend, your brother—who parts from you in anguish, urged by an imperative necessity,—who will treasure up the remembrance of every look, every smile!—who will revert to these delightful hours, and consider each moment an eternity until he again beholds you!"

"Alas! my foreboding heart has long mingled the anticipation of the hour of your departure amidst the pleasure your society has yielded us. It also whispers, that amidst that gayer scene to which Theodore's family connections and splendid fortune will lead him—the valley, the cottage, and its inhabitants will be forgotten!"

Adela sunk on the rustic seat beside them, and Theodore, throwing himself at her feet, alternately dried her tears and his own.

"Sacred and lovely memento of affection!" said he, in a voice replete with emotion. "Beloved, adored girl! when this heart resigns thy idolized image, the throb of life must have ceased, and the cold turf cover it!"

Adela shuddered,—her dream returned to her memory, with all its imaginative desolation.

"But, Theodore—my parents!"

"Will they, beloved one, forbid me to replace you in that sphere you were born to embellish?"

"But your's?"

"Alas! from early infancy I have been deprived of a mother's affectionate sympathy. But will my father separate his only son from all that can give a charm to existence! Will he sink him to despondency—to an early tomb?"

"Oh, Theodore, cease to distress me!"

"Dearest girl, then listen to reason; a year or two will finish my studies; every hour during that period that can possibly be so devoted, shall be spent in this sweet retirement; at the end of it, we will obtain our parents' mutual consent, and my Adela shall become mine for ever!"

Adela smiled through her tears. She spoke of the name inscribed on the oak —she drew from her pocket-book the lines he had written. Theodore acknowledged all;—his first visit to the cottage, his doubts, his fears, his anxiety to obtain an introduction. All was now the unclouded sunshine of mutual and acknowledged affection, and hope lent her golden hue to every future scene. Could Adela doubt, when Theodore breathed its soothing accents combined with those of impassioned tenderness, and inviolable fidelity.

On their return, Theodore mentioned his purposed departure on the following morning. Both heard him with regret. St. Clair approved his correct feeling, relative to his studies; and as they felt convinced that from inclination, he would frequently repeat his visits, they assured him that whenever he felt so disposed, he would always find—not only a humble home, but sincere friends, in the cottage on the brink of the valley.

And Theodore has torn himself from that abode of enchantment—the warm pressure of the hand from his hospitable friends,—the repeated invitation to return whenever so inclined,—the glance of expressive tenderness and regret interchanged with Adela! And every step his horse takes, now bears him farther from her. Steadily he averts his eye—another glance must unnerve his heroism;—he dares not turn where his desert flower droops over his departure, and he is no longer by her side to dry her tears.

Ralph forbears to address him, and Theodore cannot trust his voice until the violence of his emotion has subsided into some degree of calmness.

But, Adela! who can describe the perturbation of that gentle bosom amidst the solitude of its present sensations?

His farewell was yet on her ear, with all the desolation it will convey to the heart under the happiest of circumstances. Byron says:—

"————In that word—that fatal word, howe'er
We promise—hope—believe—there breathes despair."

and how justly! for, amidst the variety of human vicissitudes, who shall say it will not be the last?

Adela, pale with emotion, hastened to her chamber. She unclosed her window to catch the last glimpse of the being so dear to her artless bosom—he is gone !—and she seeks relief in tears. She then bathes her eyes with rose-water, and breathes on her handkerchief to endeavour to hide their traces, before she descends to the parlour.

"Well, Adela, our young friend is gone ;" said Mrs. St. Clair, "but, as your father and he are mutually pleased with each other's society, I think there is little doubt but he will return from time to time, to enjoy the scene he so much admires."

Adela endeavoured to reply carelessly to her mother's observation ; and, in turning over her portfolio, beheld, amongst the sketches, a set of beautiful ivory tablets, clasped with gold, and containing a gold pencil case. She saw a few lines written on the pure white of its cover, and hurried it into her bosom, that in the seclusion of the garden she might read them unobserved.

On sliding aside the leaves she read the following :—

To Adela

I leave awhile, alas ! I leave
My home of bliss—my lovely maid,
The sigh of fond regret to heave
In solitude's sequestered shade.

Enchanting vale ! where artless love
First warmed my breast, unmixed with woe ;
Sweet gliding stream and shady grove,
Far from your lovely scenes I go !

Beneath thy shade-embowering tree
Inscribed—her much-loved name you bear,
Here oft at eve she strayed with me
Through flowery glen and valley fair.

Sweet rill, the witness of our love !
Suspend awhile thy gentle flow :
Alas ! in exile doomed to rove,
Far from your glassy wave I go.

Adela pressed this treasured memento of affection to her lips, and to her pure bosom ; but, as the fairest rose is not without its thorn, a feeling of self-reproach was mingled with the pleasure this effusion of a heart she valued had given her ; and her first movement was to go to her dear mamma, throw herself in her arms, show her the tablets, and confess their mutual affection. But had Theodore authorized her to do so ? No ! Had, then, a newly-awakened feeling obtained a preference over the first—the most sacred of claims ? But again, the hand-writing being the same with that carved on the tree, might not her parents reproach him with duplicity ? His introduction, also, although entirely the effect of chance (and, alas ! one that might have proved fatal) bore so much the air of romance !

"Well," continued Adela, temporising with her own heart, "I will not betray him ; but, when we meet again, I will urge the necessity of perfect candour, and nothing on earth shall induce me to pledge my faith beyond what I have already done, without my parents consenting that I should do so. But I do him injustice," continued she, musing, "His own words plead for him : did he not say, ' we will obtain the mutual consent of our parents ?' Oh, yes ! my Theodore—my beloved friend, thy sentiments are honor, delicacy itself !—She kissed the tablets, and placed them in her bosom.

On the following morning, one of the men employed on the farm, who had been to the next village, brought a letter directed for " Edmund St. Clair, Esq."

"This is a hand entirely new to us," said Mrs. St. Clair.

"I hope poor Villars has not met with any other accident," said St. Clair.

Adela's cheek turned pale, and she offered her scissors to her father, who instantly opened it, and read as follows :—

"DEAR SIR,

"Mr. J. St. Clair's brother has, some months since, departed this life. He wrote, he informs me, at the time, not only to request your presence at the funeral, but also afterwards to invite you, with your family, to take possession of a very pretty house in his vicinity, that he might enjoy your society, which he seems to have highly appreciated.

"These letters were both entrusted to an individual, who professed to have delivered them into your hands. Some very forcible reasons, however, having since occured to deprive the parties of your relative's confidence, he questioned them closely, and observed a something so resembling confusion and prevarication, that a doubt has arisen in his mind of the actual delivery of those letters. About a week ago he was taken ill, and although his indisposition is not, I trust, serious, being merely an attack of the gout, he has since appeared to labour under a certain degree of depression of spirits, on your account, and has expressed an earnest wish to see you on several occasions. As a neighbour, I frequently sit with him an hour or two during the evening, and last night he said, ' I wish you would write to Mr. E. St. Clair, and say that I wish to see him as early as convenient ; —and, do you see,' continued the old gentleman, ' put the letter in the post with your own hands.' I assured him I would, and he seemed more satisfied.

" I am a perfect stranger to you, sir, but I feel it a duty on my own part to say, that, as there are many self-interested individuals, backwards and forwards, from time to time, I really think you do not do justice to your family in absenting yourself—to say nothing of the pleasure the old gentleman would feel at your arrival ; and he really expresses, not only a great degree of pride in your talents, but regret that a sort of delicacy on account of your altered fortune should keep you away.

I am, sir, your's respectfully,
JAMES ARNOLD."

" To Edmund St. Clair, Esq."

"Well, my love," said St. Clair, " what is to be done ? I hope sincerely he is not seriously indisposed : for had not our circumstances induced me to shrink from an appearance of earnestness to accept his friendly invitations in the first instance, I know not the man whose friendship I should so earnestly have culti-vated. Frank, generous and sincere, I esteemed him the first moment I beheld him ; and, amidst a crowd, my heart would have claimed kindred with him ; but, a too tenacious independence has stood in our way, and the individuals alluded to, have, no doubt, endeavoured to take advantage of our absence to render it a complete alienation."

" What interest can strangers have, papa ?" said Adela.

" Who can account for the actions of the selfish, and unprincipled my child ?" said St. Clair ?

" He told you, we were the sole surviving branch after himself and his brother."

" He did so."

" The individuals then alluded to, cannot be relatives."

"Undoubtedly not ; but, long may our venerable friend survive to enjoy his possessions whatever they may be."

" You will go to see him, love, will you not ?

" Why, I do not see how I can deny so earnest a request."

" You will not I am certain !—perhaps his spirits will be enlivened by your society for a few days,—and influence his recovery."

When breakfast was over, Mrs. St. Clair and Adela set earnestly to the work of preparation for St. Clair's visit ; and, although this was the first separation, and a tear would twinkle in the eye of an idolizing wife, and affectionate daughter, yet they both possessed too much generosity and self-denial to wish to deprive their venerable relative of a few hours of that society—the value of which the flight of time had hourly enhanced to themselves—and with a half smothered sigh of tender reluctance, and a warm embrace to each, St. Clair commenced his journey.

But let us return to Sir Edward Villars, whose avarice was considerably gratified by the accumulation of his uncle's wealth, in addition to his own immense possessions.

At this juncture, when his heart had unfolded itself, even to the claims of hospitality, an elderly, extremely gentlemanly, looking man called on him, and with that frank and courtly air, which evinces a perfect knowledge of the world, apologized for having been induced to do so, by a wish to make some inquiries, relative to the estate which joined Villars Park.

He spoke of his family's recent arrival from India,—and that he had been so attracted by the healthfulness and beauty of the scene around Harewood lodge, that on account of the delicacy of Mrs. Somerville's health, which had suffered severely from a warm climate, he had made up his mind to be its possessor, if money could purchase it.

Sir Edward gave every requisite information, introduced him to Mr. Irwin, and accompanied him over the grounds.

In a few days Harewood lodge was put into preparation; and, at the end of the month, although the embellishments were not completed, the family arrived in two travelling carriages; on account of the declining state of Mrs. Somerville's health, for whom immediate country air had been considered indispensable by her physicians.

A few days after their arrival, Sir Edward was taking his morning ride, when he met a neighbour, and they pursued their way together. In turning an angle of the road they encountered Mr. Somerville, accompanying a lady on horseback, and followed by a servant in a livery of green and gold. Sir Edward and Mr. Somerville saluted each other courteously in passing.

"A very fine girl," said Sir Charles Oakley, "and possessed of a fine fortune too—she will set all the young fellows in this neighbourhood on the alert. He grandfather, I understand, left her £500,000."

"Ah! indeed!"

"She is also an only daughter, and her father has amassed a considerable property in India."

"India has enriched the purse, and destroyed the health of many," said Sir Edward.

"I would not exchange health for wealth," said Sir Charles; "what are all the treasures of the east, when an aching head, and shattered nerves,—take from their possessor the power of enjoyment?"

"I am not of your opinion," replied Sir Edward, "for I certainly consider wealth the chief good in this best of all possible worlds."

"I am happy to say our sentiments are not congenial—but will you dine with me?"

"I am obliged to you; not to-day."

"Then I must bid you farewell, for I have an appointment and am already five minutes after the time."

Sir Charles turned in the opposite direction, and Sir Edward continued to ruminate as he pursued his ride.

"Miss Somerville is indeed a very fine girl, but were she not—were she deformity itself—her wealth would render her a most advantageous match for Theodore,—and setting a father's partiality aside, his fine person will, I think, give him a tolerably fair chance. I'll send for him, say nothing to him about my impressions —and let the thing take its course."

Sir Edward returned, dined, retired to his study, wrote to say he wished his son to return for a few weeks, sent off his letter; and after a few hasty strides about the apartment ejaculated, "£500,000! with what he will possess when he is of age, then what she will have at her father's death, and he is some years my senior, admirable! Heaven forbid my boy should miss such a prize."

CHAPTER XIII.

"The fool is not always unfortunate, nor the wise man always successful; yet never had a fool thorough enjoyment; never was a wise man wholly unhappy."   DODSLEY.

IT was evening when St. Clair arrived at Clair Hall; the sun shed his departing lustre on the ancient windows of the home of his ancestors, and the muffled knocker sounded heavily beneath his hand.

Some time elapsed, and he repeated it; at length a heavy step approached, and an elderly man in a plain livery cautiously opened the door.

St. Clair enquired after the health of his relative.

"Something better, sir, we think to-day."

"Is he confined to his bed?"

"No sir."

"Be good enough to deliver my card."

"Certainly, sir," said a brisk smart looking servant girl, who just at that moment passed across the hall, and proceeded on towards the staircase.

"What's that, Ellen;" said a coarse looking young woman of about thirty-five, who started from a parlour.

"I'm only going to deliver the gentleman's card ma' am."

She looked at the card, changed colour, and darting a glance of resentment at the girl, "pray how dare you presume to deliver a card to Mr. St. Clair, without first of all bringing it to me?"

"I didn't know miss."

"Very well, you know now then;" continued she, putting the card into the pocket of her black silk apron, "say that Mr. St. Clair is too ill to be seen."

"Mr. St. Clair is too ill to be seen, sir," repeated the girl; with a glance of meaning at the servant, who still held the door in his hand.

"I am concerned to hear it," said St. Clair, "but as I came to visit him at his own express desire, I should have conceived I might have been admitted."

"No one can be admitted," screamed the same voice from the parlour, "Mr St. Clair is too ill to see company!"

St. Clair departed, with impressions not the most favourable, and retracing his steps to the inn—he ordered coffee and placed himself by an open window, to enjoy the freshness of the evening.

"Mr. Arnold's opinion appears indeed to have been tolerably correct," thought St. Clair, "he has truly said 'there are self-interested individuals,' what, but the most diabolical of motives can induce so inveterate a degree of earnestness to preclude all intercourse with my venerable friend, and that in a young person! the man allowed that he was considered better to day; and, had he been seriously ill, the girl would not, I think, have tripped so readily forward to deliver the card. But I will see Mr. Arnold if possible."

At this moment the waiter entered with the coffee, and St. Clair inquired if an elderly gentlemen of the name of St. Clair lived in that neighbourhood.

"Mr. St. Clair, of Clair Hall?" said he, "yes sure! and a good sort of old gentleman too, sir, he's been ailing or so lately."

"Seriously?"

"Only a touch of the gout I believe, he has trifling attacks of it sometimes."

"Does he live alone?"

"Yes, sir, since his brother's death: he has visitors staying sometimes."

"Has he any relatives?"

"None as ever I heard of; his brothers have died off one after another, one went away long ago to foreign parts, he died too I believe. Its pity too, he's worth a power o' money! and he's got those about him as will hang on like leeches to the last. The servants come backwards and forwards sometimes you see sir; and servants will talk."

"Do they say he is confined to his bed?"

"No sir, not as I know of; at least, he wasn't yesterday morning for I saw him at the window, and very pleasant he looked too,—poor gentleman! he makes a hobby-horse of his garden; he has got some choice tulips."

"Do you know a gentleman of the name of Arnold?"

"Which Mr. Arnold sir?" said the waiter, "because you know there are two Mr. Arnolds,—there is one an acquaintance of the old gentleman."

"Where does he live?"

"At the bottom of St. Peter's Street; any one will tell you where to find Mr. James Arnold."

When St. Clair had finished his coffee, he went to St. Peter's Street; entered a very pretty garden, and knocked at the door of a genteel habitation; a female servant opened it, and delivered his card in the parlour,—a respectable elderly gentleman came out, and, offering his hand, insisted on St. Clair walking in, where his wife and two fine girls, his daughters, were taking tea.

After the usual ceremonial of introduction had passed, and St. Clair was seated,

"I am happy sir," said Mr. Arnold, " to see you here; have you seen the old gentleman?"

"No, sir! I understand he is too dangerously ill to see company."

"Who told you so?"

St. Clair related his arrival, with every circumstance concerned with his visit to Clair Hall, and impossibility of gaining admittance.

"Well, it is just as I conjectured it would be," said Mrs. Arnold, "it is now three days since Miss Crawley has permitted Mr. Arnold to see the old gentleman, and he used to be there every evening."

"Strange doings, strange doings!" said Mr. Arnold.

"Is your friendship with Mr. St. Clair of long standing?" said St. Clair.

"We have been neighbours, for years, sir, but particularly intimate during the last two."

"Has he been very communicative with you, relative to his family concerns?"

"Not particularly, any farther than what I mentioned in my letter; he said on one occasion, when he brought a work of your's for Mrs. Arnold to read, 'this is a work of great merit, the author is the last branch of our family; when you have read it, give me your opinion of it,—I think you will say he is a credit to the name.' "

"Is Miss Crawley a relative?"

"If she is, I never heard of her as such; she accompanies an elderly gentleman and lady, of the name of St. Clair, from time to time: there are two distincts families of that name, this is the Rev. Jonathan St. Clair."

"Mamma," said Miss Arnold, " the coachman at the Hall tells Hannah, that Mr. Jonathan, in speaking of the old gentleman, calls him his uncle, and that Miss Crawley calls Mrs. Jonathan St. Clair aunt!"

"This is very singular! Mr. Josiah St. Clair said, in the presence of my wife, that we were the only surviving branches of the family. He also said one brother, had died a widower without children, the other a bachelor, he himself never married. Who, then, is this gentleman?"

"Upon my soul you puzzle me!"

"It is quite an enigma," said Mrs. Arnold.

"He is the great unknown!" said Miss Arnold.

"But, my dear sir," said St. Clair, " setting all other doubts aside, by what authority does Miss Crawley intercept cards and preclude all access to Mr. St. Clair? Why does she take her station as the dragon guardian to the entrance to the hall.

"Oh, sir!" said Louisa Arnold, laughingly, "she, I understand, is the niece of the nephew's wife! but I should think Mr. Jonathan cannot know any thing of it; he is a clergyman, represented as a very pious, religious character; and, therefore, I should think, would not sanction it. Miss Crawley, on the contrary, has the character of a perfect hypocrite, selfish, and uninformed."

"Why, Louisa! I think you have been acquiring a taste for scandal."

" It is true, papa, however."

"Indeed! well, I will go to-morrow," continued Mr. Arnold, "endeavour to obtain admittance, and tell this lady frankly, what I think of her conduct."

" By no means, my dear sir! I came, not by my own wish, but at my respected relative's desire.   His repose shall not be interrupted on my account ; a day or so will, perhaps, produce a favourable change.   I will remain that period at the inn, and I shall perhaps yet see him. If Mr. Jonathan is the respectable man described, he will not throw any obstacle in the way of an interview,—if not, matters must take their chance."

"Well, my good sir," replied Mr. Arnold, " if Clair Hall is closed upon you, my door is open.   I have often heard of you,—even the girls here are as much delighted as their mother with your writings , and I must insist upon your taking up your residence with us during your stay."

Mrs. Arnold, without waiting a reply, rang for the servant.   St. Clair's port-manteau was fetched from the inn—an apartment prepared for him ; the evening passed away in the interchange of warm hospitality on the one hand, and courteous and friendly recognisance on the other ; and before St. Clair slept he wrote a few lines to his beloved Aurora and his little girl, for such he still affectionately termed his Adela.

But, as a new character has been introduced, we shall perhaps be expected to give some account of the motive capable of instigating so strenuous an exertion of vigilant arguism, at a post over which she could have no reasonable control.

We will revert to a few incidents of Miss Crawley's earliest years, that by a gradual progression of events and development of character, we may unravel the mystery.

Mr. and Mrs. Jonathan St. Clair were married late in life, they had no children ; —the lady's sister possessed one only girl, which she and her husband willingly resigned to their care

It will be asked, were they then needy ? Not at all. Alexander Crawley had drudged up, without one atom of worth or talent, from amidst the lowest of the operative class, into extreme opulence.

At the birth of his daughter, who was not the offspring of youth, he had amassed so considerable a share of wealth, that a splendid independence was certain to be the fate of this solitary scion.

How, then, you will ask, could the mother be induced to resign the exquisite pleasure of her only child's morning caress, her evening kiss of love? How forego the enjoyment of witnessing her mind's daily development—the bliss of hanging over her innocent slumbers ?

The destitute being, who sees nothing for her infant, in the dark vista of future years, but poverty and desolation, may, after a severe struggle, resign the indulgence of a mother's exquisite sensibilities to that infant's welfare ; but, even then she clasps her darling to an aching bosom, and feels, as though heart-strings were severed, when she resigns it !

What, in this instance, could induce the voluntary offering? Insatiable rapacity!   This only child possessed much—" let her possess more," said the parent ; and *more, more!* was the daily craving of this interesting germ of avarice and insensibility ! The sound produced by an attempt at utterance in other children is " ma," or "mam."   Sally's first monosyllable was " more."   In babyhood silver pleased, but gold delighted her.   If she was offered a silver or an ivory spoon, she invariably chose the silver : and, from two years of age, the little miser possessed so instinctive an impression of her own interest, that the servants called her " little Miss Graspall."

" Give a few pence to a poor blind man," said an aged mendicant, as he followed a little dog, who was his guide.

Sally ran to Mr. Jonathan—

"Blind man—blind man !"

" There my love," said he, giving her sixpence. " Go Sally—give it him prettily."

She ran to the man, and put her little hand into his hat.

He felt round the crown carefully, then put it on his head.

" God bless your generous heart, and send you such a friend if you should ever want one," said he.

The dog growled as he looked in Sally's face, he barked, growled again, and his master was obliged to pull the string thrice before he could get his little guide from the portal. Yet he still turned his head, as Sally ran to the gate, where Mr. Jonathan was standing, watching, with delighted eye, his protege's early benevolence.

" You've met with an ungrateful dog, there Sally."

" Yes, uncle, he wants to bite poor Sally !"

" Never mind, child—never mind ; that must not damp your charity. He did not seem to like your face, somehow ; but the master cannot help the prejudices of his dog, and we do not good to be thanked, but to lay up treasures in heaven !'

No. 8.

"Oh, I shall like to go to heaven, uncle, if there are treasures there! pretty silver and nice gold!"—And away she ran to her little garden.

As Sally increased in years, she became provident and careful in the extreme. With a profusion of every thing she could possibly desire, the idea alone of dispensing an atom of comfort to another, would draw tears from her eyes and sobs of anguish from her heart. She liked to have playfellows, because she could not play so well alone,—they amused her: and, as it is in the nature of infancy to be liberal, she frequently obtained little presents of toys or sweetmeats from them. Nothing, however, on any occasion, induced her to make the slightest return,—her dolls, her puzzles, her bandeloire, were brought out (in her own words) "to make them long," but returned, instantly, to her drawers.

Her cake or fruit, although she possessed a profusion of such little indulgencies, was eaten in a corner; and, if a portion remained, after she had indulged herself to repletion, it was carefully wrapped up in two or three papers, and put away for another time, where it almost universally remained until it became mouldy.

Sally had wandered beyond the lawn, and ran through a neighbouring field, in pursuit of a butterfly. A little cottager crossed her path, carrying with her a small basket of strawberries.

"Little girl!—I say, little girl!" exclaimed Sally.

"Did you call me, miss?"

"Yes, to be sure, I did!—where are you going with those nice strawberries?"

"To my poor brother, miss."

"Ah! now! give me some!"

"I would, willingly, miss—but they're not mine!"

"Whose are they, then?"

"Mother sent me, miss, to buy them for my poor little brother,—his lips are parched with fever,—he did not eat any thing all day yesterday, and mother says she's afraid he'll die. She's been crying all the morning," continued the little girl, weeping bitterly.

"Where do you live?"

"Down by those cottage."

"Ah! now give us some,—they won't be missed, you can turn 'em out and put a bit of paper in the bottom."

"For shame, miss!" said the little girl, drying her tears, indignantly, "I wouldn't deceive mother for all the world! but my poor little brother's waiting for me—I can't stay."

"Won't you, then, you stingy thing?"

"I wonder you ask me, miss, with so many in your uncle's garden!"

"Ah! but they are not yet here,—and these look so nice!"

The little cottager, finding all remonstrance useless, walked briskly on; Sally stole gently behind her, pinched her arm, and then, with a loud laugh of apparent satisfaction, tripped lightly over the meadow, and got in at the back door, just in time to place herself quietly between her aunt and Mr. Jonathan, to listen, with sanctified quietude, whilst he read prayers to the family, according to his usual observance.

Sally never failed to receive a lecture when she visited home. It was not very frequently she did so. Her father's maxim was "She's sure of ours, let her make sure of Jonathan's,—never mind mother and me, gal! that's where you must pay your court!" and she did not fail to profit by these instructions.

"Kiss your uncle, my dear, always, before you go to bed, and when you get up in the morning!"

"I always do, mother.

"Yes; but you must hug him round the neck!"

"Yes, mother, I always do; and I always run to meet him on a Sunday morning, and beg so to go to church with him, because he always is pleased with me, and gives me a shilling!"

"And what do you do with all these shillings?"

"Oh, I've got a nice little place!—I fold all of 'em up in paper, put 'em into a little wooden box, lock it, and bury it in the garden."

"But, wouldn't you like to buy a necklace or a baby-house, or something or other very pretty indeed !"

"Why, mother, father says money is the best thing in the world! and I don't know how it is, but I like the look of the money better ; what can be so pretty as a guinea, or even a shilling!"

"What good sense! I wish her father had heard her. Sweet child! always think in this way, my dear, and you'll deserve to be a rich woman : yes, perhaps even a duchess !"

"But is your uncle better to-day ?"

"Yes, mother, but he was very ill yesterday, and they thought he'd die in the night,—there'd have been a job ! Jane came and told me, this morning."

"Didn't you run into his chamber to see him ?"

"To be sure I did—leave me alone for that."

"Did you cry ?"

"Oh, no, I didn't cry, but I said I was very sorry."

"You should have cried."

"Well, mother, I will another time, but he's better now ; and he seems quite sure and satisfied that I love him better than any one in the world ; wouldn't that be a pretty joke? No! I love you best mother, then father, then aunty, (because it will be through her I shall get every thing), and then him last of all."

"You must not say so, though ; and above all, child, take care of the servants !"

"I will, mother, I will ; but Jane is come to fetch me, and I must be gone."

At fifteen, Sarah Crawley could smile when her heart was deformed by the conflicting passions of hatred and envy, and weep when she inwardly rejoiced. It may, perhaps, be supposed her education rapidly advanced ;—quite the reverse ! and with such propensities, it was, perhaps, a blessing extended to those within her contracted circle, that she was not only devoid of anything in the shape of talent, but even ordinary capacity. To the plainness of her person, Mr. Jonathan's infatuation rendered him blind ; but this he really regretted, because he had flattered himself he should see her, not only highly educated, but even a gem amongst the literary females of the day. He entreated, he gently reproved, he offered rewards,—he even wept, all was powerless to overcome so obstinate an evil.

The drawing utensils, the small library of interesting works, purchased expressly for her, the grand piano, all stood untouched and useless. Her French and Italian master, with a shrug, declared himself " *au desespoir*" and her English governess resigned her charge !

"I'm really sorry for it," said Mr. Jonathan, " because certain accomplishments are considered indispensible to a certain sphere, and I must confess I should have liked to see the girl a duchess !"

"But the poor child will fret herself ill, if she is teased, my dear, and it's not of much consequence, because our money, and her father's together, will insure her a title."

"That's true, my dear, but one should have liked a little credit reflected on one in return for what she may possess from us."

It was the wish of Mr. and Mrs. Jonathan St. Clair to have some young people, from time to time, to visit Miss Crawley, the motive for her strenuous opposition of every such invitation will be pretty obvious.

"What society can your Sally want," said she, as she threw her arm round each neck, as she sat between them, "when she'd rather be with you, than all the world besides."

But the air-built castle of attaching what the world erroneously calls nobility to their family was really not a joke ; it was a point on which the whole of them were decided. It was their daily meditation and nightly dream. Mr. Crawley visited the landlord of the head hotel in the town, and requested him whenever any of the nobility stopped there, to send an express that he might call on them, with Mr. Jonathan, and invite them.

The good man declared he " certainly would," and laughed in his sleeve at what he deemed a mania ; for the servants of Mushroom Lodge had whispered the motive of this new-born hospitality; and month followed month, and year succeeded year of unsatisfied impatience, until Sally had reached twenty-six.

"Sally does not get to look better," said her father.

"These here dukes and marquises think more of marrying a parcel of actresses and them ere gals as sing and dance, than a respectable young person of property like our Sal."

"Ah, don't tell me," replied Mrs. Crawley, "let the dukes and marquises go where they please; there's many a lord that would be glad enough to patch up his broken fortune with her daughter's;—and what matters it, isn't a title a title?"

"And do you think, mother, I'll give my hand to any but a duke? Lady Edgmont —Lady Harewood! the duchess has left town, the duchess has arrived! Oh, there is no comparison. I will never marry any but a duke."

Four more years had somewhat calmed the fever of ambition in the bosom of the Crawley family, It also drew aside the veil of infatuation from the eyes of Mr. Jonathan and his wife, and they unitedly came to a decision, that, as they had waited so long, vainly, for a duke, or a lord, or a baronet,—a knight might do, and be more within the grasp of probability."

"And what does it signify, my child," said the good Mr. Jonathan, ' 'it will still be your ladyship."

Miss Crawley smiled through her tears, looked in the glass, and unconsciously rattled her purse in her reticule.

"Some one was speaking of a Sir Edward Orville," said Mr. Crawley to the barber, who was performing his morning avocation, "does he reside in this neighbourhood?"

"I never heard of such a person, sir."

"Perhaps I'm wrong in the name;—call over to me those you know in this direction, and I'll stop you when you come to the right."

"Well, sir,—there's Sir Peter Petwin, a baronet, and married; Sir James Arlington, a baronet too, and married; Sir Henry Dainville, single, but a poor knight, for he has run through a very good fortune. He's one of those gentlemen, you see, sir, who have a taste for theatricals; that has done him no good, and although a fashionable, fine young fellow, he is very proud and very poor."

"Neither of those—neither of those," said Mr. Crawley, not much liking the emphasis on married and single! "the name will turn up when I am not trying to remember it."

This hint was quite sufficient for Mr. Crawley. He instantly dressed, and ordered his carriage, and called on Mr. Jonathan. A letter was determined on, requesting Sir Henry to do them the pleasure of a call, when in the neighbourhood of either.

This day was a day of eager anxiety, to Miss Crawley,—"lady Dainville, lady Dainville, her ladyship, your ladyship!" whispered she, Morning came, and she had not, in her own elegant style, "slept a wink." She descended to the breakfast parlour, and found a letter, directed to her uncle, who, putting on his spectacles, read the following laconic note:—

"Sir Henry Dainville's compliments to Mr. Crawley, and has the pleasure of informing him that he will find him at home, until eleven or half-past, every morning.

"4, Crescent."

Mr. Jonathan looked discontented, and a sigh escaped the bosom of Miss Crawley She, however, took the letter, inclosed it, and dispatched a servant to her father, who returned with the messenger; and as, by the time breakfast was concluded, it was half-past ten, Mr. Crawley entered his carriage, and drove to the crescent.

The person belonging to the house took up Mr. Crawley's name; and, returning, said Sir Henry requested he would walk up. This was acceded to with the utmost alacrity; and he was ushered into a scantily furnished drawing-room, where Sir Henry carelessly reclined on a shabby sofa, with the breakfast things yet before him.

He did not rise at Mr. Crawley's entrance, but motioned to him, with some degree of hauteur, to take a seat.

"A fine day, sir!"

" Very fine day, sir Henry."

" The weather is somewhat cold, for the month !"

" Very cold, sir Henry."

" May I enquire to what favourable chance I am indebted for the honour of this visit ?"

" Yes, Sir Henry,—yes, Sir Henry," replied Mr. Crawley, making an effort to rouse himself from a certain degree of overwhelming respect, with which this young man's deportment had inspired him. " The fact is, I've something to propose, Sir Henry ; and, if your impressions and mine, and my wife's sister's husband's agree—the thing is done, Sir Henry !"

At the word her, Sir Henry turned on Mr. Crawley a look of satiric enquiry, whilst he proceeded.

" My daughter, Sir Henry, is the only child of the family. On the day of her marriage I can give her £150,000. At her uncle's death (and he is not a youngster) she will have all he is worth ! about, I suppose, £200,000 more : now, if you like her, and she likes you, I don't see why title should not be placed in one scale, and wealth in t'other, and the balance struck at once !"

Sir Henry could not restrain a smile, but he considered it too good a joke not to be made the best of.

" Is Miss Crawley young, sir ?"

" Y-e-e-s."

" Is she handsome ?"

" Yes ; that is—pretty, rather pretty."

" Literary—at all literary ?"

" I beg your pardon, Sir Henry, I really don't understand you."

" Clever !—is she clever ?"

" I'll tell you what, Sir Henry, suppose you don't ask me any more questions— come and see her,—can't you come now ?"

" Not absolutely now, Mr. Crawley."

" Well, then, in an hour ?"

" Perhaps I may wait on Miss Crawley this evening."

" Be sure you do now—she will expect you !"

Mr. Crawley then took his leave, and, stepping into his carriage, drove to Mr. Jonathan's.

A few minutes sufficed to give an account of his embassy. It was agreed that Mr. Jonathan should receive him on his arrival, introduce him to his wife's niece and that he should not appear until the evening.

The hours seemed to lag on leaden pinions. Miss Crawley hesitated as to what dress she should select, and consulted with the house-maid, who had lately obtained much of her confidence.

" What does your ladyship think of your lilac silk," said the girl, with a smothered titter, " with your scarlet belt, and gold buckle; your green silk apron with black lace, your yellow scarf, and pink satin shoes—"

" And my silver flower !" said the young lady, with a smile of self-approbation, and a sidelong glance at the looking glass.

" Yes, miss,—I beg your pardon, your ladyship ; and, when your ladyship's hair is done all over in little corkscrew ringlets, the thing will be the completest in the world,"

" Well, Betsy, here are my keys, lay my things on the bed, and help me to dress,—for Sir Henry will be here, I dare say, soon after six."

The anxiously anticipated hour arrived ; and Mr. Jonathan and Miss Crawley awaited their guest's arrival, in the drawing-room. A loud ring at the gate, sent in his card, and Mr. Jonathan went to the door to receive him.

Miss Crawley had placed herself within the recess of one of the windows, behind the scarlet drapery of the curtains, so that she was not introduced ; and, being seated, the following conversation commenced.

" My wife's sister's husband, called on you, Sir Henry, respecting a proposal !"

" He did, sir, but you will pardon my making some few preliminary enquiries."

" Certainly, sir,"

" Is the young lady handsome ?"

" Of that, sir, you must judge for yourself; on this point opinions are apt to vary."

" Is she young ?"

" We leave you to guess her years, and then tell you if you are right."

" Is she literary ?"

" No, sir, few ladies are, I think."

" Is she fond of reading,—intelligent,—musical ?"

Mr. Jonathan's wishes for a title in the family, and his sincerity, had here a severe conflict.

" That is, Mr. St. Clair, can your wife's sister's daughter play upon the harp and piano, and does she sing ?"

" Why, no! Sir Henry, but that is an excellent piano, and will be her's."

" But you say she doesn't play ?"

" No."

" That's bad! Does she dance ?"

" No, sir."

" Write ?"

" Sufficiently well to manage a card of address, or invitation ; and I believe that is all that ladies of fortune aspire to."

" Bad, bad,—very bad !'

" Mr. St. Clair, I will candidly allow that fortune is, with me, a point of importance, but talent, intellect, and accomplishments, infinitely of more importance, Were I not in some degree involved, fortune would be the last thing on earth I would mingle with my choice of a bride ! adverse fate denies me this free election ; nevertheless, I will not breathe so sacred a vow at the altar, unless some degree of esteem, admiration and tenderness can accompany it.

" Can I see your niece's hand-writing ?"

Mr. Jonathan felt vexed ; nevertheless he took up a prayer-book in which she had taken some pains to write her name.

" Sarah Crawley, her book," read Sir Henry—" Bad, I'm sorry to say, very inelegant; I will, however, sir, if you please, see the young lady !"

At this moment, Miss Crawley stepped from her concealment, reddening with vexation and resentment.

" Will you have the goodness, young woman," said he, " to present my compliments to your mistress, and say I await the honour of an interview !"

Miss Crawley had darted like an arrow from the scene of defeat and confusion, before Mr. Jonathan could recover his voice.

" Why, Sir Henry! Sir Henry! that my wife's sister's daughter,—that was— Miss Crawley !"

" Indeed? I regret my observations have been so unlimited ; but you are aware, sir, I could not have been instinctively conscious of Miss Crawley's presence !

" You will, however, allow me to be sincere on this most important occasion, when I assure you, I make it a point to be so on every other. If that young person is your relative,—the wealth of empires should not induce me to call her mine! and, with this very frank avowal, permit me to wish you, sir, a very good night."

He crossed the hall, passed down the avenue, entered the gig with which his lad was waiting ; and Mr. Jonathan retired to his study, to calm his mind by an hour of tranquil contemplation.

But what became of Miss Crawley ?

She ran to her aunt—told all her sorrow, received consolation mingled with reproaches, retired to her chamber, tore off her scarf, flowers, and ribbons,—scolded the servant violently, and ultimately fell into a strong fit of hysterics : the whole family were equally disappointed, they awakened as from a dream to the consciousness of the truth of what Mr. Jonathan had at times touched upon ; namely, that talent, elegance of mind, and manner, and accomplishments, are more important than wealth : but all hope of a title was over.

Six months elapsed—a life of single blessedness was not to Sally's taste;—she had not mind to look for a world within herself. She had arrived at that period when a lady is of "no particular age," and ridicule for her absurd and misplaced vanity, seemed alone to await her. One or two of the servants had unfortunately possessed too little self-command to restrain their laughter as she passed the kitchen window; and, as the housemaid had addressed her the day after her disappointment as—"your ladyship," instead of miss,—these were all dismissed. James, however, the footman, a very serious young man, retained his place. He said "Miss Crawley would be a jewel in the crown of a prince." A week afterwards his wages were increased

It is said, that the hour of disappointment, when the wounds of slighted love are recent, is a dangerous one;—that the heart unfolds to the voice of the consoler, and a new-born hope that a portion of life's felicities may yet remain in store, is awakened. I will not vouch for the truth of this as a general assertion, although it appears realised in the present instance.

It was a lovely evening early in September; the Reverend Jonathan St. Clair had accompanied his wife on a visit to a friend in the neighbourhood; and Miss Crawley sauntered carelessly down the path that led to the stables. A row of sun-flowers grew against the gate that separated it from the paddock.

A manly voice broke upon her ear. She fancied she heard her own name; she paused to listen—she was not deceived—and eagerly caught the following part of a song:—

> "Of all the girls I knew before,
> There's none like pretty Sally,
> She is the angel I adore,
> And she's in yonder alley."

It is not to be supposed for a moment, that the servant alluded to his young mistress. His imagination, then, probably wandered to some female in his own humble sphere. She, however, felt pleased and consoled: "does he, then, know that I am here?" Her heart flatteringly assured her he did; she blushed, and stood pulling the sun-flower, she had plucked to pieces, leaf by leaf,—when he appeared.

"Did you call me, miss?" said James.

"Yes—no, James, I didn't call; I was only listening to your song."

It was now James's turn to blush, and look silly, and no one can say how far the conversation might have been prolonged, but that Mr. Jonathan and his wife returned rather earlier than expected, and rang the bell loudly. Miss Crawley quickened her pace to the parlor, and James ran to the gate. The sentiment of kindness did not diminish; the peremptory order was no longer heard—"I'd thank you, James," preceded every request, and a mutual simper attended its execution.

Miss Crawley now preferred going in the gig to her father's instead of the carriage. James drove her. It is said her visits became more frequent, and that she suffered her hand to remain within his longer than necessary, when she proffered it that he might assist her to alight. instead of waiting for him to present his arm respectfully, for that purpose. It is said, on such occasions, a gentle pressure was given and returned. It might have been a boast of the young man, already sufficiently elevated by the distinction shown him. Certain, however, it is, that his livery was exchanged for a suit of genteel plain clothes, and circumstances were in this extremely critical situation, when the Reverend Jonathan heard of Mr. Josiah St. Clair's illness; and conceiving that change of scene might tend to erase the humiliating reccollection of the past, speedy preparations were made, and the trio proceeded to Clair Hall.

CHAPTER XIV.

"There glides a step through the foliage thick,
    And her cheek grows pale, and her pulse beats quick;
There whispers a voice through the rustling leaves,
    And a blush returns, and her bosom heaves:
    A moment more—and they shall meet—
    'Tis past,—her lover's at her feet."   BYRON.

ON the following day, Mr. Arnold accompanied St. Clair to the hall: no admittance! Miss Crawley appeared at the parlour door; and, in reply to their enquiries, he was pronounced "much worse."—Can we not see him, said Mr. Arnold?—"To be sure not," replied Miss Crawley, "didn't I say yesterday, that he was too ill to be seen? well then to day he's worse! Its very strange some people can't take their answer."

Mr. Arnold in the warmth of his heart, would have reproved her severely—but St. Clair restrained him, the meanness of the self evident nature rendered her an object of beneath notice, and his feelings were of so sigular a cast, that I doubt whether millions would have induced him to contend with one who appeared to him a being out of nature, accustomed as he had been to all that was amiable, disinterested and lovely at home.

"No, no! my dear sir," said St. Clair,—" if the torch of discord is lighted, it shall not be on my account; the repose of his declining days shall not be disturbed by me." And they returned, after a walk in the environs of the town.

"All is not right there, depend on it,' said Mr. Arnold. "Where all is honourable and above board, there is no need of such watchfulness and caution; and no inclination towards violence, and the dislike that your name alone appears to have excited."

On the day following, the bound affixed to St. Clair's sojournment had expired—his soul thirsted for the retirement of his humble but happy home. Mr. Arnold's servant brought the intelligence, that his aged friend continued the same; and, with a warm invitation to this hospitable family, he bade them adieu, whilst with sincere regret they saw him depart with Mr. Arnold, who accompanied him to the coach, which would take him to the market town nearest the village.

His Adela was on the watch from her window; at the first glimpse she flew on the wings of filial tenderness to meet him. A few minutes more brought him to his peaceful retirement; and whilst he clasped his treasure in one embrace, St. Clair felt that the calm of contentment was sweeter to his soul than all that wealth or ambition could bestow.

A mind thus endowed, is above the vicissitudes of life.—" His greatness of soul is not to be cast down," in the words of Dodsley:—" He raiseth his head like a tower on a hill, and the arrows of fortune drop at his feet."

But it was not only the young farmers, and wealthy rustics, hinted at by the landlord to Ralph. It was not only Theodore who had seen Adela in the seclusion of rural home, where "when virtue and modesty heighten her charms, the lustre of a beautiful woman is brighter than the stars of heaven."

Captain Grenville, the eldest son of the gentleman of whom St. Clair had purchased his land, had chanced to see her returning from a walk with her parents: he was personally known to St. Clair, who possessed sufficient discernment to avoid the cultivation of anything like intimacy.

Sometime after, he felt inclined to pass a few weeks with a maiden aunt who resided in that neighbourhood; and, was deputed by his father, to receive some rents in the vicinity of St. Clair's cottage.

The votary of dissipation—too frequently had the young, the innocent, the fair been victims to his wiles; a finished elegance of deportment, a handsome person and a fascination of manner almost irresistible, rendered him dangerous with the inexperienced and unsuspicious. He had heard of Adela's beauty; but, although it infinitely surpassed his imagination, he beheld her merely as a lovely villager, her parents as the inhabitants of a small farm; and conceived she would fall an easy prey to his snares; he had long watched for a favourable moment, and, with the consciousness of certain success, accosted her on the evening previously to

her father's return, spoke o her matchless charms, the gaiety of a world to which he longed to introduce her, and professed himself the humblest of her adorers.

Adela's unsullied purity of heart, her native politeness, induced her to reply to his first salutation,—but her good sense and instinctive delicacy of sentiment, put her upon her guard against his protestations :—and, she firmly, with a natural dignity which astonished him, declined his accompanying her any farther.

No. 9.

" Why should you take that trouble," said she in reply to his entreaty, " those who have no enemies require not protection : in this happy and peaceful retirement, we are surrounded by friends." He still persisted, Adela's manner became more decisive—threw intrusion at a distance ; and, with a sigh, he remained where he stood, until she had entered the cottage where she mentioned her rencontre to her mother; and they mutually resolved that she should not go out again unaccompanied, during his stay in that neighbourhood.

And again Theodore is on his road to the Park, after a warm and hasty adieu to his friend Clifford—to whom he had confided the whole of his romantic adventure.

Again is he borne on his gallant steed, in the well known path leading to the fairy habitation of all his fancy could form of worth, talent, and loveliness—determined, by Clifford's advice, to throw off all concealment, and obtain St. Clair's sanction to their mutual affection. Was it it in nature to resist the temptation? impossible ! he yielded to it with a delight almost uncontrollable.

Adela was seated in the bower, where she had first listened to Theodore's vows of love and fidelity : the brilliancy of summer had given place to the mellow tint of autumn, and evening shed a pensive shade over the scene, which his presence had rendered a perfect elysium.

A pleasing sadness stole over her heart ; " Might not he be amongst those, who forget in absence, who profess a sentiment they feel not ?—Oh no ! truth, honour tenderness, beamed in his countenance ; her heart told her she must believe him, —she drew her tablets from her bosom, she read again and again the lines his hand had traced ; and, with her pencil, inscribed the following on the next ivory page.

> Oh thou ! for whom my anxious sighs
> Of infant tenderness arise,
> Oh thou ! to whom, in early years,
> I give affection's tender tears !
> Why did I ever gain thy heart,
> If fate designs our loves to part?
>
> Why do our bosoms feel the glow
> Which none but kindred natures know ;
> Congenial feelings, hopes and fears,
> Affection's throb, and transport's tears ;
> Oh why does hope such sweets impart,
> If fate designs our loves to part ?
>
> No beauties can these scenes reveal;
> Their charms with sighs of grief I hail ;
> Bright morn and evening's tranquil hour
> Have lost with me their pleasing power;
> What joy can cheer this sinking heart—
> Doomed from the youth I love to part ?
>
> I wander o'er the mead's alone,
> I sit upon the mossy stone,
> And view each scene (to me unblest)
> Which once gave rapture to my breast ;
> Ah ! what shall bid the fears depart,
> That spread their shadow o'er my heart.

A gentle sigh, and a rustling among the branches, induced her to hurry her tablets into her bosom, blushing for the confession they contained. In another moment, Theodore is at her feet ! the blissful hour's past, the doubts overshadowing the future—the whole creation is forgotten ! Adela was indeed,

> " A form of life and light
> That seen, becomes a part of sight,"

and Theodore whilst he pressed her small white hand, with the pure fervour of true devotion to his lips,—entirely forgot that he had leaped the hedge, and was the garden without having entered by the gate.

" For heaven's sake Theodore !—what will papa say ?" said the agitated girl.

" One moment beloved one, and I am gone !"

" I do not wish you to be gone !"

" Is your father at home ?"

" He is."

" Listen, then, my Adela! the few weeks I have been away from you, have so painfully evinced to me the anguish of doubt, that I have resolved to throw myself on your father's consideration, he is candour, sincerity, sentiment itself; he will allow me to unfold my heart to him; with his approbation we shall be enabled to correspond by letter, by this interchange of feeling the intervals of absence will be less insupportable; and, above all, his sanction will relieve me from the agonizing ear of other proposals !"

" Oh! you have released my mind from a weight of anxiety! almost a sense of guilt in this painful concealment.—But Sir Edward !"

" I cannot think he will oppose my felicity; he is an excellent father; and, although eccentric perhaps in some respects, his every action has hitherto seemed to have my comfort and welfare in view. But were he even rigorous and unreasonable—less than two more years will give me the power of acting for myself —and then, who shall divide us ?"

Theodore's cheek glowed with hope, a doubtful tear yet glistened on Adela's Theodore dried it, kissed the handkerchief and put it in his bosom; they arose, entered the cottage, and Adela having announced their young friend, retired to her chamber, where she awaited in tremulous agitation the result of his interview with her father.

An hour elapsed, and Adela was summoned by her mother,—she scarcely dared meet her father's benignant look of paternal tenderness, but a few minutes re-assured her,—happiness was painted on Theodere's expressive countenance,— the warmest welcome extended by her parents to their guest: he " must not depart until he had partaken of their evening repast." A feeling of mutual confidence and esteem seemed to awaken: her mother's smile of maternal love beamed on her child, the conversation chiefly fell on the past events of St. Clair's life. Theodore listened with eager interest; some of his own earliest recollections were mingled and the mutual interest first excited by an accident—the consequent interchange of warm hospitality and sincere reconnaisance seemed from the few delightful hours of this evening, to promise a duration of perfect friendship and esteem.

And Theodore had departed, he had dared press her hand even in the presence of her parents! " You will breakfast with us at eight ? without fail !" another adieu, a farewell glance—and with a foot that seemed to tread on air, he passed the garden-gate, and disappeared in the shadow of surrounding night.

When Adela returned to the parlour, she approached, as usual, to receive her parents farewell embrace; but St. Clair retained her hand, and her affectionate mother drew her towards her on the sofa.

" Stay, awhile, child, your papa has a very important circumstance to relate to you."

Adela trembled, and took her seat.

" My child," said St. Clair, " our young friend has this evening unfolded his heart to your mother and myself. He has declared an attachment, which, it appears, took its rise during the month he passed with us.

" He acknowledges that my little girl's filial tenderness, with the other domestic virtues inherited from her mother, first awakened that esteem which ripened into a solid attachment, and the certainty that she alone can ensure his future felicity. This you know, child, is the language of a romantic young man,—the future only can prove its truth! That he has not attempted to obtain your affections surreptitiously, but openly disclosed to us his hopes, his prospects, and his wishes, is so strong a proof of his honourable character, that I cannot deny his proposals the candid consideration they merit."

Adela's smiles and blushes expressed her gratitude for this parental indulgence; and, concealing her lovely countenance in her mother's bosom, she acknowledged that Theodore was the only being who had ever approached in the most distant degree, the sentiments she felt for her parents, and that those sentiments had principally arisen, first, from the sympathy his accident awakened, and next, from the admiration he evinced for her beloved father.

"Dearest child," said St. Clair, "we require no confession from a heart where all is purity; but let us clearly understand each other. That I have witnessed something like a preference above others, who would willingly have obtained our girl's favour, I cannot deny. Heaven forbid I should sacrifice her future peace to mistaken reasoning, or exert an authority which ought never to predominate, unless where the predilection is ill directed! My Adela's mind has been formed by her mother; that is a sufficient assurance, that beyond the counsels of friendship and parental solicitude we need not go.

"Education, similarity of character, mutual esteem, are indispensible in an union for life! and in these, as far as my discernment reaches, I do not think you differ; Mr. Villars informs me his property is independent of his father, who will not, he conceives, place himself in the way of his felicity; but this has yet to be ascertained, for although I do not conceive that the ambition of the parent, ought to overcloud the lives of a youthful pair, whose hearts, congeniality of sentiment, and a virtuous attachment have united; yet our Adela is a treasure we shall reluctantly resign; and heaven forbid she should enter a family unappreciated, although her virtues and her innocence will be her only dower.

"Mr. Villars is anxious to be permitted to continue his visits, and, when absent, to write to you under our surveillance during his minority. The request appears so reasonable that I cannot disapprove of it, at the end of that period, you will both be better acquainted with your own hearts, and I trust we shall never have reason to regret having conceded it."

The tears chased each other down Adela's cheek; alternately was she pressed to each fond parent's bosom; she received their blessing, and retired to her pillow, with a heart overflowing with filial tenderness and gratitude to the Creator who had condescended to grant, that the sweetest emotions of her bosom might not be in opposition to the duty she owed—the love she felt for her parents.

But another hour elapsed before St. Clair, and the anxious mother sought repose; one hand clasped in the other's they recalled the past, they spoke of the future.

Had St. Clair been in his most prosperous hour, and Theodore with nothing to proffer but the devotion of a heart so honourable—so sincere, a mind so well regulated, so highly gifted, he knew not the individual he would have preferred as the friend, the husband of his child. But fate had ordered it otherwise; a future moment must arrive which would lay himself and his Aurora beneath the turf of a humble and obscure grave, and leave her alone in the world, an unprotected, unconnected orphan, with that beauty which would perhaps expose her to severer afflictions, and an education, and sentiments calculated to render her more keenly alive to the deprivations, the loneliness of her fate.

With the utmost exertion and economy, a subsistence was all they should be likely to leave her; the self interested and mean spirit of avarice, having apparently determined to intercept the kind intentions, breathed in that sacred promise, "Let not an anxiety for her future welfare depress you: her fortune shall be my care!"

Should he then be doing justice to his child, in opposing an union consonant with the pure laws of nature and virtue? Should he sever the tender ivy from the young oak, which might ere long extend its o'ershadowing branches as its only support and protection, and leave it to perish in unheeded desolation?

Their tears mingled, they retired to rest, and the last thought of each parental breast, was a prayer for their girl, their sole surviving tie of existence.

The following morning saw Theodore, his countenance illumined with the hope that animated his heart, seated beside his Adela, and assisting her at the breakfast table. A dress of the simplest materials, but exactly adopted to disclose the perfect symmetry of a faultless form; her auburn hair, disposed in rich and asteful braids, adorned only by a white rose which Theodore had placed there; and as he gazed on her unspeakable loveliness his heart almost doubted the reality of the scene, and the bewitching hopes that in a future hour this treasure would be all his own, when they might

> " Sooth each sorrow, share in each delight,
> Blend ev'ry thought, do all but disunite !"

When their combined solicitude might strew the declining path of both their parents with roses, and present them, in the serenity yielded by the certainty of their Adela's felicity, a balm for the vicissitudes of the past.

A few days afterwards a note was delivered to St. Clair, it was from his friend Arnold:

My Dear Sir

I regret to state that Mr. Josiah St. Clair departed this life at half past five o'clock this morning: the hyena guarded the gate to the last, so that the kind offices of the friends he esteemed in life were entirely kept from him.

I say, as I before said, there is a mystery ; all is not as it should be! I think you had better come over.

Mrs. A. and the girls desire their kind regards to yourself, and Mrs. and Miss St. Clair, and

Believe me your's truly,

James Arnold.

E. St. Clair, Esq.

St. Clair perused these lines with a sigh.

"Mamma," said Adela, "do you remember your dream of the night before last ?"

"Yes love, but what has that to do with this letter ? we must not draw upon ourselves your papa's censure, for a superstitious regard to the wanderings of a distempered fancy when reason sleeps "

Adela blushed, and cast down her eyes.

"It was however a terrific dream, Mamma."

"Well, my love," said St. Clair "let me hear what has so terrified my little girl!" and drawing his daughter to his knee—he gave an attentive ear to her mother's recital.

"I found myself" said Mrs. St Clair, "in a large antiquated mansion, of which our departed friend appeared the possessor. I beheld him surrounded by friends, drawn to him by benefits conferred, and others attracted by that cheerful and open demeanour, for which he was so remarkable. In the sturdy winter of his age I beheld him wandering through his well cultivated grounds, and beautiful gardens— The scene shifted."

"A change came o'er the spirit of the dream !" said St. Clair, with a melancholy smile.

"It did love—and an awful change it was ! his friends had all vanished, a number of strange, and apparently unwelcome guests surrounded him, their carriage was in his coach house, their horses in his stables, their servants in his kitchen and other apartments, himself confined to his chamber—although not apparently sufficiently indisposed to warrant such a seclusion,—I had crept softly into that chamber—it was lofty and vaulted, I approached the canopied couch, I drew aside the curtain, I saw him in a sweet repose and the dreams of a benignant spirit seemed to hover round his couch. A foot approached, conscious of being an unexpected guest, I stepped into a recess from whence I could behold a female past the early period of youth enter ; she held in her hand a salver with a glass on it, and a phial apparently labelled as if from the apothecary, She closed the door, fastened it, and placing the salver on the cabinet, took from thence a lamp, advanced in an agitated manner to the bed, passed and repassed the light over the ᵉyes of the venerable old man, who reposed so soundly and sweetly to be disturbed by it. She replaced the lamp, went to the cabinet, and returned to the bed, entered the curtains and closed them round her. A confused noise followed. Incapable of motion or utterance, as though spell striken, I remained within my concealment, for the female's countenance inspired me with a feeling of mistrust that almost amounted to horror !

" Again the scene changed, the female was gone and I by the bedside, but I saw not the sleeper—I removed the pillows and bolster, merciful heaven ! a lifeless corpse lay before me.

" A wild shriek of agony burst from me, and I felt myself fainting—I awoke and found my Adela's tears on my cheek.

" Yes indeed, papa, I was terrified in the extreme, on going to awake mamma, previously to your return, to find her slumber perturbed and feverish, I tried in vain to wake her, and when at last I succeeded, she seemed still in search of some terriffic and distressing object; I threw myself into her arms, and she related the frightful dream which really seemed to me to have something to do with this melancholy communication."

" It is all imagination, dear child !'" said St. Clair, " your mother's mind is too energetic to attach any impotrance to its apparent connexion with circumstances which, having been the subject of discussion previously to our retiring, have shed their influence over her sleeping fancy.

" I cannot however avoid deeply regretting, that his last hours should have been attended by those whose society was evidently a restraint upon his social habits, and who, according even to his own acknowledgment, had lost his confidence."

Adela placed the writting desk on the table, and St. Clair replied to his friend's letter as follows :

MY DEAR SIR,

I bitterly lament the intelligence your letter contains, because I sincerely esteemed the departed, and consider the singular exertions of certain individuals to render him a prisoner in his own house, and by the most unequalled treachery to deprive his last moments of the soothing consolations of friendship, so complete an innovation of the rights of a rational being, that little doubt can be entertained of the motive.

My revered friend is no more! what can my presence avail at the Hall ?

I trust I shall yet have the pleasure of introducing Mrs. St. Clair, and my little girl to your amiable family. Even in our secluded valley, there are enjoyments for the mind of taste and the heart of disinterested benignity.

                    Believe me to remain,

                              Dear sir, your's sincerly,

                                        EDMUND ST. CLAIR.

JAMES ALNOLD, ESQ.

A fortnight elapsed, and again an epistle from the friendly Mr. Arnold.

MY DEAR SIR,

Every thing at the Hall has been managed with infinte snugness and caution, on the day after the funeral, not an accustomed face was seen in the house; they were all spirited away, the devil knows where, and not a domestic but those of Mr. Jonathan—who knew nothing of the matter! The Reverend Jonathan St. Clair's solicitor, arrived the day before the funeral, Miss Crawley seemed to take a very active part in the arrangement of every thing; and a fortnight had scarcely elapsed when the house was shut up, and the whole party on the wing.

The Reverend J. St. Clair's inherits everything—mark that!!

Do you really intend to let them have every thing their own way ? you certainly are a most ecentric being; but whilst I honour your disinterestedness I regret it should have fallen into such hands.

Best regards from the ladies of my family, to the lady's of your's,—they will meet I hope before the close of this lovely autumn.

Believe me, my dear Sir,

Your very sincere friend,

JAMES ARNOLD.

EDMUND ST. CLAIR ESQ.

CHAPTER XV.

" She little knew that wealth had power
To make the constant rove;
She little know the splendid dower
Could add a bliss to love."

And long and violently had an honest attachment contended with ambition in James's bosom, from the first little bewitching word of kindness sxtended by Miss Crawley.

Sarah Bleachall the laundress's daughter was blooming as the early blush ot morning,—artless, affectionate and amiable. Their parents cottages stood side by side, and many a nosegay, and many a look of love, had been interchanged over the little wooden palings that separated their gardens.

But alas! poor Sarah! the soul of man is not formed for constancy.

" The course of true love never did run smooth,"

Plutus unfolded his treasures, and angry Cupid abandoned the heart he had hitherto made his bower.

Miss Crawley had heard James's eulogium to her worth, uttered expressly for her ear, although addresed to one of his discarded companions; at a moment, when he expected to share the same fate, she had acknowledged it with a sly glance of approbation, she had listened to his song—had supposed it addressed to herself; and her looks not only promised, they proffered every thing Shakspere says

" There is a tide in the affairs of men."

James thought it would be "a crying sin" not to take advantage of that tide; and, the artless tenderness of his Sarah, the garden palings, the vows so often interchanged, the true heart and the broken sixpence, were all forgotten !

Mr. Jonathan picked up a very dirty letter in the garden at the Hall.

"It is belonging to one of the servants, I dare say, now," said he with one of his knowing winks of satisfied curiosity, which some would have called " old womanish."

He slipped it slily into his waistcoat pocket, and walked leisurely to the library shut the door, bolted it, took out his spectacles, rubbed the glasses with his white pocket handkerchief, and looked at the seal. It was of common wax, the design a heart with a flame, the motto—

" Be true to me,
As I to thee."

"Aye, aye," said he. He opened it, and read as follows:—

"DERE MISS.

" The time vares werry sloly avay since your swete presence gladened these pairts. Nothen but your kinde wow to be only mine can chere this soluntary and lonesome place. O mis, ive still got the sun flour as you pulled to peces at the stabel dore ; and the farewel as you give me wen you stepped bak for yure ridiclus, wen master and misis was in the coche, has niver bin forgot. How i envid that ere Tummus, that he got orders to go insted of me. Cum bak sune, for you can puswade master to any thinge. Cum bak, swete mis, amd i shall av pashence to wate til you can make me yourn for ever,

Your lovinge lovÿer,

" JAMES TOMKINS."

In his immediate haste to see the contents, which he imagined would let him into the love secrets of Betty or Susan, the Reverend Jonathan had not looked at the superscription. What, then, was his consternation when the fears the contents had awakened were absolutely confirmed! when he read————' To Miss Crawley !"

Grief, horror, resentment—I had almost said wounded pride contended for empire ; but I checked myself, for I recollected that nothing priestly can possess such a feeling. No, my intelligent reader, thou hast not lived to thy present period without having had frequent instances, in the annals of England and Ireland (to say nothing of Spain and Portugal) to prove that they are all humility! And do not for Heaven's sake, conceive, however doubtful or ambiguous this pious pastor's conduct may appear, at any future period described in the course of the following pages of this little work, that his nature was anything less than candid and honourable. Can a priest stoop to anything like selfishness or hypocrisy ? Never never !

But this discovery was sufficient to overturn the patience and equanimity of a saint. What ! his wife's niece ! his own protegé then, instead of becoming a duchess, would sink into the wife of a footman, " Mrs. Tomkins ?" distraction was in the idea!

At one moment he thought of sending her home to her father, disinheriting her, and doing justice to some other individuals (for a certain sense of retribution stole over his heart) ; but there are secrets, it is said, in every family, and prudence forbade. This hastily formed purpose was also argued down by the reflection of the meekness and gentleness, the utter incapability of resentment, he had hitherto been remarkable for,

" Unto him that smitheth thee on one cheek," said the pious man: " offer also the other ; and him that taketh away thy cloak, forbid not to take thy coat also."

But, he again argued, the " cloak " is not, as yet, actually taken. " I will instantly pay James his wages, and send him away." Again, he reflected that she might follow him, and thus accelerate her disgrace.

He came, at last, to a determination to conceal the thing altogether, return instantly, and consult with Alexander.

Every arrangement made for this purpose, they returned. Miss Crawley was watched with the scrutinizing eye of suspicion; her want of caution criminated her at once. A council was assembled in the reverend gentleman's study, and Alexander and Mrs. Jonathan St. Clair informed of the disgrace likely to be entailed on the family.

" James," said Mr. Jonathan, smiling benignly, on the afternoon of the same day, " Mr. Crawley is going to Liverpool ; and, as he has a particular occupation for his man Andrew, I have promised you shall accompany him. He will go in the morning coach, and you can take your place outside."

" Certainly, sir—certainly, sir," replied James, exulting at the idea of his intended father-in-law having preferred his attendance to that of his own man. He found means to slip a note into the fair hand, already his own in anticipation, mentioning his purposed absence. He reminded her that " the joys of meeting pay the pangs of parting ;" and promised to be under her window at night,

All that day Miss Crawley's attention seemed distracted, and her eyes swollen with weeping. She retired earlier than usual, and Mr. Jonathan having rang twice for James without his attending, walked round to that part of the shrubbery to which Miss Crawley's bed-room window looked. He there beheld her from his concealment, looking from her window in close conversation with her lover : and without interrupting them, returned to the house.

A few minutes afterwards she was summoned to her aunt's dressing-room, where, during the day, a bed had been prepared for her, and other arrangements relating to security made. Here her pious protector did not fail to breathe both counsel and reproof; he even wept over her, and offered up his prayers that the evil spirit might be cast out, and the damsel " made whole."

Alas! all was in vain. The pastor retired, having first carefully locked the door;

and when her rage had somewhat subsided, and her tears were dried, she sat, sullenly and silently, peeping through the grating attached to the window, until, overcome by drowsiness, she threw herself on the bed, to dream of Jamess' return; her deliverance from so unwelcome a captivity, and their union, in despite of the frowns of her relations and protector.

About a fortnight afterwards Mr. Crawley returned; but where was James?

'Ah, what had his youth with ambition to do?
Why left he Amynta—why broke he his vow?'

CHAPTER XVI.

' Twas the voice of Nature's harmony
Sweeping the chords of earth
Awakening with its symphony
The loves to a second birth.'

                                                            J. A. KENTISH.

THEODORE's life possessed an interest until now unknown.   In the bosom of the most delightful of solitudes, his ardour for study, his father's ambition, the vanities of the world, were forgotten.   To sit beside Adela in the seclusion of her rustic pavilion ; to read to her whilst her lovely fingers were employed in imitating some beautiful landscape, or group of flowers; to listen whilst her voice of music and pathos of expression gave additional charms to Byron's exquisite lays ; to wander with her, amidst her own overshadowing woodlands, was to him the summit of all earthly felicity,

Chateaubriand says, 'the elevated passions are by nature solitary, to convey them to the desert is to give them their fullest scope.'   Adela was the child of solitude ; and the purity of her manners, the pride of her character, her profound sensibility, rendered her, in Theodore's estimation, a being descended from a higher sphere, whose empire must be irresistible.

Sometimes the family of St. Clair formed a little water party in an excursion on the lake.   Sometimes they passed over to the opposite banks to enjoy the shelter of a romantic wood,   Here, in conversation, St, Clair's splendid mind gave wings to the " fairy-footed hours," or, the mellow cadence of Theodore's voice, mingled with Adela's silver tones, whilst Mrs. St. Clair accompanied them on the guitar in some of the exquisite melodies of her native land.   And long would this delirium of passion and tenderness have rendered him insensible to the existence of any other spot in the creation, than that woodland retreat on the brow of the valley ; but that the voice of friendship mingled with parental reproof came to arouse him.

Ralph brought him a letter from Clifford, which enclosed one from his father.

MY DEAR FRIEND,

            I was not astonished to find you had reached the Park, of which the arrival of the enclosed gave a sufficient demonstration ; because I know the visit you purposed making on your return.

" Where the treasure is, there is the heart also ;" and who can more sensitively feel than myself, that years fleet away like moments in the presence of a beloved object !   My hopes were like the transitory sparkle of the dew-drop, to be dashed away for ever !   A sunny hour succeeded by an eternity of night.

But why do I cast a shadow over your felicity ?   Write me a few lines, at least, my dear fellow, and let my own dark fate find consolation in my friend's " sober certainty of making bliss."

                                            Ever your's,
                                                GEORGE CLIFFORD.

THEODORE VILLARS, ESQ.

That from his father was as follows :—

MY DEAR BOY,

            Is it not very singular ?   I wrote to say I wished you to spend a few weeks with me.   I received no reply, and concluded, of course, you had set off immediately.   As one day followed another, I did not write again, because ' he is on the road, no doubt,' said I ; but every evening closed in like the former, without a shadow of your appearance !   What the devil are you thinking of ?

I suppose the fact is, that you have formed new friendships and new connexions which will render you quite forgetful to the respect you owe to your affectionate father,

                                                EDWARD VILLARS.

THEODORE VILLARS, ESQ.

Adela watched the countenance of the being she idolized, whilst his eye glanced over the letters; she saw his varying colour—she heard the sigh that escaped his bosom.

"Alas, then," said she, "the hour is come for your departure; you need not give utterance to the unwelcome tidings, my prophetic heart has long foretold them, our felicity has been of too high a cast to to admit of long duration."

Theodore pressed her to a heart palpitating with emotion, his voice faltered.

"And will Adela," said he, "regret the absence of one who adores her? will she, with sympathetic tenderness, conceive the period which divides us an eternity? will she anxiously count every hour for our re-union?"

Adela wept, and Theodore concealed his face with his handkerchief.

But as Adela's self-command exceeded her lover's, so was she first to reason down the violence of these emotions, and recall his recollection to a parent's right over a son's obedience.

"Go, then, my beloved friend," said she, "your longer delay may awaken suspicion, and occasion a prejudice against its cause, little favourable to our future felicity. But, should a parent's mandate for ever separate—"

"Cease, dearest girl—that never can, never shall be! not even parental authority shall divide us. A few weeks will find me again at your feet; and who can say but I be enabled to obtain my father's consent to the acceleration of my happiness?"

It was evening when Theodore gave and received the reluctant adieus of those he deemed his parents; for he had resolved to sleep at the inn, that he might not disturb the family by his early departure in the morning. Expressions of regret, and numberless little demonstrations of regard were interchanged, and Adela accompanied him through the over shadowed pathway that led to the gate nearest the valley.

Awhile they paused, with an ear attentive to the lay of the nightingale, which, to Adela, seemed unusually plaintive; the hand mutually and tenderly pressed, the names of Adela and Theodore at intervals repeated, the bosom alternately agitated and serene!

Who can describe the emotions of such a moment? they never trouble the repose of the soul devoid of sensibility. There are those who can conceive them.

"Theodore," said Adela, raising her tearful eyes to the moon, "a few minutes past that lovely orb was clear, and unobscured as my felicity this morning. See you not the clouds that now, in hurried succession, pass over it? Alas! my prophetic heart whispers, that these are ominous of approaching sorrow."

"My beloved! let not thy sensitive heart be too ready to anticipate evil. Oh! wa shall meet again in bliss, and our united path shall be as the stream that wanders amidst the flower embroidered banks of my Adela's native valley."

He clasped her to his breast, and departed. Adela received her parents' blessing, and retired to her chamber, but not feeling inclined to sleep, she took from her portfolio her pencil, and began to trace the features impressed on her heart. A melancholy presentiment still hung on her spirits; she placed the sketch with the others and was going to close it, when a folded paper, addressed to herself, in Theodore's hand, attracted her attention; and hastily unfolding it, she read—

THE COMMANDMENTS OF LOVE.

Oh, chase those lovely tears away,
　They quite unman my bosom now;
And whilst this last dear hour I stay
　Repeat—repeat thy plighted vow!
And yet—oh! do not chase that tear!
　It speaks of love and tenderness
And shall in fond remembrance cheer,
　When banished from thy loved caress;
Oh, promise that thy heart shall be
Sacred to all but love and me!

No other hand that hand shall press
  No other breathe that fragrant sigh,
Or read the glance of tenderness,
  Love's question, or his bland reply!
No other share thy daily thought,
  No other prompt thy nightly dream,
By magic retrospection brought,
  Affection's *fond* and *fav'rite theme*,
Nor let the vow forgotten be
That binds thy fate to love and me!

It is not necessary to say that this welcome memento of tenderness was pressed again and again by the pure kiss of affection; or that beneath Adela's pillow it raised visions, where the sunny smile of bliss enlivened their union, and all difficulties disappeared as the clouds of night before the orb of day.

She awoke, blooming and refreshed, "why should I embitter the blessings I possess," said she, "by an overweening anxiety relative to evils which never may occur!" She unfolded her heart to her Creator; she implored his protection for her beloved parent and her Theodore—arose happy and cheerful, and had just dressed when Lucy gently tapped at her door, and gave her the following note which she eagerly unclosed.

ANGELIC GIRL,

If I offend in thus adressing you, that ardent passion which defies the control of reason must plead my excuse and obtain your pardon.

I have walked, daily, through the paths you were accustomed to take, in the hope of obtaining a favourable moment to unfold a heart which has long been devotedly your own. I have wealth, but it possesses no charm for me unless you share it. Suffer me, then, to remove you from your present secluded situation to one you are formed to adorn! May I hope for an interview?

ALBERT GRENVILLE.

Miss St. Clair.

Adela's cheek crimsoned with resentment when read the above lines. The character her father had heard of him, his intrusive manner, his perseverance in the wish of following her on the evening chance had thrown her in his way, the acknowledgement that he had watched for her, terrified her extremely; she descended to the parlour, where her parents soon joined her, and put the letter into her father's hands, who instantly replied to it in the following terms:

SIR,

Your communication of this morning has been put into my hands by my daughter, whose mind is too well regulated, and too capable of appreciating her own future felicity to render my interference, on such an occasion, necessary. Permit me, however, to observe, that neither Miss St. Clair, nor her family, would be likely to encourage or countenance the visits of a gentleman whose irregularities have already reached even their retirement.

EDMUND ST. CLAIR

CAPTAIN GRENVILLE.

This letter was delivered to Captain Grenville by Lucy, at the time he appointed to come for an answer. And Adela resolved to bound her walks to their own grounds, unless in the society of her parents, or until Theodore's protection might enable her to extend them.

Captain Grenville, we have before said, considered Adela as his certain prey. Her beauty had attracted, her dignity of manner encreased his anxiety to possess her heart, he had indeed watched narrowly an opportunity. He had beheld Theodore, the companion of her morning and evening rambles, he had seen him hand her into the little pleasure boat, a few days before when with herself and her parents, they crossed over to the wood on the opposite side of the Lake. He had concealed himself, and patiently awaited their return, he had observed Ralph, conversing with Lucy at the cottage gate by moonlight, and had sought to obtain from him every possible information relative to the situation in which Theodore stood with the family. But Ralph was too deeply interested in his master's welfare, whom he honoured as a benefactor, and loved as a brother, not to be upon his guard.

"The fine gentleman," said Ralph, " is not one belonging to the village ; he may be a spy of Sir Edward's, or who knows, he may have also fallen in love with Miss Adela, and be a rival to my master—it will not be much he'll get out o' me."

Ralph was uneasy on other points. The smiles of Lucy had won his heart, and he feared for her also.

"Carry no messages from him to your young mistress, Lucy," said he ; "and do not let him get into conversation with you when I am not here, officers are always dangerous companions for village maidens."

Lucy listened to him and promised; she received a pale pink ribbon at parting, which she resolved not to wear until his return ; but the following morning, when Captain Grenville came up just as she opened the gate, she was taken so unawares, besides—a letter was not a message.

In the bitterness of his soul he had torn St. Clair's letter, "mine she she shall be," said he, " the treasure that love will not bestow, may be entrapped by art; if Adela St. Clair escapes me, she will be the first !"

But let us return to Theodore ; unobserved he had severed a lock of Adela's beautiful hair, which had escaped its confinement; he had placed it next his heart, and felt consoled that he possessed so sacred a memento.

At the early dawn of morning he arose, and having breakfasted, they rode round in that direction that led to the village—When they reached the garden gate— Theodore alighted and sprung over it, he went to Adela's dove-house, took from thence her favourite bird, and imprinted a warm kiss on its breast, resigned it to care of Ralph, who put it in his bosom.

"Sleep on, thou treasure of my soul!" said Theodore as he gazed on the little gothic window of his Adela's chamber. "Sleep on ! and may the Creator, who makes innocence and virtue his care, spread the wings of his protection o'er thee until I can claim thee as mine own."

When Theodore stopped for dinner, he took his little captive, carefully fed it, and having written the following stanzas, folded the paper and tied it with a pink ribbon round its neck.

To Adela

Go gentle envoy, pretty dove !
    And, quick as moon-beam, bear
This tribute of unvarying love,
    Committed to thy care.

And tell her on thy downy breast,
Ten thousand kisses I've imprest ;
Ge, bear them e're thy pinions rest,
    To her who fondly gave
Thee, little messenger, to cheer
Her wanderer's path from scenes so dear,
To breathe his vows—his sighs to bear
    Across you rippling wave.

Oh ! were our bosoms formed to sever ?
To live in exile ?—never ! never !

The flutterer mounted on the wing, and reached the woodlands on the valley's brow, just as Adela had retired to her pavilion, and continued her delightful task of completing Theodore's portrait, which her mother considered too exquisite a resemblance to be left incomplete. The little wanderer fluttered around her, and rested on her bosom ; she kissed it fondly, untied the billet, and read it to her parents. She now recollected Theodore had asked her, on the preceding evening, if she would give him that dove, and that she had consented to do so ; but she thought he was only jesting. "Oh I shall love the little creature more than ever !" said Adela, as she took it to the dove-house, that was sheltered beneath an arch of ivy and woodbine. She returned to her favourite retreat, and continued her delightful task.

But let us return to Theodore. It was evening when he arrived at the Park, and Sir Edward received him with warmest of welcomes. The cause of his delay seemed at first the subject of scrutiny ; but the plea of indisposition, and the purpose of having set off on one day, having led him into another, was readily received.

Mr. Somerville called in the course of the evening, having heard of Theodore's arrival, Sir Edward pressed him to sup with them, but he declined doing so, saying,

"No, no Sir Edward, I shall be happy to do so on another occasion, but Mr. Villars has just returned, you will have many little matters to talk over, and a traveller requires early repose as the conclusion of his journey."

CHAPTER XVII.

"And to be plain, 'tis not your person,
That my stomach's set so fierce on ;
But 'tis that better part, your riches,
That my enamoured heart bewitches."   HUDIBRAS.

DAY succeeded day, and Miss Crawley still peeped through the little iron gratings the most parental care of her aunt had ordered to be placed against the window. She neither heard James's voice in his general reply of ' yes ma'am," or " coming sir." She saw not a glimpse of his attractive figure passing through the grounds, nor had she the opportunity of making a single enquiry. It was to her aunt, but more frequently her aunt's husband she was indebted for her breakfast, dinner, tea, and supper, and no servant was suffered to attend her.

Solitude produced reflection, reflection recalled to her mind that her continued sullenness could avail her nothing, and might deprive her of a part of the golden store, which from childhood she had so keenly anticipated. A hint from Mr. Jonathan, whose saint-like patience was almost exhausted, had awakened her, and she determined to conceal the hatred and resentment she really felt at this innovation of her liberty, and assume the very opposite extreme of submission, as not only the means of regaining her freedom, by also of obtaining every possible source of communication with her lamented James.

This was an eventful morning—it was marked by a circumstance which gave a turn to the current of her gentle affections. Cupid was preparing yet another arrow for a too susceptible heart !

The Rev. Jonathan's solicitor had not yet completed the intricate arrangements, that had fallen to his share by the decease of the elder St. Clair, as the confidential friend, as well as legal adviser, of the above pious individual.

A slight indisposition prevented his calling for some days, and as he had a communication to make, which it would not have been prudent to trust to the post, he committed his letter to the care of one Robert Dear, formerly a poor boy, received into the house from motives purely charitable, and made useful in cleaning knives, boots and shoes.

Certain little expert tricks, however, designated "Bob," so completely (in his master's words) "a lawyer all over," that in a few years he was elevated to the distinction of a knight of the blue bag, and a useful and very devoted auxiliary he evinced himself, on many of these little confidential occasions, so likely to occur in the practice of gentlemen of this profession.

Miss Crawley saw Robert at a distance as be entered the gate, he crossed the lawn, and approached her window swinging his bag carelessly about in his hand.

Attired in the left off habiliments of his master, who was short and corpulent, he exhibited anything but a genteel figure, being tall and slender. Had the surplus part been taken out of the body of the coat, and added to its sleeves and the legs of the trowsers, the tailor might have been supposed to have had something to do with him, from his present figure that was impossible.

But Miss Crawley was no longer fastidious, she saw beneath all these disadvantages a being so capable of filling the void James had left in her heart, that, overpowered by the electricity of the moment, she hemmed twice. He raised his eyes, she smiled divinely upon him, he smiled also, and passed on to execute his commission

Miss Crawley felt inspired by the moment ; she tore out a leaf frsm her pocket-book, and wrote on it the following words :—

" Will you return again ?"

Scarcely had she written them, when a sound similar to that which had drawn his attention to the window, attracted her's ; she rolled up the paper and threw it out. He took it up, bowed respectfully, and she watched his figure until it disappeared from the gate. She still stretched her anxious sight, and beheld him with his blue bag, winding his way beside the distant canal in the path that led him into the town.

Miss Crawley now found an additional interest in the prosecution of the plan she had laid down. A new and delightful motive for deception ; and when Mr. Jonathan returned with her dinner on the tray neatly covered over, she confessed her faults so candidly, and promised amendment so faithfully, that the good man wept with joy. He sat down on the sofa, and with that sort of balancing motion for which he was remarkable in the pulpit he concealed his face with his handkerchief as in the fervor of devotion ; then removing it, he raised his eyes to heaven, and said,

" My prayer is heard !"

" My dear sir," said Miss Crawley, covering her face also, " will you let me go out of this gloomy room !"

" I will, my dear, I will," replied the pious man. " But remember, Sarah, to-day you attain your thirty-fifth year, and ought, therefore, to make reason the guide of your conduct. This time you are free, and I trust your future hours will be unmarked by the errors and follies of the past."

" Old dotard, with your follies !" whispered Miss Crawley, as she followed his deliberate footsteps down the stairs. " If I can't have a lord, I must have something ; I shan't live single for you, indeed !"

In another minute she was in the parlour, and seated between her credulous protectors, who each took a hand, perfectly satisfied with the sincerity of her apparent meekness and contrition.

But let us return to Robert. He sought the retirement of the lane, to read the contents of the scrap of paper.

" Will you return again ?" What could she mean ? It must be Miss Crawley ; and her smiles were too inviting, too unequivocal to admit a doubt of her wish to become better acquainted.

" I must turn this forward lady's advances to account," said Robert, laughing heartily.

He waited a little while, opposite the gate that led to the stables, and Peter came out with a basket to go into town to the market.

" Good morning, Mr. Peter," said Robert, " how are you ?"

" Good morrow to you, Robert Dear," replied Peter.

" How are all the family ?" said Robert, " for I didn't see the old gentlemrn, so I left the letter."

It may readily be conceived that this last question was prompted by curosity; for when Robert called to mind the iron gratings, united to some other singular appearances, it struck him forcibly that Miss Crawley was mad.

"All tolerable, thank you," said Peter, in reply to the above inquiry, "only master's a little vexed like about Miss—that's all."

"Miss Crawley! why, what's the matter with her?"

"Why haven't you heard? didn't you know she tumbled over head and ears in love with James? He's reason enough to wish he'd never seen her, for the old folks have spirited him away, God knows where, and shut her up. Aye, and if I had my will, there Madam should stay. Throwing our her snares, indeed! for a lad, ten or fourteen years younger than herself, at least; and engaged to as pretty a gal, too, as ever trod on shoe leather! All the money in the world should never ha' made me have her such a close fisted, mean spirited, virago! She wouldn't give a penny away to save a poor creature from starving, bless you! though she's got more money now, than she knows what to do with, and is to have £200,000 from her father, and all master's, I suppose, though she is no relation to him, as one may say, and he's got those of his own,—yes, his own name too, as would be a credit to him, if he behaved as he ought! But she'll take care to keep them away. It surprises every one to see how she bamboozles him!"

"Is it possible?"

"Yes, sure! She makes lots of fun of him behind his back; you'd split yonr sides to see her sometimes; and when he turns round, she looks for all the world like a saint! But won't you come and have a drop o' nothing, Robert? I'm going into town."

"No, thank you, Mr. Peter, not to-day; I shall be this way again, shortly, I dare say."

Here they separated, and Robert communed with himself as he wound his way homeward. Every thing seemed to authorize hopes he could not have dreamed of, a few hours before. That the lady was desperately anxious for a husband, her advances to a servant of the establishment, and that servant so many years her junior, was an evident proof. The obstacles that had divided them had evidently instead of rendering her less anxious, set her heart wandering in another direction, and he was the fortunate being, who, in so critical a moment, had been thrown by favouring fate, in her way. Would it not be worse than insanity not to take advantage of it; £200,000 from her father, and all the Reverend Jonathan's, which, by a recent arrangement, had been so enormously encreased! Why, were she age, deformity, ugliness itself! he would become her devoted slave, her passionate adorer!

In vain did Susan's charms, her loves and faith, her tenderness when Robert had nothing but a heart to bestow; her promise to be his, and his only. In vain did her nightly watching and daily care, when sickness had visited his solitary pillow, present itself; with her generous sacrifice of an entire half year's salary, to pay the little debts he had contracted, and procure him the comforts he then required. His heart bitterly reproached him with his purposed infidelity, for he loved her warmly, passionately, sincerely! and she was, really, a very handsome, and a very devotedly affectionate girl.

"But then," replied the demon in his heart, "if I do not desert her, if by assuming what I do not feel, I can support her I love in affluence, in a sweet retreat where I can visit her unknown to any one!—but will Susan consent to be any thing less than my wife?"

This doubt awakened a mingled feeling of guilt and pain; but it was instantly silenced by the idea of the worldly benefits, the baubles and frippery, by which he could repay the anticipated abandonment of every bitter feeling; and the devoted tenderness which could render her an easy prey! Then, with all the cold-hearted premeditation of an attorney's factotum, he took out his pocket-book and pencil, and prepared the letter he intended delivering on the following morning,

"MY DEAR MADAM,

"I have passed the night in a state of delirium over the dear little note you did me the honour to drop into the garden.

"What am I to understand by your question? Does Miss Crawley wish me to return? Her smile would almost authorise the presumptuous hope. Give me your commands, madam, and I will pass through the furnace of Shadrach, or stem the whirlpool of Maelstrom, to execute them! When will you admit to the honour of an interview the most devoted of your admirers,

"ROBERT DEAR."

Miss Crawley had wandered through the grounds in the evening. Every sound drew her anxious eye to the gate; but no signs of the young man with the bag! Perhaps he did not understand her. She regretted she had not held out a more explicit encouragement. She sighed as she passed the walk leading to the stables, and saw the sun-flowers that had so often witnessed James's vows of love and constancy. He was gone for ever! and who could say, if the one who might have filled his place in her susceptible bosom might ever return? She wandered to the house sulky, and sad; and complaining of a head-ache, retired early to her chamber.

No. 11.

At morning's dawn Miss Crawley arose, and haunted with fears lest the young man with the blue bag might come, and, imagining she was still there, contrive to throw a note into her aunt's dressing-room, which, in her own elegant language, would "put the old fellow o' top of the house at once;" she continued to saunter near the gate, that she might intercept his entrance.

At length he arrived; he offered the letter, which she eagerly received and slipped into the pocket of that eternal black silk apron; she gave him a smile in return. Robert went to the house to await the Reverend Jonathan's commands; Miss Crawley retired to her chamber, to read her letter, to kiss it joyfully, to write the following sentence: "Meet me this evening, at eight, at the reservoir;"—and, watching at a window, under which she knew he must pass, she rolled up the paper threw it out when he appeared. He took it up, put it in his pocket, kissed his hand, and Miss Crawley proceeded to the parlour, and took her seat at the breakfast-table, between the credulous Mr. Jonathan and his equally confiding partner.

At the hour of eight, Miss Crawley met Robert Dear at the appointed place. The extreme fervour of the one to be opulent, and the other to be married, set aside all those little sentimental perturbations which might have been supposed at a first meeting, to have delayed, or thrown a feeling of reluctant delicacy over an explanation. The poles are not more distant than were such tremors from the lady's bosom; and as to the gentleman, it was really too good a thing to be left to the casualties, that, in the event of delay, might spring up to prevent his wishes.

Vows of eternal constancy were given and received;—a letter proposing himself as son-in-law to Mr. Crawley was agreed upon;—and another to the Reverend Jonathan.

Miss Crawley arrived before her protectors had returned from their visit. Robert wrote his letters, sent them, and called on the following morning for his reply.

Old Mr. Crawley left Mushroom Lodge, and arrived at the Reverend Jonathan's before mid-day. They compared their letters, wondered at the young man's impudence, threatened to have him turned out of doors by his employer; and the fair culprit was called upon to account for so strange an adventure.

"How's this, Sal—how's this?" stammered the enlightened Mr. Crawley; "is your brain really turned?"

"Are these the proofs of returning rectitude?" said the Reverend Jonathan.

"And what," replied the young lady, with the most unblushing effrontery, "is there so very remarkable in my wishing to be married? I'm sure I've waited long enough for a duke or a lord—I must have som-thin."

"His words, then, are true—'by Miss Crawley's desire;'" said the horror-stricken pastor. "Is this thy love to thy parents? and have not I been as a father, brother,—nay, even as a husband, to thee? My very spirit groans over the impurity and perverseness of this wandering lamb."

"Is this your wish, wench?" said Mr. Crawley.

"Yes, sure," replied his hopeful daughter.

"Then I say," rejoined he, "that you are an impudent baggage. What! a fellow without a sixpence or a coat to his back?"

"I can buy him a coat!" said Miss Crawley.

"Quite lost—quite lost!" said the mother, and echoed the aunt. "She must return to the dressing-room."

"I do think you fancy you've got a child to deal with," said Miss Crawley, "I will have Robert Dear, and I won't be locked up in the dressing-room, there then!"

Mr. Jonathan again groaned,—by his slow mode of bending forward, and sideway, alternately, on his chair, he now evinced the agony of his mind; his colour varied, he cast up his eyes to heaven, applied his white handkerchief to his face, and was half ready to exclaim in the bitterness of his soul, "Give not that which is holy unto the dogs, neither cast ye your pearls before swine, lest they trample them under their feet, and turn again and rend you."

" Think, Sarah," continued he, " think what I have done for you ! more, even, than I can answer to my own conscience ! Think, unfortunate child, of the reproach you thus cast on your parents ! Will not the world say, By their fruit shall ye know them ?"

In vain did the aunt jog her, in vain whisper her not to irritate Mr. Jonathan. In vain did her mother promise for her, her father insist she should give up so insane a scheme; Miss Crawley persevered in her resolution. Her parents returned home, and just arrived at Mushroom Lodge, in time to kick the intended son-in-law down the steps, and out of the gate.

This was very humiliating, but it had a favourable effect in the furtherance of Robert's splendid prospects. It put him up to the turning o account a trifl ng secret of which he was in possession—" what love fails in, fear frequently accomplishes;" and he made his way to the Reverend Jonathan's.

Miss Crawley was in her chamber, when Robert Dear was announced by Peter.

" To be sure, my love, you won't see him ?" said Mrs. Jonathan.

" Why not, my love ? perhaps a few pounds and a little salutary reasoning may convince him of the cruelty of disgracing so respectable a family. But, there is another reason, he is the only one entrusted by my friend Quibble to fetch and carry our most important communications; he has perhaps come on business."

" I hope you will see Mr. Quibble to-day, my dear, and have the insolent vagabond turned out of door."

" That, my dear, will depend upon circumstances."

Mr. Jonathan sent for Robert to his study; the severest reproaches, the bitterest replies, were heard by Miss Crawley, whose ear was closely applied to the key-hole.

" Little did I think," said the good pastor, " that when I received you, Robert, as the meek, trusty and confidential messenger of my worthy friend, I was communing with a 'wolf in sheep's clothes.' "

" I'll tell you what, sir," rejoined Robert, " the less we allude to hypocrisy the better. We will say nothing about ' wolves in sheep's clothing,' lest the idea of ' false teachers' should occur to us ; one part of that impressive paragraph cannot easily be separated from the other ! I have met with an insult from Miss Crawley's father, which, in all the poverty with which you have reproached my origin, I never until this day endured—and, I will be very candid with you, I will receive no compensation but,—"

" Well, well," hastily interrupted the amiable Jonathan, " I will take the compensation into my own hands. If five or ten pounds will be of any use to you, Robert, or even twenty, on condition you will see Miss Crawley no more."

Here the Rev. Jonathan's discourse was stopped short, by the triumphant sneer that curled the lip of the exulting Robert.

" Twenty pounds, Mr. Jonathan! No, nor fifty, nor a hundred! no £100,000 ! I will have Miss Crawley, and you shall consent to it, and her father shall consent to it!"

He approached the reverend gentleman, he whispered a few words in his ear ; what were those words we know not, but the effect was magical !—The redness of face vanished ; a ghastly blue-tinged, death-like paleness succeeded; he trembled with a thousand emotions more direful than rage, but tears came to his assistance —he covered his face, and waved the young man to retire.

But Robert remained motionless ; he felt at that moment, that, place all the wealth of this worthy and opulent family in one scale, and that odd mysterious power which his manner, and the effect of his few magic words seemed to arrogate in the other, that the dross would fly up, and the power, however treacherously acquired, preponderate.

At length the excellent man, in a voice half choked with emotion, called Robert to him.

" I will consider of your proposals, Mr. Dear," said he, " call on me to-morrow at this hour."

" No, sir !" replied Robert, "I will have my answer to-night! aye, and a promise too under your hand, and that of Miss Crawley! and understand me, old boy! —no spiriting me away! I'm prepared against all that sort of manœuvring ?"

Upon this he entered the ante-chamber, where the lovely Sarah awaited him with a laugh of exultation.

" Will you walk with me round the grounds, my love ?" said he, with an embrace.

" I will," said Miss Crawley—" we will leave old hunks to talk over his consent with aunty, and when we return, everything will be snugly settled, I'll warrant ye!"

"See," said Robert, " what a little power in the hands of a lover ardent, faithful, and passionate as myself, can effect !"

Miss Crawley peeped in at Mr. Jonathan. " We will be with you, my dear sir, in five minutes," and tying on her bonnet she placed her hand within Robert's, who pressed it to his heart, promised to forgive her father, and they strolled together round the lawn, garden and shrubbery.

When they returned, the venerable pair were seated at the table, wine, glasses and fruit before them,—pens, ink and paper. The traces of indescribable anguish were on each countenance, but they received Robert with studied politeness ; and an hour's conversation, as it quelled the storm in their bosoms, produced, if not a certain degree of good-fellowship, yet something so very like it, that a common observer would have been easily deceived. We are entirely ignorant of the behind-scene machinery which had power to work so singular an effect, but certain it is, that the promise was signed, sealed, and delivered that night !

An interview with Mr. Quibble, in which, although some reproaches intervened, and the Rev. Jonathan was heard to say, " whom the Lord loveth he chasteneth," and "thy will be done," all ended amicably enough.

Mr. Crawley was convinced there was no " striving against the stream," and the marriage was fixed for the following month, with the promise that, instead of the lady taking his name, he should take hers.

No expense was spared to effect this desirable change, which would, Mr. Jonathan said, prevent the fall, from a duke to a lawyer's drudge, getting wind, and rendering the family more ridiculous than they already were.

An establishment was prepared for the happy pair—an elegant secluded cottage, built, furnished, and presented to the too confiding Susan, who now vied with her rival in silks, ribbons and laces. And the hours the bridegroom could steal from the chain avarice and ambition had imposed on him, were here devoted, and a welcome relief from the ignorance, petulance, and vicious selfishness he found at home. Susan's parents, although poor, had nurtured in her bosom sentiments of the purest morality, and she felt, amidst this change in her destiny, that she would rather ten thousand times have shared a hut with Robert as her husband, than all the comforts and conveniences of her present existence, amidst those constant reproaches of conscious guilt, that had already faded the rose from her cheek. In vain did he whisper, with the wiliness of Satan, that, should he ever be free from his present shackles, " Susan should become honourably his." Her parents slept in the grave, her heart was cold and joyless, and he might have said, in the language of Shenstone,—

" Poor artless maid! to stain thy spotless fame,
Expense and art and guile united strove,
To lure a breast that felt the purest flame,
Sustained by virtue, but betrayed by love.'

CHAPTER XVIII.

"I know within the blushing rose
A cankering worm is often found;
And even while its sweetness blows,
Its leaves with thorns will most abound!"

MR. SOMERVILLE dropped in whilst they were breakfasting, with an invitation from the ladies to a family dinner, and the gentlemen prepared for a ride; after which Theodore devoted an hour to his first sitting to a miniature painter. He then dressed, and accompanied his father to the Lodge.

They were announced, received by Mr. Somerville, conducted to the drawing-room, and Theodore introduced to Mrs. Somerville, her daughter, and daughter's companion.

Mrs. S. appeared in the decline of life and health; her daughter's companion was a genteel-looking young person without any personal attractions—and the heiress? we will draw her picture.

Miss Somerville was tall and graceful, her complexion a clear brunette, her black eyes, unusually fine, were shaded by dark fringes, and required their shadow to tempt their brilliancy. Her arched brow gave dignity to her countenance, and her lips, unclosing to welcome Theodore, displayed one of the finest sets of teeth in the world—her dark hair was tastefully disposed, a bandeau of pearls and emeralds crossed her brow, and corresponded with her dress, which was composed of rich green silk.

Thedore could not avoid acknowledging her a very fine woman, but it was not the style of beauty to interest the heart; and when he took her hand to conduct her to the dining-room, his fond imagination recurred to his Adela, in whose unadorned loveliness, whose hourly improving mental and external graces all his hopes, desires and anxieties centred.

The table was spread with that sort of luxury which carries with it more the air of a banquet than a family dinner, and the conversation turned on India, its climate, the regretted friends the ladies had left behind, and various little incidents attending their voyage home.

Mrs. Somerville said she had not yet invited any company to meet Mr. Villars on the present occasion, because she herself felt there was more friendship in a snug family party, and although this was a first introduction they had long ceased to be strangers.

Sir Edward smiled, Theodore bowed to the compliment, and the beautiful Belinda turned aside her head, Theodore imagined, to hide a blush.

Mrs. Somerville said she hoped, in a few days, however, to introduce Sir Edward and Mr. Villars to a few of their friends. The ladies retired to the drawing-room, and it gave great pleasure to Sir Edward to observe that the sound of the harp induced Theodore, in about half an hour after, to follow them; and he positively prolonged those topics apparently most interesting to his hospitable host, and loitered over his wine, with a view of "giving his boy" an opportunity of making his own way in the young lady's affections. So that it may be very naturally conceived, that when the elder gentleman entered the drawing-room, and saw Miss Darlington at the piano, the beautiful Belinda displaying her fine figure at the harp, and Theodore standing beside her, apparently wrapped in an ecstasy —he considered his golden visions realized.

But Theodore's imagination was far differently occupied. The air he had heedlessly turned over was Adela's favourite; it carried him back to the cottage on the brow of the valley. In vain were a thousand studied graces introduced—he saw, he heard but Adela; and when she concluded, and awaited with downcast eyes his commendations—if for a moment he was lost, the two fathers, the mother, even the young lady herself, were certain that there could not be stronger demonstration of a new-born passion. Theodore, however, recovered himself, blushed, declared her performance inimitable, and thanked Heaven internally for the entrance of the tea equipage, which released him from his embarrassment; and he took his seat beside Miss Darlington, to assist in doing the honours of the table.

After tea, Belinda proffered to accompany Mr. Villars in a ramble through the grounds, to show him some improvements of which she had been the directress; and Sir Edward, as he watched them from the window, in rapture anticipated a thousand tender disclosures of the heart, and positively determined that they were " formed for each other !"

An elegant supper, with more music, concluded the evening; and Sir Edward retired highly elated, and his son weary and uninterested to his pillow.

On the following day they dined *en famillé* at the Park, and strolled together through its capacious and fine gardens; and, although it was the decline of the year, a variety of autumnal flowers yet emitted their fragrance.

On the following morning an excursion into the country was proposed, but Theodore declined accompanying them under the plea of a head-ache, because his miniature was to be this day completed, and he wished to enclose it to his Adela. Sir Edward, therefore, accompanied Miss Somerville on horseback, the rest of the party went in the barouche; and Theodore, retiring to his study, wrote as follows:

" To ADELA.

" The pang I felt at parting from the idol of my soul required no accumulation, yet it met with a severe one. Adela! I observed a stranger passing to and fro in the direction of your cottage. This I conceived might be chance, and argued my jealous fears into tranquillity—but Ralph tells me he made some inquiries at the gate, during the last few happy days I enjoyed your society. He is not of the village, I am persuaded, he has the air of a dissipated man of fashion. My Adela! listen not to him for a moment, he can have nothing in view but the winning of those affections which are pledged as mine, and mine only! but why do I for a moment doubt my Adela, whose strength of mind is equal to her gentleness,—she will not consign to despair a heart so truly devoted!

" Adela! was my little messenger faithful to his charge? did that rosy lip kiss the plumage mine so fondly pressed at the moment it took its flight to where my anxious hopes so tremulously lingered?

" The beautiful hair is set in the form of a heart; neither night nor day does it quit my bosom.

" In the enclosed morocco-case my beloved girl will find the resemblance of her Theodore; will she sometimes look on it? will she allow it a place in that pure bosom?

" When will the hour arrive when I shall behold my Adela the mistress of my paternal mansion, and beloved by my father as the adored wife of his son? I dare not trust myself with the anticipation, or I shall no longer be able to endure the delay.

" Present my warmest regards to our parents; and what to my rose of the desert?   " The heartfelt devotion of her

" THEODORE."

This having been carefully enclosed, was consigned to the guardianship of Ralph, who, with a store of ribbons and a new gown for Lucy, set off for the village, where his honest heart was equally a sojourner.

And Theodore's anxiety was not without reason. If Captain Grenville no longer wrote, no longer addressed Lucy with inquiries respecting her young mistress; if in a rage he tore up St. Clair's reply to his insulting letter, he was not less resolved upon carrying his purpose into execution; he now hovered about under the cover of darkness, and on the night after Theodore's departure Adela was awakened from her slumber by the sound of music beneath her window. She listened, and heard these lines accompanied in a superior style on the guitar:—

SERENADE.

Oh, say not that it cannot be,
All things are possible for thee !
Midst direst dangers I'd advance,
To gain one sweet approving glance ;
O'er Alpine mountains climb my way,
Through burning deserts gladly stray !
To thee, sweet maiden, could I prove
That all is possible to love !

During the first moments of awakened recollection, the idea that it was Theodore occurred to her, for his form, sleeping or waking, was ever present. But the thrilling tones, the mellow cadence of his voice, were too well remembered. Who, then, could it be ? Captain Grenville's letter, his inquiries of Lucy, rushed on her mind, and, trembling with indefinite terrors, she hid her head under the bed-clothes. In about half an hour it ceased, and she sunk into a perturbed slumber.

On the following morning, she mentioned this circumstance to her parents.: Lucy was again cautioned, the boundaries of their own grounds prescribed to Adela, and a new regulation entered upon, that of locking the outer gate previously to the family retiring, in future.

It may well be conceived that the dove, the tablets, the stanzas written by Theodore's hand, were her constant and cherished companions ; whilst St. Clair and his endeared Aurora, leaving ill-acquired wealth, with all its heart-corroding self-reproaches to the worldly-minded, looked forward to their Adela's union with one whose congenial virtues would prove her solace when they should be no more.

And Ralph has arrived at the cottage ; he has delivered the little packet enclosing the letter, he has been invited to sup and spend the evening with Lucy, to whom he has given his little offerings of affection. And Adela having put her letter into the hands of her parents, and suspended the miniature around her neck, concealed it in her bosom, and retiring to her chamber, replied as follows :

" TO THEODORE.

" And can my beloved friend for one moment encourage so injurious a doubt ? can a heart modelled by such a mother, directed by such a father, be supposed capable of being misled by the dissolute and worthless ? not another word on the subject, I command you, dear Theodore ! there was a talisman in Adela's bosom even before the faithful and treasured resemblance she has just placed there.

" Do not ask me how I received my bird, for I must not tell you. It was always a favourite, it is now Theodore's also, and possesses a double claim to my care.

" Let us not, my valued friend, be too sanguine in anticipating the future ; the present is too delightful in the interchange of congenial feeling to be embittered by the thoughts that will intrude,—I dare not, a sentiment of anguish indescribable swells at my heart, and the flowers which you have woven in the wreath formed for the future are gemmed with tears ! I will not reflect—but, oh, Theodore ! your father is yet ignorant of our affection. Well ! at any rate our hearts cannot be divided !

" You will say I am melancholy, but these reflections are mingled with a tenderness that has banished my displeasure, for I really could have reproved you for the commencement of your letter, had not the thought of the miles that sever, the vicissitudes that may yet divide us, pleaded for you in the heart of your

" ADELA.

" P.S. Those beloved parents whom Theodore affectionately designates his also, desire me to express, on their account, all that affection and esteem can dictate."

Theodore had watched anxiously for Ralph's return, and ten thousand kisses were imprinted on the exquisite lines traced by the lovely hand of his Adela. So lost, indeed, was he to anything below the ethereal regions of love and sentiment, in which he was imparadised, that Sir Edward had sent twice, and ultimately was obliged to come himself, to remind him that it was Belinda's birthday, and that they had been invited to join a select dinner-party, which was to precede a ball and supper, to which the first families, for many miles round the Lodge, had been invited.

A superb and newly-decorated suite of apartments were thrown open. Luxury and splendour reigned around. The beauty of the exotics, the music, the gay and lovely faces—it seemed an enchanted palace, where youth and pleasure "weave the light dance with festive freedom gay," and Belinda, the presiding goddess of the scene, in white and silver sparkling with brilliants, shone the "fairest of the fair."

"Does she not look handsome to-night," said Sir Edward, in a whisper to his son.

Theodore allowed her beautiful, and his father felt not only satisfied, but even certain, that on this auspicious night his fair favourite's conquest would be complete. Alas! Sir Edward's heart was not formed to feel that it is one thing to dazzle the eye, and another to attract the heart.

But Belinda smiled on him; she yielded him her fair hand in the dance—his arm encircled her waist in the mazes of the waltz, and they mutually excited the despair and envy of the unmarried fair ones, and the gay flutterers who fail not to cluster around the shrine of fortune and fashion. But here was an attraction of infinite power, an arrival from India, her grandfather's heiress—and Belinda was a beauty!

Theodore also had long been a most desirable alliance in the eye of every parent and guardian of the fair damsels in that circle. But the heart, in the first instance unawakened, and afterwards devotedly, passionately, indissolubly engaged, had baffled every indirect pursuit and hidden snare, and he still gazed on the half-blown, full-blown, and over-blown graces surrounding him, with as much indifference as if looking on a parterre of tulips, or a cluster of our friend Miss Crawley's favourite sun-flowers.

"A devilish happy fellow that Villars!" said a tall moustachioued lounger, as he raised his glass to have a better view of the heiress, as Theodore conducted her to one of the sofas, and presented her with a glass of negus; "so much beauty united with what is still more attractive, has then at length aroused him from his apathy?"

"Why, my dear fellow, would you have had him like yourself, over head and ears in love already fifty times? you forget that he is yet in his minority, and"—

"Oh," interrupted another, "young Villars is one of your sentimental eccentric beings, who permit their exquisite sensibilities and love of solitude to mingle the mellow tint of autumn with the beauties of spring; he is, in fact, a nondescript."

"There you see, Lady Emily," said Miss Dacre with malignant exultation, "your interesting insensible is at length captivated."

"Who would have imagined," said Lady Charlotte Herman, "that he would have been won by a beauty in Miss Somerville's style?"

"You allow her a beauty then," said Miss Dacre.

"Why, no one can deny that she has fine eyes."

"And beautiful teeth," said Miss Dacre; "she may be what is generally considered handsome, but she is certainly not interesting,—she has not the sylphide delicacy, the air of pensiveness. I should have expected in the chosen of Theodore Villars."

Lady Emily looked languishingly.

"In your own style, for instance," said Lady Charlotte.

Their several partners now advancing, checked the farther observations of these amiable friends; and Theodore led the exulting Belinda to join them.

The supper-rooms were magnificent, every luxury procurable was there lavished; it was profusion arranged by the hand of taste, and they seemed to vie with each other.

The dancing recommenced, and was continued until the earliest tinges o morning succeeded the shadows of night, and Theodore and his father were amongst the last loiterers of the company, who took coffee with the family, previous to their departure.

It was not in human nature to be insensible to the unequivocal demonstrations of Belinda's preference during this evening.

If she hung on his arm, it was with a degree of tenderness not to be mistaken; when he took her hand to lead her to the saloon, she suffered it to remain within his with apparent unconsciousness; then suddenly, as if recollecting herself, withdrew it with confusion. If he looked on her, her eye was averted, and a sigh more than once had escaped her.

On the following morning, Sir Edward sought an explanation with his son, during breakfast.

"Miss Somerville looked like an angel last night."

"Sir," replied Theodore, whose thoughts were in another direction.

"Belinda, did she not dance gracefully?"

"Yes, sir."

"She has an exquisite voice too."

"Her singing is very well."

"And is she indeed," continued Sir Edward, "a very charming woman, just such a one, Theodore, as I should like to see your wife."

No. 12

This was coming to the point, but it did not surprise Theodore, because he had anticipated that his father was veering thither, and he did not reply.

"What do you say, you sly dog, eh?"

"To what, sir?"

"Why, to proposing for Miss Somerville, to be sure!"

"You seem to think, sir, that it is only requisite to propose, in order to be accepted. Miss Somerville will have many aspiring to the honour of her hand, and I am not disposed to enter into any such engagement at present."

"Oh, nonsense! where fortune, beauty, the approbation of friends, every thing is likely to conspire to render the thing eligible,—why, the sooner the better! and I think there is not much danger of your being rejected!"

"I really think, sir, your parental partiality misleads you," said Theodore retiring, glad of any excuse to prevent the continuance of the subject.

"But stop," said Sir Edward, securing a button of his dressing-gown, "we must not forget to wait on the ladies this morning."

Theodore assented; and having dressed, they went together to the Lodge.

They found the ladies fatigued from the exertion of the preceding night. Mrs. S. was replacing some drawings (which she said were her daughter's) in a portfolio, Miss Darlington was selecting some new music, and Belinda arranging some choice and exquisite flowers in an Indian vase.

A sprig of blossomed myrtle had fallen from her hand. Theodore stooped for it, and would have replaced it, but she received it with downcast eyes; and he perceived in the evening, when he assisted her to mount her steed, that the myrtle had found a place in her bosom, whence it had apparently protruded by chance.

After a pleasant ride in the environs, the party returned to a collation at the Park, and having accompanied the ladies to the portal of the Lodge, Theodore retired to his chamber, where, having had a few minutes' conversation with Ralph, on the subject of his anxiously anticipated return to the Woodland Valley, he sunk to repose.

CHAPTER XIX.

And the tressell'd foliage green
        Rears its waving canopy;
Through each branch, the garish sheen
        Is mantled in its rainbow dye.

Sacred to love that verdant bower
        Where the rose and jasmine 'twine,
Where bends the lily's spotless flower,
        And truth's pure gem adorns the shrine.

                                        F. A. KENTISH.

"'Tis my friend Arnold," said St. Clair, hastening to the gate to receive him, as a chaise drove up to it, and in a few minutes a blooming girl, about Adela's age, was introduced as Louisa Arnold; and a sincere welcome given and received by all.

The hospitable table was spread, and the interchange of perfect friendship, and an immediate prepossession in each other's favour, spoke, from brilliant eyes, the language of warm and unsophisticated hearts.

Enchanted period! when the vicissitudes of life have not chilled the fervour of the pure heart—when the vision of hope has not been set aside, or the dark realities of character awakened suspicion that shall sleep no more!

Adela had never, until now, possessed a female companion of her own age; and her young heart unfolded itself to the charming novelty in a very fascinating manner; she performed the duties of hospitality with so much frankness and grace, that Louisa threw her arms around her neck, and said—

"You really are a dear, delightful girl! how sorry I am Mr. Josiah St. Clair did not live to see you just as I do, at this moment, for then he would never have parted with you. You would have been mistress at the Hall, and we should always have been together!'

Adela returned her embrace, and told her she must rest during that evening; but, on the following morning, she would lead her through so many delightful scenes, and show her so many animate and inanimate objects endeared to her by their association with her earliest recollections, that she was certain she would allow it possible to be very happy without being very rich.

During the evening Mr. Arnold informed St. Clair that the Hall had been shut up carefully ever since the Reverend Jonathan's family had so mysteriously and suddenly left it. That a dismissed female servant of the above gentleman's, in passing through the town to London, had encountered a servant of his; and from their gossip, the whole account of Miss Crawley's marriage and previous intrigue had transpired. That the family had become the ridicule of the neighbourhood, as much on account of the Reverend Jonathan's ducal vision, as the humiliating rejection their proposals met from Sir Henry. That old Alexander had died in a fit occasioned by disappointed ambition. That no one could behold the bride without a satiric smile of contempt; that she had recently become sullen and gloomy. "In the pious pastor's style," continued Mr. Arnold, "we may, indeed, say, He gave them their request, but sent leanness into their soul;" for, it appears, that since that period she has been, hourly, more the prey of hungry avarice and jealous doubts and suspicions, which occasioning incessant wranglings, have rendered their home a scene of splendid misery.

That Mrs. Crawley repines over every sixpence laid out in the necessary expenditure of the family,—portions out the provisions to the servants, who are, therefore, changed weekly, and has given orders that every beggar shall be whipped from her gate.

That Mr. Crawley seldom spends an evening at home—that he frequently passes a week at a time away from his bride, who, not having been visited by any of the ladies in her vicinity, would stand a chance of living almost entirely alone, but for the Reverend Jonathan's consolatory visits, to whom it seems she bitterly complains of her husband's desertion, ingratitude, and neglect.

"As you have made your bed, Sally, so you must lie on it," is generally the good man's reply.

"Some say," continued Mr. Arnold, "he feels a delicacy, and some even a fear of remonstrating, possibly the latter; for, between ourselves, although the reverend gentleman possesses the power of willing away about £400,000 to whom he pleases, yet Mr. Crawley holds, it seems, some higher power, of that mysterious and indefinable nature that is not to be disputed!"

Conversation led them into a late hour, when Mr. Arnold would fain have retired to the inn, not to disturb the family arrangements; but Mrs. St. Clair had ordered it otherwise.

The servant was sent to sleep at her mother's; her bed was prepared for Mr. and Mrs. St. Clair; theirs resigned to Mr. Arnold; and Adela and Louisa retired to the chamber with the little painted window and muslin curtain, which Theodore had so often watched with the tender interest of anxious solicitude.

The beauty of the surrounding scene, on which Louisa gazed with delighted admiration, welcomed them forth; and Mr. and Mrs. St. Clair with Mr. Arnold had just placed themselves at the breakfast-table, when Louisa and Adela entered from their ramble, glowing with the freshness of a fine October morning,

Adela had gathered a nosegay of the last fragrant flowrets of the declining year, to present to their guest; and they partook of a breakfast of every little rural delicacy the farm could produce, with an appetite increased by the warm welcome and varied conversation of their elegant entertainers.

Mrs. St. Clair and the girls passed the hours preceding dinner in reading and music. St. Clair conducted his friend over his little farm, and took him to see the school-house, and other village improvements. In the afternoon St. Clair, Mr. Arnold, Adela, and Louisa, took a long country ramble, and on their return found Mrs. St. Clair waiting tea for them. The evenings had become chill, and the cheering fire threw a glow of exquisite comfort through the parlour window, as if to welcome their return. A little concert sped the evening hours rapidly away, and after an hour's conversation after supper, they all retired to share that repose rendered sweeter by health, exercise, and self-approving hearts, which avarice and injustice, even on their pillow of down, and canopied in state, seek in vain!

A week elapsed in the interchange of friendship amidst a scene that seemed to Mr. Arnold and his daughter a terrestrial paradise. One mystery still was unravelled, and as curiosity is said to be a female failing, we may permit Louisa Arnold to have felt a slight touch of it. She had on several occasions pulled at the black ribbon, suspended round Adela's neck, but it was secured,—at night she looked slyly through the curtains, and observed her companion take the treasured secret, inclose it in a little morocco case, and place it beneath her pillow. A few hours were now (notwithstanding their united entreaties for a lengthened visit) to separate these tenderly attached young friends. Louisa had unfolded the inmost recesses of her heart to Adela, but that one secret had not been confided to Louisa.

"Is that your papa's miniature, Adela?"

"No, love."

"Your brother's?"

"No, love." And Adela's cheek was suffused with crimson, as she continued, "It is the resemblance of a friend."

"Ah, Adela! a very dear friend, I imagine; may I not look on this highly favoured memento of friendship?"

Adela drew the miniature from her bosom.

"He is extremely handsome," said Louisa.

"He is talented and amiable," replied Adela, "and that worth which has obtained him the friendship of my parents, cannot fail to secure him my esteem."

"Dear, charming, happy Adela!" said Louisa, "in the bosom of this peaceful retirement, with such parents, such a friend, such claims on the esteem, the admiration of all who behold you! I am aware that you have indeed not a wish left ungratified. Long may Heaven spare you these unmingled blessings, and suffer your Louisa now and then to share them with you."

Adela clasped her friend to her bosom, a rustling in the path behind the harbour disturbed them, a voice repeated :—

"Dear, charming, happy Adela!"

They started—It was not Theodore's voice; they removed the foliage that separated the harbour from the lane that ran behind it, but no one was visible.

They returned to the parlour, for the unwelcome hour drew nigh, and St. Clair having placed some friendly remembrances of his daughter's pencil for Mrs. and Miss Arnold, together with some baskets of the finest fruit their orchard yielded, in the chaise, the parting cup was pledged, and Mrs. St. Clair's tear of tender interest mingled with those the girls could not restrain.

Louisa waved her sad adieus as they turned from the village; both father and daughter declaring that rustic dwelling an earthly paradise, and the family of St. Clair beings as superior to the present possessors of their departed friend's property, as the summit he Alps from the Valley in the Woodlands.

Adela thought with terror of the repetition of her friend's words. It seemed to her to be the voice of Captain Grenville, and not imagining she ought to render her beloved parents uneasy by the idea that he yet haunted her path, she pressed her lips to the treasured resemblance of her heart's chosen friend; breathed a prayer to the Creator for his protection, and resolved to avoid even the arbour until she was certain her persecutor had left the village.

Captain Grenville had returned to his paternal habitation, after the disappointment contained in St. Clair's letter, not an iota deterred from pursuing the point he had in view, some particular business requiring his presence there; but particular business also recalled him. His aunt, who had resided about a mile and a half from the Valley, had paid the debt of nature, and he was sole heir to all her possessions, which, as a reimbursement to some very heavy losses at play at this critical moment, was far from an unwelcome event. In his own words "she was a good old soul," and he was "rather partial to her," because she had been indulgent to his follies from infancy—but he was infinitely more partial to his pleasures, and had no sooner given orders, and seen every arrangement in fair train for the funeral, than he was again on the wing after Adela, who had inspired his heart with a much more ardent passion than it had ever before been susceptible of. And as he had resolved to win over the servant to his aid, in obtaining an interview with her young mistress, he watched morning and evening to intercept her path.

Lucy was the daughter of very humble parents. Mrs. St. Clair had sent her to the village school shortly after her arrival at the Valley, where she had been taught to read; she had her also properly instructed in those sort of domestic occupations which would render her a useful servant at the cottage. When Ralph came thither to his master, and with letters to her mistress, he from time to time had brought her a ribbon, a pair of ear rings, or a handkerchief, and as he was a handsome lad, and wore a very handsome livery, she thought she should be the envy of every girl in the village if she could possibly secure him as her sweetheart. With this view she paid all sorts of attention to Mr. Ralph; plucked him the prettiest nosegay in the garden, placed his chair beside the bright fire in the kitchen, and smiled so invitingly upon him, that he could not fail to believe her desperately in love with him.

Now Ralph had opportunities of seeing many really pretty young women in his own station, from time to time, both at the Park and in its neighbourhood, and Lucy had not the slightest pretension to prettiness. She was a little snub-nosed girl; lively and merry, because her young lady left her nothing to wish or to care for, and as she put on her best gown when he was expected, curled her hair, for the first time she ever thought of such an embellishment, in a number of little corkscrews, that gave you the idea of a French dog, and mounted the green ribbons he had given her in her bonnet, Ralph fancied she loved him sincerely. He could associate nothing but simplicity with the image of a village girl. "Brought up under the same roof with Miss Adela," said he, "she must be innocence herself!" and he almost pledged himself never to forsake her.

St. Clair had, during the last year, obtained her father a situation as porter, at a warehouse in the neighbouring hamlet, so that when she obtained permission to visit her parents, she had to cross a field and a lane. Captain Grenville soon found this out; he also discovered that the servant at the cottage had a ruling passion, that it was a love of finery; he exulted in the prospect it offered him, and began to turn it to his own advantage.

If he saw her going into the hamlet, he took another path thither, insisted on Mrs. Lucy choosing a pretty dress, or a shawl for the winter; recommended scarlet as best suited to her complexion (which although of that indefinable cast, which has in fact no appropriate term) he did not fail to compliment, and during their walk homeward, obtained from her all the secrets that concerned, and a great many that did not concern the family, with a promise that she would assist him to an opportunity of conversing with Miss Adela. "I can have Mr. Ralph's presents, and the Captain's too," said Lucy, as she entered the gate, "why not?" and it was by her connivance he had entered and stationed himself beneath the window, on the evening of the serenade. On the night of her friend's departure, the remembrance of Captain Grenville's voice, and the determined purpose these constant interruptions to her liberty and repose evinced to annoy her, banished sleep from her pillow—and she resolved to caution Lucy still more impressively This faithful attendant, however, anticipated the subject, by bringing to her bed-side a paper, which she said she had found in sweeping the path by the arbour. It contained the following lines :

"ADORED ADELA,

"Have you then no compassion? neither your father's reply to the letter you so cruelly disclosed to him, nor your own obduracy, shall destroy my hope of one day possessing the pleasure of sharing with you that fortune, which without you is devoid of worth.

"Place a few lines in reply in the hedge, and do not drive to desperation

"Your devoted

"To Miss St. Clair.   "ALBERT GRENVILLE."

Adela felt a mistrust of Lucy steal over her mind, as, with a glance of penetrating scrutiny, she saw her eye fall under hers.

"Take this paper," said she, "place it in the hedge, and never on any occasion presume to bring me another."

"If I find one in the garden, Miss, can I help it?"

"No, you cannot help finding, but you can sweep it away. If however you had been careful to lock the gate, according to papa's orders, we should have had no intruders. It would give some trouble to climb the portico, and the hawthorn hedge is high enough to be a sufficient security."

Lucy blushed, and went to execute her commission, but all Adela's fears and anxieties were forgotten; Theodore alighted at the gate, a few steps bore her to his arms, and she was clasped to a heart she valued beyond existence.

Mr. and Mrs. St. Clair had not yet risen, and Adela and Theodore sat on the sofa beside the fire awaiting them.

But Adela saw the cloud of care on that countenance, which was too much the index of the heart to deceive her.

"Theodore," said she, "something has occurred!"

"No, love."

"Why do you turn away your eyes? Your father has forbidden—"

Her heart palpitated so wildly, she could not proceed. Theodore turned on her a look of indescribable tenderness—she burst into tears.

"My beloved! why these tears? nothing has occurred. Oh, smile again! and give the promise of our approaching felicity. Say you will be mine! say you will put it beyond the power of fate to divide us!"

"Dear Theodore! reflect for one moment that nearly a year is wanting to the time proposed by you to papa. Oh! your eyes are wet with tears, my prophetic heart has foretold it all, and we must part—for ever!"

"That, dearest girl, can never be! but your father is coming, meet me in the garden after breakfast, and there I will be more explicit."

Adela went to her chamber to recover her calmness, and left Theodore to receive her father. Her mother soon after came down, and breakfast had commenced before she had sufficiently recovered her composure to join them.

Theodore was sincerity itself, and although he had, on this occasion, more self-command than Adela, a sadness so unusual stole over him, that St. Clair perceived it, and rallied him upon it. Theodore smiled, attributed it to the late hours and scenes of festivity at the Park, in which he had been obliged to engage, whilst his inclination would have led him in another direction, and taking St. Clair's hand,

"Is it necessary to remind my father and my friend," said he, "that where the treasure is, the heart is also?"

Breakfast concluded, Theodore hastened to the garden, where Adela awaited him.

But we will return to the Park, and inform our readers of an interview, which Sir Edward had with his son on the morning after the Somervilles had supped at the Park.

"Theodore," said his father, "you need not, I think, return to Oxford."

Just as you please sir, but why not?"

"I have something else in view for you."

Theodore raised a glance of inquiry to Sir Edward's countenance.

"Yes, you may look, my dear boy, but I wish you to propose for Miss Somerville, and marry her out of hand, before some fortunate fellow carries off the prize."

"You really astonish me, sir! what, after merely a few days' acquaintance? strangers to each other's natures, dispositions and inclinations, pardon me if I say that such a thing would be premature in the extreme!"

"Not at all—not at all! do you know what she possesses when she arrives at the age of twenty-one, and she is now twenty, her father's wealth must be her's also! premature as it may seem, let me tell you it is too good a thing to be left to chance! every one can see she loves you, and there is not so lovely a girl for fifty miles round!"

"You certainly will give me time for consideration, sir."

"A week only—a week only! and mind, my dear fellow, I expect your obedience."

Theodore inwardly shuddered at this innovation of every thing in the form of that liberty which is the lifespring of the heart, but his affections were no longer at his own disposal; and somewhat sullenly and ceremoniously moving to his father, he was retiring, when it occurred to him to mention his purpose of visiting a friend for a week.

"You will then have determined on acting according to my wishes," said Sir Edward. "It is not possible you should be serious in opposing an alliance, where wealth, beauty, every thing conspires to attract and to charm. But you are a sad sly dog, and, like a boarding-school miss, must be coaxed into following your own inclinations. But we will spend this evening there, previously to your temporary absence."

Theodore assented, and the evening beheld them bending their course to Harewood Lodge.

The intelligence of Theodore's purposed departure had travelled like wild-fire from Sir Edward's valet to the housekeeper; from the housekeeper to the steward at the Lodge; from him to Miss Somerville's maid; from her to Miss Darlington. No wonder, then, that on entering the drawing-room, they found Belinda gazing so pensively on the surrounding scenery, that she either did not, or did not seem to observe their arrival. Her hair unadorned, her plain white robe, with no other embellishment than that very sentimental sprig of myrtle.

Mrs. Somerville, Mr. Somerville, Miss Darlington—all were immensely concerned at Mr. Villars' intended return to Oxford.

"He is not going to Oxford, madam," replied Sir Edward, "merely a visit to a friend, which will not detain him from us a week."

Miss Somerville gave a languid smile.

"Come, young lady," said Sir Edward, "you must favour my son with one of your delightful songs before we take our leave, although to others that week will soon pass, to him it will seem an age!"

Miss Darlington sat down to the harp, and Belinda, smiling on Sir Edward, sang the following air:

> Thou fond delusive syren, hope away!
>   Ne'er shall thy smile delude my bosom more;
> Fled are thy pleasures, closed thy dawning day,
>   And every fairy prospect clouded o'er;
> No more shall Fancy paint in colours gay
>   The future scene, delightful, calm, and fair,
> In sad reality they fleet away—
>   And what remains but sorrow and despair?
> No longer at thy voice this breast shall glow,
> The sigh of rapture rise, the tear of transport flow!

At the last stanza Belinda's voice faltered; she arose and retired, Miss Darlington following her.

"Belinda is extremely unwell to-day," said Mrs. Somerville, "an unusual melancholy has hung over her spirits during the whole of the morning."

Sir Edward expressed the greatest possible sympathy, and hoped the young lady would recover and again favour them with her society.

Theodore regretted that Miss Somerville had exerted herself for their gratification, at a moment when suffering under indisposition; and her mother left the room to inquire respecting her.

But Belinda did not return during the evening, and Theodore set off for the Valley on the following morning.

CHAPTER XX.

Like music borne on by the blast,
    As a sprite to its cavern'd home,
When the thunder-roll following fast
    Sheds o'er it a darklier gloom;
Or the dimpled smiles of a seraph maid
    In the 'joyance of youth so gay,
'Till by lightning her lover is laid
    A blacken'd corse by the way.   F. A. KENTISH.

AND Theodore had unbosomed his heart to his Adela;—tremblingly had she dwelt on every accent; but, when his father's mandate reached her ear, with the short term of a week only left for decision, every hope seemed expiring within her, and her prophetic fancy recalled her dream with all its soul-subduing imagery. The past and the present seemed as nothing, and of what value was the future, since it was likely it would be passed in absence from the chosen of her now hopeless heart?

"Oh, speak!" said Theodore, "beloved girl, speak!—say you will be mine,—say that an immediate union shall indissolubly unite us?"

"Alas! I fear papa will never consent to it, unsanctioned by your father. He will conceive a private marriage inconsistent with the honour he has hitherto preserved unsullied. I fear even to name it to him, lest it should embitter the last few dear hours fate has left us."

"And can he then, love, so soon have forgotten his own feelings? Oh, his soul is attuned to the tenderest sentiments of sympathy;—he is too just to imagine that a parent's avarice should be permitted to overcloud the felicity of his offspring!"

"Pass this week with us, dear Theodore," said Adela, "and say nothing to my parents until you have used all your eloquence to awaken the father in Sir Edward's heart. He may yet relent; if he remains inflexible—if he will not defer this union, then return, and we will, together, throw ourselves at the feet of papa. Oh! I will recal his hours of anguish—of inquietude, when the thought of being separated from mamma, clothed every future hour in the hue of despair! If he sanctions it—I will be yours! But let us not hasten calamity; let this week, at least, be devoted to that felicity we may never more be permitted to enjoy!"

Theodore clasped the agitated girl in his arms. Their tears mingled, but her very soul seemed wrapped in the preserving that given week tranquil, and he obeyed.

The winter was hastily approaching; the trees waved their almost leafless branches, and the yellow and withered foliage strewed those paths, which, in the lustre of summer, they had trodden with hope and ecstasy.

Day succeeded day in that interchange of feeling which is indescribable. Theodore's ardent gaze, the sigh that would not be repressed—Adela's suddenly starting tear bespoke that within the bosom "which surpasseth show;" and six days of that treasured week had already vanished as a dream!

Ralph arrived with a letter ; and Theodore went to the gate to receive it from him. But, as though he had not already a sufficient subject of anxiety, the inauspicious form of Captain Grenville glided past. Ralph had been making some observation to Lucy, and he just caught her reply—" one of Miss Adela's lovers." He heard not another word but receiving the letter, dismissed his servant to await his orders at the inn ; and, hurrying into the garden, read the superscription, in his father's hand—" To Theodore Villars, Esq. Woodland Farm."

" My father ! and positively addressed to the farm ! How has he obtained this unfortunate information ?"

He tore open the letter, and read as follows :—

" THEODORE,—I am aware of your connexion with Farmer St Clair's family. I make all due allowance for the human heart ; and Miss St. Clair is, I understand, although very pretty, yet a very designing girl ; but it will not answer my purpose that she should inveigle you into a marriage which would disgrace your family. Home, therefore, you must return, or I shall order my horses to be put to, and come after you. Do not put my patience to the test, at a moment when I am feverishly anxious on the point you know. No reply to this :—but your immediate presence will be received by your still affectionate, though offended father,

" EDWARD VILLARS."

No. 13.

Theodore's cheek was flushed with mingled emotions. He was aware, that to hesitate would be to draw the curtain of night over his dearest hopes ; for if his father arrived with his present feelings, the high-minded St. Clair would not, for an empire, permit a thought of his daughter forming an union with the son of one so sold to avarice, so incapable of appreciating her ! Adela's delicacy would shrink under his glance of cold-hearted worldly-mindedness, and all the sympathy of her benign parents be lost in the indignant feelings of wounded honour. Alas ! a moment's delay was not to be thought of. He closed the letter, and put it in his pocket : a slip of paper fell at his feet ; and, imagining it had fallen from his hand-kerchief, which he had drawn forth to dry the starting tear, he hastily returned it, and went to meet his Adela, who came to call him to the parlour, where her mother was waiting tea for them.

He endeavoured to rally his spirits, and avoided mentioning his father's un-propitious discovery (for which he felt half-ready to accuse his faithful servant) ; but spoke of his departure by day-break, and supported his depressed spirit by the prospect of his proposed return in a few days, and decided upon the point of acting independently where an interest, dearer than life, was concerned.

The evening found Adela with a flushed cheek, and throbbing temples. She did not complain, but her anxious mother saw the emotions of her heart in every glance, and endeavoured to persuade her to retire to her chamber to take an hour's rest.

" No, love,—not to your chamber," said Theodore, " shorten not the few hours of this sweet evening—repose on the sofa ;—no sound shall disturb you."

She consented : and he sat beside her, clasping her lovely hand, whilst her fond parents interchanged a glance of tender remembrance of former years, when they met at Sebástiano's cottage. Supper was spread, but Adela could take nothing ; and when her mother accompanied her to her chamber, Theodore whispered that he should not depart until mid-day on the morrow, and not then unless she was somewhat recovered.

Adela returned his look of tenderness, and retired to weep away the night. She, however, arose early, and met her lover in the parlour, where her parents found them, in deep and earnest conversation. St. Clair saw the emotion of both hearts ; he trusted it was one of those clouds that pass away before the sunshine of assured felicity.

Breakfast concluded—the hours between that and an early dinner were spent by Adela in languor and pensiveness, whilst Theodore, clasping her slender waist with his encircling arm, drew many a picture of anticipated bliss, which he urged in the language of an enthusiast " could not fail to be realized."

" And if my father disapproves," continued he, " in another year, I shall be independent, and, until then, we can live in seclusion. Smile then, my beloved ! smile again, and promise you will not give way to the fear of evils which never will arrive."

Adela turned her eyes to his, but it was the smile of an April morn. The hospitable St. Clair sought to enliven a meal, hitherto passed in festivity : but his young guest's cheerfulness was evidently assumed ; and Adela sad and thoughtful. It passed, the horses were at the gate,—the last embrace was given, the half-uttered farewell was breathed,—and he was gone !

She hastened to her chamber window, she looked to the winding pathway that circled the valley's brow, where they had so often wandered together. Every moment now bore him farther, her eye

> " Grew frozen with its gaze onvacancy,
> 'Till—oh, how far ! it caught a glimpse of him,
> And then it flow'd—and phrenzied, seem to swim
> Through these long, dark, and glistening lashes, dew'd
> With drops of sadness oft to be renewed.
> He's gone ! against her heart that hand is driven
> Convulsed and quick—then gently raised to heaven."

And she threw herself on her bed in an agony of tears.

Let us now, for a few minutes, revert to Captain Grenville, who, it may be remembered, repeated Louisa Arnold's apostrophe to her young friend, whilst, at the same time, his dark and revengeful spirit planned the changing the paradise of sweets he witnessed, to a scene of desolation.

He had discovered from Lucy, whose propensity to listening had assisted her to this and other novelties, (for, from Ralph, everything concerning his master was at all times sacred) that Theodore had been introduced there by accident ;—the mutual affection and engagement that had arisen from that introduction, and Sir Edward's address.

This rendered him still more anxious to obtain, by artifice, that which he despaired of winning from affection. And Adela scarcely ever visited her favourite haunt that he did not place himself behind the hawthorn hedge, to watch her footsteps, and gaze on her beauty.

It may be remembered that a letter had accompanied the miniature ; that it was Adela's constant and cherished companion, and that she delighted to retrace those tender sentiments in her solitary rambles.

These, the arrival of Louisa had interrupted, but they were again drawn forth on her departure ; and, although the once embowering trees were almost divested of their foliage and the path leaf-strewn, Adela still sat in her bower—still gazed on those idolized features, and read again and again her Theodore's welcome epistle.

Summoned to the house, hastily, by her mother, she had heedlessly dropped the letter. Grenville was, at that moment, in the lane, waiting a favourable opportunity to place his letter in the hedge, according to previous arrangement, and saw it lying in the path. Ardent as his curiosity was, he could not, with propriety, make an aperture in the hedge and it was too high to leap over ; he saw Lucy approaching, and gave her his letter.

" What paper is that in the path, my dear girl?"

Lucy stooped, picked it up, and unclosed it.

" I declare, sir, I can hardly see ; but I think it's from Mr. Villars to Miss."

" Come, come—give it to me, I'll tell you in a minute !"

Lucy gave it ; he looked at it ; she held her hand to receive it ; half a sovereign was placed there instead. Lucy thought the captain a charming, generous gentleman, wondered, from her heart, what on earth Miss could see in Mr. Villars, and tripped off to answer the bell ; delivered the letter the following morning, and Theodore's unexpected arrival prevented, not only Adela's missing what she had lost, and rendered her insensible to everything on earth but her love and her despair.

Meanwhile Grenville retired to a neighbouring inn, eagerly perused the letter which disclosed Theodore's secret attachment, his restless fears, and many other little circumstances capable of being wrought up into a state of utility to aid his dark design.

The project of writing to Sir Edward was no sooner thought of than executed ; but this was not all : " the displeasure of the parent," said he, " will only add fervor to their passion. Jealousy envenomed, heart-coroding jealousy must mingle her devastating influence :" and he watched his moment as anxiously as the shipwrecked mariner looks for the dawn of day.

CHAPTER XXI.

Love reigns a very tyrant in my heart,
Attended on his throne by all his guard
Of furious wishes, fears, and nice suspicions.   OTWAY.

BUT Theodore's was not his wonted welcome home. He had changed his trovelling attire, taking his coffee, and having vainly sent to apprize his father of his arrival, he was preparing to seek him, when he received a summons to attend him in his study, and was received with the extreme of *hauteur* and coldness.

"Well, sir! and what have you to say for this innovation of every thing decent and honourable?"

"I cannot conceive, sir," replied Theodore, "that my visiting a friend for a week, can have any thing to do with impropriety, much less dishonour."

"How then, sir! is your understanding with Miss Somerville and her family ot to be taken into consideration?"

"I never professed to have any particular understanding with Miss Somerville, sir; and, if I had paid her those attentions due to a lady from a man of education, it was more from a deference to your impressions in favour of that family, than any inherent inclination of my own, and assuredly never went beyond the limits of courtesy."

"Theodore—this is a paltry evasion! You know my wishes, my intentions, do not oblige me to make them commands. Miss Somerville must be your wife! speak not a werd! I will not have you reply. Leave me : when you can be reasonable, and then only, I will see you."

Theodore saw the nature of his father's feelings. Bacon says, "The ripeness or unripeness of occasions must ever be well weighed;" and, wishing to gain time to prepare himself for the assertion of that liberty of choice he could not resign: he retired to his chamber, where his honest servant attended his orders.

"Well, Ralph," said he, "this discovery of my father's is rather an untimely one; if my knowledge of your fidelity from infancy would not render such a suspicion next to impossible, I should imagine it could have proceeded from no one but yourself."

"Betray my master!" exclaimed Ralph, with a flush of indignant sorrow, that set his features in a glow; and Theodore would have given half his possessions to have recalled the unkind and heedless expression, as he continued, in a faultering voice—

"If you please, sir, I'll send William to you, to-morrow, when you are at leisure to see him. Mayhap he'll serve your Honor better, and he's long envied me my place."

"Are you, then, desirous of leaving me?" said Theodore in a softened accent, "wilt thou quit thy master when he most requires thy fidelity?"

Ralph's heart was in his eyes.

"Why, as to that, your Honor, you are the best judge whether, from the time when her ladyship took my poor mother, and your now disgraced servant, under her protection, up to a few minutes ago, when I felt proud and flourishing in your favour; if I have ever done any one thing, or uttered one word to give your Honor cause to mistrust my faithfulness : but, forgive me, sir, I can't, indeed I can't serve your Honor any longer, after this disgrace.

"Why, my poor fellow, you take a hasty word much too seriously: I do not suspect you," and he extended his hand to the honest lad, who seemed perfectly happy at this restoration to his master's favour; and their imaginations vainly wandered in search of the engine of malignancy, that had wrought so painful a change in the hues of the present moment.

The following morning brought a message from Sir Edward requesting his son's presence at breakast. The commencement of this interview was affectionate on the part of the father, and calm and pensive on that of the son. But when the insinuations of the former, relative to the purity of the disinterested tenderness of Adela, and the honour of her father, aroused him,—he insisted on being made acquainted with the name of their base traducer, that he might pursue him to the farthest point of the habitable globe.

"Why, do you not mean to say, that your professions for Miss St. Clair have gone beyond a little flirtation?"

"I mean to say, sir, that Adela St. Clair is a being, whose name it would be sacrilege to breathe at the same time with the insulting term you have just uttered! I mean to say, sir, that the brilliancy of her mind, far more than her soul-subduing beauty, has bound me hers for ever! and that her parents, so far from dishonouring my family by their alliance, would not receive additional lustre by the possession of an empire!"

"Mad—mad, by Heaven! But do not, boy, fancy me so." And he arose, foaming with rage, which seemed likely to subvert reason. "Hear me, Theodore!—either abandon this girl, or the heaviest curse that ever parent heaped on child shall be thine! and all the evil that wealth can influence or exert, shall pursue her parents until the turf shall cover them!

Theodore heard not the last of these words; for so instinctive a horror had he of anything like a malediction, from the lips of a parent, that he had rushed from the room.

Sir Edward ordered his horse, and rode rapidly so far out into the country, that his servant imagined he had some important appointment, for which he was afraid of being some hours too late. Judge, then, of his surprise, when, having reached a certain point, he turned round, and rode as leisurely back.

But let us return to Theodore; he sought the solitude of his study, determined to visit the Lodge no more, and, assured by reflection that his father would never consent to his union with the chosen of his heart, to gain time, and await a seasonable moment, when restored calmness might enable him to plead his own cause. He purposed returning in a few days to the Valley, and claim his Adela's promise. But he must first prepare her for this; and he wrote as follows.—

"To Miss St. Clair,

"Adela—my beloved, my idolized girl! has thy heart mourned my absence as I have thine? Has the bloom which thy Theodore's departure chased, revisited that cheek? Oh! has the rose returned, with its exquisite tint, to say that I am less regretted? But it bloomed there before thy wanderer paid his devotions at that holy shrine of innocence and purity; why should I repine that I alone witness not its renovation?

"Adela! I have a severe trial for thy gentle heart, but its fortitude is equal to its gentleness, and it will not abandon me. My father is inflexible! avarice and ambition have usurped the empire of a heart which once felt as a parent, he will not listen to reason! I come therefore to claim thy sacred promise. 'We will throw ourselves at the feet of our parents, and, if they consent, I will be thine.'

"At the village church, we will pledge our sacred vow in the presence of the Creator, whose laws are those of truth and nature; our parents shall accompany us, and trust me, love, when my father is aware that we are indissolubly united, his tenderness will return, and a perfect reconciliation follow as inevitably as day succeeds to night: repeat then that sweet assurance, and a few days shall give my Adela irrevocably to her   "Theodore."

Having despatched Ralph with his letter to the Valley, with throbbing temples, and a body wearied by mental agitation, and want of rest during the two last nights, Theodore threw himself on the sofa in the study, and fell into a heavy slumber.

Nor were Sir Edward's feelings in a much more tranquil state. That his son had arrived, it was impossible to conceal; that he was not in a state of mind on that day, at any rate, to pay the visit of courtesy which would be expected, he felt painfully certain; and nothing but a falsehood could, he thought, save at once his own hopes, and his son's credit. He therefore calmed his mind, and smoothed his brow sufficiently to call at the Lodge, and express his son's heartfelt regrets, and that an indisposition, tending to fever, obliged him to keep his chamber for a few days. Much concern was expressed by all, and the fair Belinda turned aside to conceal a pearly tear.

But deception is always dangerous, and it sometimes occurs by a sort of fatality, that we are encountered by the very evil assumed.

When Sir Edward returned to dinner, he sent to call his son; Ralph was absent, Theodore's bed-room, and dressing-rooms were vacant, and his study locked; none of the servants had seen him, and the housekeeper only for a few minutes after breakfast, they therefore conceived he had gone out.

Theodore, however, still slept heavily until evening, the last embers of the fire were extinguished, and he awoke with a giddy head and rapid pulse—he arose, and threw open the glass doors that led to the terrace, which now could boast of no adornment excepting the evergreens by which it was surrounded, and the few plants which the gardener's care had not already removed to the green-house.

Finding himself worse, he rang the bell for a light and retired to his chamber, where his excellent friend the housekeeper visited him, and having insisted on his taking the remedies she considered most potent, in the event of colds, (which she trusted was the only source of her beloved young master's indisposition) and which she felt certain, when taken in time, no one was more competent than herself to cure, she went to Sir Edward, to pour her anxieties in his ear.

Wishing to make a memorandum, previously to retiring, Theodore drew forth his pocket book—a paper fell from it, did this bewildered sight deceive him, or was it addressed to Miss St. Clair? How came he in possession of this!—Long and painfully he taxed his memory, at last, it occurred to him, that on the afternoon of his departure, he had taken up a paper in his path, deeming it his own; and on preparing for his journey, had placed all unconnected notes together in his pocket-book.

"Would it be honourable to unclose it?" yet it was not St. Clair's hand, and from whom else excepting himself, could, or ought Adela to receive letters? (the character was bold and masculine,) Adela had no brother, no acknowledged relative, no male friend excepting himself; and to him she was sacredly affianced! Gentle Reader! expect not such an effort of philosophy in the ardent bosom of so youthful a lover. He opened it; and if he overstepped the bounds of honour, a bitter retribution awaited him in the following lines:

"To Miss St. Clair.

"The arguments you use, my love, are sufficie ntly powerful to quiet the fervour of my jealous fears, whilst I see your visitant walking by your side, sharing your society and received as a favoured guest in family.

"You say ' he will only remain a few days,' and that you will meet me at our wonted place of appointment, even on the evening of his departure. To me that time will seem an age! only rendered supportable by your candid and cheering explanation in our last delightful moonlight ramble. Adieu, dear girl,

"Your devoted
"Albert Grenville."

Attendant spirits! who make innocence your care, where were ye—when watching Theodore's footsteps to the garden, on the receipt of his father's unwelcome letter from the Park, the cold-hearted designer contrived to throw this base deception in his way? with the smile of a traitor he saw him unconsciously take it up and slip it into his pocket mechanically, but into his pocket it had gone! and would be likely to raise a storm in that bosom—which would never subside!

Nor had the demon of mischief checked his flight at this successful feat. By the promise that he would introduce Lucy to a friend, (who had caught a glimpse of her at the gate, and become so desperately enamoured of her, that he would doubtless marry her, and make her a lady at once,) he so wrought on her vanity and weakness of intellect, that he bound her his for ever! and a more willing auxiliary never existed. The first letter which would arrive could not, he feared, be intercepted, but the reply might! a little practice would enable him to imitate Miss St. Clair's hand, the "dear little Lucy," could manage by being the bearer of her young mistress's reply, to slip his in its place, and he instantly prepared one sufficiently soul-harrowing to sever their hearts eternally.

But here the principle and the agent were equally disappointed. Ralph would give his master's communication to none but Miss Adela; and Miss Adela, who had recently mistrusted her gentle handmaid, would consign her reply to no one but Ralph. So that the following lines, traced by that pretty white hand which had always excited his wonder and admiration, were sacredly and securely transmitted.

"To THEODORE VILLARS, ESQ.

"No, my beloved friend, you shall not find me unequal to the hour so long anticipated. I hold my promise sacred, and from the lips of my parents we will receive our doom. I have forborne to disclose to them the contents of your letter, until your presence shall support me ; but they expect you, and I anxiously await your arrival.

"Alas ! my Theodore, I dare not ask what may be that destiny ! shall we together hail the return of Spring, and watch the unfolding of the pale pink blossoms of the almond tree that shades our favourite retreat ? or will our hopes be 'as the flowers that fade and wither away,' when the dew no longer refreshes nor the light colours them ? But why does my foreboding heart thus anticipate the hour of desolation ? let thy presence chase these sombre reflections, and speak peace to the soul of thy   "ADELA."

CHAPTER XXII.

> And didst thou not thy breast to his replying
> Blend a celestial, with a human heart?
> And love which dies as it was born, in sighing,
> Share with immortal transports?   BYRON.

AND now every moment was counted, no hand moved the gate, no footstep pressed the path—no horseman appeared in distance, that Adela's cheek did not glow with a deeper hue, and her heart palpitated more wildly.

"Our young friend will be here to-day," said St. Clair, as he looked down the Valley.

The dinner was ordered an hour later, the hospitable matron had destined several little delicacies to be added to the usual simplicity of their table, and Adela's dark auburn tresses were yet more richly and tastefully disposed.

The dinner hour passed, she walked through the path that led to the valley, and leaning her arm on the gate, fixed her anxious eye on the distant prospects. It was a fine December afternoon ; the last rays of the departing sun shed its reluctant glory on the spire of the distant village church ; where, haply in a few days, a parent's hand might present hers to the fondly cherished friend of her heart. The leafless branches, encrusted with white frost, glittered in its last golden rays, and the indurated pathway sounded beneath the heavy steps of the way-faring passenger.

Oh ! he comes—his horse approaches with the fleetness of an arrow ! Ralph follows—they have passed the hill ; a few minutes more will bring him to the Valley ;—why did my heart doubt his punctuality !

No ! again is the tearful eye cast down, again sinks the heart in disappointment ; and she turns aside with increased vexation and disgust, for the individual her fancy had pictured as Theodore,—was Captain Grenville. Evening brought the social hour of tea, the windows were closed, the curtains drawn. Alas ! there was a time when those two loved parents, on either side that cheering fire, formed her universe of hope and felicity. Why is there now, an aching vacuum in the heart, a want of comfort in that once dear home ? why is she absent and confused—and her ear turned instinctively to every sound from without.

Adela, Adela ! were such sentiments as those recently awakened in thy heart unalloyed by such moments as these, earth would be a paradise ! But the dew glitters on the bramble, and a serpent often hides amidst the flowery couch that invites the weary traveller to repose !

"Something has, no doubt, prevented him ; but he will be here to-morrow, girl !" said St. Clair, when she came for her farewell embrace, previously to retiring to her pillow, where she breathed her artless prayers for her lover's safety ; and, pressing his resemblance against her pure bosom, slept—to dream of a joyous morrow.

But that morrow came not. Day followed day, week succeeded week ;—winter had infolded her loved native valley, the verdant plain, and gently rising hill, in his fleecy mantle,—the wind howled in melancholy murmurs through the dry and leafless branches, and even the evergreens were enveloped in a thick covering f snow.

And Adela's cheek rivalled its whiteness—Theodore came not ! not a line pleaded a cause for the delay, and her bosom became a scene of yet deeper desolation than that with which the present season had clothed the face of Nature.

And many an hour of doubt, and scarcely repressed apprehension at this singular change of their young friend's conduct, visited St. Clair ; and many an excuse did the still unshaken friendship of the mother urge for this long delay, which her husband's reason rejected, for woman's heart is the home of the purest friendship, the most steady fidelity ; and it is not until the last hope has vanished that the absent will reclaim the esteem which appearances would almost banish, that she resigns its holy influence.

Nor were these doubts in St. Clair's mind unmingled with starts of resentment, at the possibility that would sometimes occur, that Theodore's professions of attachment to their daughter, might have been a specious mask.

"Oh, never, never !" said his gentle advocate, "it cannot be,—sickness or accident may have prevented, but his countenance is too true an index of the heart. Theodore is anything but ungrateful and insincere : and, if he lives, we shall yet see him ?"

January and February passed ; the boisterous month of March commenced ; and Adela, who concealed and nurtured her grief in her own bosom, had frequently been importuned, by letters from Grenville, which Lucy failed not to throw adroitly in her way, not one of which obtained a perusal. The heroism of a daughter's love veiled the pang she carried in her bosom, beneath an appearance of cheerfulness ; but her languid eye and pallid cheek betrayed it, and St. Clair at length came to a determination to accept his friend Arnold's warm invitation as far as regarded his daughter, trusting that a variation of scene and change of air, might produce a salutary effect ; when one morning, at breakfast, the following letter was laid upon the table :

"Sir,

"Your plan to induce my son to marry your daughter has, I am happy to say, been timely prevented.

"A trifling indisposition, which confined him some time to his chamber, has brought reflection to his aid ; and it is now at his entreaty I write, to say that he begs leave to decline all further communication with your family.

"This is still more indispensable, as his union with a young lady of high connection and immense wealth, is fixed for an early day in the approaching month.

"Enclosed you will receive the little gifts presented by Miss St. Clair to my son ; they are very pretty, and specimens of much taste and ingenuity : they are accompanied by a few lines, dictated by my son, for, in consequence of a violent rheumatism in his arm, he cannot do more than affix his signature.
                                   "I am, Sir, yours respectfully,
"To Farmer St. Clair.   "EDWARD VILLARS."

Accompanying was a slip of paper, containing these words :

"Adela—farewell ! A few days will now make me the husband of another ; but this will not deprive you of the good wishes and friendly remembrances of
                                          "THEODORE VILLARS."

Roused by the familiarity of the address, the insolent style, the hateful contents, St. Clair's wonted presence of mind had so far abandoned him, that, unconscious that Adela was standing within the recess of the little painted window, which was shaded by its blue winter drapery, he read it aloud to Mrs. St. Clair; and had arrived at the last line, when a faint shriek recalled him to recollection, and he caught the lifeless form of his beloved child in his arms.

It is impossible to describe the scene which followed. The mother, bathed in tears, kneeling beside the sofa, where reclined the only hope of their declining years—like a flowret cut down in the morning; St. Clair, the injured, the indignant father, with sparkling eye, flushed cheek, and clasped hands, vowing to pursue to the farthest verge of the earth, the destroyer of his daughter's peace.

He seized the first moment of returning animation to carry his innocent sufferer to her chamber, where he left her to weep in that fond maternal bosom, and

returned to the parlour, where he drew the curtain, to exclude the unwelcome light of that day of bitterness. Who, at this moment, could feel so keenly as that high spirit, what it was—

> " To sit and curb the soul's mute rage
>   That preys upon itself alone ;
> To curse the life which is the cage
>   Of fettered grief, that dares not groan,
> Hiling from many a careless eye,
>   The scorned load of agony."

And the evening had arrived before his outraged heart could reason itself into sufficient self-command to see his Adela and her sorrowing mother.

No. 14.

But we will revert to the period when Ralph returned from the delivery of Theodore's letter, with Adela's reply, and found him in a state of delirious fever.

In vain, when he had gained admittance, did he go to his bed-side, take the hand extended him and bathe it in his tears. Not the slightest glance of recognition cheered this faithful domestic. He looked anxiously around the room lest any letters should have fallen that might betray the correspondence wit "Miss Adela." He sought for the keys, took the letter which he saw beneath the pillow, and without casting a glance on its contents, put it, with that of which he was now the bearer, in the desk; the key he suspended to a ribbon round his neck, and resolved that no power on earth should induce him to part with it, until his master's recovery. He then concealed the desk, as far as possible, under the bed, that it might escape Sir Edward's eye, and took his seat behind the curtain, that he might watch every change, anticipate the slightest wish, and await the first dawn of returning reason.

It must not be supposed that Sir Edward did not feel some slight touches of remorse at the state in which he beheld his son, for he loved him as much as such a heart could love; but wealth, the ruling, the predominating passion, was ascendant. Plutus shook his bags, and the cry of parental feeling was stifled; nor was he utterly insensible to a sense of retribution, when he found the fever no longer a fable.

But the good that should result from all this evil (no matter how much duplicity —how much meanness, might bear him onward to the subversion of every honourable or moral feeling, until the Somerville wealth, both from India and in England, should be safely lodged in the coffers at Villars Park), would, he thought, wash the transaction white as the silvery path of the milky way.

He, therefore, left Theodore to the care of the good housekeeper and his attentive Ralph; and received Mr. Somerville's visit of condolence. He took an opportunity of whispering a fear that a feverish anxiety, lest his son's intended proposals should be rejected, had brought on his present delirium, and, to stamp the assertion with the appearance of greater reality mentioned his having, on two or three occasions, called on the name of Belinda.

This had the desired effect. Mr. Somerville was pleased, his wife flattered,— the beautiful heiress denied herself to her numerous intimate friends, and daily sent her maid to inquire respecting his health, and to gather every possible information that concerned her imaginary lover.

CHAPTER XXIII.

What could that aching bosom ease,
    What cheer the night of his despair—
The conflict of his soul appease,
    Or chase the vow engraven there ?   F. A. Kentish.

On the evening when that amalgamation of treachery and falsehood awakened the demon, Jealousy, in Theodore's bosom, and banished reason from her throne, —in the agony of his mind he had thrown indignantly from him, everything that immediately occurred to him as in any way blended with her idea; these were, a beautifully shaded purse, finely wrought by her hand, and a ring of her hair, clasped by a small brilliant heart.

They had attracted Sir Edward's eye, as he sat by his son's bed-side, and held his burning hand; and having gathered from his wanderings that they were Adela's he took them up, and slipping them into his pocket, resolved to turn them to account.

During many weeks the fever raged with undiminished force; and although some transitory gleams of reason gave hope of its ultimate restoration, yet the smallest circumstance, that, either directly or indirectly, recalled the past, threw him into the most terrific paroxysms; and his exclamations of despair, his pathetic lamentations and reproaches to his still lamented Adela, drew tears from every eye, excepting his father's.

Belinda's inquiries and messages were received and repeated by Sir Edward, without eliciting the smallest notice, or exciting the slightest reply. And, at the end of two months, (during which Ralph had scarcely left his master an hour, and when he did, it was only to take a slight refreshment or snatch a few minutes repose, that he might be enabled to return to his station) although the fever had subsided, he remained in a state of languor and weakness; the shadow of his former self.

This was the first moment that Ralph had dared present Adela's letter. The name alone, having, until then, been dangerous to mention, he trembled as he took it, unfolded and wept over it. Ralph was pleased at this change, and hoped the first day of sufficiently renovated strength would lead him again to the Valley; for, although he had not received a reply, he had anticipated the anxiety "Miss Adela" would feel, and had written a letter to Lucy, mentioning his master's illness.

Ralph took the present opportunity of restoring the key of the desk, which he brought to his master, who warmly approved his fidelity and prudence.

"How happy will Miss Adela be to see your honour restored to her, out of the grave, as one may say. Why, you were looking quite charmingly this morning; and a week or two at the cottage, under the care of that excellent lady, Mrs. St. Clair, will bring you about again nicely."

Theodore groaned with irrepressible emotion.

"Alas! my good lad," said he, "never more shall we bound over that verdant hill, or trace the windings of that beautiful valley. Read these lines!——Adela St. Clair won the heart that adored her only to wither its hopes and abandon it to desolation! Adela St. Clair is a cold-hearted syren! a serpent in the form of an angel!"

He sunk back in his chair, and covering his face with his handkerchief, wept convulsively.

Nor did the eyes of Ralph trace those hateful lines without overflowing with the many tears of indignation; and whilst his respect for that more than master,—that friend he held dearest on earth, kept him silent, he inwardly vowed to see Lucy no more—to guard his heart against woman's perfidy, and do all in his power to chase from his master's mind the memory of the valley and its inhabitants.

At length Theodore was urged by his father (whose care and tenderness during his illness, he knew could not be lost on such a heart) to change the solitude of his chamber for the *boudoir* which had once been his mother's favourite retreat, and ever held by her son as a sacred retirement; for there stood her harp —there her portrait was suspended.

The sofa was drawn to the fire, which shed its warmth around, and gave a hue of comfort, which, for a moment, soothed the sufferer; and he was reclining, listlessly writing detached words, sentences, and names on pieces of paper, when his father entered.

"Come, my boy," said he, "this is something like; you begin to look yourself again!"

He glanced over the paper, felt relieved that his son was not writing a letter, and observing a slip of paper on the ground, with "Adela, Adela," and at some distance below "Theodore Villars," as in the trying of a pen; he eagerly took it up, and having twisted it carelessly together, slipped it imperceptibly, into his pocke .

At this moment a gentle tap at the door announced a visitor. Sir Edward arose, and the fair Belinda entered, leaning on her father's arm, interestingly pale and her unadorned jetty ringlets parted on her majestic and unruffled brow. She addressed him in tones of the tenderest sympathy, took her seat beside him on the sofa: and Sir Edward apologised for retiring to his study for a few minutes, where he made the following very honourable arrangement:

He drew out the paper, left the first "Adela,"—carefully erased the second ; wrote the repulsive announcement of his son's intended nuptials ; and this filled the space, the leaving unfortunate signature at the bottom. He wrote his own insulting letter—enclosed the purse of Adela's work, and ring, (for which he had taken care to have the brilliant extracted) and, with a smile of demoniac exultation, sealed and dispatched the parcel. Ralph's letter to Lucy (describing his master's lamented illness) she had put into Captain Grenville's hands, who had made her a present to destroy it, and keep the intelligence it contained a secret ; so that this was one of the many instances where malignity and cunning triumph over honour, innocence, and candour : and the unhappy Theodore's hopeless situation was not lkiely to plead his cause in the heart that (however cruel she might deem his desertion) yet beat for him with unabated, but hopeless fidelity.

Miss Somerville was now Theodore's constant visitant, and sought by every little art to while away his sadness ; she threw her fine arms over the harp, (which Sir Edward had ordered to be restrung,) and sung him many a cheerful lay, as if to welcome his return to health.

The most beautiful roses from the conservatory at the Lodge, the finest fruit from the hot-houses, were regularly brought ; the latter to tempt him by their beauty to taste them, and the former to adorn his favourite chamber. But Theodore's heart was cold and ungenial : and if, as a young and a very fine woman, he repaid her unequivocal attentions with courtesy, in the solitude of his chamber he unburthened his overflowing heart. He blushed for his weakness, but there was that lovely image yet fondly, tenderly cherished, and although reason, insulted pride, outraged tenderness—all things conspired to tear it thence, its every chord yet vibrated to her memory.

Even Ralph had ceased to speak of her : he who had looked so anxiously forward to see his master's chosen one the lady of the Park, now shuddered at the deceit that had thus miraculously for his master's honour been unfolded ; and Theodore's bosom continued the uncheered abode of inconsolable despair.

"It is strange too," said Ralph, "she looked so innocent I should as soon have expected to see an angel from heaven capable of deceit as Miss Adela ! but I always said those military scoundrels were dangerous acquaintance for Village Maidens. Poor girl ! he'll soon give her cause to rue her change, from such a husband as my poor master would have been to such a jacknapes. I fear he'll never forget her ! but who can wonder ? Why Miss Somerville, with all her flummery, and money, and jewels, and all that, isn't fit as you may say to be her hand-maiden, and then, instead of master paying his addresses to her, as Sir Edward wishes, why she quite courts him ! with her flowers and her fruit, and her fine singing, and fly-away whirligig stuff ; there was some pleasure in listening to poor Miss Adela, but we're all mortal as one may say, and if angels fell—why shouldn't an angel in woman's form ? I never look at my dear lady's portrait but I think she's like enough to be her own veritable daughter, and intended still to be my master's wife, if that wasn't now impossible."

But although Theodore, in the insanity of that overwhelming moment, had cast from him his ring, and his purse, and on recovering his reason, finding they were not in Ralph's possession guessed something of the truth—he had not torn from his bosom the heart suspended by the braid of her beautiful hair, and had now no longer energy to do it.

"Alas!" said he, " Adela St. Clair is faithless ! her tenderness was either assumed or light as the summer breeze,—but the villain for whom she has abandoned me is devoid of sentiment, devoid of honour—for a time he may pay his devotions at the shrine of her beauty, but remorse will soon dim its lustre, and he will then desert her ! Oh why ?▶continued he, clasping his hands in the agony of the moment, " why did I not watch over her guileless innocence and secure her mine, before the destroyer crossed her path ?—who, incapable of appreciating her mind, will ere long abandon her to the reproaches of a yet keenly sensitive heart, and she will drop into an early grave, the victim of irremediable despair."

St. Clair too—the respected, the honoured St. Clair, and his tenderly esteemed friend who had stolen into his affections by her maternal cares for his welfare, appeared to his mind's eye lonely and desolate.—He dared not pursue the thought he took the little heart in his hand, and placing it next his own, as though it possessed a balm to ease its aching emotions, he wept himself to sleep.

Nor did Sir Edward omit, in conjunction with the family at the Lodge, to form many little social parties as his own son's strength increased. Sometimes at one mansion, sometimes at the other. If Theodore felt inclined to take a drive out in the carriage, Belinda was ready to accompany him; if disposed to remain at home, she would sing or play for him. If, at his father's earnest instances, he at times accepted their invitations, their daughter's extreme anxiety for Mr. Villars' recovery was the constant theme of both father and mother; if he admired a group of flowers or a landscape, " They are my Belinda's," was the reply; if an air of peculiar sweetness, " It is my daughter's, who is a devoted admirer of painting and music."

April passed, and May, delightful May, with her unfolding buds, and fragrant blossoms, her flowery carpet and early treasures, arrived to awaken joy in all but the desolate and abandoned of hope; and who might claim their kindred, if not those devoted ones formed for each other, yet doomed to pine in exile, in that exile, deprived of the consolation of a fervent faith in the honour, the purity of its idol.—Oh! that had divested the pang of half its bitterness and mingled balm in every tear! Now it was guilt, meanness, the most abject degradation, to cherish either memory, yet how shall the heart struggle against itself?

And not a moment which might be rendered favourable had once escaped. Sir Edward; arguments, reproaches, entreaties, even tears were not wanting to urge his claim in favour of Belinda.

" Was she not wealthy, beautiful, amiable?"

True, she seemed all these, but alas! she was not Adela!—Adela! who with all her apparent transgressions on her head, must be

> " Loved till life can charm no more.
> And mourned till pity's self were dead!"

Yet ah! if she with such a seeming could fall off—But what availed it? If a union must be formed. If a parent's curse must follow the rejection of a choice in which the heart could have no share. If denied the consolation of devoting the remainder of a joyless existence to the memory of that one and one only! of what importance to him with whom he passed the few short hours, that separated him from the tomb!

Theodore no longer opposed his father's will, he made no professions of passion or even attachment; his soul was too sincere to assume a sentiment which he did not feel; and although he at times wondered that Belinda's apparently warm affection could feel itself repaid by his unvarying calmness; although he could not fail to recur to St. Clair's native dignity; who seemed reluctantly to extend even the hope of his one day possessing that treasure, which neither wealth nor elevated station, but innate worth alone could win from their arms, and that soft, retiring, native loveliness,

> " That would be wooed, and not unsought be won,"

little favourable either to the Somervilles or their daughter; yet he conceived such characters might exist; and at his father's entreaty he was at last induced to propose for her hand, but it was under the following promise,—

That £5000 should be advanced by Sir Edward from the property bequeathed him by his uncle; and placed in Mr. Edmund St. Clair's hands for his daughter's use. This, he urged was an indispensable duty, having promised her marriage,— for Theodore had not only buried Adela's supposed melancholy dereliction in his own bosom, but had imposed a sacred silence upon Ralph—alas! whispered this honourable, this devoted heart, even if he marries her, their souls can never assimilate, he is a disipated reckless villain, and she will ere long return, a heart broken mourner, to the Valley.

Sir Edward at first shuddered, at the devotion of so large a sum ; but a moment of reflection, and his smile of satisfaction returned.

"Agreed ! agreed !"

" To be put into my hands for this purpose, on the day previous to the solemnization of this sacrifice," said Theodore.

"An union with a beautiful heiress, a sacrifice, uncourteous boy !" said Sir Edward, laughing off his evident vexation, " well, agreed! I've no objection in ife."

CHAPTER XXIV.

For should affection cease to cherish
The heart I've given to thy care,
Soon like the fading flower 'twill perish
That shrinks before the wintry air.

But we will return to the Valley. A violent struggle of contending emotions had overpowered Adela's fortitude, but it was not until, with a feeling of concentrated agony, she had listened to the full extent of her affliction : not a syllable escaped her, and it was not until the last line—not until the name subscribed by the hand of the individual in whom she lived ; not until he had aimed the arrow, that she unfolded her bosom to its venom, and, with a shriek so piercing, so plaintive, that it sunk into the soul ; that the memory of her almost incredible affliction abandoned her :—

Conveyed to her chamber, her parents, gentle care restored her ; she did not complain, but wept in silence while she listened to the persuasive and consolatory arguments of that affectionate mother,—and at length, closing her eyes, appeared to sleep.

The day passed in bitterness, the domestic regularity of Mrs. St. Clair's well-governed little domain, was altogether interrupted, as if in sympathy with their feelings it seemed to close in earlier than usual. And the wind whistled so loudly and wildly through the leafless branches without, that St. Clair had twice tapped at his daughter's chamber door, before his afflicted partner unclosed it. His first impulse was to press her to his bosom, whilst he tenderly inquired how fared their child. If congenial souls spring to each other to participate the hour of joy how much more tender is the unison in that of sorrow !

" Yield not to this unexpected reverse," said Mrs. St. Clair, as she returned her husband's embrace, " for this delusion in character we deemed so perfect, this destruction of our Adela's fairy vision is, indeed, a bitter one. You will not forget, my Edmund, the duty we have to perform in supporting her spirits, and teaching her to look beyond this transitory scene for comfort and repose !"

"My Aurora! thy gentle admonition shall not be unheeded ; I have overcome my first emotion, and can shake off the designing villain : however the coils of his apparently candid and superior nature, his professions of disinterested affection for our girl, united with the apparently unsophisticated warmth of youthful friendship, had wound around my heart, for I could have loved him as a son, and, dying, resigned her to his arms in security and bliss ; but it is done ! I have shaken him off. His father, too, is beneath the notice of a man of honor and feeling ; it were pollution to breathe his name ; it were degradation to touch so mean, so contemptible a wretch! Did he, then, suppose that St. Clair's daughter, the grand-child of Don Manual de Mello, and my honoured father, whose legitimate pride would have shrunk from an alliance with a family, whose only claim to distinction is the possession of a few petty, paltry thousands would consider herself honoured by becoming one of them? Pshaw!

"But, my love—he is a stranger to ourselves and our history. He addresses my husband merely in the character of the inhabitant of a humble cottage, on the brow of a valley.

"But his son might have informed him better. Ah! had he, in reality, united to so much native talent, all the honour, truth, generosity of sentiment he professed—had St. Clair been emperor of a world, and he the lowliest peasant on the brow of that mountain—Theodore Villars alone should have possessed the hand of Adela. But, my beloved, we will forget him, and breathe our ardent vows to our Creator, that our dear girl's purity of mind has not been sullied by such an union."

Mrs. St. Clair approved her husband's resolution, whilst he, assuming a tranquillity foreign to his heart, informed her, that he had been infringing on her dominion, by dispatching her hand-maid, Lucy, to her father's for the evening.

"I observed her," said he, "listening, on the stairs, on two or three occasions. Family affliction should be sacred; and, if I possess any knowledge of the human countenance, that girl's character has not recently improved.

Mrs. St. Clair's impressions were similar. She roused up the fire in Adela's chamber, and carried the tea equipage thither, whilst St. Clair sat by the bed-side, and dropped the tear of unutterable sympathy on the hand of his apparently sleeping sufferer.

Mrs. St. Clair closed the window-curtains, and veiled the lamp, that its light might not disturb her daughter's repose.

But Adela slept not; she had not slept; the tears had continued to chase each other through her closed eyes dark lashes, down the pure ivory of her colorless cheek. She had heard her father's impressive words; she resolved to expire rather than add to the agony her parents had already experienced. She breathed a prayer to her Creator, and although the tumults of such a heart are not easily subdued, filial tenderness gave her courage; and, unclosing her curtains, she gave a hand to each, and each fondly returned its pressure.

"You have eaten nothing to-day, love. Our hearts have also taken from us all inclination for refreshment, since breakfast. Will you take some tea?—it is quite ready."

"Oh! I have been very wrong, dear mamma; I have given you an infinity of trouble and sorrow."

"Say not so, my treasure! how can you have been culpable? No! you are the object of our tenderest sympathy."

"We have met with a traitor," said St. Clair, "who, under the mask of the most elevated sentiments and purest affection, has stolen into our hearts! Yes! he won thy mother's and mine also. Never mind! he shall not desolate them; thy mother's he will not, for where duty and maternal tenderness calls, she is more than woman! mine he cannot—for do I not still possess my beloved ones?"

"Nor shall he mine!" said the heroic and enthusiastic girl, "are not my parents my world?" Then, sinking back, she faintly added, "it will now be a crime to cherish his memory!—pardon me, dear papa, this last tribute to the hours gone for ever! and I will indeed be all your own!" And Adela wept in her father's arms in an agony of emotion beyond the power of utterance.

But she checked the indulgence of these unavailing tears, and making an effort to assume the appearance of tranquillity, she said, softly,

"I am more composed,—I am indeed, now, quite calm, and ready to attend you to the parlor."

No, love, you yet require rest,—remain where you are. Your mother, with her accustomed sympathy in the feelings of those she loves, imagined we should be more comfortable and secluded here. Lucy has gone to her father's,—the tea has been prepared by your own fire-side, and we are our Adela's guests."

Adela smiled pensively; she sought to renovate her parents' cheerfulness by an arduous exertion of fortitude. But night came. Lucy returned, with the eye of scrutiny, the listening ear, and the air of assumed concern for "poor dear Miss Adela!" The fond parents retired to their chamber, and the youthful mourner was left to the solitude of her pillow, where unrestrained sighs and torrents of tears repaid the task she had imposed on herself.

But sleep did not once visit her eyelids; with eager interest she reverted to the past, half ready to ask her own heart if this affliction might not be a retribution for some forgotten or thoughtless dereliction from the path of duty? No! the retrospect was calm as the sky of a summer evening, unspotted as the down on the cygnet's breast! need it be whispered to so pure a heart—that the Creator's love is seen even in his chastenings! She bowed her lovely head in humble submission, and continued to recall every year of her calm and delightful existence before chance had thrown Theodore in that path which he alone could have had power to desolate. Why, when he had shared her parents' hospitality, did he not return to his father's boasted splendour and the desirable alliance prepared for him? why did he, with so much warmth, claim their unproffered friendship,—her father's consent, her mother's favour? and oh! why seek the responsive sentiments of a heart, which until that fatal hour had slept calmly and purely in the halcyon dream of innocence, her sole aim, her parents' love, her heaven of felicity, their smile?

How should she now meet their anxious wishes? how hide from their view a heart joyless and withered? She drew the miniature from her bosom, her tears fell on the crystal that covered these once—ah! still loved features! She arose and paced the room in agony, and in the morning her mother found her hand burning, and her temples throbbing with fever.

During that month she was incapable of quitting her chamber. She wept not, she never mentioned his name, and her parents also carefully avoided it. Alas, in vain! Adela fixed a glance of melancholy interest on the mountain, the stream by which they had so often wandered at moonlight. She silently watched the silver-tinted landscape; and the sigh of the ill-concealed desolation of the heart moved the muslin that veiled her bosom.

April passed with its transient smiles and sparkling tears. May unfolded the pale pink blossoms of the almond-tree that shaded the bower, and when she could steal from the solicitude of her fond parents, it was there she wandered, to indulge in her "soul's sadness." But Adela's cheek no longer surpassed their mild tint; her eye was languid, her cheek pale! and even the libertine, whose licentious passion had caused all this woe, trembled when he beheld her. His inquiries had been unremitting, he had remained concealed in the vicinity of the cottage, and anxiously watched the renovation of her health, in order to seize her as his prey, and, for this purpose, the designing, the ungrateful Lucy was regularly bribed and deceived by a thousand visions of future grandeur.

But Adela had almost forgotten such a being existed. She employed the first hours of returning health (if merely the absence of fever could be called so, for she remained weak and incapable of active exertion,) in returning to her usual little domestic avocations. Again she guided the pencil; again "turned the tuneful page," and again smiled, although these smiles were as "roses o'er a sepulchre."

Her parents sought, by every possible means, to restore her to peace, and cast into oblivion one they conceived unworthy her care; and so far from regretting his alliance, they felt grateful that she had escaped from so versatile, so unprincipled an individual.

Adela sat by her window: the exquisite freshness of the landscape, with its early emerald tint, the unfolding flowers, the song of the little birds, who again fluttered and warbled their lay of love amidst the branches that shaded her window deeply affected her, and the tears so long suppressed, streamed down her pale cheek.

Oh! if May thus overpowered her with its balm-breathing gale, how might she endure the luxuriance of that month when every scene must recal him whose memory it were now crime to cherish!

This was a new reflection—it startled her; she must make an effort, or be lost to those whose sole earthly felicity was centred in their child; and at the impulse of the moment she arose, and, taking from her writing desk the tablets, ring, and numerous other little valuables—Theodore's gifts—she placed them with his tear-

bedewed portrait, in a morocco case. This she folded in paper, tied it up with a mourning ribbon, and sealed it with black wax, resolving never more to indulge herself or her sorrows, at the expense of her duty.

This was self-command! and thou who hast known what it is to obtain such an empire over the heart, will feel how sweet a consolation mingled with her tears, and allow that one such hour surpasses in worth all the wealth a long life of prosperous guilt can bestow.

St. Clair had written to his friend Arnold, accepting his pressing invitation, and mentioning his daughter's declining health.

Mr. Arnold's reply assured him, "every individual in his house would de-lightedly devote themselves to Miss St. Clair's amusement and comfort," and tha
No. 15.

he should be with them on the following Sunday or Monday, accompanied by his " little Louisa," to escort her back.

This event produced some additional occupation at the cottage, and the hurry it occasioned flushed Adela's cheek ; but it was a hectic glow, and her anxious mother trembled as she beheld it.

On the approaching week, then, she was to leave the Valley, for the first time since her infancy ! her beloved parents, and those dear, those accustomed haunts, whence if—

> " A song, a flower, a name, at once restore
> These long-remembered scenes, when first they drew
> The attention,"

it were salutary to remove. Yet, oh ! how large a share of philosophy did it re-quire from a heart so wedded to its home, so replete with sensibility !

On the Saturday previous, everything was in train for her visit, as well as the reception of the welcome guests' of the day or two preceding her departure ; and Adela sat listlessly playing with her dove, around whose neck a mourning ribbon was tied, when a messenger arrived with a letter ; and, having delivered it, rode off.

St. Clair retired to his chamber, dreading to unclose it in his daughter's pre-sence. A Bank of England note fell on breaking the seal, and he suffered it to remain on the ground, whilst he read as follows :—

" To EDMUND ST CLAIR, ESQ.

" Theodore Villars requests his ever-honoured friend will accept the enclosed on his daughter's account, and retain it until the hour, which, he fears, is not far dis-tant, when it may be rendered useful to her.

" Should she never need it—then Theodore Villars trusts those ever-regretted friends he once hoped to call by a dearer name will not disdain to retain it, as a token of the remembrance due to those hours. But why recall them ? they are past !"

And what was it ? The amount, no doubt, before mentioned. No ! my as-tonished reader, a single note of fifty pounds.

A feeling of unutterable scorn, an expression of infinite contempt, curved his lip.

" And dared the scoundrel then, veiling the hateful principles of his cold and reckless heart in the language of sentiment, combine insult with injury ? Dared such a being outrage the sacred name of friendship ? dared he proffer money to my noble-minded child ?—why, were he capable of presenting her with the treasures of the East, rather would she repose on the bare earth, and eat the bread of toil ! rather would she perish than (under such circumstances) share them !"

St. Clair walked to the parlour, and presenting the letter to his wife and daughter : " read," said he, " my girl, and return thy grateful aspirations to Heaven for an escape !"

Adela read ; her eye was tearless, her cheek pale, her brow calm.

" Do you reply to this, papa ?"

" Merely a few words, my love, enclosing his insulting, his paltry proffer."

" Wait then a moment, I have also an enclosure to make."

St. Clair saw the triumph in her expressive eye, and, when he received the little black-sealed packet from her hand, imprinted the pure kiss of parental pride on her polished brow. He retired, enclosed his daughter's parcel, and wrote as follows :—

" The family of St. Clair feel themselves most happy in having escaped the contamination of an union with duplicity and dishonour. Every memento which might, by chance, at any time have recalled Mr. Villars to memory, is, with his insulting enclosure, returned. Adela St. Clair would disdain to accept an empire from such a hand; whilst her father lives, not a desire of her pure heart shall remain ungratified; when he is no more, her talents will secure her that independence, which will be cheered by a guileless heart, and a bosom void of reproach."

St. Clair's parcel despatched, let us return to the Park, where grand preparations were making, for the day was fixed. A smile of triumphant joy sparkled on Belinda's countenance; all was delightful hurry at the Lodge, and Miss Somerville's magnificent dresses and splendid jewels were a subject of enthusiastic admiration to the many who had claimed the title of her particular, her bosom friends, since the short period of her family's arrival from India. Every lip wore a smile to welcome her, and Sir Edward was the picture of exulting satisfaction.

But there was one amongst that festive, that happy throng, whose lip wore no smile! and had his father possessed a heart, it must have bled whilst he gazed on the pale and interesting countenance of a son, who was evidently a prey to the consuming anguish, attendant on an insurmountable, yet hopeless passion.

Ralph saw and sympathized sincerely; he shunned the festivities of the servants' hall, and mourned in secret; for he plainly saw his master's happiness was overclouded for ever. Much as he had blamed her, the remembrance of " Miss Adela" had always carried with it, if not a favourable impression, at least a feeling of regret; and it really seemed next to impossible that so sweet a countenance could hide a treacherous heart.

On the day preceding the nuptials, at his father's desire Theodore presented Belinda with some exquisite brilliants which had been his aunt's; he then claimed his promise.

Sir Edward brought the stipulated amount to the study, and seeing the letter ready to enclose it, had just put it into his son's hands, when Belinda appeared at the door.

"Come, Theodore, shall we walk in the Park?"

"I will be with you instantly, Belinda."

"Oh! give me the letter," said Sir Edward, "you have enclosed the note, and directed it, I see; I'll seal it for you and send it off; come, you cannot keep a fair lady waiting!"

He took the letter: Belinda smiled, and, putting her hand within Theodore's arm, they passed down the steps that led from the terrace.

Sir Edward hastened to his study, where he changed the five thousand for five hundred, and had closed it, when he paused:

"This is a sad, a melancholy waste of money! Lord! why, fifty pounds would do just as well, and be quite a fortune for a village girl! If the boy is a fool I am not."

He again unclosed the letter, substituted fifty, sealed it and sent it off—went to his son and the bride elect, and accompanied them to the Lodge, where they were to sup with a select party.

The next morning, decked in sunshine and flowers, arose on the bridal day! a day of joy to Belinda, of an agonizing sacrifice to Theodore!

In going to his cabinet for the ring, two half-blown roses fell from a paper; they were withered and drooping, and, with an electric shock that almost subdued him, he recognised them as the first Adela had gathered him, and which he had treasured as a sacred vestige, as an invaluable though melancholy pledge! How deeply did he then feel that she was still the idol of his heart, and that the espousals which were that day to bind him to another, were powerless to command its devotion; that

> " True love never yet
> Was thus constrain'd, it overleaps all fence:
> Like lightning, with invisible violence
> Piercing its continents; like heaven's free breath
> Which he who grasps, can hold not; liker Death

Who rides upon a thought, and makes his way
Through temple, tower, and palace, and the array
Of arms: more strength has Love than he or they;
For it can burst his charnel, and make free
The limbs in chains, the heart in agony,
The soul in dust and chaos!"

A cold, a death-like dew stood on his forehead; there was a feeling of guilt, of perjury in the step he was going to take of despicable weakness in coinciding with such a command, although a father's! Oh! that death might interpose! But death heard not his prayer; the measure of the youthful sufferer's disappointments was not yet full.

Sir Edward came to remind him that the carriage waited to take them to the Lodge, where an elegant breakfast awaited them; and the fair bride glittering with jewels, moved under her silvery veil like a splendid constellation.

Adela! hapless, lovely Adela! thy Theodore, the being most dear to thy soul, is even now at the altar! It is true his eye is averted, his cheek pale, his voice faltering. It is true thy image, in all its innocence and beauty, rushing on his memory, has for the moment annihilated all in the universe beside! but he has breathed the vow of fidelity and love, once pledged as thine and thine for ever!

CHAPTER XXV.

You know not half the horrors of my fate!
I might perhaps have learn'd to scorn his falsehood;
Nay, when the first sad burst of tears was past
I might have rous'd my pride and scorn'd himself;
But 'tis too much, this greatest, last misfortune.

TANCRED AND SIGISMUNDA.

MRS. ST. CLAIR, not knowing precisely at what hour her expected guests would arrive, resisted her husband's and daughter's entreaties to accompany them in a walk on the Sunday evening preceding the week of Adela's purposed journey; and, Adela leaning on her father's arm, retrod paths that renewed many a too fondly cherished remembrance.

St. Clair felt her hand tremble in his, as he drew it through his arm, and sympathised sincerely with the conflict then passing in a heart of which he knew all the sensibility and worth: they had descended into the valley, passed the wood, and paused to rest at a stile that led to the high road, purposing to pass round and return by the border of the lake, when Lucy ran forward with a message from her mistress, requesting St. Clair to return for a few minutes as she merely wished to say two words to him, and that she was to stay with Miss Adela till her master's return.

St. Clair walked hastily back, but was scarcely out of sight and hearing, when two men leaped over the stile, threw a large cloak over the trembling and horror-stricken Adela, whose cries were stopped by its close envelopement, and bore her off with them to a chaise-and-four which waited in the adjoining road.

St. Clair, on his arrival at the cottage, found no such message had been sent; and, hurrying back, found both his daughter and servant gone. He inquired at every cottage, of every villager—no one had seen them, perhaps they had returned! but what could have induced such a message. He was the last being on earth to be joked with: had St. Clair been reduced to the most abject penury, his countenance and deportment were such as to command the highest respect from prince or peasant.

Was the girl mad, then?—Alas, no! his arrival at his once happy home, banished that apprehension to give place to the certainty that she was not only unprincipled and ungrateful, but decidedly vicious,—and the distracted parents, when they found every article of Lucy's apparel gone from her chamber, were but too well convinced she must have had a deep plan in view, when she framed the falsehood that separated their absent daughter, from her father's care. Every moment now added to their agony of mind; the neighbours gathered respectfully round, all anxious to devote their lives, if requisite, to the recovery of their patron's daughter, their endeared and lovely benefactress. One of their sons entered at this moment; with the utmost sorrow he had heard of Miss St. Clair's absence, for he had met a chaise-and-four, with the blinds drawn down, driving furiously down the western road; and shortly afterwards, Captain Grenville's servant on horseback, apparently in great haste.

All was now a horrible certainty! The suspicions that had at first glanced on Theodore, vanished. Captain Grenville then, was the villain—the utter destroyer of their already disturbed repose—the robber of their soul's dearest treasure.

Mrs. St. Clair fell from one fainting fit into another; and St. Clair left her, with his tears on her cheek, in the arms of an excellent being, the wife of a neighbouring farmer, scarcely recovered; and, putting his pistols into his pocket, he mounted his horse, and, accompanied by the husband of the good woman before-mentioned, rushed forward, resolved to rescue his daughter, or die in her defence.

When Adela's senses returned, she found herself supported by the arms of Captain Grenville, who had removed the covering from her face, and was using every possible medium of restoration; he even let down part of one of the windows, for now, alas! they were passing across a track of country where he knew her cries would avail her little; and of this he assured her, when he found she indignantly shrunk from his embrace, when she exerted all her strength to extricate herself from the envelopment which held her captive, and heard her pathetic exclamations for her beloved parents.

"For what new calamity has my joyless existence been protracted?" said the distracted girl, and she relapsed into the insensibility from which she had only temporarily recovered.

About midnight Adela awoke to all the horrors of a state of captivity. She found herself lying on a sofa, Grenville on one side, kneeling, and fervently pressing her hand to his bosom; Lucy on the other. Her fainting had continued so long, that they were apprehensive, in consequence of her weak state, the terror and fatigue had occasioned her death; and they mutually congratulated each other when they saw her eyes unclose : but she averted them from Grenville with horror, and fixing them on the youthful traitress, inquired the meaning of her present situation. Then raising herself with all the strength her agitated frame could collect, she commanded her oppressor to quit the chamber.

There is so much real dignity in virtue,—it is so irresistible when it, radiates the countenance of a young and lovely female, that despots and tyrants have trembled beneath its glance. Here it awed the libertine, although it could not reclaim him. It blended the respect due to a higher order of beings with the warmest passion of which such a heart was capable; and so much had the last few hours heightened his adoration, that he would have given worlds to have gained her hand, but that was impossible!

Being so, however, he had determined to possess her : for this purpose he had long remained in ambush, watching his moment, whilst his little artful auxiliary took care to inform him of everything that transpired, or was likely to transpire, at St. Clair's cottage.

For this purpose he had taken this elegant retreat, and furnished it in the style he conceived best suited to a refined taste. And even the library was so selected, as to mingle the choicest productions of the sage, the poet, and the philosopher.

This envied treasure was now in his possession ! Theodore no longer his rival! her former affection for him overcome, or sinking under a just resentment and outraged pride (the very moment most favourable to his hopes).

Her brave father far away ! but then, she was scarcely convalescent from a long and severe indisposition! and there was a something of ethereal delicacy in that lovely form, that whispered "there is a power more resistless than thine, which many free her from thy grasp."

Grenville's selfishness was alarmed; he resolved to assume the sentimentality of a hopeless lover, and to have an infinity, of patience, in order with the greater certainty, to secure his victim. He, therefore, submissively left the chamber.

Adela repeated her question; and, assuming a spirit which she was far from possessing at that moment, insisted on knowing by what detestable chicanery she had thus been thrown into the power of that being, of all others most the object of her abhorrence.

Lucy was awe-stricken by the decided manner of her mistress. She had taken her lesson from Grenville, and mingled hypocrisy with her numerous other vices; for she dared not acknowledge the part she had taken in his scheme.

"Dear me, Miss,—how shou'd I know that ar'n't a witch nor a fortune-teller? —if you're to be pitied,—why, so am I! they've carried me off, too, haven't they —and taken me from my poor, dear, honest parents, and God knows when I shall see them, or you yours again!"

Here the finished hypocrite raised her apron to her eyes, and seeing the tears stream down Adela's cheek—

"Dear me!—my dear Miss Adela," continued she, "pray now don't take on so! I'd go through fire and water to serve you: didn't I run after you, frightened to death as I was, when the Captain ran away with you in his arms? and didn't I get run away with myself at last,—only because I wouldn't leave my poor dear Miss Adela? Pray look on me again, Miss, as you used to do! Do you think, after all master's warnings about both John and the Captain—and after all you've said, I'd have anything to do with such wickedness?"

Lucy accompanied her expostulation with so many tears, and so much apparent grief, that Adela's resentment subsided, her suspicion vanished, and although she had always considered her a vain, silly girl, her compassion and benignity towards her attendant from infancy returned. She extended her hand to her, and began to arrange her ideas, and reflect how their united exertions might free them from so perilous a situation.

A gentle tap at the door disturbed her reverie. She ordered Lucy not to open it on any account; but John, Captain Grenville's servant, rendered it unnecessary, by unclosing it, and calling Lucy. He begged pardon, and said his master had merely sent him to say that there was a fire in the next room, which he thought Miss St. Clair would find agreeable, as she yet remained an invalid,—that coffee was waiting there, and that her mistress might feel assured that no one would enter either of those apartments, unless the bell summoned their attendance. He added, in retiring, that the Captain had left the house, and would not return until the following day.

Adela arose; she tried the door, it was fast. She fastened it inside with a bolt: —she took the small silver candlestick from the table to explore the chamber. Lucy dried her eyes, and pursued an investigation equally minute, although of a different nature; for while her mistress was employed in trying every door, and seeking how an escape might be effected from the windows, she was extolling the beautiful carpet and wardrobes; the elegantly carved bedstead, with its rich and tasteful drapery, looking glasses, and sofa.

Adela heard nothing but the sighs of her lamented parents, rendered desolate by her absence, on the first night she had ever been an exile from home! She saw nothing but the medium, through which she fervently trusted she should be enabled to escape, and find a shelter in their arms!

What, then, was her despair, to see the windows secured with small iron-bars; that they looked into a garden, spacious and surrounded by a high wall, which, alone, would be insurmountable! The moon also, hid her face, and inauspiciously prevented any object beyond being visible.

Lucy threw open the folding door that led to the next apartment; a bright fire shed its rays on a Persian carpet of brilliant colours, the flowers and fruit of which seemed to rise from its surface; an elegant piano and Spanish guitar; a superb Grecian couch, chairs, and cabinet of tastefully wrought rosewood; elegant mirrors; books and music, elegantly bound; drawing case, and writing desk.

Lucy was declaring that—" only for being taken there against one's will like, —it really was a pretty place, and all Miss Adela's heart could wish," when a glance from the despairing girl, and a sigh of agony, checked her.

On a table, before the sofa, was placed an elegant tea equipage, a silver urn with coffee, and every little luxury which might induce the cheerless captive to partake of refreshment. Two wax lights, in silver candlesticks, and a note placed beside them, where it could not be overlooked, addressed to Miss St. Clair—

" My Adored,

" Forgive this rash step—for I cannot live without you! My presence shall not, however, distress you—I shall pass the night some miles hence; so sleep peacefully, I implore you, and take the repose you so much require.

" Believe me—I will not intrude into your presence, until you permit me to enjoy the felicity of an interview."

"Albert Grenville."

Adela indignantly tore the paper. She tried the windows—they were screwed down, and she sat down to weep; when Lucy suggested to her, that she had taken nothing since the day before, at dinner, and then not sufficient for a sparrow. That if she gave up to grief, and took nothing, she'd never have strength to escape, but fall into a weakness and die away from her parents.

" Now do take a cup of coffee, Miss," said she, " and a bit of something; and as we sha'n't get away over that 'ere lonely road to-night, let's make all safe and go to bed, and I'll answer for it we'll get away, by hook or by crook, to-morrow!"

Adela possessed a strong mind; but her fortitude had nearly abandoned her. Was there, then, no alternative, to the awaiting morning in that detested abode? Her heart sunk within her.

Yet there was reason in Lucy's observation: she felt how powerfully the body influences its pervading spirit; and that the weakness of the one is capable of enervating the other. She knew that her present situation require the concentrated energies of both. As Lucy had drawn the sofa to the fire, she reclined her weary and trembling limbs; for although it was the delightful month of June, her recent indisposition, united with the late hour, to render her chilly. Lucy drew her chair to the table, and Adela took a cup of coffee and a biscuit, whilst her handmaid satisfied the keen appetite her journey had given her, in such a style of entire forgetfulness of the past, or care for the future, as to excite astonishment in one whose heart was a scene of mourning and desolation.

When Lucy's repast was finished, the first point was to barricade the doors: the piano served this purpose in the drawing-room, and the wardrobe in the chamber; for Lucy was strong, although a thin, slight-looking girl; and she managed, with very little assistance from her mistress. They threw open the folding doors; and Adela, whose consideration for others never, either in mental or bodily suffering, abandoned her, recommended her attendant to lie down beside her, although neither undressed.

Lucy was asleep in a minute, and Adela, left to her own reflections, steeped her pillow with tears. In the silence of the night, she unfolded the inmost recesses of her sorrowing heart to her Creator, and her soul became calm.

" Benign and heavenly Parent," said she, " thou, who in the splendour of thy omnipotence, disposest of events, and governest futurity; yet carest for the smallest atom, amidst the multitudinous worlds surrounding us! Thou! who measurest creation at a glance, yet temperest the wind to the shorn lamb! support the fortitude of my beloved parents through this terrific night. Inspire them with confidence in thy protecting mercy, and the most perfect dependence in the principles they have inculcated in the heart of their child! dry their tears, and spread thy protecting shield before us; for without thee, Creator, we are nothing!"

And did not another sentiment mingle with that prayer? Alas! that outraged —that gentle heart was too pure to retain resentment towards one, once so fondly cherished. She pitied, she implored blessings on his future hours; although she shrunk from the idea that they were to be devoted to another. But years must revolve before such a mind as Adela's can hope to drink at the Lethean stream.

Adela's ear was alive to every sound through the night; but, even when the house was in perfect stillness, not a momentary drowsiness closed her eyelids.

Twilight at length cast its hue of sober sadness through the curtain window. It was a wet morning; but she felt faint and feverish, and, anxious to inhale the freshness of the breeze, she arose, gently raised the sash, (which being barred, was not screwed down, like those in the other apartment) and drawing a chair, sat pensively reclining against it.

Presently a heavy foot passed beneath, and an alternate singing and whistling, sounded on her ear—as of some rustic, employed in cultivating the grounds. This continued about a quarter of an hour, when a second footstep approached.

"Early at your work, I see, Master Jenkins. Why didn't you come into the kitchen, and shelter from the shower?"

"Why, no," replied the other, "master's anxious to have this finished, d'ye see, and I don't much mind wet."

"Yes," rejoined the first speaker, whom she now recognised as John, "all's been hurry these two or three days. I think master wishes to have the mistress home: he thought she'd never get well at them private mad-houses!"

"Ah, he's much to be pitied! I hear she's a pretty young body."

"Yes! he married her when she was just turned sixteen: the year after they'd a fine little boy, but he died;—and grief for his loss turned her brain, and she's been mad as a March hare ever since!"

"Is the Captain at home? I want to speak to him."

"No: he'll not be here 'till after dinner; but I must go and ask Lucy if her mistress is ready for breakfast."

"What—have you got a new servant?"

"No; she's only Mrs. Grenville's nurse or keeper—or whatever you please to call her,—but I call her a very nice young woman; and as I think I hear her stirring, I'll be off."

Adela was petrified:—the whole horror of her fate was now disclosed to her! Was it not sufficient that she was torn from her parents—must she also be designated mad? Yes! it was too evident that this was an assertion promulgated purposely to prevent all possibility of an escape from his deep-laid snares.

Many a doubt also stole over her mind respecting Lucy. She seemed to sleep so easily, to feel so contented, that, notwithstanding her tears of last night, she could not avoid doubting her fidelity,—and how should she prove it? If she were to be depended on, by mingling with the servants she might engage one of the few males in their interest, and a plan for escape might be easily formed: but could she place confidence in one so trivial, so versatile?

Adela again threw herself on the bed, and closing her eyes, seemed to sleep: presently Lucy awoke; she got up, tried the wardrobe doors, opened one of them, and investigated its contents. She took out several pieces of silk, lace, and muslin; scarfs, flowers, and ornaments;—tried them on, and appeared delighted with her own face and figure in the glass. A tap at the door induced her to hurry every thing rapidly into its place; she stole softly into the adjoining apartment, and the following conversation took place:

"Is your mistress awake?"

"No,—sound asleep."

"What makes you look so pretty this morning, mistress Lucy? You rested well, I daresay; I slept not a wink for thinking of you!"

"Ah now, Mr. John, there you are again, with your wheedling ways; but you'd better keep your compliments for your equals. I should be badly off, indeed, to take up with a footman."

"Footman, Mistress Lucy! you did not talk in this way, when you used to walk to the church and to the fair, with Mr. Ralph!"

"Well but I've got better things in view now, Mr. John, I assure you. The Captain tells me all his secrets, and places all his confidence in me;—he doesn't place me on a level with servants! besides—a friend of his saw me, and fell desperately in love with me! He was called to London to receive a large fortune, left by his uncle; and when he returns we shall be married! Then I shall look

down on the lower orders, and ride in my own coach, and scold my own servants and if Miss Adela calls on me, I shan't speak to her.—A servant indeed! No Mr. John, I'm not so ridiculous as you think me!"

John laughed heartily—Adela could scarcely restrain a smile; although now the veil was withdrawn; she could not, without anguish, behold the picture so young a heart, so deeply depraved, presented.

Lucy was then Captain Grenville's accomplice; ready to undertake anything or gain! And Adela now found that it was upon herself alone she must depend for her escape from a prison, rendered still more terrific by this certainty.

John descended the stairs, Lucy continued to dust and arrange the room; and Adela determined (should she ever again behold her dear native valley,) to combine her father's interest with parental authority to draw this poor deluded girl

No. 16.

from the destruction to which her vanity and ambition were consigning her ; but till then to conceal the discovery she had made.

"Will you take your breakfast, Miss ?" said Lucy, undrawing the curtains.

Adela assented, she arose and went into the next room. She took a cup of chocolate, but had no inclination to eat, and cast her tearful eyes on the spacious gardens, in all the luxuriance of June, for a feeling of despair stole over her, when she saw them surrounded by a wall, better adapted to a convent, a prison, or a receptacle for bewildered reason, than a country retirement.

Lucy said there was a young woman in the house, that she should like to get better acquainted with, "because, Miss," continued she in conversation, "I shall get into the secrets of the house, and find out which way, and at what hour, we can get away, and about the roads, and all that ; and perhaps, Miss, if we gave her a trifle, she'd help us off."

Adela saw through the artifice ; but prudence kept her silent, and she coincided, as much from a wish to conceal her sentiments, as to enjoy the luxury of solitude.

The blinds were drawn down, and the windows up in the chamber, which was an advantage denied to the front room ; and hearing a female voice, she leant forward, and caught the following conversation.

"When did he come?"

"You couldn't have got out o' sight of the cottage—poor gentleman ! he seemed so troubled, so wretched for the loss of his daughter, and had travelled so far with the good-looking farmer-like man he brought with him, that I got out the breakfast things again, and made them a cup of tea ; they said they had been on the road all night, and the gentleman took it so kindly that he slipped this sovereign into my hand, and said if we could find out his poor dear girl, he would reward us to the utmost of his power !"

Adela's heart beat tumultuously, she ran to the next room, and wrote the following words on a paper.

"I am that unhappy girl, torn from the arms of the best of parents. Good woman, be my friend ! I also will liberally reward you : be cautious, be silent ! but give this paper to the gentleman at the cottage."

When she gently removed the foliage, the gardener's wife looked up.

"Who's that at the window?" said she.

"Only poor Missus," replied the good man, "you mustn't mind her, Beckey ; she's crazed, poor thing ! but quite harmless."

Adela could not fail to be shocked at this observation, but she had caught the young woman's eye, and threw out the paper ; she could not read it, but her husband could make it out sufficiently to see 'that all was not fair and above-board.' He shook his head, put on his hat and jacket, and accompanied his wife back to the cottage, whilst Adela, wrapt in a vision of renovated hope, eased her overflowing heart in tears of joyous gratitude.

In about a quarter of an hour the gardener returned, she saw John conversing with him at the gate as he let him in, and locked it upon him ; her spirits sunk, and her misgiving heart assured her she was betrayed. In a few minutes however, he approached the window, smiled, touched his hat, looked round to see no one was at hand, and fixing a note on the end of a wand, raised it to the window.

Adela tremblingly seized it, and had just time to conceal it in her bosom, when Lucy entered with a basket of fruit.

What should she do if this babbling girl should commence one of her long narratives ? her impatience would render her frantic ; how should she contrive to get rid of her?

"Those roses beneath the drawing-room window are very beautiful, Lucy."

"Yes, Miss, I'll go and gather you one."

She set off, and Adela fastened herself in the chamber, and read as follows :

"My child, my beloved girl ! support thy fortitude, thy father is at hand ! in a few hours he will clasp thee to his heart and restore thee to that anxious mother who is now mourning and desolate. Be calm, be happy! and leave the rest to parental affection."

Adela kissed these welcome lines again and again, she laughed and wept alternately; and having made her toilette, sat down awaiting her father's arrival. Lucy returned with the roses; they seemed to breathe hope with their refreshing fragrance, and one she placed in her bosom.

An hour elapsed, another and another, her heart palpitating wildly as she fixed her eyes on the gate,—but her father came not, and the fond hopes, only a few hours before awakened, were now darkened and over-clouded by the agonizing fluctuations of hope deferred.

CHAPTER XXVI.

"Ah me! that e'er
Our home we left! my birds already call
For their Viola. Would that I could hear
Their matin song once more! yes, let us home."

But we will return to the cottage in the Woodlands, and trace the heavy-footed hours that elapsed from St. Clair's departure until the present moment, where the desponding mother passed a night of agony, starting at every sound, and listening to every footstep.

"I shall see her no more! my child is lost to me for ever!"

"Nay, do not say so, my dear madam," said her sympathising companion. "If master returns without our dear young lady, then it will be time to despair! but he'll find her fast enough, and my good man will stand by him to the last drop of his blood."

Night closed in, the rain poured down in torrents, it pattered amidst the foliage, and bubbled down the pathway.

Mrs. Ashton made a fire in the parlour, and put the kettle on in the kitchen, whilst Mrs. St. Clair placed slippers, and every article requisite of wearing apparel in readiness; for "alas" said this fond mother, "should she even be restored to us in her delicate state, she will never recover the damp of this night."

"You must not give way to these fears, madam," said her consoler, "Mr. St. Clair has got his cloak, and my good man (not knowing but they might be out all night) took his top coat over his arm, on account of the cloudiness that came over; miss will be taken care of, they'll not let her get wet, I'll be bound!"

Every requisite arrangement made for their anxiously desired return, the despairing mother sat down and wept, until the sun's earliest rays shone doubtfully through a sky, over-clouded as her hopes.

Let us follow St. Clair and the honest farmer, Ashton, who had declared it his intention to go with him to the world's end. There was not an individual in the village who would not have done the same, for this was to the inhabitants of that retired and simple spot a public calamity. Adela had been from infancy their benefactress, their ministering angel! every female eye was wet with tears, every youth in the village ready to raise his sapling in defence of the idol of all their hearts. Few amongst them had dared raise their hopes to St. Clair's daughter, but those who had been rejected as lovers, her candour and condescending sweetness had secured as devoted friends.

The agonized father hastily expressed his grateful acknowledgments for the proffered aid of the young; he shook hands with the aged; and, mounting his horse, was, in a moment, out of sight.

Burning with rage, resentment, horror, for what might be his daughter's fate in such hands, he rushed forward in the way the chaise had taken; but having proceeded a considerable distance, the road branched off in three different directions : which was he to take? One was a lane, no carriage could pass down that : but how decide between the other two? for, in consequence of recent showers, both roads were deeply imprinted with the wheels of the carts that had passed to and fro, from the villages and hamlets to which they led.

" Let us take our chance, sir," said Farmer Ashton, and a lucky chance it was, for, they had not gone far when they found a slipper, which both recognized as Lucy's, "and depend upon it, sir," said the good man, "that girl has had more to do with this business than is to her credit—my wife has noticed her gossipings with the Captain, and his man ; and her fine shawl, ear-rings, and frippery, they all look very suspicious; and young girls in her station are better attending to their occupation within doors, than chattering about the affairs of master and mistress, such as heaven blessed her with, to such a giddy fly-a-way good-for-nothing extravagant fellow, as the Captain, but what's that?"

They reined in their steeds, farmer Ashton alighted, and St. Clair's tears started as he received his Adela's reticule.

" Thank Heaven, we are then in the road they have taken! Divine justice will not permit crime and treachery to triumph over innocence and virtue! Solitary and unfrequented as the road across this wild and rugged way, we shall yet trace them ! a father's vengeance will yet be hurled on the head of the oppresser!"

About two in the morning they arrived at a small inn by the side of the road, into which they turned.

St. Clair inquired if a carriage and four had passed. They were answered in the affirmative; and, as the blinds were closely drawn down, the landlord thought it was empty ; "but a few minutes afterwards," he said, "a man in a large great coat stopped to take something; he had a young woman with a cloak on behind him, on the pillion, she had the large cape thrown over her head in the form of a hood."

" Did the young woman seem to be carried away reluctantly?" said St. Clair.

" Not at all sir, not at all—she seemed quite jocular, and was laughing about the loss of her slipper, and a reticule."

St. Clair having insisted on farmer Ashton taking something to prevent the effect of the wet, that had already drenched them, they rode off again in the direction the carriage and horseman had taken ; the former, horror stricken at so great an extent of depravity in one so young ; the latter heaping a thousand imprecations on the " little forward conniving hussey."

About day-break they reached a straggling village. They there heard that a carriage and four had passed up through a wide lane, that led to a retired villa, which had not long been uninhabited, but taken about two months since by a gentleman who had laid out a large sum of money, in beautifying the house and grounds ; and thither they bent their way.

The anxious father had travelled through the night, unconscious that he was wet to the skin, unmindful of weariness, insensible of hunger.

His child, his lost, his loved-one, in the power of a villain ! and the despair in which he had left her mother, were the only earthly events he was alive to.

In vain did his kind-hearted companion use every argument to cheer him, in vain proffer everything hope could dictate. A cloud heavy as night hung over his heart, which he feared would never more respond to the touch of joy.

It was about six in the morning : the sun began to chase away the clouds and shed its lustre on the sparkling gems, they brushed away in passing, from the intrusive woodbine and brier rose, when they reached a solitary cottage, and seeing a young woman with her baby in her arms at the door, they inquired " if a chaise and four had passed that way."

" No, sir, not to-day."

" When did you see one? this way is not much frequented, I believe."

" Why not much, sir; sometimes we do not see a passenger for days, and as for a coach, not once in a month, the high road leads round there, as far almost as you can see ; last night, however, Master brought Missus home, in a chaise and four : she's been very bad, poor lady, and he thinks that change of air will bring her about."

" Who is your master ?"

"_That is, he's not rightly my master ; only as he has employed my husband for the last two months, as gardener, we call him so."

" But who is he ?"

" Oh sir, he's an officer in the army."

" His name ?"

" Grenville, sir, Captain Grenville."

St. Clair and his companion exchanged glances.

" Where is your husband ?"

" At the Villa, sir, working in the garden."

" My good woman, I have been all night in search of a beloved child, who has been torn from my arms. Say nothing to your husband, but that there is a gentleman at this cottage who would speak with him. Should it be in his power, by inquiry or otherwise, to assist me in recovering her, I will compensate his kindness to the utmost extent of my capability !"

" Certainly sir, certainly, but as the kettle boils, I'll just put you the breakfast on the table, and you can serve yourselves, for you look quite faint and tired ; I'll slip on a clean apron, and put baby into the cradle ; and, if that other gentleman will just touch the rocker, she'll be quiet till I come back."

" No, give me the little wench," said Ashton, " I've brought up too many my own, to let her lie fretting there."

The breakfast-table was spread in a minute ; the heart-broken St. Clair prevailed upon by their mutual entreaties to take his seat by the fire, and the young woman (in whose hand he had slipped a sovereign,) off to the Villa with her heart full of joy, and calculating upon the nice things the treasure she held would buy her husband and her baby. And, as St. Clair took the smiling innocent from Ashton's arms, a manly tear fell on his cheek,—for memory reverted to the moment when his Adela's infancy promised nothing in the vista of future years, but peace and joy. Alas ! how had that futurity been blighted by the very individual he had conceived best calculated to secure it ! The purity of her gentle bosom had rendered her an easier prey to desolated hope ; and her artless beauty had only marked her a more distinguished sacrifice, to the worthless wretch who now held her captive.

And why had he given his innocent child the appellation of wife, but to render her more securely his own, and to close the ears of strangers who might have compassionated her, more completely to her entreaties for aid.

St. Clair's first impulse was to throw himself in Grenville's way, demand his daughter, and call him to an awful and retributive account ; but his Adela's delicate state of health, so recently recovered from so long an indisposition, and her anxiety for her father, urged him to pursue a different line of conduct.

" Let us get the young lady off quietly first, my good sir," said Ashton, " let us restore her to the care of her mother ; and you can then revenge this villanous action to your heart's content."

St. Clair saw the prudence of this plan—Jenkins arrived : a few moments exchanged suspicion into certainty ; and during their consultation it was determined that as this honest fellow was then employed in nailing up a passion flower, and training a vine round the windows of the chamber, he could easily remove the screws that secured the bars, leaving them in their place for a favourable moment, and all the rest he would engage to manage.

" But it must be done secretly, and by degrees ; for you see, sir, with my family, I shouldn't like to be thrown out of employ."

St. Clair perfectly coincided with the necessity for caution. He sent his note the friendly fellow returned to assure him he had delivered it, that he understood the captain was going to pass the night out, and " it would be better perhaps to write a little bit of a note, to tell miss she must have patience till evening."

"Yes," said the good-natured Ashton, "or the poor dear will think we've forgotten her, and pine away like a bird in its cage."

St. Clair wrote a few consolatory words, urging her to take refreshment, and support her spirits—"for that night, would, he trusted in the Creator, restore her to his arms."

Adela received this dear memento of a father's solicitude, in the same way she did the former, and sat pensively watching the good gardener in his avocations. How little did she imagine, that whilst she heard him knocking in the nails to secure the shreds that restrained the vine's vagrant branches, he was covertly removing the barriers to her freedom. Had she known it, the live crimson would have rushed to her pale cheek, and her heart would have beaten wildly; for independently of the fibres of that sensitive heart, that were wrung to anguish by this first separation from those who were dearer than its life spring, Adela possessed that inherent love of liberty, which should animate the bosom of every female. She was worthy such a father, and formed to be the bride of a hero.

But the fragile, the delicate exterior, was not equal to the energies, the powerful emotions of the gem it enshrined; sorrow and ingratitude had well nigh emancipated it from the traummels of mortality, and, although she had been partially restored by parental love, this last outrage had nearly overwhelmed her. Her temples throbbed, her head ached violently—and she reclined on the sofa in the drawing-room, and closed her eyes as if sleeping.

Lucy entered with the housekeeper, who regularly let her in and out with the key, a young woman brought up the tray to lay the cloth, and, conceiving her mistress asleep, the following conversation took place in a whisper.

"There, you see, I'll put the captain's note there, she can't help seeing it when she wakes, can she? Is he returned?"

"Returned! why he's not been out, he only pretended he was gone out, that she might not be frightened, for, he says, she's frightened out of her life at him, and he knows those about him won't blab."

"So it seems" said Lucy, "but I haven't seen him all day, where is he?"

"In his own chamber; he expects to take tea with madam this evening, but dinner's ready, and if I stands gossiping here, cook will ring my ears instead of the dinner bell."

Adela trembled: the wretch was then in the house—had been there all night! an unversal tremor pervaded her frame. How should she prevent her father meeting him? What that beloved parent's determined valour and unquenchable resentment would be she well knew; and resolved not to evince the smallest inclination for escaping before Lucy, lest violent measures should bring on an encounter, which she felt certain would end in death!

When the dinner was arranged, Lucy called her gently; and, although too ill to feel inclined to eat, she partook of a fowl, and half a glass of wine, that she might not sink into absolute incapacity to undertake the blissful event the evening promised her.

Adela read the note, it was to entreat the favour of an interview: she wrote these words in reply.

"To Captain Grenville.

"Miss St. Clair is too severely indisposed to see Captain Grenville to-day; to-morrow evening she may perhaps be somewhat recovered, if permitted to remain in tranquillity.

'Monday 4 o'clock."

Grenville had never received a line from Adela, until this moment—an appointment made by herself! (for so his vanity construed it,) oh! that to-morrow were arrived! How should he endure the weary interval! well—he had fortunately precisely hit upon that mode of conduct best suited to her nature, which would have recoiled from intrusiveness or presumption, and he must pursue it; nay, now the severity of her resentment had subsided, even evince some degree of indifference, he would spend the evening with a friend about a mile and a half distant; return at dusk, glide in, and remain in the apartment to which he had hitherto confined himself until the blest—the warmly anticipated to-morrow He wrote the following words .—

" MY SULTANA,

" As the most devoted of your slaves I obey you !— I go to visit a friend unt to-morow.   " ALBERT GRENVILLE."

Adela saw him mount his horse at the gate, and, retiring to her chamber, told Lucy she might pass the afternoon as she pleased, for she required repose.

About five o'clock Lucy rang the bell, and the housekeeper, who had invited her to tea, came to unlock the door and secure it after her ; and she tripped down to boast of her brilliant prospects to Mrs. Hacket and John, who called in the gardener to take a glass of wine with the " ladies."

Jenkins expressed himself delighted at John's hospitality ; but, as there was so snug a party, he must give something towards the merry-making, and would, with the ladies' leave, just run home and fetch a bottle of " famous stuff," given him by the butler at the Grange.

" The ladies" smilingly assented, but Mrs. Hacket proposed that the housemaid should just step up with the urn, and Mrs. Lucy take up the tea-things, and set everything ready for madam, that her visitor might not be interrupted when they had all sat comfortably down ; " which was," she said, in her opinion, " one of the most disagreeablest things in life."

When Adela heard the door tried, she unbolted it within, and felt pleased when she observed the lock again turned upon her. Having replied to Lucy's question, " whether she would wish for anything else at present," in the negative, she said she should take a cup of tea, which might possibly relieve her head, and then sleep for an hour or two; that she should bolt the doors ; and did not wish to be disturbed.

Adela took her seat at the solitary tea-table : ah ! where were now those love-beaming faces that used to cheer that delightful hour? that fond father, that tender mother to whom her inmost heart was unveiled ? where was he, who once blended the anxious care of father, brother, friend, in one sweet, one soul-subduing sentiment ? Ah ! wherefore this reflection ? was he not even now perhaps another's ? could a heart so versatile have ever been worth a sigh? but

> " Ere such a soul regains its peaceful state,
> How often must it love, how often hate !
> How often hope, despair, resent, regret,
> Conceal disdain; do all things but forget!''

The tea concluded, the social party below placed a table at the door, and they set in for an hour's conviviality ; certain of not being interrupted by the captain's return until twelve or one in the morning at any rate ; and they alternately sang, laughed, and jested, until the clock of the neighbouring church struck nine. Jenkins had pushed the glass about so freely, that Mrs. Hacket and her fair friend had both sunk back in their arm chairs, in the most delightful repose possible, and John's eyes were heavy and drowsy.

" Another glass, Mr. John ?"

" Why, Mr. Jenkins, you don't drink any yourself !"

" I took half a bottle with the butler, before I left."

Another glass,—and Mr. John snored profoundly.

Now for the keys !—no time was to be lost,—they must be in John's pocket ; —no ! in the housekeeper's—as far off as ever ! Well—never mind—such a favourable moment must not be lost !

The nails ready for the rope ladder were in the wall, the ladder he used for nailing up the vines in the garden ; and, although he would rather open the doors for the young lady, yet " what must be—must," and he hastened to give the signal to St. Clair, who waited the event in the lane.

Adela heard the ladder against her window,—the good gardener ascended,—the iron bars miraculously yielded to his touch. She listened to his assurance that he came to restore her to her father, who awaited her in the lane. She stepped on a chair, from thence to the window-sill, her small foot was on the ladder; and, with the lightness of a sylph, she descended, and followed her guide over the lawn to the side wall, to which he carried the ladder. Tremblingly she ascended it ;—she saw her father awaiting her—his gentle arms encircled—his soothing voice animated and consoled her, and she again breathed the invigorating, the soul-inspiring air of freedom!

Having received the sincere congratulations of the good Ashton, and accompanied by Jenkins, they reached the cottage in the lane, where a chaise awaited them. On the restoration of her reticule, she gave her purse to the hospitable Rebecca. St. Clair liberally rewarded her husband ; and, having yielded his horse to Ashton's guidance, they commenced their journey, for the agitation of Adela's mind had renewed her fever; and he trembled lest this, their sole surviving pledge of connubial love, should have been restored, only to be lost to him for ever !

And whilst St. Clair wrapped his daughter in his cloak, and supported her in his arms, and that now happy girl listened to his voice, and felt conscious of his protection, the past was lost to oblivion; and the fondly anticipated moment, which would restore the wife, the mother to their arms—alone the image of the future !

They had half crossed the Heath, when, suddenly, Ashton rode up to them.

" We've a couple of horsemen in the rear," said he, " perhaps the captain and one of his fellows,—who knows? he calls loudly enough to us to stop !"

" Will the villain, then, dare expose himself to a parent's just resentment ? but, should he, my Adela's presence of mind must not forsake her !"

" Alas! my dear papa,—of selfish terrors you will not suspect me ; but where will be your child's fortitude when that valued life may be in danger ?"

" Fear nothing, Miss," said Ashton, " we are well armed."

" In the cause of innocence," said St. Clair, " and Heaven will nerve a father's arm in defence of his child !"

St. Clair ordered the postilion to stop, sprang from the chaise, and seizing both his pistols, stood before one door, whilst Ashton, equally armed, placed himself before the other.

" Scoundrels!" exclaimed a voice, which Adela but too well recognised, " resign the lady you have taken from my house and her home ! resign her, I say, this moment, or it shall be your last !"

" Villain !" replied St. Clair, firmly maintaining his ground, and throwing himself before him: " lay thy sacrilegious hands on her, and by Heaven I'll lay thee a corpse at my feet, for she is my daughter !"

" I have a stronger claim, for she is my wife ! so restore her, or take the consequences !"

His companion advanced : there was a violent rush at the door ;—St. Clair disarmed one. Adela shrieked wildly for her father. The report of pistols sounded on her ear. She sunk, lifeless, to the bottom of the chaise ; and Ashton having discharged his only remaining ball, (which slightly grazed Grenville's arm,) reached his friend in time to receive him in his, wounded, and apparently expiring.

" Monsters !" exclaimed the warm-hearted fellow, wiping the cold dew from his forehead, " ye have murdered the best human being God ever created ! His persecuted child lies there also, beyond your power—for her Creator has taken her to himself! but Heaven's curses will pursue ye !" continued he, bending over his friend, " for if my life is spared, not a nook in this wild world shall shelter ye from justice !"

Morning shed its earliest twilight on the death-like features of St. Clair, and the blood streamed from his wound. The assailants interchanged a few words in

French; they mounted their horses, and were out of sight in a moment, and left poor Ashton with his wounded friend, and apparently lifeless daughter.

When Adela revived, she found herself at a little inn, by the road side, attended by a young girl and an aged woman. She entreated them to conduct her to her father. They tried to persuade her to remain for some time, in order to recover her terror and fatigue.

"The gentleman has had the ball extracted from his shoulder," said the land-lady, " and make yourself easy, my dear young lady; for if he can but get a little sleep, and we can but keep off fever, there is no doubt of his recovery!"

All seemed to Adela a terrific dream. Merciful Heaven! had her beloved father, then, been wounded in her defence? She rushed forward—she met the good Farmer Ashton at her father's door. He unfolded, in cautious accents, the melancholy truth, and in another moment she was kneeling by his bed-side, and covering his burning hand with her tears and kisses. Ashton informed her of everything that had occurred: that Grenville, having supposed her father no more, and her own recovery doubtful, had fled. That the postilion, whose terrors had induced him to conceal himself in a hedge, had crept out when he found the enemy quitting the field, and proffered his services in assisting to remove his wounded friend to the nearest habitation, which fortunately proved to be an inn near a town, where an

No. 17.

eminent surgeon was obtainable; and that he could assure her, if his mind was kept calm, there was very little doubt of his recovery.

"But, my dear Mr. Ashton, can we not send to inform mamma of our fate? My heart bleeds to think what she must have endured. Melancholy as the tidings we have to convey, yet that beloved mother must not be left in suspense."

"I will go myself, my dear young lady. Mr. St. Clair is asleep;—do you think you can bear the fatigue of sitting by his bedside till I return? I'll be off and back again in a couple of hours."

Adela heard nothing but what concerned her father, saw nothing but his wound, was apprehensive of nothing but his danger. The highest degree of health could not have inspired more energy: and having insisted on Farmer Ashton's taking that sort of refreshment best suited to his fatigue and exertion, he departed, and left her to the tender solicitude that yet sleeping father's precarious state could not fail to inspire.

Adela sat beside his pillow: she gently drew aside the white dimity curtain to contemplate those beloved features; calm and pale, that best of fathers reposed—the serenity of his soul reflected in his features the spirited character of which had been mellowed not destroyed, by the usually defacing hand of misfortune. Yes, he slept sweetly, for his last thought had been his Adela's safety,—his last hope the power of restoring her to her beloved mother; who, he doubted not, would be there at day-break.

The morning (and it was a brilliant one) shed its first golden ray through the white curtains that were drawn before the casement. A neat carpet, a few rustic chairs, and a table, formed the furniture of this humble apartment; and three beautiful geraniums mingled with the deep variegated leaf, and scarlet and lilac flows, so as nearly to shade the light. And she patiently awaited the moment when she might present the refreshing draught to his parched and feverish lips.

At length he awoke; an embrace of inexpressible tenderness---a silent tear—words are nothing to their eloquence! But where are those heart-thrilling accents?

"Where---where are they?"

And the fond, the anxious, the trembling mother clasped to her bosom a creation in itself,---her all of earthly felicity!

The kind-hearted Arnold had arrived late on Monday evening, with his Louisa, who mingled her tears with Mrs. St. Clair, whilst her father went to Lucy's parents, and in every direction that held out a hope. Lucy's parents knew nothing of her. He used every possible argument to arouse the heart now a prey to cheerless despair. No one thought of rest; and Louisa sat by the window during the night, where she listened to every sound, and was the first to announce the good Ashton's arrival, who, finding Mr. Arnold ready to accompany Mrs. St. Clair and his daughter to the inn, remained to take charge of the farm, and his good wife of the cottage. And St. Clair welcomed his friend, who warmly and sincerely sympathized with his past and present sufferings.

"Call not the present suffering!" said he; "is not our child restored to our arms? have I not her mother by my side?—my esteemed friend, and the favourite of all, my Adela's chosen one, to cheer the solitude of a sick chamber? They talk of quietude, but I have slept and am refreshed. The society of those I love and esteem is a balsam for every wound---a balm for every care! So,---Adela, love, throw open the middle door, order breakfast, and we will take it —en famille."

But Louisa saw that her friend's animation was more mental than bodily. She took her place, when breakfast was over. St. Clair was left to repose. Adela submitted to the entreaties of her beloved parents and friends, and retired to take an hour's sleep. Louisa sat beside her, and passed away the time with a book. Mrs. St. Clair watched the hour for administering her husband's medicine. She awaited the doctor's arrival, and crept on tiptoe from one chamber to the other, to attend her two invalids, whilst Arnold remained in the little sitting-room, that opened out of St. Clair's chamber, to write to his wife; inform her of the varied and melancholy occurrences of the past day, and that he should not leave his friend until the following evening.

CHAPTER XXVII.

Whither have fied,
Those hues of heaven, that canopied his bower?
But thou art fled
Like some frail exhalation, whilst the dawn
Robes in its golden beams.—SHELLEY

THE marriage ceremony performed, the bride and bridegroom partook of an elegant entertainment at the Park, and set off for Beechwood, where they passed the first month of this propitious union.

But, the husband won, the fair Belinda seemed to suspend these little sentimentalities, that, although they could not win a heart devotedly engaged, yet, at least, claimed a feeling of friendship and consideration. She became haughty, petulant, expecting, and capricious: her jewels must be reset; every arrangement at Beechwood be remodelled; a favourite shrubbery torn up to plant a garden; a wood, where he had delighted to wander with his lamented uncle, cut down; even his faithful Ralph became an object of her dislike and suspicion; and Theodore longed for the moment of their departure for the metropolis, when he hoped some new whim might put him, at least, out of her immediate recollection. But there new follies, new extravagances, assailed him. For some time, in order to drown the reflections brought by solitude, he accompanied her in the round of dissipation in which she engaged; but he reflected that his wife yet wanted some months of being one-and-twenty, and he was yet a minor. The sums his father had advanced since his arrival had occasioned, if not discontent, at least expostulation!

Mrs. Villars's parties were attended by the first votaries of fashion. "The beautiful Mrs. Villars," the very darling of *haut ton*, continued to be a splendid novelty: the knocker in Grosvenor-square resounded to morning calls, the hall table was covered with cards, and her rooms crowded when they were thrown open to select parties of her particular friends. The designing saw that vanity was her ruling passion, and resolved to profit by it; the avaricious (for even woman's bosom is not insensible to this deforming propensity) and a regularly initiated *coterie* of female gamesters, alternately invited her to their houses, solely with a view of plunder.

The admiration her peculiarly majestic style of beauty attracted, had turned her head; and when Theodore found it requisite, by his absence, to discourage this eternal routine of dissipation, she rarely ever passed a night at home, and the greater part of her day was passed in repairing the ravages of the night.

Theodore ventured to expostulate: "I do not wish, Belinda," said he, "to debar you from amusement: see your friends (if such you term them) but suffer some degree of reason to be your guide. This continued dissipation is ruinous; your health must yield to it; and our circumstances, so far as regards present convenience, for you are aware we are now dependant alone on advances made by my father.

In vain did he reason. Belinda evinced the most violent resentment. "Was she, then, to be governed like a child?"

Theodore's heart recurred to the feminine sweetness, the purity of his Adela's mind; and, retiring to his study, a silent, settled melancholy took possession of his soul.

The next plan was to get rid of Ralph. This, Theodore long resisted; but sighs, tears, and hysterics were called in aid. Poor Ralph discovered the source of contention, and urged his master to send him away for the present.

"And, although it is worse than death to me to leave you, sir," said he, "yet this may pass off, and mistress will not leave you a peaceful hour until I am gone."

Theodore's soul recoiled from this innovation on everything feminine or reasonable, but his was a wayward destiny, and he sat down to write to his friend Clifford in the following terms:—

"MY DEAR CLIFFORD,

"I told you I was wretched; I told you that, much as you had repined at your fate, it was a heaven of felicity compared with mine. The ties of your tenderness were severed, but memory still left her halo of purity around each lost one! Thou canst still behold, in fancy, thy Zephyrina as an angel of light; she still treasures thy memory with unfading constancy; whilst I—it is madness to breathe her name! But, were this all, the bondsman—not the bridegroom of another—a being who even denies me the consolation of esteeming her! Her follies have daily increased; and, for a long time, 'she is young and thoughtless,' said I, she is my wife, and has some tenderness for me. Although my soul is wedded to another, what love cannot give shall be compensated by attention and consideration; for I alone am to blame in weakly coinciding with so unjust a command. Was it my instinctive horror of a parent's curse? Was it revenge towards the syren—St. Clair's daughter? Alas! can that word be breathed with her name? Was it with the idea that the daily intercourse of domestic life with a young, and, certainly, a fine woman, would wear her memory out of my heart and brain? Oh! madness! to the devoted there is but one woman in existence—and thou, Clifford, thou canst feel this truth. Mrs. Villars passes her day in her chamber, her night from home. She never meets me, unless some loss at play renders conciliation—and, above all, cash—a matter of importance. Her whims accumulate; and, above all, she has fallen upon one that has afflicted me deeply. You know my poor Ralph: you are acquainted with his history! Her waiting-woman has whispered in her ear the tale of the Valley—that he was the bearer of my letter to Adela, and hers to me—and she insists on his instant dismissal.

"This, then, is the boon I ask of your friendship: take this poor fellow into your service, for the present,—let him be your attendant; and, sometimes permit his honest, unsophisticated heart to unburthen itself of its kind feelings for an unfortunate being, who considers him more in the light of an early companion, and the tried friend of after years, than as a servant.

"But do I not know the heart I address? I could not make such a request to another. Have not congenial sorrows awakened congenial sympathies? Has not the arrow of affliction bound our hearts in closer unison?—and may we not hope to find, in that friendship which time can but improve, the only balm for widowed hopes and broken faith?

"Write to me instantly, and believe me, ever yours,

"THEODORE VILLARS."

With a liberal amount, which the disinterested fellow would fain have refused, with many a gift of unshaken regard, Ralph took the letter from his master's hand. His lips trembled, he dared not trust his voice to express his gratitude, his devotion. He drew his hand across his eyes, and rushed from the house, whilst Theodore locked himself in his study to indulge the regrets he could not overcome.

The morning visits, the bustle, the constant ingress and egress of milliners, mercers, and jewellers, rendered the house in Grosvenor-square a scene of continued confusion. The authoritative presumption of Mrs. Villars's maid toward individuals who had grown old in the service of the family, pained and disgusted him. He resolved to exert a too-long dormant authority in checking these innovations. The most unequivocal expressions of indignation and resentment were the consequence ; and Theodore secluded himself in his own apartments, until Belinda might be sufficiently calm to listen to his expostulations.

But one day followed another, and no such favourable moment arrived, " Mrs. Villars was not yet visible." The dissipation of the night rendered repose necessary during the greater part of the day. Shopping and morning visits must take up a part of her time ; then select dinner parties ;—a masquerade,—the opera, or card parties : thus every hour was engaged, every moment dedicated to some new folly.

A letter from Sir Edward, inviting them to spend the autumn at the Park, was a real relief to Theodore ; and as it was accompanied by a present to Belinda, (perhaps the first individual who had ever elicited a spark of liberality from him) most welcomely it arrived ; for, as she said, it enabled her to pay a portion of her debts of honour, incurred at play.

Sir Edward expressed his intention of giving a grand *fete* in October, in honour of his daughter-in-law's birth-day, and all these pleasing and flattering events put Belinda in such good humour, that she absolutely gave her husband the meeting in the drawing-room, for a few minutes ; although Lady Rattleton had affectionately called to take her up in her way to the Duchess of Daugerfield's, and was then waiting in her chariot at the door.

Short as the period allowed him to express his sentiments, Theodore threw a degree of decision into his manner that rather startled her ; and, placing her brilliantly decorated and snowy hand on his arm, she smiled so bewitchingly in promising amendment, that he hoped her errors might be more of the head than of the heart.

But it was impossible the health, so recently restored, should not fall a sacrifice to the silent anguish that preyed upon his heart.

> " Give sorrow words,—the grief that dares not speak,
> Whispers the o'erfraught heart, and bids it break !"

And Theodore's pale cheek and wasted form seemed to promise a speedy conclusion to his silent affliction.

The medallion with Adela's hair was still in his bosom ; her portrait (sketched by his ever-regretted friend, St. Clair) which he had taken from her portfolio, hung elegantly framed in his study, dressed in the simplest attire, a rose, the only adornment of her beautiful hair; her dove (his little messenger in happier hours) pressed to a bosom that rivalled its snowy down in whiteness. He gazed on those lineaments of ethereal loveliness, that speaking expression of soul-touching innocence, until his " very senses ached," and a nervous fever confined him for several weeks to his chamber.

Perhaps it may be conceived, according to the tenor of Belinda's former conduct, that she declined seeing company, administered every medicine, and devoted her every hour to cheer his solitude and soothe his sufferings. Far otherwise ; no daily offerings of fruit or flowers were now brought to invite and please by their fragrance and beauty. It is true she visited him once each day ; told the physician she " hoped there was no danger," sent her maid before she went out for the evening, to inquire " how Mr. Villars found himself," but Pleasure called her votary to a gayer scene than a husband's sick chamber ; and, with a solitary exception, that she did not receive company at home, she still laughed, danced, sung, and visited as usual.

CHAPTER XXVIII.

> Why did she love him? curious fool, be still!
> Is human love the growth of human will?
>
> BYRON.

LET us return to St. Clair and his little social circle.

A few hours' rest were all that Adela would be persuaded to take! and as her considerate mother had brought with her a small portmanteau, containing everything requisite, Louisa and herself made their toilette, and repaired to the apartment where St. Clair still slept, and where his affectionate wife and the warmhearted Arnold watched by his side, administering his medicines, and anticipating his slightest wish.

Refreshed by his slumber, the father, husband, friend, awoke; and, with that elasticity of spirit which arose against the pressure of pain and adversity—his smile of benignity renewed the most pleasing hopes in those around him.

"Why do you close that middle door, my dear Aurora?" said he; "it faces the open window, whence I can behold this sunny season in all its splendour. The distant corn-fields—green moutains, and embowering woods. Let me see those faces most dear to my heart; and sickness will take its flight to the chamber of luxury, and to the abode of dissipation."

In the evening, Farmer Ashton came to see his esteemed neighbour and to give an account of his stewardship, bringing some of the best fruit the orchard yielded. The next morning his good wife paid her visit, and presented the choicest flowers to refresh the invalid's chamber. To impress the maternal kiss of love on the cheek of her dear "Miss Addy," and to raise her grateful thanks to Heaven for her restoration to her parents, her friends—ay, and to all the attached and grateful hearts of the inhabitants of her native valley.

Mr. Arnold returned on the following evening; but granted his friend's entreaties for Louisa's stay some few days longer; during which she shared Adela's bed, and her mother's cares for her dear father.

The ball had struck and fractured the clavicle, and lodged in the shoulder; but so skilful was the surgeon, so temperate his habits, and so unremitting the attentions of his wife, his daughter, and her young friend, that, at the end of a fortnight, it was conceived perfectly safe to remove him by easy journeys to the Valley; where they found all the comforts of that elegant retreat in readiness to receive them. And monarchs might have envied the heartfelt congratulations that awaited the friend, the father, the patron of a happy and industrious peasantry:

> "To bless mankind with tides of flowing wealth,
> With power to grace them, or to crown with health,
> Our little lot denies."

But St. Clair's eventful history will furnish an example, with how little a liberal heart, a talented, an independent, a philanthropic mind, may become a benefactor.

On the morning after the family of St. Clair were reinstated in their cottage, with many regrets on both sides, the gentle Louisa returned to her home, whence her father had made another excursion to visit his friend and to fetch his daughter, that she might give place to her mother and sister, who were anxious to pay their visit of congratulation and condolence. Their minds were frank, no worldly selfishness, no paltry and affected considerations of etiquette, checked the pure stream of friendship in hearts that were nature's own, and they felt that their father's friend, his estimable wife, and their desert flower, merited all their attention, respect, and sympathy.

And the dear little Louisa was gone, the flowers her hand had gathered the evening before, to place in the urns, drooped, to Adela's fancy, for the gentle friend no longer smiled on the scene, no longer breathed the accents of sympathy, to soothe the incurable anguish of her heart.

The breakfast was laid by the open window in her mother's chamber; and they waited her father's waking to share it together.

Mrs. Ashton just stepped up to the door to bring a newspaper.

" It's not to-day's nor yesterday's, my dear Miss St. Clair, it may be a week or two old, but I always find a something amusing in a newspaper, so I left my master at breakfast, and ran in with it."

Adela thanked her with a smile and whisper, and had retired to a window to run over its contents, when her mother beheld a death-like hue overspread her already pale cheek, the coral tinge deserted her lips, her eyes closed, and, with a sigh, she fell to the ground.

Mrs. St. Clair raised her daughter, bathed her cheek with her tears, and, with the aid of Mrs. Ashton, carried her to her chamber, where, in a few minutes, she revived.

Her affectionate mother made no inquiry respecting the cause of her sudden indisposition. Adela attributed it to the weakness arising from the recent painful events, and assured her if she would return to her chamber, lest her papa should awake, she would instantly join her, as she already found herself much better.

On returning to the table, the newspaper caught her eye, and, looking over the marriages, the secret was unveiled at once, in the following lines :—

"Theodore Villars, Esq., of Villars Park, to Miss Somerville, of Harewood Lodge."

The indignant feeling of the moment may be easily conceived; but Mrs. St. Clair instantly sent away the paper, and concealed her daughter's indisposition, for St. Clair awoke, and how dear was that life, which depended on the calmness of the present moment !

But what became of the dissolute Grenville? He returned to the villa about half an hour after Adela's departure, accompanied by his friend, who merely proposed riding over with him, as he was determined not to stay. When, however, his repeated rings at the gate were not answered, it occurred to him all was not as it should be; they leaped the gate, and passed round to the side-door leading out of the housekeeper's room.

There he found Lucy, Mrs. Hacket, and John sleeping on the grass; he instantly ran up the principal stairs to Adela's apartments.

He called in vain, and obtaining no reply, burst open the drawing-room door and found his captive flown; on entering the chamber, and seeing the bars removed from the windows, he raved like a madman. In vain did he call John, and endeavour to rouse the female servants from their sleep; a snore, a yawn, or an incoherent exclamation was the only reply. He took his friend's advice to commence an immediate pursuit, and with this purpose they remounted and proceeded across the heath.

The attack we have described, and Grenville resolved to carry Adela back with him, or die in the attempt; when St. Clair fell, and his friend seeing his arm slightly wounded—Adela lifeless at the bottom of the chaise, and her father to all appearance dead—he in French exclaimed, " By Heaven ! Grenville, this is a bad business, flight is our only alternative ! you must not go home, but return to my house, and remain *incognito* until we know the result."

As the horrors however of the consequences, attendant on an abduction of so serious a nature ; the probability that he had killed St. Clair, and might be apprehended in a few hours, the evidence of the farmer and the postilion ! the delay of a moment would be dangerous. He therefore rode back to the Villa ; collected everything valuable, which could possibly be conveyed away about his person, took a hasty leave of his friend, and never stopped until he reached the Isle of Wight.

There he found a Spanish vessel getting under weigh, to sail for the southern coast of Spain, and he got hastily on board of her, with a view of proceeding to a relation in the Island of Malta ; and residing there under a feigned name, until he could hear from his friend the result of his criminal enterprise.

Blowing a stiff breeze from the east, they soon cleared the Channel, and reached

the ocean.   But in passing the Bay of Biscay, with a strong gale setting towards
the shore, they were momentarily in danger of being wrecked.   In this situation,
when every moment was expected to be the last, the many misdeeds that had
crowded his short career appeared in terrible array ! the innocent hearts he had
deluded,—the confidence he had often betrayed ! but above all, the forms of St.
Clair and his daughter, arose in his mind as if to beckon him to the hour of final
retribution.   It was indeed an awful night, even to the guiltless, but they weathered the gale ; in the morning passed the Straits of Gibraltar, and reached the
serene and tranquil waters of the Mediterranean.   Grenville's spirits now revived
—laughed at his recent superstitious forebodings, and revelled in the prospect of
pleasures yet to come.

But his happy anticipations were transitory: a sailor aloft espied a vessel
making all sail towards them ; the master with his glass soon discovered her to be
a Tunisian Corsair, and, with the utmost consternation, he communicated the sad
intelligence to the crew, for he was unprovided with the protecting pass.

All their endeavours to beat to windward were vain ; the pirate closed rapidly
upon them ; and, after a six hours' fruitless exertion to escape, she came close
alongside, her shrouds filled with men, ready to board and capture them.

Seized with desperation at the prospect of slavery, for the remainder of perhaps
a protracted existence, Grenville seized a handspike, and in a fit of unavailing
despair, knocked the first man down who leaped the bulwarks. This act of insanity
drew upon him the immediate vengeance of those who followed ; and they
instantly drove him headlong into the sea, where he would inevitably have perished,
had not the Corsair's commander noticed he was not an ordinary individual belonging to the crew, and, therefore, from the consideration of ransom, worth preserving.

Thus rescued a second time from a watery grave, he was ironed and sent on
board the Tunisian ; and, on landing, sold as a slave, to proceed to a distant point
in the interior of the empire of Morocco.

CHAPTER XXIX.

Alas ! what hast thou done ?
Thy rash credulity has done a deed,
Which of two happiest lovers that e'er felt
The blissful pow'r, has made two finished wretches.—THOMSON.

THEODORE felt satisfied, by the unvaried tenor of Clifford's letters, that his faithful servant would find in him not only a master, but a friend.   He forbore to make
any complaint of Belinda to his father ; he avoided breathing a word respecting his
illness, and above all to Clifford, because he knew that if it came to poor Ralph's
ear, nothing could keep him from returning to attend him ; he therefore deferred
the visit from time to time with various excuses, but, about the middle of September, preparations were made for carrying it into effect.

And a still greater degree of bustle was the order of the day at the Park ; for
this one, this great occasion—the celebration of the heiress's birth-day ! the period
which would bring Sir Edward's hopes to maturity—no expense would of course be
spared, no source of varied and elegant amusement neglected.

Sir Edward himself overlooked the whole arrangements.   Whoever called, early
or late, found him superintending the workmen, or in his grounds, which he purposed should rival the splendour of an Arabian Night's scene of magic and enchantment !

It was the last day of a brilliant September, and every one expected, each
moment, the announcement of Mr. and Mrs. Villars's arrival.   Sir Edward was
taking a late breakfast, when a footman entered, to say that an individual below
requested an interview.

"What is he like?" said Sir Edward.

"I can hardly tell you, sir," replied the man; "but he's a queerish-looking subject, and seems very anxious to gain admittance."

"Well—show him up."

On entering, Sir Edward found his servant's description tolerably correct; for he scarcely gave him time to inquire his business, before he proceeded to inform him, he had been told, in the neighbourhood, that he would be as likely as anybody to inform him where he should meet with "Master Somerville."

"With Mr. Somerville? Why, at the Lodge, certainly."

"Ay, ay; Sir Edward," replied the man, rather familiarly, "there I've been, but aint disappointed at not finding him; because it's not the first time by many he's had the start of us some hours."

"The start of you! What mean you, sir? And why take the liberty to come and make these inquiries of me, when the family can give you the information you require?"

"The family, sir! I should like to get hold of 'em! They're all off as clean as can be; and the house as close shut up as though it had been empty the last century."

No. 18.

"They've, no doubt, left for the metropolis; but I'm surprised they did not take leave of me, previous to their departure."

"For London, sir! ha, ha! Mr. Somerville, or Mr. Woodville, or Mr. Thornton, or whichever of the string of *aliases* now in fashion with him, knows better than to proceed there; for, if he did, we should lay hold of him in twenty-four hours."

"I'm at a loss to understand what you mean, fellow! Mr. Somerville is a man of large fortune and of high respectability, and must, therefore, be at liberty to go whithersoever he pleases."

"You'll excuse me, Sir Edward, but I doubt every syllable of that,—though it's nothing new for him to carry a high head while he can, wherever he takes up his abode, though it is seldom for long at a time."

"Well, sir," said Sir Edward, rising angrily, "either quit my house, instantly, or explain yourself in more intelligible terms, for I am too much interested in what concerns that gentleman's welfare to be left another moment in suspense."

"I'm sorry for it, Sir Edward, I'm sorry for it."

"And why the devil are you sorry for it?"

"Merely, Sir Edward, because I have the trifling matter of a warrant in my possession for his apprehension, upon a number of wholesale frauds committed by him in several parts of the kingdom, and many of 'em of so serious a nature, that I'm not certain they don't amount to forgeries!"

"Good God!" exclaimed the baronet, "you don't say so: 'tis impossible!"

"Possible, or not possible, it is so, however; and Mr. Somerville has figured under so many different names these last two years, that we've found it plaguy hard to trace him. It's clear enough he has an understanding with some one at the public offices, who seasonably advises him of what's going on, that he may decamp before he is reachable."

Sir Edward heard no more. He darted from his chair, pale as ashes,—folded his arms, knit his brow, and paced the breakfast-room with hurried and hasty strides.

"Accursed avarice!" exclaimed he, "I have ruined my boy! I have, then, forced him into an union with a nest of swindlers!"

"I hope, sir, you are only joking; you can't have been such a fool as to oblige your son to marry one of that old scoundrel's daughters!"

"I have—by Heaven!"

"Then your Honor is the greatest flat he's met with in his travels: for, although he's often tried this, it's only now he's been able to manage it. He's got two daughters: the eldest's plain, rather—the youngest's a handsome, personable wench enough, but both are cunning Jezabels, and aiders and abettors in all the rogueries of the gang. There are old heads on young shoulders; and, if what you say is true, your son's a ruined man, to a certainty."

Sir Edward ran up and down the room, like one distracted. Disappointment, conscious guilt, the deepest humiliation, oppressed him almost to suffocation. At length he paused, and eagerly exclaimed,—

"I think you said his name is not Somerville."

"That I'll be sworn, unless the last's the right one,—and that's not very likely to be the case."

"Well, then," replied Sir Edward, breathing more freely, "we shall, I trust, still escape, for she was married to my son in that name. But, how can the designing villain have proceeded, to his present period of existence, without falling into the hands of justice?"

"God bless you, sir,—such things are done every day—more's the pity for the families of the industrious tradesmen they ruin! I'm told he was once a man of fortune; but being lured into Crockford's, that sink of infamy, he soon became insolvent, grew desperate, and has, ever since, been connected with a number in the same circumstances; who, for the greater part, live in a magnificent style, play into each other's hands, and practise at their own residences similar enormities to those which worked their destruction in the first setting out. Unfortunately for the town, there are those amongst them that few would be likely to suspect, because they figure under titles that do not, now-a-days, always carry honor or even honesty with them."

"Well, my good friend," said Sir Edward, "you know, by what I have said, how we have been entrapped by them, that it's not very probable I should know of their retreat. But I thank you, sincerely, for your information : accept this note, and I wish you a good morning."

Bowing—the officer received the five pounds ; and Sir Edward, burning with shame, resentment, and remorse, shut himself up in his study to tranquillize and arrange his ideas.

In a few minutes he became sufficiently calm to see the necessity of conveying the above intelligence to his son, declaring his intention of applying immediately for a divorce, and concluded by observing,—

"I am rightly served. Had I permitted you to follow the dictates of those inclinations, which have never, until these Somervilles appeared, been in opposition to my wishes, you would now have enjoyed not only health, but felicity ! Hasten to me, my dear boy, and let us reflect on the compensation yet possible to be made by your—

"Sorrowing Father,
"E. Villars."

Theodore had just received a message from the fair Belinda ; she awaited the pleasure of his company to breakfast, and, presenting her hand with one of her most winning smiles on his entrance, expressed her delight at his recovery ! During the repast she informed him she had taken leave of her friends, and should devote every remaining hour of their stay in London to his welcome society.

Theodore was too sincere to make any other reply to those warm advances to friendliness, than that dictated by politeness due to a female ; her past and present conduct formed so glaring a contrast,—her dissipation, her extravagance, her heartless manner since their residence in London, and above all, her hatred to poor Ralph, had utterly deprived her of the small portion of his esteem she once possessed, and secured the empire of Adela in all its melancholy influence.

Having breakfasted, she proposed a morning ride, and arose to dress for that purpose ; Theodore took up a volume of Shelley, as most congenial with the anguish of his heart, and read whilst he awaited her return ; but scarcely had she closed the door, when, glancing towards that side of the sofa she had left, a small letter-case caught his eye. Taking it up, the silver clasps flew open, and presented to his view two letters, the one directed in her father's hand to "Mrs. Villars," the other in her own, to "Miss Brown, Post Office, Dover," containing a bank note.

Was his wife then sending away money, when only the day before she had applied to him for the payment of debts, which his father's really liberal amount would not cover? This was mysterious : and then, who was this Miss Brown? Such a correspondent had never previously come to his knowledge! The letter was not sealed, and enclosed the half of a £500 Bank bill.

This might well create suspicion. He took the letter-case and retiring to his study, closed the door, and read as follows :—

"My dear Belinda,

"Our retreat is again discovered. I have received this intelligence from our official friend ; so that, unless we are off from the Lodge in six hours, we shall have a visit of no very conciliatory nature. I have received your remittances, with my portions from Rattleton, Dangerfield, and the rest, together with your fudge losses, so that we are pretty well in funds for the present crisis.

"Our very peculiar circumstances having obliged us to assume the name of Somerville, your marriage is not, of course, legal ; but, as we have succeeded in entrapping young Villars, I trust his heart will be too securely yours to permit him to take advantage of this ; so that your mother considers you are fixed upon this titled and ancient family. Should this, however, not be the case, there is no alternative, but make the best of the arrangement.

"We shall repair, without delay, to Dover, and you can address your sister as Miss Brown, at the Post Office of that town You may enclose her whatever you may have got together,—and remember, jewels and other valuables are easily converted into cash.

"Many days coannot, I fear, elapse, without Sir Edward being made acquainted with our deporture, as well as with the cause of it; but in the event of an immediate *denouement,* which might render it requisite for you to leave hastily, you had better proceed to join us at the above port; and, should we have sailed, follow us in the first packet to Ostend.

"Yours affectionately,

"J. Somerville.

"To Mrs. Villars."

The letter to her sister (who it seems had officiated as companion to the heiress, under the name of Miss Darlington) merely stated, that she enclosed half a five hundred pound note for her father, whose letter had come safely to hand, and that the remainder should follow by the next post.

Theodore perused, and re-perused these letters, and the contents transfixed him with horror: it was assuredly a terrific dream. No; he held them—looked on them; he could not doubt Belinda's writing, and that the other was her father's he well knew.

And was he then united to a woman connected with such a family? By a mere chance the veil had been drawn aside, which had concealed a regular system of fraud and villany; the principal actors in which proved to be individuals who passed in the world as persons of fortune and fashion.

One sentence in Somerville's letter had, however, elicited a hope that the marriage would be found illegal; and pointed to a prospect of indulging his regrets throughout his future existence in an uninterrupted solitude.

Decision was now indispensable; all further imposition must be resisted; and his first step was to write a letter explanatory of what had happened to the bank, containing the half note; with instruction that if any person presented the other, he might be detained.

He was upon the point of enclosing both these letters to his father, when an express arrived from the Park, making him acquainted with every particular of the Somervilles' character and flight.

Theodore was calm but decided; he arose and returned to the boudoir, where he found Belinda awaiting him.

She arose from the sofa as he entered, and coming forward to meet him, playfully touched his cheek with the small wrought gold head of her riding-whip.

"You fugitive," said she, "why, I've been waiting for you at least ten minutes. I was just coming to scold you for your neglect, I assure you. Have I not been quick?"

"We will not talk of fugitives, madam," replied Theodore, with a repulsive glance that seemed to penetrate her conscious bosom, and almost threw her long accustomed effrontery off its wonted equilibrium, "until I have read you this communication from my father, and have heard your reply!"

Belinda threw herself again on the sofa, and as Theodore proceeded in Sir Edward's narrative, expressions of astonishment and terror, tears, sobs, and lamentations, alternately interrupted him.

When he had concluded, she arose, threw herself at his feet, and seizing his hand, said—

"Is it possible my Theodore can suppose me possessed of the slightest knowledge of these events? Oh! believe me, I am innocent! Papa has had a propensity to play from his youth; he may have had losses, sufficient to involve his own circumstances in ruin; but I know him too well to imagine he will have wasted the fortune left me by my dear grandpapa."

" And you know nothing of all this ?"

" Absolutely nothing !" and she raised her fine eyes beseechingly to his counte nance.

Theodore looked at her with a degree of disgust increased by her beauty, which only rendered her a more dangerous and destructive medium of mischief, and diisengaging his hand from her grasp—

" Stop, madam !" he exclaimed, "and before you give farther demonstrations of your duplicity, read your condemnation in your own hand. Behold your father's letter, your own to your sister, and judge if, after having become acquainted with these treacheries and deceptions, there can ever be any farther communion between us ?'"

A violent fit of hysterics followed this impressive appeal. Theodore left her to the care of Macdonald, and retired to his study ; when there, he wrote to his father, enclosing the letters that had so singularly come into his possession, and was just going to send them off when Ralph entered.

A tear sparkled in his eye, when he saw the change in his beloved master's appearance, and he listened with intense interest to the recital Theodore thought due to his long-tried fidelity.

" Well, then," said Ralph, " that accounts for my meeting Macdonald and her mistress (for, begging your honour's pardon, I could never call her mine) at the corner of the square, stepping into a hackney-coach, and attended by two men with trunks, portmanteaus, and travelling bags."

Theodore rang the bell, sent off his letters by the servant, who had brought his father's, and inquired of Mrs. Hilton, the housekeeper, if Mrs. Villars was at home ?

The good woman appeared relieved by this question—of a weight which evidently pressed on her mind, although respect had kept her silent.

" Mrs. Villars, sir ! do you not know, then, she is gone ?"

" No, Hilton, I did not know she was absolutely gone ; although, after what has transpired, it does not surprise me."

" Well, sir, I'm glad poor Ralph has come back, and I hope he'll stay, for your pale countenance has long made my heart ache. I told Joseph how ill you have been, and I dare say Sir Edward will be here in a few days."

She then retired, and Theodore wrote to Clifford his reasons for detaining Ralph at a moment which rendered him so necessary to his comfort.

Mrs. Hilton had long felt disgusted at the innovation of all the comfort and order too long prevalent at the family mansion ; she had shrunk from the insolence of Macdonald, and was indignant at poor Ralph's dismissal, who was equally a favourite with herself and with the housekeeper at the Park ; but above all, she was afflicted at the neglect of her young master in illness, by turning night into day at so serious a period.

The messenger from the Park had whispered to her privately some of the reports regarding the Somervilles as well as their flight ; and this induced her, when Macdonald came with a message from her lady for several articles of plate, to mislay the key of the chest ; so that when she took a round through the apartments, chiefly occupied by the lady and her woman, she found some silver candlesticks, spoons, forks, and the coffee-urn used at breakfast, were the only articles at present missing ; but Mrs. Villars' wardrobe and jewels had been rapidly and carefully packed, and not a vestige of either remained.

CHAPTER XXX.

For love's an essence of the soul,
That shrinks not with this chain of clay;
But lives beyond the stern control
Of withering time and pale decay.

                                        MOORE.

THE first moment of calm consideration which St. Clair's unfortunate illness left his daughter, was devoted to urging Lucy's parents to go instantly and fetch her away from a scene which could promise her nothing but destruction. But the kind intention was unavailing, for when they reached Grenville's villa, accompanied by the good Ashton, they found the house shut up, and every individual had flown.

This formed an additional source of regret to the gentle-hearted girl and her benevolent parents; for, deeply as she had outraged their goodness, they had sheltered her from infancy, and would have sacrificed much to reclaim her.

Although St. Clair's mind rose with an instinctive elasticity against the pressure of pain or misfortune, he was no longer possessed of the constitution which had hitherto added to its energetic tone. He was no longer capable of taking an active part in the superintendence of those arrangements, where a master's eye is indispensable.

The expenses of an illness that kept him confined to his chamber until the end of November, the loss of some of his finest cattle, and other untoward circumstances, tended to give him a disgust for a scene, now only replete with melancholy recollections of former happiness, and, if not prosperity, at least of that competence, which left little to well-regulated minds to desire. But the chief motive which decided him to new arrangements, was his Adela; for time, instead of lessening the impression which Theodore had made on her heart, seemed to add to its force; and although she sought by every effort of a mind, naturally energetic, to combat its power, although she tried to vanquish the unwelcome intruder, he made the inmost recesses of her heart his citadel, and there resisted all opposition.

Mr. and Mrs. Arnold sincerely sympathised in the anguish this relapse occasioned; and Maria and Louisa urged her to spend a few weeks with them, where every hour should furnish some pleasing variety. But Adela never failed to assign a sufficient reason for declining their affectionate invitations. Her " dear papa was yet unrestored health;" her beloved mamma's anxiety on his account would, she feared, sacrifice hers also, if she were absent. She must remain to read to them, and, with her guitar, to pass away their hours of solitude, to mingle her voice with its tones in the melodies they loved. And oh, how deeply did its now plaintive expression reach the soul, with the foreboding, that the fragile, the lovely form they gazed on, would, ere long, cease to enchain a spirit too ethereal, too pure for this sublunary sphere.

But Adela was unconscious that another fascination mingled with filial tenderness. The scenes, rendered sacred by Theodore's partial praise; the tree whereon he had engraved her name; the arbour where they had listened to the nightingale's lay of love; all possessed an enchantment that threw its chains over a heart, which not even his inconstancy had power to alienate. Those scenes were again changed by winter's desolating hand—the tree, leafless, the arbour, deprived of its flowers and its foliage. Even the nightingale had sought a sunnier clime, yet her footstep pressed those paths; she still wept amidst those recesses.

Akenside could fully appreciate such feelings. His description of the irresistible magic of hopeless grief, in his "Pleasures of Imagination," evinces it, when he says :—

> ' Ask the faithful youth
> Why the cold urn of her whom long he loved,
> So often fills his arms? so often draws
> His lonely footsteps, at the silent hour,
> To pay the mournful tribute of his tears?
> Oh! he will tell thee that the wealth of worlds
> Should ne'er seduce his bosom to forego
> That sacred hour, when, stealing from the noise
> Of care and envy, sweet remembrance smoothes
> With virtue's kindest looks, his aching heart,
> And turns his tears to rapture."

The notice of the marriage, which had so unfortunately met her eye, had inflicted a severe shock, which she had summoned all her fortitude to resist; but the languor that followed the exertion left her in a state of renewed weakness and of oppressive melancholy.

St. Clair conversed with his friend on the subject of his purposed removal; and although he regretted the adverse circumstances which occasioned it, he not only saw the prudence of the arrangement, but its necessity. He observed the hourly change in Adela's manner and person. The latter wore evident traces of consumption, and would not every varying season, amidst that sweet retreat, renew recollections too fatal to be encouraged? Mrs. St. Clair, too, seemed decided; and Arnold turned his attention to the method he conceived best calculated to render the removal convenient.

In the first instance, Miss St. Clair must not be aware of the purposed change of residence, until the thing was effected. She must, therefore, return with Mrs. Arnold and Maria. In the next, he possessed a commodious house very near his own, and this he insisted his friend should occupy.

St. Clair felt the value of the heart in these considerate proffers. The first he gratefully accepted; the last, with equal acknowledgments, he declined. This, under any circumstances, St. Clair's native independence must have shrunk from, because Mr. Arnold would not hear of receiving anything in the shape of rent. He urged, that emoluments was not a matter of the smallest importance to him, and that the gratification of seeing their families thus united would leave the obligation altogether on his side.

But St. Clair had yet another motive, not less powerful. Circumstances rendered a retired cottage the only abode he could now aspire to; and highly as he valued his friend's warm attachment to the welfare and interest of his family, his pride recoiled from his witnessing the smallest deduction of the little luxuries and comforts they had hitherto enjoyed.

Adela had yielded to the united persuasions of her parents and friends. She had returned with Mrs. Arnold and Maria; and Mr. A—— remained some days to render himself useful in accompanying St. Clair in his search for a residence. But so fondly did he linger on the hope of yet securing him as a neighbour, that he threw all sorts of objections in the way. "These rooms were not sufficiently lofty to admit of free respiration; those much too small; the entrance to the other too contracted, and every way inconvenient." Nothing pleased his fastidious anxiety, and he at last returned, exulting in the idea that, although he had not turned St. Clair from the project of becoming a hermit, he had gained time. And as he would receive no denial of spending their Christmas with him, and of passing with them the last week of Adela's stay, he left the rest to the all-powerful persuasion of Mrs. Arnold and the girls.

On the day following the departure of Mr. Arnold, St. Clair set earnestly about the search for a residence, and discovered a pretty, retired abode, in a hamlet about twenty miles distant. It was situated in the midst of a garden, and consisted of a parlour, a kitchen, and two chambers, newly painted and papered, at a low rent, and, although humble, every way convenient.

Mrs. St. Clair approved her husband's choice, and she looked joyfully to this entire change of scene as the only hope of restoring his peace in their child's health and tranquillity.

Necessity, as we have said, rendered a retirement yet deeper than their former elegant seclusion yielded them important. The sale of the farm, and its surrounding lands, stock, implements, and superfluous furniture, had left an amount so much less than they calculated on, that the strictest economy would be indispensable.

And how could such hearts endure to live amongst those they could no longer benefit by employment, nor in any way aid in their necessities.

A week sufficed for their removal. Scarcely was there an individual who did not receive some little token of remembrance; but particularly the Ashtons, and from all those faithful and really-attached beings they concealed the precise day of their departure, to avoid a parting which would be too painful. And so affectingly did these good creatures evince their grief, when the moment arrived, that the St. Clairs felt thankful their friend's prudence and foresight had spared their Adela's feelings on the occasion.

A few hours after their arrival at their new residence, with the assistance of a neighbouring cottager, they placed everything in its proper order. The white walls of the kitchen were adorned with utensils that equalled silver in brightness; the blue and white china arranged in regular gradation on the shelves. The holly branch peeped forth its crimson berries from amidst the dark green glossy foliage that interspersed the various articles of utility that decorated the mantel-piece. The white curtain shaded the casement, and the fire shed its comfortable rays over the cherry-coloured floor. The parlour, opening from it, was covered with the long-accustomed carpet, which appeared scarcely the worse for wear; the same hearth-rug, sofa, tables, chairs, pictures, books, vases; whilst the blue merino drapery shaded the casement, and added warmth and comfort to the whole.

Their own bed-room was got ready for the occupation of the night, and the morrow devoted to the placing everything in the most fastidious order for the return of their beloved girl.

Her little cabinet, her wardrobe, her painted blind and curtains, drawing-case, writing-desk, and guitar were all neatly arranged, and the room carefully aired for her reception.

In three days Mr. and Mrs. St. Clair were as perfectly settled in their new abode as though they had resided there for years; and, having locked up their cottage, which was well secured on all sides from within, they placed it under the guardianship of their landlord, whose dwelling was situated at the bottom of their garden; and, in conformity with their engagement, they proceeded to the habitation of the friendly Arnold.

CHAPTER XXXI.

But thy credulity has ruin'd all;
Thy rash, thy wild—I know not what to name it—
Oh! it has proved the giddy hopes of man
To be delusion all, and sickening folly.   TANCRED AND SIGISMUNDA.

WE left young Villars deserted by his fair bride, and attended solely by Mrs. Hilton and Ralph, who seemed to vie with each other in solicitude for his comfort, from an affection which had increased from his infancy.

His eye still retained its languor, and a fever yet hovered over his nerves; but the perfect stillness observed by every individual in that spacious mansion, contrasted with the bustle and confusion prevalent during the last few months, soothed and relieved him.

For several days succeeding Mrs. Villars' departure, numerous accounts were presented for jewellery and other valuables, the amount of which would have astonished him, considering the sums she received from himself and his father for the purchase of such articles, had not the letters, so opportunely fallen into his hands, made the matter evident.

Nearly a week had elapsed, and Joseph again arrived from the Park, with a few lines from Sir Edward, written in a dull, unsteady hand, and enclosing a remittance, which he said, "he could not help fearing he would require."

He entreated he would hasten to him; for an awful impression hung over his mind that they should never meet again.

This communication was accompanied by a letter from the housekeeper, informing him that Sir Edward had been, for some days, confined to his chamber with an attack of fever; that he frequently addressed his son as though present, and evinced the most impatient desire for his arrival, when not under that illusion. She expressed the most affectionate anxieties for her young master's health, and presented her grateful prayers for the restoration of that peace which, from his earliest hour, had formed her tenderest care.

No. 19.

Theodore did not pause in the indulgence of unavailing repinings over these letters, although his heart was keenly alive to the mental and bodily sufferings of a parent, to whom his happiness and convenience had recently seemed a matter of little importance.

He sent Ralph to arrange every account transmitted to him, for Theodore would not permit any one to suffer a loss by debts, contracted in *his name*. He set off in the evening, and only waiting to change horses on the road, arrived at the Park at the close of the following day.

It was sunset when they entered the gates. He alighted, and took his way through a shrubbery that led to the principal entrance. The evening breezes sighed amongst the branches of those trees, beneath which he had so often sported in childhood; and the spirit of melancholy seemed wailing amidst their deep recesses.

On reaching the mansion, so impressive a degree of silence reigned around, that his footsteps echoed along the hall as though the home of his infancy had been deserted, and death held his court amidst its ancient and lofty chambers. A thousand superstitious apprehensions crept over his mind, when Ralph returned, accompanied by Mrs. Stafford, who, with a thousand expressions of joy at his appearance, begged him to be of good cheer; for, although her master was certainly in danger, if any thing could occasion a favourable change, it would be his son's society.

With a light footstep young Villars followed to the chamber, on which the last rays of the setting sun shed their golden lustre. He approached the bed, withdrew the curtains, and, bending over his sleeping parent, pressed his parched and burning hand to his lips and bosom. A tear fell on that pale and emaciated cheek, and a prayer of filial piety ascended to the throne of mercy for his restoration to health and peace."

" He still sleeps," whispered Mrs. Stafford; and Theodore awaited the conclusion of his slumber with anxious expectation, nor would he quit his pillow, either to change his dress, or take refreshment.

About midnight he awoke, and Theodore heard him exclaim,—

" My son will never arrive! but I cannot wonder; have I not sacrificed all his hopes of earthly felicity? Has he not been cut down like a flower? Does he not wither like the grass of the field?"

" No! my beloved—my honoured father!" said Theodore, sinking on one knee by the bed-side, " your son is with you! No other eye shall, in future, watch over you,—no other hand bring you refreshment. Forget the past! Nothing shall again divide us, and, for my sake, endeavour to recover!"

" Alas! my boy," said Sir Edward, " it is all too late!" and looking anxiously round he continued in a whisper, "the wealth which was the point of attraction, has eluded my grasp! Through life all was sacrificed to it;—a thousand mean and dishonorable actions now arise in terrible array against me!—even thy peace was not held sacred;—and see! the demon avarice mocks me!—All has fled, and shame and disgrace are mingled with our name!"

Here he began to wander. No one but Ralph and Mrs. Stafford were admitted to the chamber, and the physician having ordered a composing draught, he sunk into a heavy slumber.

Theodore kept his station by the bed-side, and morning peeped through the gothic windows, without sleep having once visited his eyelids.

The housekeeper ordered breakfast in the drawing-room, as nearest Sir Edward's chamber, and insisted on her young master taking some repose. To this he objected, but at length, finding his father more tranquil, he consented to lie down on the sofa for a short space of time, leaving Ralph as his attendant.

Sir Edward slept heavily. The certainty of his son's presence had overspread his mind with a calm to which it had long been a stranger; and Theodore sunk into a dreary repose, which transported him to the Cottage in the Valley. Again in fancy, he guided his steed through the winding path, dismounted, and leaving him to graze on the little hill, leaped the hedge. Again he was in the garden, in the flower-embroidered arbour. He called Adela. She replied not. He flew to the cottage; but what a scene met his view! Mutes stood at the gate: young girls, in white, passed before it scattering flowers—St. Clair and his heart-broken wife were the mourners!

Suddenly an aged man started from the crowd, and sternly advancing towards him, "Is it not enough, traitor," said he, "that thou hast destroyed her? Comest thou hither to add poignancy to the desolation of such an hour?"

He heard no more; a pang worse than that of death assailed his heart; the vision fled; he awoke; and covering his face with his handkerchief, wept in the agony of his soul.

When Theodore had sufficiently calmed his perturbation, he returned to his father's chamber where he found Mrs. Stafford and Ralph, who told him Sir Edward had awoke to take some refreshment, and had sunk again into the same deep sleep. He dismissed them from their charge, and in the solitude of that lonely apartment ruminated on the sombre imagery of his vivid dream.

The most harrowing presages arose out of these wanderings of a distempered imagination.

"And is it thus," said he, "the year has revolved? my fondest hopes blighted, my fairy prospects of bliss converted into the reality of woe. Betrayed by love—sacrificed by ambition; and to complete the desolate picture, am I to be the last of my race—a solitary mourner over a parent's tomb?"

And these fears were not unfounded, for although Sir Edward's tranquillity, his willingness to take nourishment, which he had previously rejected, and his disturbed slumbers, during the first days of his son's return, had awakened hope, they were succeeded by a most alarming relapse.

Sudden fits of violent passion, restlessness, and remorse destroyed the effects of his son's care, his tender consolations, and philosophical reasoning.

"When death took my beloved mother from us, my dear sir," said Theodore, "we were all to each other. Let us forget that any individuals have presented themselves to alienate those feelings. Many happy hours may yet be in the vista of future years.

Affecting, and hapless reasoner—forget! And did thy accents urge on another that which thy heart found so impracticable? But, if thy wonted sincerity abandoned thee at such a moment, the pure motive of filial love, by which it was prompted, will plead its cause with the severest censor."

"Oh! that I could recal the past," said the repentant, "oh! that I had permitted thy heart to make its own election! Such a mind could only have been guided by virtue, honour, and reason. Oh! that I had permitted myself to be persuaded; for I have wrecked your peace! I have divided you both for ever!"

But a sad, heart-rending disclosure awaited that generous—that devoted heart;—for, mildly grasping his hand, Sir Edward related the receipt of the anonymous letter, secretly, from Grenville,—the return he had secretly made of the little gifts of Adela's regard,—his own insulting communication to St. Clair,—his barbarous conversion of his son's name to his own sordid purpose—the changing of the £5,000 note for £50—St. Clair's indignant and spirited reply, with the return of the money, tablets, miniature, and everything which might recal a being they now conceived too contemptible to merit a place in their memory.

Theodore lost, for the moment, all command over his feelings. He wept in the fulness of his heart; his emotions penetrated Sir Edward's soul; but he had imposed upon himself this bitter task, as a just retribution, and the cold dew hung on his forehead when he concluded his tale of agony.

"And now, my son," said he, "I shall die content; my only wish is, that my days may be prolonged to see this inauspicious union rent asunder, and the tomb may cover the remains of thy unhappy father!"

These words acted like electricity on Theodore. He felt how deeply humiliating such a moment must be to a parental heart; and, with an effort of honourable self-control, he shook off all traces of the despondency that but too powerfully pervaded his soul. And, taking his father's hand, he entreated him to be calm, and be assured he should never revert to events now best consigned to oblivion.

" Only think of renovating your health and spirits, my dear sir !" said he, " if my happiness is dear to you, reflect that my father's recovery will be the sole medium of of its restoration."

Sir Edward grasped his hand in silence, but his wandering eye, disturbed slumber, and increasing restlessness, evinced the unsettled state of his mind. He was feverishly anxious to see his solicitor upon the subject of the divorce, but Theodore would not permit such matters to be discussed during so eventful a period.

One week followed another, without producing any improvement. The fever had left him ; but a gradual decay seemed consuming the principles of life.

Meanwhile Theodore was unwaried in his care. If Sir Edward spoke, no voice but his son's responded. If his parched and pallid lip thirsted for the refreshing draught, it was the hand of his son that brought it ; he smoothed his pillow, watched his sleeping, and cheered his waking hour !

The excellent hearted Mrs. Stafford found it necessary to take care both about his sleep, and his food, for neither occurred to him unless positively insisted on by her maternal care, and when he did steal a moment's absence it was devoted to a solitary ramble amidst scenes, desolate as his own prospects ; for the commencement of December had not left a leaf on the dry and withered branches ; and the wind whistled hoarsely through the desolate shades of his native woodlands.

And all seemed a desert, like that in his breast ! he scarcely dared turn a thought to Adela ! he once conceived, that could he believe her yet innocent, yet faithful, although separated from her by adverse fate, some consolatory reflection would have mingled its balm with every tear.

His father's confession had greatly exculpated her ; she might have just reasons for her apparent insensibility ; might not the author of that mysterious letter, which traduced her father so basely, have also fabricated some demoniac tale to alienate the faith she had so fondly plighted ? But why reflect ? He was yet the husband, and she perhaps the bride of another ! for with what meanness, what baseness, what *ingratitude*, what a *total want of soul* must his memory be blended, in those hearts, whose esteem he would not have exchanged for an empire.

Christmas had passed without a sign of the usual festivities of the season being apparent at that ancient mansion. For although the kindest inquiries had been made, cards left, and visits of condolence paid, since Theodore's return, he had altogether secluded himself to that wing of the edifice, in which his father's apartments were situated.

One cold and tempestuous evening, about the middle of January, the lawn covered with snow, and the servants crowded round the blazing fire in the hall, were speculating on the odd changes in the Somerville family, and the disgrace to which their master's name had been subjected by such an alliance. One observed their young master was broken-hearted for the loss of a young lady he was obliged to resign, in obedience to his father's commands ; that Sir Edward's remorse would shorten his existence.

The aged nurse declared she had heard the same wailing in the principal corridor, that frightened every one on the night preceding her dear lady's death ; that she heard the door leading to the mausoleum bang to, without hands, as she passed through the grove at the end of the shrubbery, so that she was *certain* they would not be long without a death in the family.

" Our master has seen many prosperous and varied days, and takes things more to heart than when he was younger, or he would have sunk in despair when my lady died, she was so amiable."

The wind whistled through the ancient avenues, with a violence capable of rooting the trees from the earth, and the porter hesitated whether he should proceed to the gate, the sound of whose bell was scarcely distinguishable, amidst the violence of the blast ; a second and more violent peal induced him to venture towards it, when an old sailor presented himself, who had brought a letter to Sir Edward.

We will leave him by the fireside to which he was hospitably invited, and accompany Joseph to the dressing-room door, where he delivered the letter carefully into the hands of Ralph.

Sir Edward, that evening had a fancy to sit up an hour, by the dressing-room fire, and thither his son and Ralph had carefully conveyed him; he seemed enlivened and refreshed by the change; Theodore's countenance was illumed with a melancholy pleasure as he arranged the pillows in his large easy chair, and folded his flannel gown around him, when Ralph delivered the letter to his master.

"It is doubtless a petition," whispered Theodore, "let the poor fellow go into the servants' hall, and have whatever refreshment he chooses."

"What is that?" said Sir Edward, with a vigilance his son would fain have eluded, until he could investigate its contents; for he feared everything that might produce excitement, "a letter!—read it out."

Whatever it might contain, the risk could not be greater than the evil which would ensue, from an opposition to his wishes. Mrs. Stafford and Ralph retired, and Theodore, in a voice which required all his energy to command as he proceeded, read as follows:—

"HONORED SIR,—I take the liberty of writing, to inform you of the awful end of my poor mistress, for I suppose you have not yet heard it.

"I went with her to Dover, and we got there just in time to embark with her family in the Heron packet, for Ostend. But the sinful are not always fortunate, for the vessel was wrecked on entering that port, and every soul, but a sailor and myself, perished. He returns to England, and promises to deliver this at the Park.

"I think it my duty to say, sir, that my mistress ordered me to pack up everything valuable I could get together, but I'm sorry now I had anything to do with it, for as everything is lost, nobody is any the better for it.

"I knew nothing of the danger, till I felt the dreadful shock of the vessel against that pier, and in less than five minutes all were drowned; for, although hundreds of people were in view, they saw the vessel go to pieces, without giving the least assistance.

"They tell me that the bodies of my poor lady and her family floated out with the tide, so that they were deprived of Christian burial, and I wish I'd never seen them. The little money I had about me will be gone before I can get back to Scotland, for I've been confined to my bed, upwards of two months, with hardly any hope of recovery.

"I remain, sir, your honour's humble servant,

"To Sir Edward Villars."   "HELEN MACDONALD."

During the reading of this letter, the countenance of Sir Edward underwent a thousand different expressions; he struck his forehead, his frame shook convulsively; a maniac laugh burst from his lips.

"Thank Heaven, they're gone!—thank Heaven, they're gone!" he exclaimed, "you are now as much divorced, as though you'd never been united."

Theodore shuddered—he tried to calm his father's emotions; emotions too strong for the shattered state of a frame dilapidated by the sickness of blighted and disappointed avarice.

Theodore turned aside to conceal the horror with which the sudden and wretched fate of one, who, however hateful her vices, had once shared some portion of his esteem; of one, to whom his vows had been plighted, although his heart could not respond to them.

Deeply did he deplore the turpitude of the mind which had inhabited so fair a form, and whilst he lamented an event which had summoned her with the yet more guilty authors of her existence to their final account, at a moment when it was perhaps most requisite to make their peace with Heaven, he inwardly breathed a supplication for them to the throne of mercy.

But his father's sudden exultation had overpowered his strength; it was requisite to remove him to his chamber, and Ralph was summoned to assist his master ; Sir Edward having since his illness preferred his attendance to his own valet's.

When Theodore saw his father in bed, and Mrs. Stafford watching beside him, he proceeded to the drawing-room, sent for the sailor, and questioned him upon the melancholy occurrence ; his replies recalled to his mind the account he had read of the loss of the Heron, in the heavy storms that had occasioned so many wrecks on the coast. He gave him ten pounds,—recommended him to the hospitality of Joseph, and urged him, as the night continued tempestuous, not to leave the Park until the morning.

The poor fellow received this unexpected bounty with gratitude ; he went down to enjoy the cheering fire in the hall, whilst Theodore returned to his father's chamber, and found him again confused and delirious.

Dr. Selwyn remained till the morning, when slumber steeped his senses in forgetfulness, and left a pause to Theodore for reflections that had thronged on his heart in hurried and painful succession.

About mid-day Sir Edward's eyes unclosed ; he appeared tranquillised and happy, and his son seized this moment to awaken his mind to those benign sentiments best suited to so awful a moment.

Theodore became eloquent as he proceeded ; the warmth of filial piety gave energy to his language ; it beamed in every feature !

Sir Edward was soothed into deep attention, his passions were subdued, and his soul elevated with the hope of peace, when, taking his son's hand,—

"Do you think," said he, "I shall ever recover? "

"I hope there is not a doubt of it, my beloved parent," replied Theodore. "I trust we shall together enjoy many a ramble amidst the gardens and woodlands, in which you have so many years delighted, long before summer puts on her gay attire, and the groves spread their luxuriant branches to receive us."

"Never more!—never more! But, hear me, Theodore,—will you promise me to make St. Clair's daughter your wife? Will you promise when the tomb has closed over me to do this act of justice to my memory? Tell her, that although avarice seduced me into a crime, which the justice of the Creator did not fail to punish, the completion of my wishes would, I feel, never have brought me felicity. Tell her I have not ceased to suffer the deepest remorse, from the moment of your ill-assorted union; for the silence of night has whispered her name to my heart ; tell her, that had life been spared me, her happiness, combined with thine, would have formed my greatest care ! and that the blessing of thy departed parent will hover over the altar where your vows are plighted !"

Here his strength failed him ; Theodore's heart throbbed tumultuously with varied emotions. What would he not have given that his father had entertained these sentiments a few months back ! Alas ! the cup of Tantalus could not have been more tormenting to his thirsty lip ! But he forbore to say the restitution came too late, and he turned from the impression that incessantly haunted him ; had he seen Adela's nuptials with Grenville performed, he could not have felt more certain that she was now irrevocably his, and lost to him for ever !

This was a powerful effort of self-command, but it was triumphant, and the heroic youth, with a melancholy smile, expressed his sense of the affectionate feelings that then sincerely actuated his father's intentions. With a heart interiorly withered by despair, he appeared to coincide in his every wish. He listened to every plan formed, with almost the earnestness of childhood, for their future felicity ; and he felt his anguish relieved when his father's hand relaxed, and he fell into a repose,

"Calm as the infant's on its mother's breast."

CHAPTER XXXII.

There is a smile, a woe-fraught smile,
  Which more than sighs or tears can speak,
It says "no more can hope beguile
  The heart despair has doomed to break."

The world may pass unheeded by,
  Nor heed the pang that lurks beneath.
Thus turf and flow'rets please the eye,
  Yet hide the dark abode of death!

The St. Clairs arrived at Mr. Arnold's on Christmas eve. Their approach had been anxiously anticipated on the two days previous, and the welcome they received was replete with the undisguised warmth of sincere friendship.

St. Clair called his friend aside, and mentioned the arrangements he had made, which the latter lamented deeply, because his wife and the girls were regularly prepared for the attack, and he had felt certain they would come off victorious. But since you will not consent to become as near neighbours as I trust we are warm friends,—since you will not permit us to serve you in our way, you must command us in your own.

St. Clair's expressive countenance spoke, more than words, his sense of the excellent Arnold's kind-heartedness. Adela flew into the arms of her parents; but the crimson glow that had tinged her cheek from joy at their arrival faded in the marble paleness it had worn since her illness. She was, however, uniformly cheerful, and sang, conversed, and joined in every amusement, in gratitude to those kind friends, whose only care seemed centered in the consigning to oblivion her past sorrows.

A social family dinner gave place to a little entertainment, which a party of their young friend were invited to partake in. The carpets had been taken up in the drawing-rooms, the floor chalked in various flowers and devices, and the folding doors thrown open for dancing. Both families sat conversing by the fire-side, whilst the girls retired to dress for the evening.

Adela varied the arrangement of her hair, from the style so peculiarly her own, by a few graceful ringlets on each side, that fell carelessly from the knot above, confined by a comb set in cameos. A rich clasp of the same secured the braid across her forehead. Her ear-rings and bracelets were similar, for Mrs. St. Clair had, on this occasion, presented her with a small casket of the only little valuables the wreck of their prosperity had left her.

A Swiss dress, of puce-coloured Gros de Naples, was adapted to display her small waist, the exquisitely turned ankle and pretty foot, which the white satin shoe and silk stocking could not adorn; and when she had suspended her father's miniature to her gold chain, and had drawn on her white kid gloves, her dress was complete; and formed a characteristic contrast with the blue silk dresses, and flower-woven tresses of the lively Maria and the gentle Louisa.

At eight o'clock the greater portion of the company had assembled, and after partaking of tea, coffee, and other refreshments, dancing commenced, and the true spirit of festivity animated every countenance.

Adela commanded her feelings. She would have given much to have been permitted to seclude herself in the dressing-room, with a book, until the party had dispersed; but she was conscious the anxious eye of the parents she idolised —the friends she loved—was upon her; and no foot tripped so lightly—no form glided so gracefully amidst the young and happy votaries of pleasure.

The question of "Who is that lovely girl?"—"Who are the St. Clairs?" was frequently addressed to their hospitable host and his family during the evening.

"Relations of my departed friend."

"At the Hall?—I declare I thought as much," said an old gentleman, "why, there's the family features exactly! How is it they suffer such a fine mansion as the Hall to be shut up?"

Here Mr. Arnold took the inquirer by the arm, led him into the adjoining apartment, and a long conversation ensued, which only ended by a third inquirer approaching with a similar question.

The first dance had concluded. For the second Adela's hand was engaged to a young gentleman, who, with his sister, were guests to a neighbour, and to whom the invitation had beeen extended. They were introduced as Mr. and Miss Clifford.

Adela had never heard of Theodore's friend. But the pensive cast of his interesting sun-burnt countenance bespoke a mind, with which, in sorrow, her own seemed to claim kindred; and the few minutes she was permitted to converse with his sister, gave an inclination to both to prolong the acquaintance.

But as St. Clair had hinted to his friend his wish to be as little known as possible, Adela was conscious that their present circumstances would place a bar to their extending their friendly connections; and this threw an air of mystery over expressions which might, in happier hours, have ripened into friendship.

Clifford had heard of Adela, he had heard of St. Clair and his admirable wife, he had heard of the Valley.

It so happened, amidst the throng of guests that crowded the hospitable mansion, Mr. and Mrs. St. Clair were not particularised to him by name; but when he entreated Mrs. Arnold to introduce him to their daughter, he started at the name of St. Clair.

Why did he start? Were there no other St. Clairs in the world? Adela St. Clair was now, by his friend's heart-rending account, the wife of Captain Grenville; yet such was the form, the face, he had described.

What finished elegance of manners!—what an eye beamed beneath the dark eye-lash that seemed to veil its lustre!

At the conclusion of the dance, he led her to a seat, and went to fetch her a glass of negus. He had presented it to her, when his sister approached, and uttered a few words in an under tone. He answered in the negative, and Adela caught one word only of her reply. But that word changed the hue exercise had given her cheek into a death-like paleness. The glass fell from her hand: and, but for the supporting arm of Clifford, she would have sunk to the ground.

Miss Clifford was alarmed; she ran to call Maria and Louisa, who came to her assistance. Adela tried to rouse herself, and, anxious to escape from public observation, she retired to her dressing-room with her young friends and Miss Clifford, where, having entreated them not to let her parents know of her sudden indisposition, she gradually recovered, and, in about half an hour, returned to the company.

"But you shall not dance again to-night. I wish I had not permitted you to do so at all," said Maria.

"It was extremely imprudent, after Miss St. Clair's illness," said Louisa.

Clifford had approached, anxious, yet happy, to hear of her recovery; for her sudden fainting had alarmed him.

That it occurred at the moment when his sister had mentioned his friend's name seemed to realize the suspicions that had darted across his mind.

But it appeared she had just recovered from a long illness. The exertion of the evening might well, then, have occasioned a relapse: and although, beautiful as Theodore had described his village maid, there was a something so soul-subduing, so intellectual, so like his lost Zephyrina, in his fair partner, he could not believe her the inconstant, the thoughtless, the versatile Adela!—the heartless wanderer who could abandon his valued friend for such a being as the dissipated Grenville! —Impossible!

About one o'clock the dancing ceased, and the company assembled in the large parlour to supper, where all the delicacies of the season were profusely spread. The ladies took their seats, and, as the company was numerous, the gentlemen waited on them, and partook of their kind entertainer's hospitality as they could.

Never was a party more social—never did mirth and hilarity more inspire every individual in sympathy with the welcome they received.

Mr. and Mrs. St. Clair had only seen their daughter once or twice during the night; and then she had glided to them to inquire respecting their health, and received their caution not to fatigue herself.

But Clifford had scarcely lost sight of her a moment; his eye had followed her pale, interesting countenance. In conducting her to the table, he had placed her between his sister and Louisa Arnold. He devoted all his attention to the lovely trio until they adjourned to the music saloon; and the gentleman who had accompanied them having taken his sister's hand, he gave an arm to each of the other ladies of their own little party.

They found Miss Arnold at the harp; and Adela, at the repeated entreaties of her friends, sang the following air :—

No. 20.

Sweet rose! when the first radiant blush of Aurora
Thy bosom in fragrance and beauty hath drest,
In every fond zephyr thou find'st an adorer,
To sport 'midst thy foliage, and die on thy breast.
In the balm of thy youth's early freshness I've found thee,
The butterfly woos, and the wild bee hums round thee;
The queen of the valley all nature has crown'd thee!
Praised, courted, and flattered, adored, and carest.

Ah rose! lovely rose! when calm evening shall banish
Those charms, that to grace and endear thee combine;
Alike shall the bee and the butterfly vanish,
And Zephyr his fond adulation resign.
Nor the dew of the morn, nor her smile shall restore thee,
Nor the plaint of thy nightingale, wildly sung o'er thee,
Tho' his faithful heart then alone shall deplore thee,
And live on the memory of all that was thine.

The voice ceased : but her auditors still paused in enchantment on the silvery sounds. The words were St. Clair's—the style of the music deeply plaintive, the vocalist scientific and perfect. The music of the spheres seemed to steal from the beautiful lips that unclosed to give it utterance.

Clifford was wrapped in mute delight ; such had Villars described the voice of his syren. But no! this enchantress must be his Zephyrina's sister-angel! Were she, indeed, Adela, his friend's loss must be irreparable! How deeply should he sympathise? But, alas! was not the die cast? If she were yet free, was not Villars now the husband of another? And with an exertion, to hope it could not be, and that his friend had not lost such a treasure, he awoke to the consciousness of passing events.

So deeply had Clifford remained absorbed in the above reverie—so much was his imagination engaged with his lost Zephyrina, his friend, and the Maid of the Valley, that several ladies had sung, and Louisa had taken her sister's place at the music before he awakened to a knowledge of what surrounded him.

" Oblige us, dear Adela, with papa's favourite song."

" Adela!—it was, then, the same. Alas, poor Villars!" and his generous heart ached for his friend, whilst he listened to the following air :

Vainly wouldst thou break thy chain,
Vainly flutter to be free,
Yield to doubt or jealousy;
Or wander like the changeful bee
From flower to flower 'midst Flora's blooming reign,
In vain is thy attempt—thy wish in vain!
To her, once fondly loved, thou shalt return again.

Thou canst not in oblivion shade
Those days, that ah! too swiftly flying,
Beheld us in our native glade,
Thy heart upon my faith relying.
No! memory is my friend, and she
Will not let thy heart be free!
Her living pencil forms no trace in vain,
To her, once fondly loved, thou shalt return again !

The voice of renewed applause covered the cheek of the lovely Adela with a momentary crimson. Clifford was silent ; he knew not what opinion to form of the exquisite being before him. On one point he was decided,—that Villars should never be informed of this singular rencontre, and as his sister had never heard of the St. Clairs until this night, although she had frequently seen Theodore, it was not likely to occur through her medium.

The guests departed: when the last carriage had driven from the gate, it had struck four, and the two united families encircled the fireside, previous to their retiring to repose. And an hour of real pleasure is that when friends meet unrestrictedly and hearts assimilate.

It may well be conceived that the families were not assembled very early on the following morning, and Clifford's card was amongst the first on the hall table.

Christmas-day thus passed in the old social style of conviviality; and music and conversation whiled away the hours unconsciously.

During the week, although Mr. and Mrs. Arnold declined all invitations on account of their guests, Adela yielded to the solicitations of her young companions, and accompanied them to two balls given in the neighbourhood; and deeply did they regret the arrival of that day, when no farther entreaties could prevail with St. Clair to delay their return to the calm seclusion of their sequestered home.

But the prospect of meeting in the summer, if it could not chase the regret of parting, yet it extended some consolation. The walk amidst Nature's calm recesses, the rural festival, the dance on the green!

"Oh, we will wish away the moments, dear Adela!" said Maria.

"And sing the song she has taught us, and remember every word she has spoken," said the weeping Louisa, "and we shall think every hour an age, until we meet again."

Adela received the almost parental embraces of the good Arnolds; she passed from the arms of one dear girl to those of the other; and when she entered the chaise, she waved her hand until their much-loved forms were no longer visible.

It was evening when they had arrived within a mile of their home, and St. Clair took this opportunity of mentioning the necessity of leaving the farm.

"When we first retired thither, my child," said he, "two hundred and fifty pounds was all the vicissitudes our fate had left us. The land I purchased for a trifle, but that amount you will of course conceive could not go far in such a speculation. For building and other expenses I was obliged to obtain a loan, which the success that attended the undertaking enabled me soon to repay. My girl is aware how the uninterrupted succession of years of competence and rural felicity has been succeeded by one of loss, disappointment, and sickness, as though fate had resolved upon overclouding the calm lustre that had promised to gild our declining day."

"Oh, say not so, my dear papa," said Adela, "your recent illness requires repose, a smaller cottage, without that extent of land, will suit our convenience infinitely better; and why should not the same felicity attend us everywhere whilst we are together?"

"And will not my child regret the scenes of her infancy?"

"Dearest papa—with you and mamma I possess the world; will not the interest excited by my earliest recollections of your tenderness be renewed wherever we may go? May not the friends, who esteem us for ourselves, extend their smiles to the cottage, as to the palace? And what other sentiment is there worth cherishing? —what other sentiment is there that does not end in sorrow and delusion? Believe me, I feel the *necessity* for leaving the Valley."

"Your father, my Adela, has anticipated all your feelings: he has spared you the parting regrets that pain without relieving those fate has doomed to sever; and we are now going to a dwelling—humbler, perhaps, but I trust not less happy, and where a much shorter distance will divide us from the hospitable friends we have just left."

St. Clair felt his mind relieved by his daughter's firmness and affection, although it was not more than might have been expected from the usual tenor of her conduct. When they alighted, he gave an arm to each of his beloved companions; and, having passed the garden, unlocked the cottage door.

The sound of the chaise had brought their landlord's servant with a light. Her mistress had ordered her to kindle a fire, and to render herself useful on Mrs. St. Clair's arrival. And Adela, whose smiles expressed her perfect satisfaction, accompanied her mother over their new abode.

At so chilly a season time was requisite to air the chambers, and they encircled the cheering fire, before which Adela's hand had spread the table with such refreshments as the cottage afforded; and the friends they had left, the events of past years, with their own little plans for the future, made them unmindful of the flight of hours, until the clock recalled to them that it was considerably past their usual time of repose.

CHAPTER XXXIII.

Yes, yes, 'tis I, 'tis I alone am false!
My hasty rage, joined to my tame submissions,
More than the most exalted filial duty
Could e'er demand, has dash'd our cup of fate
With bitterness unequall'd.   THOMSON.

THEODORE felt hope revive in his breast, whilst he watched the calm that succeeded his father's confession. He fondly trusted, that, during many years of serenity, his tender solicitude might yet cast into oblivion the many painful occurrences of the past; but the bitterest self-reprobation mingled its sting amidst his reflections; that, had he resisted so unjust a claim upon his obedience, although his father might have retained a momentary resentment, reconciliation would have followed,—Adela might have been his bride, and his father now flourishing in the sturdy winter of his age.

But a constant stupor overwhelmed the senses of Sir Edward. He awoke seldom; when he did, he appeared perfectly conscious of his son's unremitting care—a smile of perfect satisfaction illumined his altered features, and thus he remained until the end of April, when his spirit left its earthly tenement for ever.

Theodore wept over the remains of his parent. His fatal avarice—the destruction of his early hopes—the deception practised on his confiding heart—all were forgotten. The little indulgences when they were together during his infancy—the parental caresses lavished on his earlier years—his self-imposed penance, and acknowledged dereliction, alone remained on his memory. "And oh! my parent!" he exclaimed, as he wept in bitterness over his lifeless corse, "why has not this joyless heart preceded thee to the tomb of our ancestors?"

Ralph watched every change of his master's sorrowing countenance. His was the most impressive consolation:—it was not expressed in words, but silent sympathy.

Nor were the kindest attentions of the venerable Mrs. Stafford wanting. A mother could scarcely have watched over him with deeper anxiety, or have felt more sorrow, as she contemplated his soul's sadness pourtrayed in his countenance.

"I wish, sir," said Ralph, as he conversed with the old steward, "I wish you could persuade master to send for his friend Mr. Clifford. He has known sorrow himself, and would be better able to console him than any of us."

"You had better suggest the thing yourself, my good lad. Who would be so likely to be listened to by Sir Theodore as his early favourite? I should feel most happy to see his attention drawn aside from the weight that has overwhelmed him during the last few months of sickness and sorrow. Alack-a-day—that I should have lived to see Villars Park such a scene of affliction, and the young master cut down, as one may say, in the flower of his youth!"

Ralph succeeded in his entreaty, and a few lines brought the consolations of the most sympathetic friendship in Clifford's arrival, who, having assisted in performing the last melancholy obsequies, turned his attention to the recalling a naturally energetic mind back to the duties he yet owed to society.

Theodore unfolded the inmost recesses of his soul to Clifford. Who was so capable of sympathizing with his trials—of awakening hope's inspiring beam?

But would it be mercy to do so until the doubt relative to her supposed union with Grenville was perfectly elucidated? He was convinced it would not.

It was the commencement of May when Sir Theodore Villars and his friend wandered beneath the groves that surrounded the park. The branches had again put forth their emerald foliage in all the renovated beauty of that delightful month. They conversed on life's vicissitudes—on the various events that had succeeded their first introduction; and Clifford, reverting to Sir Edward's last request, urged upon the hopeless mourner the necessity of ascertaining whether Adela was yet free.

This he did from a double motive: the assurance that she was indeed irrecoverably engaged, would perhaps recal him to the necessity of making a vigorous effort to consign her memory to oblivion. If, on the contrary, the same deception had been practised on him that had roused the indignant reply of the noble-minded St. Clair, his friend might yet be happy.

An inquiry in the neighbourhood might be prudent, previous to an attempt of renewing a friendship so unfortunately checked in its meridian; and he proffered his assistance in an *eclaircissement* which had now become indispensable.

Theodore felt the sacredness of a promise to a dying parent; and, although with a heart abandoned by hope, he acceded to his friend's considerate proposal.

Clifford was to depart on the following day. His road lay within about a mile of the village; and Theodore resolved to accompany him, but not with a view of venturing to the habitation of St. Clair, where he felt conscious that nothing but resentment and contempt could await him. Clifford had been summoned home, to be present at his sister's nuptials with her cousin Edward, who had recently arrived from the Brazils. Much had he importuned his friend to accompany him home, to spend a month at his father's country seat; but he declined it. Alas! said he, my dear friend, my mourning habit is too much the picture of the desolation of the soul, to be a fit accompaniment of bridal festivity; yet think me not insensible to an event in which that fraternal heart is so deeply concerned; my prayers mingle with yours for their felicity, and at a future hour I will return your friendly, your consolatory visit.

They travelled slowly, beguiling the way with retrospections little cheering to either, and resting to take refreshment at the prettiest villages that interspersed their road. But, when they arrived within a mile of the scene of all his former bliss, Sir Theodore's spirits failed him, and he acknowledged his want of fortitude to proceed. Clifford therefore undertook the task of inquiry. "I will return to enjoy your satisfaction," said he, "if the intelligence I bring you is good; if the reverse, you will not forget, my dear Villars, that suffering is the lot of human nature. The Creator often in mercy denieth our wish.

' How distant oft the thing we dote on most,
From that for which we dote,—felicity!'

"This, although a village inn, will accommodate us for the night, as well as our servants and horses—I will return and sup with you,—after an early breakfast, bid you adieu and proceed on my journey, since I cannot prevail upon you to accompany me."

Clifford's servant remained, and Ralph, who was required as guide to the Valley, attended him.

It was sunset when they wound round the verdant hill on which stood the farm, with its vineyard, garden, and orchards; but the gate was closed, and all was silent. The order and beauty once remarkable in these pleasant grounds were no longer visible, and Ralph observed, that Miss Adela's favourite plants were absent from the paths and windows; grass and weeds now mingled and intruded themselves amongst the flowers, that but peeped forth amidst the solitary scene; the untrained vine, mingling with the ivy, tended towards the ground, and with a sigh the poor fellow could ill repress, he acknowledged his fears that they had departed.

"But let us inquire," said Clifford, and tapping at farmer Ashton's door, a stout, florid looking country girl appeared.

" Can you tell us whether Mr. St. Clair's family still reside at the farm ?"

" Oh no, sir ! they've removed, but if you'd give me the world I couldn't tell you where they're gone."

" Is your master at home ?" said Ralph, " I should think he'd be likely to know."

" No sir, master and mistress are gone into Lancashire, to see their daughter, and won't be back this fortnight, I dare say."

" Was Miss St. Clair married before they left ?"

" Married ! Oh no, sir ! everybody expected to see her buried rather ; if you knew her, your heart would have ached to see the change,—she went into a decline."

" I thought she was to have been married to a Captain Grenville."

" Oh no, sir, she never could bear the sight of him. I've heard my mistress say, he ran away with her, poor young lady ; her father and master got her safe back. But the fright and the fatigue overcame her, she got worse, and Mr. St. Clair got worse of the wound he received in saving her from the ruffians. Then they could no longer bear the sight of a place that had cost them so much sorrow ; they all went away, nobody knows where, and many an aching heart they left behind them."

Clifford shared, with the most painful sympathy, the intelligence he should have to convey. Ralph wept as he reflected how lovely a creature had been thus cropped in the spring of her beauty, and doubtless laid in the dust ; that she had been still faithful to his master and falsely accused, enhanced this feeling of pity and regret ; and he cast a glance of melancholy remembrance af the arbour, when Clifford turned his horse's head in the direction of the inn. Of Lucy he thought with resentment, certain that she must have been an accomplice in the plot against his master, and much he feared, he never would survive the intelligence it would now be impossible to conceal from him.

Theodore had awaited their arrival with a beating heart ; but he possessed too much penetration, not to read his fate in the countenances of his friend and his servant, and returning the grasp of Clifford's hand,

" I anticipate your intelligence," said he, " she is united to Grenville."

" No—she is not married, and let it console you that she never felt inclined to unite her destiny with his. But——"

" Alas ! then, how have I been deceived ! and is it too late to compensate my injustice ?"

" That, my dear Villars—that is the subject which will call for your philo-sophy ; yet I dare not conceal the melancholy truth, Miss St.Clair's mental sufferings considerably injured her heatlh. Captain Grenville, after having been repeatedly repulsed, surprised her, and forcibly carried her away. Her father was severely wounded in rescuing her from the power of the villain, and months of illness fol-lowed ; the Valley became a terible remembrancer of past bliss and present affliction. St. Clair disposed of his farm, and they left it for some far distant spot, no one knows whither."

It is impossible to describe the contending passions that shook the frame of the unfortunate youth,—remorse, regret, rage, despair !

" Oh ! that I had never crossed her path to darken her morn of bliss ! That I had shared the tomb of my lamented mother !—Or that with the earliest dawn of reason, I had abandoned the home of my ancestors, and sought a distant clime ! Yet, had I candidly applied to her father for an explanation, instead of yielding to the jealous phrenzy of the moment, I should have withstood the unnatural inno-vation of my liberty, she would have been mine, and we had all been happy. Alas ! unavailing repentance !—St. Clair, the philosopher, the patriot, the affec-tionate father ; his gentle, his enlightened companion, and the treasure of my now desolated heart—doubtless share the same tomb."

Theodore arose, in the agony of his soul he paced the room ; the tears chased each other down his cheek, and he implored death to silence the emotions of a heart, in which hope was extinguished for her, ·

Clifford forbore to offer a word of consolation in this moment of bitterness ; at a future hour he trusted the voice of reason might be listened to; he permitted him uninterruptedly to weep, and he retired to his chamber, which opened out of the same apartment, that his perturbed spirit might neither be disturbed, nor excite the notice of those who might chance to enter.

It had not occurred to Clifford, to inquire of the girl the date of their removal from the Valley; so that he conceived it most probable their rencontre must have taken place, previously to that fatal abduction, with all its melancholy consequences Of what avail would it now be to renew the agonizing recollection of all the fasci nating attractions, too evidently lost to him for ever?

In another hour Theodore joined his friend, presented his hand, entreated him to pardon the irresistible ebullition of sorrow, and assured him he would, in future, be calm, and seek in his friendship a balm for the afflictions they had both so deeply endured.

"You have often said, my dear friend," replied Clifford, "that were Miss St Clair innocent of the deception you imagined she had practised on your devoted tenderness, you would feel consoled; you are assured of her innocence, and although I cannot bid you hope, on account of the declining state in which she has been described to have been, when departing from the Valley, yet lament her not as lost. Many have been spared, over whom the angel of death appeared to hover, certain of his prey. She may yet be restored to you—the same country contains you! No edifice reared by superstition immures her in a living tomb! No fiends of selfishness and hypocrisy watch, with dragon vigilance, their slowly consuming victim! you, my friend, may yet hope—a chance may throw you together, should she still live; and then, the voice of reason, the pleading of unvaried affection, shall restore you to each other!"

Theodore became calm; the supper remained almost untouched,—the friends separated for the night, which to Theodore was sleepless; and, after breakfasting at an early hour, they bade adieu to each other, with the prospect of meeting in a few weeks at Clifford's paternal habitation, when the gay and happy bridal guests should have returned to their respective destinations.

"A good man is merciful to his beast." Clifford proceeded on his journey in a chaise, leaving his servant to return with the horses, when they had rested sufficiently; and Theodore remained until the following morning, when he retraced his melancholy way back to the Park.

CHAPTER XXXIV.

Oh, what are the miseries of the most abject poverty, in comparison with the gnawings of this man's heart?—DODSLEY.

ADELA, in the seclusion of their deep retirement, in the performance of her filial and domestic duties, in the perfect resignation of her pure soul to the will of he Creator, found that calm "which surpasseth show."

To banish the memory of one, whose idea seemed entwined with the very principles of life, was a thing impossible; but a spirit of pure and natural religion chastened her anguish and almost subdued her sorrows.

It is truly said, that occupation is the best antidote to hopeless affliction. Adela suffered not a moment to remain unemployed: and if she indulged in retrospection it was only in the solitude of those hours when sleep fled her pillow, or when she awoke from visions of beauty and bliss, to the reality of withered hope and blighted affection.

But the altered circumstances of her parents weighed heavily upon her; the productions of her pencil were not so beneficial in that retreat, as they had been in their former vicinity to a town of importance.

Heaven had granted her prayer, in the restoration of her father's health, her dear mother's also had infinitely improved. Why then should she remain an incumbrance when her exertions might be rendered available in bettering their condition? The services of the little girl who came an hour or two daily, were all her mother would require. Yes; she might furnish them with many of their former comforts, and evince to their anxious hearts her capability of obtaining an independence, although it might be a humble one. With this impression she wrote to her young friends entreating them to assist in obtaining a situation as governess in a family, or as companion to any lady who might consider the few accomplishments bestowed on her by parental love at once acceptable and available. Her letter was bedewed by the tears of this amiable family. The reply was an entreaty that she would come and reside with them, and be as another sister. This was, of course, declined, with the warm sentiment of gratitude and increased esteem it merited, for Adela never resolved without reflection. And, as the good Arnold said on a former occasion, since she would not permit them to serve her in their way—he set in good earnest about serving her in her own. The first advertisement, to effect this, was replied to by several individuals, anxious to secure the talents and capabilities described by the warm-hearted Arnold.

Mrs. Arnold waited on several, and the situation which appeared best suited to the retired habits, the benefit, and above all, the comfort of their young friend, was in the family of a widow, who resided about ten miles distant, in an elegant retirement, and devoted all her time to her two daughters, the one sixteen, the other five years of age.

Louisa wrote to inform her of the success of their inquiries, assuring her that the only consolation her determination had left them was, in the idea that an hour would, at any time, bring her to their arms, and they should not fail to embrace it frequently.

Adela found it very difficult to bring her parents to coincide; but much as the separation cost her, where duty called her resolve was not to be shaken; and, consoling them with the recollection that she should be less than half way between their cottage and the habitation of the Arnolds, and that every leisure hour should bring her to their bosoms, they reluctantly complied. Mrs. Arnold accompanied and introduced her. The parties were mutually prepossessed in each other's favour; and the following Monday was fixed upon as a new era in Adela's existence.

Nor did the generous Arnold fail, in a visit to the cottage, to force upon the acceptance of his third daughter (for such he ever termed her) a purse, which might be serviceable, he said, on such an occasion; nor Mrs. Arnold and the girls, to present her with many an elegant memento of their disinterested love.

In vain did Adela protest against these expensive proofs of their kindness towards her;—in vain did St. Clair disapprove; the Arnolds were not to be denied, and their hearts seemed so much in their wishes for her welfare, that, to coincide, was unavoidable.

But the three days previous to her departure—those treasured hours devoted to filial and parental tenderness, every moment of which would, in absence, be a gem in the diadem of memory! The farewell embrace of her beloved father, who accompanied her to her destination:—the pearly tears of maternal tenderness that mingled with her's as she sobbed an adieu on their bosoms—the prayer of parental love! Oh! it ascended to the throne of that sublime Creator to whom the secrets of all hearts are unveiled, and the balm of consolation was shed over them by that Power which setteth bounds to the ocean, and saith unto the stormy winds—"Be still!"

But Arnold did not confine his friendship to gifts pressed upon their family favourite. In the indignant wrath of his heart he took his pen, and wrote the ollowing letter to the Reverend Jonathan St. Clair:

"Sir,—As an individual long known to every branch of your family, as a Christian and a father, I conceive it my duty to make you aware, that, from the unanticipated, unavoidable, and unmerited losses of Mr. Edmund St. Clair, his daughter, a very accomplished young lady,—instead of being in her proper sphere, is obliged to accept the appointment of governess, to avoid remaining any longer an expense to her parents.

" I feel this highly improper and derogatory to their respectability. That you will feel ashamed of such an alternative, I do not anticipate, because it is not usual with men of your profession to possess such a sentiment, it being generall epugnant with your natures to assist even a parent in misfortune.

" You cannot now, however, plead ignorance of this event, although I am awa e it will be a matter of perfect indifference to you, because Mammon is the priest's divinity. I never knew an instance to the contrary, and will not venture to consider you an exception, whose feverish anxiety for gain increases hourly, although on the confines of eternity. " I am, sir, yours respectfully,

" JAMES ARNOLD."

Mr. Arnold's observations were severe, but neither harsh nor ill-timed; because, since his appointment as a magistrate in the town, in the vicinity of which he resided, the Reverend Jonathan's nature, or rather what had hitherto appeared his

No. 21.

nature, had altogether changed. He who had always appeared anxious to be considered a philanthropist by the surrounding community had now laid this apparent inclination aside, regardless of present opinion, or of future fame, having reached the goal of his hitherto concealed ambition.

In opposition to all his previous professions and precepts, he had been for some time industriously persecuting all the agricultural labourers around him, to obtain the tenth part of their miserable annual income ; and several had even been taken from their families, and consigned to the horrors of a prison—not because they were immoral, but because they were too indignant to satisfy the hungry cravings of his avidity.

Alas! that those who profess to be the champions of humanity—whose precepts oppose injustice, or cruelty to man or beast, should be the very first to transgress— to harass and oppress the one, and, for amusement, hunt down and destroy the other.

On Sunday, the clergyman, from the pulpit, uses his utmost eloquence to awaken his flock to the duties of their various stations, to mutual piety and forgiveness, to the beauty of mercy! On Monday, he consigns the unfortunate individual who, in opposition to the laws of nature and humanity, he deems his debtor, into a cold and solitary dungeon! And with his dog and gun, he pursues the harmless tenants of the spray, or hunts down the timid hare, exulting in its dying agonies.

Self-defence is one law of nature : the preservation of life in a sacred duty. The savage throws his quivers and his bow across his shoulder, and penetrates the woods in pursuit of a subsistence. The cravings of hunger—the customs of savage life—authorise this necessity ; but in the sons of luxury the same pursuit, and particularly for diversion, is a crime, but doubly so in a minister of the gospel. The arrow of the savage cleaves the air—a moment puts an end to the existence of his victim— whilst the civilised part of mankind protract its close by all the horrors of accumulated and refined tortures.

It is not one of the least evils of aristocratic usurpation that immense tracts of land remain uncultivated, as a shelter to the wild animals they selfishly monopolise as one of their sources of brutal gratification. Such land being kept for ever untilled is a serious injury to the community ; but more particularly to that class whose necessities require that every medium of abundance should render the requisites of life easily obtainable.

Arnold's letter could scarcely have arrived at a more unfortunate period ; an amalgamation of peculiarly untoward events having occurred to ruffle the usual placidity of Mr. Jonathan's temper, and to render his narrowness of soul still more contracted.

Mrs. Crawley having declared herself in a highly interesting situation, the Reverend Jonathan suggested the propriety of her widowed mother residing with them, that the anxiety of overlooking the economy of her household might not occasion a dangerous degree of excitement. He was aware of the intensity of his *protegée's* feelings on this point, and urged, with appropriate earnestness, that as the minds of mother and daughter were pretty congenial, this confidence might, at so critical a moment, be reposed in her.

Robert assented with cheerfulness to this proposition—nothing could be more consonant with his feelings. It would be precisely the arrangement which would leave him an unlimited disposal of his time ; and as Mrs. Crawley's stipulation, that her mother should pay a handsome amount for her subsistence, was acceded to, all parties were satisfied.

This post was found to be no sinecure. At five in the morning the bell regularly summoned the servants. A few minutes afterwards another, which communicated with the old lady's chamber, reminded her of the propriety of trotting down with the key, that the proper quantity of coal only might be portioned out for the breakfast-parlour and kitchen. She then returned to her room, was summoned again to attend the servants at their breakfast; and she then passed the time, until her daughter's morning repast, in prying through the grounds, counting the plants in the conservatory, or investigating the proceedings of the dairy-maid. Thus, each servant was made the object of suspicion ; and in a discussion relative to some trifling economy, |she accused her mother so unequivocally of conniving with the servants, that her patience became exhausted, and she resolved to return to her former domicile, and there again to enjoy a repose suited to her declining years.

Robert Crawley was quite the reverse of penurious, and incessant contentions were the consequence. He had been lifted, as it were by magic, into extensively opulent circumstances. The profession to which, in early years, he had looked forward as the *acmé* of his wishes, was now no longer needed. Reading was a bore, his wife's petulance and meanness insupportable.

For Susan, who passed in the village where she resided as Mrs. Dear, he began to weary; the sooner, perhaps, because she evidently drooped under the degradation of conscious guilt. And the rich Mr. Crawley was the last man on earth to submit to reproach, although only conveyed in a glance.

His resource, therefore, was the society of the low associates with whom, in earlier years, he had been accustomed to mix, and with them he passed days and nights in a series of outrage and extravagance.

In gratitude they praised him for his wit and vivacity, lauded his generosity, and courteously styled him " Sir Robert." Through the medium of his servant, this title got into the neighbourhood, and as " Sir Robert and " my Lady," they became universally dubbed in derision.

Anxious to enjoy the amusements of the metropolis, he frequently resorted thither for weeks, with a few of his chosen friends, where his expenditure was so unlimited, that he was frequently arrested for the debts he had suddenly contracted before he had time to apply to his banker for the necessary sums.

Mrs. Crawley, disgusted with pursuits that led him eternally from home, and exhausted so much of that wealth which was her idol, had written to the Reverend Jonathan requesting his immediate presence.

Having left his horse at an inn on the road, he pursued his way to his *protegée's* mansion, wishing to surprise and please by his sudden appearance.

His cheerfulness, however, at the prospect of spending a day tranquilly with Sally, in Robert's absence, quickly abandoned him. Tears, lamentations, and hysterics assailed him on his entrance. He replied by reproaches—she by urging the necessity of his immediate interference.

" How can I interfere?" said the Reverend Jonathan; " I would not venture to take such a step. You were resolved to have him—well, your wishes are accomplished. If you refused your friends' advice, I am not to blame; and all the counsel I can now give you is, that as we all know the reckless and determined character of your husband, you do not provoke him to hostility, but make the best of a bad business, and submit with Christian patience and becoming resignation."

Here the lady's resentment became ungovernable. She forgot the respect due to her protector; and, muttering his wrath, he ran from her presence, and made the best of his way back to the inn, ruminating upon the folly of " casting pearls to swine."

Leaving the scene of vexation and disappointment, and unconscious whither he was proceeding, he advanced to the stable, and, in a tone of impatience, desired the ostler's assistant to bridle the horse, and bring him out without delay. The lad obeyed, the magistrate mounted, and off he rode in high dudgeon.

About half an hour after he had departed, a traveller gave the ostler directions to get his horse without delay. The horse was equipped and brought to the door. The traveller paid his bill, and was preparing to mount, but, finding it was not his own horse in waiting, he loudly exclaimed against the man for what he conceived his stupidity.

The ostler submissively assured him he belonged to no one else, and solicited him to mount.

This added to the traveller's resentment, and, in the act of chastising him for what he presumed an insolent joke, the horse started, kicked, and flung so furiously that the man fell beneath him, and every one concluded Joe had ceased to be an inhabitant of this sublunary world.

Disentangled and conveyed into the house, he was found to be more terrified than injured; and he was, therefore, summoned into the presence of his master to account for this singular incident.

The ostler declared he positively knew nothing of the matter, and that it really must be the gentleman's horse, for it was the only one remaining.

The traveller lost all patience, broke into execrations at the prospect of losing one of the finest horses on the road, and they all adjourned to inspect the object of this strange disturbance and confusion.

The innkeeper was well acquainted with the absent horse; he had frequently admired him, and had repeatedly offered two hundred pounds as a price he would willingly have given to possess him.

"I wouldn't lose my horse for five hundred pounds," said the gentleman. "I am in a hurry to pursue my journey; either you are playing me some trick I really do not relish, or you have suffered some one to steal the horse from your stable; but, if he be not restored to me in a few hours, I will demand four hundred pounds as his purchase, for it is not likely I would consent to receive him back at any price, after any one had retained, and had ridden him, but for a single day.

On hearing this the innkeeper was in a state of consternation; he ran about from stable to stable, to ascertain whether he had been transferred in mistake, but it was all in vain; nor would any of his guests own the sorry figure which now stood as miserable in appearance, and as patient as an overworked jack.

At length it occurred to the innkeeper, to inquire what horses had come in during the day; and this brought to the ostler's recollection, that an elderly gentleman had put his horse up in the same stable, which they could no longer find.

The boy confessed the gentleman had ordered him to bring the horse out half an hour before, but that he did not know which road he had taken.

This intelligence increased the general consternation, for as no one knew the gentleman who had made this excellent exchange, little doubt was entertained but that the horse was gone for ever. As the only prospect, however, of recovering him, the innkeeper ordered his ostlers, stable boys, and postilions to saddle each a horse, and gave them instructions to proceed at a full gallop in different directions out of town, and not to stop until they had got thirty miles on the road, if they should not be fortunate enough to come up with the delinquent previously.

Terrified at the probability of having so large an amount to pay, with the acquisition of an animal scarcely worth ten shillings, he jumped upon the best horse he possessed, whilst the traveller, quite as eager to recover that which he preferred

> To everything in life,
> Except his wife,"

as hastily vaulted into the saddle of the sorry pledge that had been left behind, resolved on accompanying the innkeeper.

But to set out with him was one thing—to keep up with him another. The one was high mettled and all agility, the other dull, heavy, sulky, and sullen, whose legs had not been put in motion beyond a trot for many a year. Off went the innkeeper full gallop on the route, but whip and spur were used to little purpose to keep the other up with him.

This was natural enough; for when we compare the pace to which he had been accustomed, with the feats now expected of him, he no doubt imagined himself himself ridden by the prince of darkness, and instead of proceeding in a direct line onwards, he flew from side to side, ran backward, kicked and snorted, so that he was soon left very considerably behind.

And the innkeeper had eagerly continued rapidly to advance, regardless of every obstacle, and equally regardless of his companion. Nothing presented itself to his fancy but the unfortunate consequences of his ostler's negligence, and the amount it was likely to cost him, when, in about half an hour, he happily beheld the object of his pursuit. Delighted with this unexpected success he increased his speed, crying out, "Stop! stop!"

Hearing these terrifying exclamations, the Reverend Jonathan was horror-stricken. He looked behind, and seeing some one on full stretch pursuing him, with so terrific an outcry, he had little doubt but a highwayman was in his rear, and saw no medium of escape from robbery and murder, for no protecting hand was nigh.

The Reverend Jonathan's mind had been so completely disturbed and ruffled by his visit to Mrs. Crawley, that he had not yet discovered his mistake ; and, fully aware of the habits of Dapple, he knew there was little chance of escape. Life, however, is dear to every one, and as money is yet dearer than life, and both were equally cherished by the reverend gentleman, he instinctively gave the supposed Dapple the whip. But his terror was only equalled by his astonishment, for off full stretch went he—off went his hat! and, being mounted on a much finer horse than that behind him, had he been indeed the thief they took him for, the innkeeper would have had little chance of overtaking him.

This freak in the usually tranquil Dapple was so astounding, that it became a hasty question with him, whilst he seized on his ears for safety, whether he should suffer the animal to break his neck, or the highwayman to blow his brains out and rob him.

The anticipation of a bullet is, however, so horrifying to some people, that almost any other risk is preferable ; so on went both horses at full speed, the innkeeper vociferating, " Stop him ! stop him !" and the clergyman leaving his horse to his own discretion to effect his escape.

The turnpike man, seeing the pursuer and the pursued—one bending over the neck of his horse, the other using every possible exertion to come up with him—calculated that something, of course, must be wrong, and suddenly closed the gate, just as the Reverend Jonathan was upon the point of passing through.

Had he done so earlier, the horse would inevitably have leaped it ; but he was so startled at the sudden slam, that round he went with his rider on his back, who, not anticipating any such circular evolution, was pitched headlong into a hedge, rolled down into the ditch below, from whence he called out loudly for assistance. The innkeeper having recovered the horse, thought of nothing but securing the rider ; and having extricated him from his awkward predicament, contrived to draw him to the turnpike gate. Here he accused him of purloining the horse ; and as he was without a hat, and splashed so as to take from his appearance everything like respectability, it was in vain that the reverend gentleman protested the innocence of his intentions, related to them the nature of his visit, and the consequent distraction of mind which had prevented his discovering his mistake.

Innkeepers are not unaccustomed to very plausible fictions, on occasions where it is intended to render them a prey to the dissolute and the designing ; he was, therefore, the last man in the universe to accredit what he heard. He accordingly insisted on the turnpike-man procuring a constable, and off the Reverend Jonathan was marched to a neighbouring magistrate, in spite of all his protestations.

Fortunately for this pious man, amidst this accumulation of humiliating circumstances, he was conducted sufficiently near the vicinity of his home to be recognised after some slight explanation, rendered necessary by the burlesque *tout-ensemble*, which would have rendered his identity doubtful to his most intimate friend.

The gentlemen he sent for were familiar with his oddities and eccentricities ; they knew the marriage of Sarah Crawley had blighted his ambition of uniting nobility with his wife's family, that other vexatious circumstances weighed heavily on his mind, and therefore conceived it very possible that such a mischance might occur in one of his moments of abstraction.

The innkeeper, exasperated at what had occurred, could not bring himself to believe that the decision was not partial ; nor would he be satisfied that the brother magistrate should be set at liberty, until the assurances of the gentlemen then present were backed by those of several others from his neighbourhood.

By this time the traveller, burning with vexation and resentment, had contrived, by dint of whipping and spurring, to reach the same spot ; not, however, without having been dislodged from the saddle six or seven times on the road, from the obstinate beast's disinclination to proceed onward ; and, delighted at the recovery of his horse, he jumped on him and proceeded back to the inn without a syllable of further explanation ; whilst the innkeeper, eager to inform him of all that had happened, pursued as closely after him as he had just previously done in quest of the same horse.

Clothes, and his carriage, having reached the reverend gentleman, he retired to a room, where his servant, who could scarcely restrain a laugh, assisted him to cleanse and change, and he returned home in a fit of profound pondering over the singular events of the few last hours.

"Whom the Lord loveth he chasteneth," repeated the pious man, devoutly crossing his arms on his breast, in reply to his wife's hurried inquiries, and he retired to his study, firmly resolved that it should be the last time he would obey the peremptory call of Mrs. Crawley, to interfere between herself and her dissolute husband.

It was precisely in this situation of affairs that Mr. Arnold's letter arrived, and it will be readily conceived unwelcome enough. He took off his spectacles, rubbed the glasses, put them on again, turned it this way and that to read the motto, and at length he broke the seal.

"What's that to me," said he, soliloquising,—"what's that to me? Why does this individual interfere?—what's that to him? He's so authoritative—one would think he knew more than he ought, but that cannot be either—that I should think is impossible."

He wiped the perspiration from his brow, and some reflections, not the most self-approbatory, passed in hurried succession; the comparison of one, by nature vulgar, on whom all the advantages of education had been absolutely thrown away—immoral in her feelings (for what else could they be judged from her earliest, her more recent associations?) without one trait of decent feeling; ungrateful, and even gross in the remarks that had transpired during the last resentful hour they had passed together. But why complain of an evil brought on voluntarily?—was not the die cast?—was there any retreating?

How different was St. Clair's daughter according not only to Mr. Arnold's description, but even general report, for his curiosity had not failed to inquire respecting the individuals he hated; and he had heard of their misfortune with an exultation that added considerably to the enjoyment of his own selfish gratifications, splendid mansion, and luxurious table.

"Why should I," said he, "who have built my house upon a rock, heed those who are the outcasts of heaven? Edmund St. Clair has raised his edifice upon the sand. 'And the rain descended, and the floods came, and the winds blew and beat upon that house; and it fell.'

"What is that to me?—did not other circumstances prevent, their poverty alone would be an insuperable bar. Now poor Sally, with all her failings, would still have been rich, had I not suffered her aunt to adopt her, whereas these people have now been poor for years! No matter, no matter! I should not, I think, under any circumstances, have felt inclined to disgrace myself in this way; but if I would, it is no longer in my power." So saying, he tore the letter into twenty pieces, and proceeded to arrange his sermon for the morrow.

CHAPTER XXXV.

" The forest depths, by foot unprest,
  Are not more sinless than her breast;
  The holy peace that fills the air
  Of those calm solitudes is there."

ADELA, invested in her new arrangement, in the exertion of talents which now, on her beloved parents' account, bore an additional value, in cultivating the taste and completing the education of her elder, and in forming the mind of her younger, pupil, had little leisure for unavailing sorrows or distressing retrospections.

A few hours had sufficed to render the amiable widow and her fair inmate perfectly at their ease with each other.

Whilst vulgar and narrow minds hesitate over the paltry considerations of etiquette, pride, circumstances, souls of a superior order assimilate at once. There are few such; but when they do appear, the votary of fashion and folly would do well to throw aside her superficial graces, and acquire the easy elegance that flows from a cultivated mind.

Mrs. Drayton was delighted with the acquisition she had by chance, as it were, made for her girls, and Adela felt partly consoled in her self-imposed exile, by her flattering and friendly reception.

Miss Drayton was with her mamma in the drawing-room on the evening of our heroine's arrival, for the youngest retired early. Everything around gave an idea of the correct taste and elegant mind of the mistress of the mansion; and the hours preceding supper stole imperceptibly away in those mutual inquiries natural on such an occasion, and a thousand little plans formed by an anxious mother for the future.

In parting for the night, Mrs. Drayton said she trusted Miss St. Clair would feel at home and consider herself with a mother and sisters, who would find it a felicity to lighten the cares devoted to their benefit, by all the amusement and variety in their power to bestow.

Adela replied with a smile, that her favourite sphere was study and seclusion, and that her highest reward would be the satisfaction and improvement of her young friends.

Miss Drayton was an interesting and delicate girl, whose studies had been, in the mother's words, retarded by an illness resulting from the bitterness of sorrow on the loss of her father.

Adela pressed the hand she held, and felt she should love her for the cause of her indisposition. She had not an opportunity of seeing the younger until they had retired for the night. Miss Drayton's chamber opened out of that destined for Adela, and, retaining her hand,—

"Come," said she, "and see my sister. My brother Charles is at school; you will be pleased with him when you see him, because he is a favourite with every one; but I am sure you will admire my little Rosalie. She is sleeping now, but she will have a thousand little anecdotes to relate to you in the morning."

Adela approached the bed,—she drew back the drapery that shaded it, and beheld a lovely child, apparently about five years of age. Her dark eye-lashes formed a striking contrast with the clearness and freshness of her complexion, and one of her glossy ringlets had escaped from her nightcap to wanton on the snow of her dimpled shoulder. Adela kissed her affectionately, and the young ladies separated for the night, mutually pleased with each other.

But it was not only the early rays of the sun that peeped into Adela's chamber in the morning. About six, the moving of the handle of the door, and the cautious tread of gentle footsteps over the carpeted floor, attracted her attention. The curtain was withdrawn from the head of her bed, and a pair of brilliant eyes fixed on her.

Adela recognised, in her little visitant, the beautiful child she had seen the night before, and half closed her eyes to observe her more leisurely.

She gazed on her instructress for some minutes, and kissed the hand that rested on the pillow, then, gently retiring, with the exclamation, "she is very pretty, and I am sure I shall love her,—for she does not look at all cross," returned to her chamber, and gently closed the door.

At seven o'clock every one in the house was stirring. Adela arose, and whilst the attendant assisted Miss Drayton, and dressed Rosalie, she made her toilette, and as Caroline proposed a walk, and her little sister tied on her bonnet, and took her hand, they wandered round the grounds until half-past eight, when they met Mrs. Drayton in the breakfast parlour.

The windows opened on parterres of flowers that seemed to vie with each other in fragrance and beauty; and many a little warbler came fearlessly round to peck the crumbs scattered for them by the little Rosalie.

Mrs. Drayton was delighted with the specimens she saw of Adela's drawings.

" Her Caroline," she said, " had a peculiar taste for that delightful art, and would now possess a chance of ultimately excelling." French and Italian had been conjointly her study, when the loss of a lamented father set everything aside; and years of illness following, they were obliged to visit one watering-place after another, anxious to preserve the only individual capable of yielding her the smallest consolation in this her solitary widowhood.

" A master," she said, " attended three times a week for the harp; and if Miss St. Clair would give her daughter some instructions on the guitar, and in singing, it would indeed be an advantage."

" But all this, my dear Miss St. Clair," continued Mrs. Drayton, " must be done at intervals, and not rendered a labour to you. The extreme delicacy of your complexion assures me, you require as much management, rest, and recreation as your pupil; and whilst you are devoting your talents to her, and she is availing herself of your gentle instructions, it must be my part to watch over the health of both.

" As for this little gazelle," continued she, drawing her fingers through Rosalie's jetty ringlets, " she is almost too wild for anything. She has been like a tender exotic, and much care, and incessant daily and nightly watching (with the Creator's goodness) have been requisite to make her what you now see her. She can, however, read,—she has a pretty notion of drawing—a voice that may be made something of by cultivation. Time may do much for her under so elegant an instructress; and, if we can allure you to remain with us, we shall feel your society a valuable acquisition.

Adela replied to these courteous and encouraging observations by the assurance that no exertion on her part should be wanting, and immediately took possession of the boudoir, which was to be devoted to their studies.

A small library of well-chosen authors, a pair of globes, a variety of maps, drawing implements, a harp and guitar, were here arranged in due order; and here their mornings passed rapidly away, every hour increasing the tender interest, of the one, and the affectionate gratitude of the other.

At one o'clock they were summoned to take refreshment, and afterwards retired to dress. Music and drawing occupied the remaining hours until the dinner-bell rung, which was usually at four; and the remainder of the day was devoted to exercise and recreation.

Sometimes they took a drive in the carriage to see Mrs. Drayton's son, a fine youth, whose rapid improvements under an enlightened instructor seemed to promise the realisation of all his fond mother's hopes. Sometimes they entered a beautiful pleasure-boat, and in a sail on the river, which wound its way at the bottom of their spacious grounds, enjoyed the beauty and freshness of the surrounding scenery, or wandering in the neighbouring meadows, inhaled renovated health and beauty in every breeze.

If the skies were overcast they retired to a pavilion, at the end of the garden, which overlooked the river. Here Adela read some exquisite lay or moral tale, or mingling her voice with Mrs. Drayton's harp, or accompanying herself on the guitar, beguiled the tear of sensibility from the eye of the amiable widow, and a sigh from the breast of the gentle Caroline, as she clasped her Rosalie in an impassioned embrace.

Mrs. Drayton visited little, although much courted by a highly respectable circle, amongst whom she had for many years resided.

But the loss of her lamented husband, the death of her father, and, ult   i the sudden disappearance of a beloved and only brother, about a year ago, had bound her to solitude, and endued her character with a peculiar interest to a heart so well acquainted with affliction as Adela's.

Not many months elapsed without producing a striking change, not only in the acquirements, but also the health of Miss Drayton. The benefit of a few hours devoted daily to any pursuit is really magical. Adela rendered everything a pleasure, and her example was worth volumes of precept.

The little Rosalie began to read her native language correctly. She had commenced the rudiments of the French; already her little fingers began to wander over the strings of the guitar, and she had acquired some of the first lessons.

Caroline was delighted; for her sister was dearer to her than light or life, and

their affectionate caresses were united with the warm acknowledgments of their mother's esteem, for their lovely and unassuming inmate:

> "To tempered wishes, just desires—
> Is happiness confined,—
> And deaf to folly's voice attends
> The music of the mind."

And that peace was Adela's—for although another could never succeed Theodore in such a heart, she had acquired so much empire over herself, that not only her health, but even a large portion of her serenity had returned; and no sooner was

No. 22.

the resolution formed, which the pure feeling of filial piety had suggested, than every hour brought its reward.

The multitude of her occupations had in a manner stolen her from herself, and the delightful certainty that this disposal of her time would not only restore to her parents the comforts of which their recent vicissitudes had deprived them, but even prove a blessing to their declining years, surrounded her heart with a sentiment of unalloyed felicity. Her health improved, the mild lustre of her eye returned, and the pale rose of health again appeared on her cheek,

" Diffusing bloom and every nameless grace."

The salary produced by the present arrangement did not exceed fifty pounds annually; but this she resolved should be solely devoted to her family.

Her wardrobe was already well furnished, not only by the affectionate consideration of her parents, but the kind-hearted Arnolds had added every little elegance adapted to superior society.

The small Spanish casket, her dear mother's present, contained every ornament she would need. Her newly-acquired friend had presented her with a gold watch, as a token of her perfect satisfaction and increasing esteem.

The purse which the excellent Arnold had given her contained twenty sovereigns. These she carefully laid aside; and, having added her first quarter's amount, she presented it to her parents on the next visit to her paternal abode.

Adela had seen her parents monthly since her departure; and oh! what bliss, what a holiday of the heart were those visits! how she counted the hours for their arrival! how reluctantly did they see them glide away! Such moments are indeed gems, and the heart which has mourned the absence of those who are its life-springs can alone appreciate them.

These affectionate parents would fain have laid aside this amount, as the commencement of a little fund for their child; but she would not permit it. She insisted on seeing everything purchased that might be conducive to their comfort. And Adela, where her heart was interested, was not to be denied. Clasping them to her breast, she assured them of her restored tranquillity, and the smile of seraphic sweetness that irradiated her lovely features, convinced them that their beloved girl was indeed again all their own.

Nor had she neglected to visit the Arnolds—or they to fetch her, according to promise, frequently, to their hospitable home. And so judiciously did Adela dispose of her time, that she was not only enabled to correspond with her young friends, but to continue her own studies, and acquire a proficiency on the harp and piano, which her correct theoretical knowledge of music considerably facilitated.

" I am now no longer a speculator," said the exulting girl; " a future hour may enable me to provide for the idolised authors of my existence, should fate be unwearied in her persecutions."

" Rosalie is not a family likeness," said Adela, as she finished the united portraits of the sisters, " her mamma is brilliantly fair—so is her sister, whose shining dark brown tresses form a striking contrast with the jetty ringlets of our little brunette."

Mrs. Drayton sighed. " There is a melancholy tale attached to our sweet Rosalie's history," said she; " she is not belonging to our family, although entwined with the warmest affections of our hearts. No one in this part of the country, but myself and my children, are aware that she is not mine,—nor would I, for worlds, with her sensitive feelings, she should ever know she was not her Caroline's sister. But our hearts, my dear young friend, are too congenial to admit of concealments. I will relate to you her history; but we must select the hour when she has retired to repose. I am certain she will drop a tear of tender sympathy over the fate of a little orphan, who is unconscious of being so, who has never been sensible of the caress or the smile of a parent."

" You say, my dear madam, this sweet child has never known any other tie of affection than that which binds her to her mamma and her Caroline? Ah! unconscious of her loss—how can she be unhappy—sheltered in the bosoms of such a protectress—such a sister?"

"There are, however, melancholy—very melancholy incidents appertaining to her history. We will sup in the pavilion, dispense with the attendance of the servants, and either Caroline or I will relate it to you."

CHAPTER XXXIII.

BUT the history of the little Rosalie contains so many incidents connected with the five years preceding the present period, that we will not only revert to that period, but even to the hour that beheld the elegant Mrs. Drayton the bride of the chosen of her warm and devoted heart.

The following year beheld them the parents of a daughter, the young lady mentioned in the preceding pages ; and a son, the youth who now promised, by his rapid improvement and amiable nature, to be at once the comfort of his widowed mother, and protector of his Caroline and Rosalie.

The death of Mrs. Drayton's father added considerably to the possessions of a family already opulent, and gave, with the pang it occasioned, an additional power of dispensing blessings to the children of adversity, to whose claims both hearts unfolded with congenial benignity.

But, as a picture of the family we have introduced, we will revert to the few days preceding the thirty-second anniversary of his birthday ; who, as the best of fathers, husbands, friends, formed the felicity, not only of his own family, but a large circle bound to him by benefits which wealth alone has not the power to bestow.

"Let me see," said little Charles, turning aside the shining curls of his flaxen hair, and looking at his sister with the cherub smile of health and happiness, "to-morrow will be the third, Agnes says, the next day the fourth ; yes, Thursday will be the fifth, and papa's birthday."

"Mamma, you know, has her present ready ; for when papa presented uncle Albert with his watch, because he admired it, and uncle Albert gave you his, mamma begged him not to purchase another, having chosen one as a birthday gift.

"Uncle Albert has purchased an elegant dressing-case. I have long been saving up my money for a beautiful gold clasp, and Agnes has worked me a purse to put to it. But you, Caroline, are so very close, so cunning, that you will not tell me what you intend to give papa."

Caroline smiled at her brother's address, and, taking his hand,—

"Shall I tell you, Charles," said she, " why I am so cunning and so close as you are pleased to term me ?"

"Do, dear Caroline !"

"Well, then, if Charles was not prudent enough to keep a secret of mamma's, which happened to come to his knowledge, what chance would one of mine have ?"

Charles pouted and looked vexed.

"I do not understand you, sister."

"Don't you? I will remind you, then. Do you remember the day when Lady Ann Castleton called on mamma, to tell her of the provision made for the unfortunate family of the Stapletons, even to the children's clothing, which, being a great gossip, she described ; and all (said she) 'as it were by magic, by the hand of an unknown benefactor.' You started forward, and, unable to restrain yourself, even by the respect due to mamma's presence, exclaimed with earnestness,—
'Oh! I can tell your ladyship, it was my dear mamma. These were the very frocks that were cut out in mamma's dressing-room, and my sister, and Agnes and Jane made them all ! Jane says it was mamma sent the furniture and beds and all, and papa that paid the money that freed the poor sick father from that horrid

prison.   You cannot, surely, forget this, Charley, or mamma's reproof and displeasure, or that I obtained your pardon; for, although you were very wrong in disclosing what mamma's silence alone ought to have convinced you she wished concealed, yet I pitied you because I knew it was the love you bear to our dear parents, and the pride you take in their goodness, that led you into the error."

"Yes, I do remember now, sister, but I did not like that mamma's goodness should not be known, and even, perhaps, somebody else be praised for it."

"My dear Charles, mamma and papa do not wish their actions published to the world.   Have they not repeatedly told us that those acts of kindness that are coupled with vanity lose half their worth, and that one sigh breathed in secret over the unfortunate is worth them all?"

"Well, I know, dear mamma and you are quite right, and I am wrong; but you know, sister, you are much older than I am, for you were eleven last month, and I am only seven."

"Yes, love, for that reason I hope that when you are a little older, and think a little more, with your goodness of heart, we shall find you all papa, mamma, and I can wish you."

*   *   *   *   *   *

"God bless me," said Mrs. Hawkins, arranging the cards she held in her hand, "is it possible?   I really do not believe it.   I don't consider this weather cold at all.   For myself I find every winter milder than the last, and expect," continued she, laughing, "that we shall have one continued summer in a few years.   But what are trumps, Mr. Gruffland? these odd stories make one quite stupid."

But there were some amongst that society, whose sentiments did not correspond with those of the fat, elderly lady; and a manly and rather stern voice in some measure disconcerted her self-complacency in replying,—

"Yes, madam, every winter is doubtless less severe than the last; where hourly increasing comfort exerts its magic power in casting the past to oblivion.   Few, whilst their limbs are wrapped in elegance and ease, reflect

> 'How many shrink into the sordid hut
>   Of cheerless poverty,'

or, whilst they share the banquet of luxury, how many (ten thousand times their superiors) sink unheeded and unaided, as in the instance now so touchingly described by my friend!"

These words, and the impressive manner in which they were pronounced, had the effect of electricity.   One lady dropped a tear, another raised her embroidered handkerchief to hide—the absence of so graceful an effusion; all felt that the reproach so appropriately addressed to Mrs. Hawkins, was perhaps equally applicable to themselves, and the energetic speaker retired amidst the applauses of the very few enlightened and worthy present.

Nor was Frederick Montreville, whose warmth of feeling had thus hurried him away, merely a speaker on the occasion.   His steps were turned to the lonely dwelling his friend had described; his soul of benevolence, whilst he mourned over the desolation before him, concerted the best medium of recovering and protecting the innocent bereaved ones.   And well might such a scene excite the commiseration of colder hearts.

On one side of the damp and comfortless chamber, on a little scattered straw, lay the unfortunate victims of want and despair.

Together they had shared every gradation of adversity, from the successive delusions of "hope delayed," to the last closing scene of pining hunger, woe, and death.

Together they had received the last sighs of their two little ones lying beside them; and, although they had devoted the last morsel to them, the spark of departing life yet hovered over this solitary remaining pledge of their ill-fated affection.

Their sufferings, however, closed, and a neighbour, wondering that no one of the family appeared to pay for the last loaf she had been induced to concede them, (coupled with much coarse rebuke and overbearing insolence), had gone to demand it.

She found the door on the latch; entered, and witnessed the melancholy scene. She, however, speedily absented herself, much alarmed lest she might incur some trouble on the occasion; she did not wait to see whether any spark of existence remained, or if anything could be done for the little sleeper, who lay apparently as lifeless as the maternal bosom on which it unconsciously reposed.

"Other people, however," said she, "may do as they please :" she therefore left the room-door unclosed; and a gentleman, passing to the before-mentioned party, observing her singular gesticulations, and attracted by the piteous cries of the infant sufferer who had just awakened, entered.

He took the little solitary being from the icy bosom, which its parched and feverish lips yet pressed for its wonted sustenance; its plaintive moan struck to his heart, and hastening to the woman who had before denied her assistance, he induced her, by the promise of a sovereign, to take charge of the little orphan, to procure it some warm milk, and keep out all intrusive curiosity until he should return with his family sugeon.

"Oh certainly, sir," replied the *disinterested* Mrs. Linton, "certainly! it does one's heart good to be of service to people, when they can do nothing more for themselves!" and on closing the door after him she continued, "it's monstrous lonely, though, only that the gentleman seems that he'd pay me well, and Mercy can mind shop, as she does when I go to chapel."

The kind-hearted stranger returned with the surgeon, but life was altogether extinct, and, repeating his injunctions, he departed with the promise of a speedy return.

Mrs. Linton followed her orders most implicitly; she made a fire, warmed some milk, and even fetched some flannel of her own in which she wrapped the little orphan, who was voraciously receiving the refreshing draught, when young Montreville arrived, as we have before mentioned.

He took the little innocent in his arms, and whilst he brushed away the tear that would start to his eye, he determined never to abandon it.

"How could Egerton," said he, "with so generous a heart, shake off the effects of such a scene, sufficiently to bear even for a moment with the mere chit-chat of the society I have just left! His excuse was, that by mentioning the calamity he had witnessed, he had hoped to make many friends for the helpless orphan. Alas! how little does he know of the general feeling of human nature! A momentary ejaculation of surprise, a start of selfish terror at the idea of death; and before the cards are again given round, the little innocent may share the desolate grave of its parents, for any interest that they will either take or feel in its preservation. There are, however, some few exceptions, whose benign and pure spirits redeem humanity; Egerton will soon be here, and I will await his arrival."

Montreville turned to contemplate the features of these unfortunate victims of calamity. The unspeakable calm described by the inimitable Byron, of this their

" First dark day of nothingness,
Their last of danger and distress,"

possessed a something so impressive, so sacred, so touching to his feelings, that a peculiar interest attached to every thing relating to their fate.

The tranquil expression of those features was perfect repose; it seemed to say, " We have endured a severe struggle, but it is past! Our solitude has been uncheered, and our last hours deserted, because we were unfortunate. But our lives were unsullied by guilt or dishonour, and we are now sharing eternal felicity."

The two little ones, whose death had preceded their parents, were cautiously covered with all that could be collected from the wreck of what they had possessed, to shield them from the chill of the damp walls, and broken casement, in the last fond effort of parental love, to preserve them.

A pitcher, which the weak hand of the owner had vainly attempted to carry for water, lay dry and vacant, and no vestige of food was visible. An inkstand was upset amongst the straw ; and Montreville drew from beneath the arm of the unfortunate father, a pocket-book and an unfinished letter.

The pocket-book contained letters, evidently from early connexions, written in reply to those, probably requesting the exertion of that sort of interest which might have produced a subsistence for his family. All were expressive either of the " sympathy they felt for the reverses of so esteemed a friend," or the " regret that nothing had yet fallen in their way," or that they had " so many claims," or that their " circumstances were not what they appeared, which they deeply lamented on his account;" but all were crouched in terms of the highest respect and esteem.

" So much for human nature," sighed the benevolent youth. He took up the half-finished letter ; it was apparently addressed to some intimate friend of earlier years, and replete with dignified yet pathetic reproaches.

The hurried succession of unfortunate events ; the exhaustion of their last resource ; the heavy visitation of a rheumatic fever, with the debility succeeding, which had rendered all exertion impossible, were here affectingly described,—the death of two lovely, patient innocents within a few hours of each other.

" I do not reproach you, Stanley," said the unfortunate writer, " with the acts of kindness, of brotherly regard, conferred upon you in your hour of adversity; because I felt it at once a pleasure and a duty to divide my house, my purse, my all with you, and if I esteemed you in the days of our happy boyhood, your misfortunes gave you a yet stronger claim.

" How little, then, did I dream of a heart devoid of one worthy, one generous sentiment ; or, that you could be aware that my family were absolutely perishing, or the want of that aid, which amidst your profusion you could not even have missed, and which might have been extended, without deducting one single luxury from yours !

" Should this letter, Stanley, ever fall into your hands, it may awaken the remembrance of days gone by. But it will be then too late.

" My Rosalie's features already wear the semblance of death ; her languid eye scarcely recognises the heart-broken husband, of whose existence her devotion and tenderness have formed the charm.

" Our innocent babe vainly moans for its wonted nourishment.

" The hand of death is upon me."

A few unintelligible words followed, and the generous-hearted Montreville, deeply regretting that the knowledge of these melancholy circumstances had not arrived earlier, folded the letter, and placed it carefully with the rest in his pocket-book.

The little orphan's hunger satisfied, it lay warmly enveloped in Mrs. Linton's lap, when a gentle tap was heard at the cottage-door, and Mrs. Drayton and her daughter entered.

She had heard of the foregoing tragic events through the medium of their medical attendant, and had apologised for her absence to a number of visitors, because she feared lest a moment's delay might lessen the benefit she wished to confer.

Caroline's tears streamed over the little sleeper, as she knelt before it. All the wife, the mother, arose in Mrs. Drayton's bosom, as she contemplated the lifeless sufferers ; and, having conversed for some time with her young friend, he readily undertook to execute some little commissions relative to the departed. She then took the baby from Mrs. Linton, and unfolded her cloak, sat down by the fire, and laid it comfortably on her knee.

" Mamma," said Caroline, her eyes still shining through their tears, " this is indeed a melancholy scene !"

" To lament it is in vain, my Caroline ; we have unfortunately arrived too late to render our assistance available."

" But this poor baby ?"

" It is to that alone we can now be of any utility."

" Dear, dear mamma, she has no one left to love, to protect her, to attend to the little wants, do let her be mine !"

"Dear child, you know not what you request; remember, your education is but commenced, and this little one (if we can recover her) will require so much care, so much constant attention, that everything else, I fear, will stand the chance of being neglected."

"No, dear mamma, I will rise earlier, and sleep later: I will be more anxious in every acquirement, that I may instruct her. I will, when she grows older, teach her all you have taught me. Charley shall be her playfellow, and I will be her sister. Oh! I will try to make her forget the cruelty of the world, and the loss she has suffered."

"Rather say, my love, that we will endeavour to conceal from the innocent creature all that might cast a cloud over that felicity she may yet share, if virtuously educated. That is, in the event of our being enabled, by much care, to restore her; but this little, wasted, delicate form, excites a doubt whether we shall effect it."

"All things, you know, mamma, are at the disposal of the Almighty; and I think He will restore her."

"Well, my Caroline, dry your tears. Your heart appears so deeply interested in your request, that I cannot deny it to you. The baby shall be yours, unless any unforeseen circumstance occurs which may bring forward some relative to claim her, and I trust this will be her last hour of adversity."

The little Rosalie (for so they called her from her unfortunate mother) awoke. The arms of her young benefactress received her; and Mrs. Linton, who was ready to go anywhere for money, was dispatched with a note, ordering the carriage, and a female servant, to attend Miss Drayton home.

The baby was enveloped in some fine new flannel, and a large warm camel-hair shawl, bought expressly for the purpose.

Caroline pressed it to her innocent and pure bosom, and, sinking on her knees beside the parents of her little charge,

"Unfortunate parents," she exclaimed, "if, from your abode of felicity, you can behold the hearts of mamma and her Caroline, let all anxiety for your darling vanish;—mamma has permitted me to become her protectress."

The carriage had just driven from the door, when Frederick Montreville and his friend Egerton arrived; and Mrs. Drayton remained to consult with these gentlemen relative to the last melancholy duties to the departed.

The events mentioned in the preceding pages had occurred just a week previous to the conversation between Caroline and her little brother, who felt extremely anxious to know why so many conferences were held in mamma's dressing-room.

Agnes told him he must not pass the corridor, on account of a sick visitor, and he did not make any further inquiry.

He, perhaps, hoped, by this forbearance, he should ultimately arrive at his sister's secret about papa's birth-day present.

At length the day arrived. The beloved father, the soul and centre of an affectionate family, received the gratulations of all (excepting one) at the breakfast table. Caroline alone was absent. Mrs. Drayton presented her husband with a superb plain gold watch;—uncle Albert with an elegantly inlaid dressing-case; —little Charles in a new suit of clothes, made expressly for the occasion,— proudly took his seat on his papa's knee, and received a kiss in return for his pretty purse.

But where was Caroline?

"Has my sister, then, got nothing to give to poor papa?"

"Yes, Charles, Caroline will be here presently."

At that moment the door unclosed, and Caroline entered. Her dark brown hair, parted on her forehead, fell in shining ringlets on her exquisitely-formed neck. Her white dress had no ornament, and formed a striking contrast with the long mourning-robe of the lovely infant she held in her arms. Every one arose in astonishment, except Mrs. Drayton, who knew all that was passing in her daughter's bosom.

Caroline passed forward to her father. She bent on one knee; and, raising her supplicating eyes to his countenance, she elevated the infant in her arms, whilst with a voice almost inarticulate with emotion,

" Dear papa," said she, " your Caroline presents you with a little orphan, whom mamma has permitted her to protect!"

Mr. Drayton bent over his daughter. He kissed her beautiful forehead, and clasped her fondly with her little adopted one to his heart.

"Be it so, my Caroline," said he; " your mamma well knows that the most grateful offering I can receive from my children is an act of virtue and benevolence !"

Alas! for the uncertainty of sublunary bliss!—little did that happy circle anticipate that in another year that idolized being would be snatched from their arms.

Mrs. Drayton's mind was naturally energetic. For her husband, or her children, she could have left the luxuries of a splendid home, and have passed mountains or traversed deserts without a murmur. Here her philosophy abandoned her. She repressed her grief until the last pious duties were performed ; but no sooner had the tomb closed over the idol of her heart, than the violence of her grief became uncontrollable, and a fever, which lasted many weeks, followed.

The little Charles had been removed by his tutor, who sought, by every medium of consolation and reason, to reconcile his young heart to this, its first sorrow. But no one could separate Caroline from her widowed mother—her daily nurse— her nightly attendant,—she smothered the anguish she endured from her irreparable loss ; and the first dawn of restored reason disclosed to the sufferer her Caroline, seated by the bedside, with her little orphan on her knee, silently and attentively watching over her.

What a moment was that !—they wept together and felt consoled; and the little orphan rested alternately in each bosom, as in the sympathy of infantine tenderness.

Mrs. Drayton's brother was naturally gay and thoughtless, but he loved his sister sincerely, and had devoted much time to her sick chamber ; but, when he found she was no longer in danger, he superintended the removal of the establishment into an elegant villa in the country, and departed whither the arrangement of his own affairs called him.

But poor Caroline's health had been sacrificed to her feelings, and it was now that her mother overcame her affliction, and travelled about, from place to place, with her, for the benefit of change of air and variety.

Nor were Charles and the little Rosalie excluded from the travelling party. Nor did the latter, who hourly improved in health and beauty, fail to entwine the bonds of tender interest around the hearts of her generous benefactors.

At the close of the year Mrs. Drayton and her young family returned to their villa, little Charles to the house of his instructor ; and the acute pang of sorrow began, in the course of a few succeeding years, to soften into sadly pleasing remembrance. Caroline's health improved, and her spirits were sufficiently restored to perform the duties she had imposed on herself at so early an age. But, even amidst this prospect of peace, care would intrude. And the affectionate Mrs. Drayton had first to lament her brother's irregularities, and ultimately his disappearance. It was at this period she chanced to glance her eye over the advertisement relative to Adela. She replied to it, and what followed brings us up to the present period, where we behold Mrs. Drayton, her Caroline, and the young instructress in the pavilion on the banks of the river. And the hour of eleven had sounded on the bell, before the interesting narrative of the little orphan had concluded.

CHAPTER XXXVII.

There is a grief that cannot feel,
It leaves a wound that will not heal.
My heart grew cold—it felt not then,
When will it cease to feel again ?—MONTGOMERY.

THEODORE, we have said, retraced his way to the Park, and passed the lovely
month of June, in the deep solitude of scenes endeared to his recollection from
infancy.   He shunned society, although courted by the neighbouring families who
were all anxious to form parties to enliven the evident depression of his spirits,
which they attributed solely to his recent loss.

To him life was joyless. He abjured the world, and resolved that his solitude should only be varied by the visits of Clifford, whose society was endeared
to him by a similar fate.

Ralph silently and unobtrusively attended his master's seclusion, he studied his

No. 23.

wishes, anticipated his slightest inclination, and anxiously sought everything most likely to interest and vary the scene; and vowed, in the warm attachment of his faithful heart, to devote the remainder of his existence wholly to his unhappy master.

In vain did the venerable steward, and the affectionate Mrs. Stafford, urge that "time would do wonders." Alas! the idol in his heart still reigned—still was likely to reign unrivalled. The smile of spring recalled her dawning beauty. The wonders of nature, that *mind* which surpassed in his estimation, all the other works of the Creator!

For days he hung over her portrait in the extreme of despondency. The little gifts, once accepted by a confiding heart, and rendered sacred by her possession, were his daily, his nightly companions. Ah! too late his remorse. Hurried on by the blind infatuation of jealousy, he had not sought an explanation whilst yet it might have restored them to each other.

With unavailing regret he turned to the tablets—wept over the lines traced by her gentle hand, and transcribed the following effusion of despair on the succeeding ivory page:—

> Yes—yes! thou art gone! and the wretch who deplores thee,
> Too reckless to succour, too heartless to save—
> Would fain his last tear of repentance shed o'er thee,
> And share the repose of thy desolate grave.
>
> Thy heart was too pure for the heart that possess'd it;
> So pitying heaven has severed the tie:
> Incensed at the bosom that wrong'd and distress'd it,
> Neglected its pleadings—and left it to die.
>
> Ah, fool! not to know that o'er virtues like thine,
> (Which once formed my happiness, pride, and my joy;)
> Pale envy's dark myrmidons ever combine,
> And what they can't emulate, blight and destroy.
>
> Those who envied my lot, or repin'd at thy worth,
> Thy soul-beaming beauty, ah! cropp'd in its bloom,
> Now may smile to behold thee, reposing in earth,
> And the hopes of thy lost one enshrined in thy tomb.
>
> For ah! thou art gone, and I vainly deplore thee,
> In vain, on thy name I distractedly rave!
> Oh, when shall this heart, wrung with anguish, burst o'er thee?
> Oh, when shall I share the repose of thy grave?

But his melancholy reverie was interrupted by Ralph, who, seeing the traces of anguish on that expressive countenance, silently placed on the table the following letter:—

To Sir Theodore Villars,

In disclosing the following melancholy event to my valued friend, believe me, I rather seek to teach him to support his sorrows with becoming resignation, than to unload my heart of the weight that oppresses it.

My soul's cherished idol—my long-lamented Zephyrina, is no more! and the glimmering ray of hope that, against all probability, would still hover round my heart, is at length extinguished.

I think I hear your friendly accents bid me be comforted. I think I hear you say, I may have been deceived by a report circulated by her heartless relatives, and the bigots who held her in their cruel bondage! Alas, my friend, it is *too true*!

My cousin, who in the pursuit of his own felicity, forgot not mine, proceeded to Lisbon, on his return from the Brazils, to claim my sister's long-promised hand. He there devoted some time to the strictest inquiries relative to the Senora Lenora, and her mother. By mere chance, he met with a creole of the former lady, who informed him of the name of the convent to which my lost angel was consigned, who died two months after the period which put me in possession of her letter, and the melancholy pledge of her ill-fated tenderness.

But the Creator did not permit her guilty relatives to revel in her wealth, or exult over my despair. A malignant epidemic swept off the mother, daughter, and half their attendants. A distant branch of the family, to whom they had long been inimical, inherit the whole of their possessions.

> "These—these were they whose souls the furies steeled,
> And cursed with hearts unknowing how to yield."

Alas! my gentle girl! and was this, then, to be the close of the visions we so often formed together of a happy future? Thy last moments, uncheered by the voice of tenderness or sympathy, and to complete the desolation of thy fate, thy sacred ashes are mingled with alien earth,

> "By foreign hands thy humble grave adorned,
> By strangers honoured—and by strangers mourn'd."

Poor Edward forbore to relate these sad events to any but my mother. She entreated him to conceal, and would still have done so, but for one of those chances that occur daily.

An old correspondent of my father's met him, was, of course, invited home, and in a conversation which Edward vainly tried to check,—the fever, with the numerous families it had swept off, was mentioned; and, amongst the rest of its victims, my relentless enemies. But do not accuse me of exultation, although a dawn of hope awakened schemes never to be realised. Yes, my friend—I had determined to visit Lisbon, and endeavour, by bribing those who had admittance to the gardens, to enable me to see her, to assure her of my undying love, "and who knows," said I, "perhaps even free her from the hateful shackles of superstition."

My affectionate parents exchanged glances descriptive of the most painful emotions. Alas! Edward felt it was no longer possible to conceal the fatal secret :—

Come, I beseech you, my dear friend. My sister has been given to the arms of one who will form her felicity, and appreciate her unassuming goodness. My father has accompanied the bridal party, but my mother cannot be persuaded to leave me alone under my present desolate feelings. This dear parent wishes to see you : hasten to us, and if we cannot teach each other philosophy, we can, at least, diminish, by participation, the evils of a fate too singularly similar.

Your's with unvarying esteem,

GEORGE CLIFFORD.

Sir Theodore keenly felt the renewed anguish of a heart, the value of which had evinced itself in the hour of sorrow. The claims of such a friend, so situated could not be disregarded; and the day following saw him preparing for this visit of condolence.

It was evening when the chaise stopped to change horses, at a road-side stable; and Sir Theodore Villars, weary with the confinement of the vehicle, walked forward to inhale the breeze which seemed, by its freshness, to relieve the weight on his spirits.

He had not proceeded far, when the cries of distress and infant wailings met his ear, and drew him from the path he had taken into a narrow lane.

The sounds proceeded from a miserable hovel; and, as the door stood half open, he considered it a duty to enter and inquire if he could be the medium of aid to the sufferer.

An aged female advanced, with a new-born infant in her arms, which she vainly endeavoured to soothe into quietude.

"Oh, sir," said she, "ours is an affliction beyond your power to help, although we thank you sincerely for your generous wish to do so. After a lapse of more than a year, it is only *this morning* we have been enabled to trace our unfortunate daughter—and we have, I fear, only *found* her to lose her for *ever!*

"Yesterday she gave birth to this poor little innocent, and this morning, at daybreak, the barbarian who betrayed her, has deserted her."

At these words she made way for him to enter. A man, apparently bent with age and sorrow, sat by the embers of a wood fire, and on a miserable pallet lay an emaciated female, who seemed to be at the last extremity.

"Be comforted, good woman!" said Sir Theodore, addressing the aged mother, "want, and an absence of the comforts her situation demands, have, no doubt, combined with the events you have related to bring her to this afflicting situation, —take this purse, procure her proper nourishment and clothing, and she will yet, perhaps, recover, and accompany you home, reclaimed by suffering."

At these words the unfortunate girl raised herself convulsively from her pillow, a wild scream burst from her lips, and the names of Villars, St. Clair, were mingled with heartrending sobs and piteous wailings.

Sir Theodore approached the couch. Merciful Heaven! did his eyes deceive him—or was it St. Clair's servant? Were those Lucy's features; nipped and rendered haggard by the hand of death, that so unexpectedly met his view?

She motioned him to approach her, and, in tremulous accents, supplicated his forgiveness for the injury she had done, not only himself, but her young mistress.

"She wanders," said Sir Theodore, "how can the poer girl have injured me?"

"Oh, yes!" replied the heartbroken penitent, "deeply and without repair have I injured you, but the Almighty has visited my sins on my head, and not *only* mine, but on this poor baby's, who will be left fatherless and motherless."

She then proceeded to state the various gradations of deception and vice into which Grenville's promises and her own avarice and vanity had led her—her mistress's cautions and reproofs—her incessant attempts to throw the captain's letters in her way,—introducing him into the garden to play beneath her window; with all the numerous arts of chicanery in which they had acted in concert.

But how agonisingly did she rivet the attention of her auditor, when describing the evening she was surprised, when awaiting her father's return, and made captive by their previous arrangement.

The last throb of parting existence seemed centred in this soul-harrowing moment; and the dying girl dwelt earnestly on Adela's unshaken fidelity to her absent friend—her energetic conduct—in terms, although rustic, yet deeply pathetic. And Sir Theodore wept at the truth now unveiled to his view.

Adela's mysterious disappearance was not forgotten, nor the confusion of her mind, when awaking from her trance-like slumber. She could not detail the encounter on the heath, (of which he had already been informed by Clifford,) because she knew nothing of it; but the sudden departure of the captain, his friend's arrival to pay off the servants, cast *her adrift, unrewarded* for her performance, in this hateful drama, she related as clearly as a frame exhausted by misery, a soul racked by the united terrors of a future state, and *too late* repentence would permit.

She concluded by acknowledging the justice of Heaven; for induced by her deserted and hopeless condition, expecting to be pursued by the resentment of a justly incensed master, and dreading to return to her parents, she had accepted the protection of Captain Grenville's servant; who, after a series of ill-treatment, brought her to that wretched hovel to expire with her baby, divested of all human aid.

And here it was her unhappy parents had discovered her.

In their search for her, they had met the villain a few hours after his desertion. They recalled the period when Lucy, innocent and happy, under the protection of the excellent St. Clairs, had frequently, in her visits to them, been conducted home by this young man, contrary to their advice and caution; they enquired of him if he knew anything about her, and he directed them to the spot where he said he understood she was residing, although he had himself not seen her for months.

Sir Theodore shuddered, whilst he contemplated the hapless victim of a traitor's guile, and her own ambitious and confiding folly. But the violence of her emotion had exhausted her. Her mother gently raised her, whilst her father presented a small quantity of wine to her parched and pallid lip, in the hope to revive her. Unavailing care! the hand of death was upon her; she turned her eyes on her infant, breathed a prayer, and they closed for ever!

"Sad close of a life commenced in innocence!" sighed the generous youth, "may thy sorrows have expiated thy transgressions!" and presenting ten sovereigns, in addition to what he had before given, he took the address of the disconsolate pair, and leaving them to their mournful duties, rushed from a scene, which had recalled his earliest vision of perfection in all its melancholy splendour.

Alas! the unshaken faith which had survived even the abandonment of his, and all the opprobrium with which appearances must have shaded his name! the lustre of mental and personal loveliness unequalled, were now beneath the turf of a lowly and unheeded grave.

He returned to the chaise, where Ralph awaited him wondering at his delay, and, having recommenced their journey, he related his sad adventure; the confession the succeeding sad events had elicited, and its fatal conclusion.

He also mentioned his purpose of providing for the support of the infant, who could not be responsible for its parent's errors; and as an orphan, he considered it truly an object of compassion, thrown in his path as a refuge from future destruction.

"Your honour is very good, and ready to heap benefits even on an enemy," said Ralph, his voice faltering with suppressed emotion.

"Should I," replied Sir Theodore, "of all others be unmerciful? I who have been the cause of all this woe. Had I sought an explanation it would have been granted. Miss St. Clair had been mine, the family yet at the Valley, the villain Grenville's schemes defeated, and his unfortunate, although guilty accomplice perhaps now the happy wife of some honest rustic,—yes, I alone have been the cause of all this desolation."

"Not the cause, my honoured master, not the cause, but the sufferer on all sides for the deceit of others."

A manly tear stole down his cheek, which he hastily dried, to descend, and give the requisite orders at the inn, at which Sir Theodore purposed resting for the night.

CHAPTER XXXVIII.

She wept the days when hope's gay-hue
　　Its golden lustre lent;
And breathed a lay to memory true
　　As o'er her harp she bent.
Ah reckless! he who could forego
　　Truth's purest, holiest shrine,
Or teach the pearly tears to flow
　　From those sweet eyes of thine!—F. A. KENTISH.

TIME with Adela glided rapidly away. Mrs. Drayton's was a mind that improved upon acquaintance, and Caroline and her little Rosalie hourly advanced in all the fondest parent could desire. The pleasure the former evidently felt in her society, the fond caresses of the latter, their regret when she left the villa to visit her parents, their unfeigned joy at her return, assured her she might place this interesting family on her list of friends. Nor was Charles less a favourite, or a less ardent candidate for Adela's good opinion. At once charmed with his little Rosalie's improvement, and emulous to succeed in the studies assigned him, an additional ardour seemed to animate every exertion.

" And for this," said the happy mother, " for this we are indebted to you, my love.   Oh ! that their beloved father had survived to witness and share my satisfaction."

Mrs. Drayton's associates were selected with that discernment which marked her every action.   We have said she sought not a host of worldlings, because she hated mere professions and bounded her circle to the few really estimable.

Amongst these were Mr. Egerton and his sister, and Mrs. Montreville and her son Frederick, the elegant youth we have before introduced to our readers ; and these usually came to pass a few weeks at the villa, during the summer season.

But it was not possible that such attractions as Adela's should be encountered by the heart alive to that beauty, which receives its brightest lustre from the mind, harmlessly.   Her unassuming elegance, her dignified simplicity of manner, the silver tones of her voice, had stolen into the soul of Egerton ; and he anxiously sought to discover whether her heart was disengaged, that he might lay his, with the splendid independence to which he had recently succeeded, at her feet.

Caroline's birthday was always set apart by her fond mother as a little festival.

It was at the commencement of July, when a cloudless sky was reflected in the glossy river that flowed beneath the windows of their favourite pavilion, and a profusion of fruit and flowers spread their vernal treasures, and unfolded their beauties, regaling the sense and refreshing the gale.

A select dinner party, to which some neighbouring families were invited, and a *Bal Champetre*.   All was frank and elegant hospitality on the part of the fair hostess, and real festivity on that of her favoured guests.   Egerton was a candidate for Adela's hand, young Montreville presented his to the interesting Caroline, nor amongst the graceful and the fair, that shared that evening's entertainment, were Charles and his little Rosalie excluded ; young and happy, beautiful as angels, they seemed the personification of love and innocence.

Garlands of flowers were tastefully suspended from the trees ; the Pavilion, concealed behind their umbrageous shadow, formed the orchestra, and the dancers tripped, in gay and graceful measure, upon the smooth and verdant carpet spread by nature.

An elegant supper was prepared, beneath an awning at the end of the lawn, which was brilliantly illuminated ; and, notwithstanding the late, or rather early hour at which the party separated, Egerton retired to a sleepless pillow.

On the follow morning he sought a private interview with Mrs. Drayton, and, unwilling to leave his ardent hopes to chance, amidst so many admirers, he entreated her interest in his favour.

" My esteem for yourself, as well as that I bear your family," replied Mrs. Drayton, " demand sincerity ; were my young friend's heart disengaged, I know not the individual on whom I should see it bestowed with so much pleasure. But alas ! I fear it is not, and indeed I have been made to understand that it has been an early prey to sorrow.   Nevertheless, you have my permission to unfold your wishes to her, conscious as I am of the honour and integrity of the sentiment which actuates you."

And Egerton sought with tremulous agitation this *eclaircissement.*

Adela was too candid to encourage hopes she could not realise, but when she destroyed the fascinating imagery, raised by the most disinterested and tender of passions.   She changed her empire in his heart, to that of an esteem pure and unchangeable as the virtues by which it was inspired.

Miss Egerton felt her brother's disappointment severely, for she was a most affectionate sister ; to her he had unfolded his hopes and their recent destruction. She had wandered into the garden, she had heard the sound of the harp from the

Pavilion; the voice it accompanied was too sweet not to be Adela's, and she paused to listen to the following *rondeau*.

Oh, place this rose amidst the gold
Of thy soft braided hair;
Nor wake amidst its crimson fold
The fairy sleeping there.

It must not near this heart be placed,
Its fond vibrations soon
Would that enchanting slumber chase,
And dearest! yet 'tis noon.

Then place this rose amidst the gold,
Of thy soft braided hair;
Nor wake amidst its crimson fold
The fairy sleeping there.

It was Theodore's! written in one of the gayest moments of elated hope on an occasion when she had presented him with a rose.

Alas! the flower, those few dear lines had celebrated, together with those happy days, were alike no more! and, she reclined her graceful head over the harp, to conceal the tear that was not to be repressed.

"Too truly," said Miss Egerton, "has Mrs. Drayton spoken. This interesting girl cherishes a hopeless passion!"

She paused until she saw the tear dried, and the benign smile of resignation restored, and, entering the Pavilion, requested she would take a turn with her beside the river.

"My dear Miss St. Clair," said she, "you are born to inflict sorrow as to communicate felicity. To us your influence has been of a mingled description, commencing in joy to end in sorrow. We had already designated you as the presiding goddess of our little domain, but poor Horace has told me all! and he can have little chance of the restoration of his tranquillity whilst he beholds you, or even the scene to which your presence has given so many charms. We shall depart this evening, will you not permit a farewell?"

"Alas!" said Adela, "how much too highly does the partial favour of my friends appreciate the talents of a simple girl, already dead to all joy; but that which emanates from her duties and the felicity she is capable of imparting to her parents, and the few valued individuals who have honoured her with their esteem."

"You will see my brother then?"

"I am not an advocate for adieus, but how can I deny a request made by Miss Egerton?"

When Adela returned to the parlour, she saw Caroline behind her mother's chair, and Rosalie on her knee; a letter was unfolded before her, and joy and sorrow seemed struggling for the ascendancy in her attractive features.

Caroline congratulated her mother, and Rosalie, kissing away her tears, exclaimed, "Uncle Albert is safe. Now I shall see Uncle Albert?"

Adela would have retired, but Mrs. Drayton extended her arms to her.

'Who is so capable of sympathising with our present feelings, as our dear Miss St. Clair? My brother, whom I had mourned as lost, has written me a few hasty lines to inform me that he has been from England, to which he has only a few days ago returned, that he is broken in spirit, and declining in health, having suffered severely from a bad climate, and only remains until his strength is sufficiently renovated to enable him to join us."

"He concludes by saying, that he will not enter into a detail of the adventures which have so long detained him from us, even previous to his absence from his native land, for they have been so similar to an Arabian Night's adventure, that they will form a topic for the astonishment of the girls and boy, on a wet evening in the Pavilion, or a fireside story, when winter has wrapped the gardens and fields in his mantle of snow."

Adela felt interested in everything that could give joy to her favourites ; and their friends, who had been on a little excursion in the neighbourhood accompanied by Charles, entering, they united their congratulations.

In the evening, Mr. and Miss Egerton departed ; the former entreating that although another more *happy* individual might possess her heart, he might carry the assurance of her esteem into his exile, which would only be cheered by the remembrane of the *few delightful hours* he had been permitted to enjoy her society.

Adela permitted him to imprint a kiss on her hand, and bade him adieu with a melancholy sweetness, that smoothed the certainty that fate had destined them a different path through life, which to him was now divested of every prospect of felicity.

Miss Egerton embraced her tenderly, and the girls waved their adieus until the carriage of the Egertons was no longer discernible.

On the following morning the Montrevilles also returned to their home, previous to a visit they purposed making to the Continent, and Caroline remained pale, pensive and thoughtful.

The anxious eye of the most affectionate of mother's read the cause of this sadness. The mutual preference between these amiable young people had long been evident, although *unacknowledged ;* Caroline's innocent heart was unconscious of the nature of its own sentiments, but she felt happy in his presence, and uneasy in his absence, whilst Frederick was " ages gone " in a passion which he felt was his fate. He had disclosed his heart to his mother, she warmly approved an inclination which had its origin from the moment they *met* in the cottage—where the little Rosalie was rescued from a fate so desolate, and every hour had added to that tender interest. But Caroline was yet too young to become a bride.

" We will pass a year on the Continent," said Mrs. Montreville, " and if at the end of that period, you both retain your present sentiments, *then* I shall delightedly receive my favourite from the hands of my Frederick as a beloved daughter."

After their departure, Mrs. Drayton called Adela to her dressing room.

" I have an idea," said she, " of making a little excursion. My brother is at Liverpool, the journey will benefit you all, and remove the depression from Caroline's spirits ; have you any objection to accompany us ? we shall not be absent more than a fortnight."

" Certainly not," replied Adela, " the change of place need not interrupt Rosalie's studies ; I will, however, if you will permit me, apprize my parents of your wish."

It was determined they should depart in two days, travel in Mrs. Drayton's carriage, and take apartments for the period of their stay. These matters arranged, Adela prepared to return to her father's, obtain their approbation, and pass the night and the following day in their beloved society.

Her visit was unexpected as it was welcome, alternately pressed to each fond heart, they gazed with delight on the rose which had returned to her cheek, and which was brightened by the joyful emotion their presence occasioned. They did not disapprove of the journey, for the change of air would be beneficial. If only for a fortnight, she was frequently longer than that away from them ; and would be under unquestionable protection. What then should cast a cloud over those delightful hours, devoted to the blissful communion of three such hearts ?

———

CHAPTER XXXIX.

Her midnight meals in secrecy she takes,
Low murmuring to the moon, that rising breaks
Through night's dark gloom ; oh ! how much more forlorn
Her night, that knows of no returning morn.—BLOOMFIELD.

ADELA made many little arrangements, tending to the comfort of her parents before she left them on the following evening ; she cheered their hearts with the prospect of being ultimately enabled to return, and quit them no more. Her spirits were no longer chained by affliction, and although memory cast her halo of pensiveness over that pure and lovely bosom, the pang it sometimes renewed was mellowed by time, and alleviated by conscious rectitude. But alas! the hour of parting, that unwelcome hour will arrive; and the carriage, that Mrs. Drayton

had sent for her young friend (accompanied by a note, entreating her not to delay her return, and a present of game, and the finest fruit obtainable for Mr. and Mrs. St. Clair, of which she solicited their acceptance) reminded her that time has wings.

Mrs. Drayton had awaited the arrival of her favourite with extreme impatience, for she much feared her parents would object to her going with them. Besides, the girls' arrangements and her own were made, and several little presents in readiness for Adela, which she considered suitable to the occasion.

On the next morning they were on the road at five, and the weather being extremely fine, the whole party enjoyed the variety of scenery through which, in the words of Charles and Rosalie, "they seemed to whirl," high in expectation, and buoyant in spirits.

They stopped only to change horses, and to take refreshments, which a servant always rode forward to order in the best possible style; and they put up for the night at the principal hotel in a town in Warwickshire, for the little ones had laughed and talked themselves to sleep; and after an early supper, they retired to repose. But poor Caroline passed a sleepless night, and in the morning her mother found her indisposed and languid. The journey, therefore, for that day was delayed. On the next she was worse, and medical aid was summoned; and, on the third, Mrs. Drayton determined not to extend her journey, but ordered a search to be made for private apartments, where they might at once await the restoration of Caroline's health, and her brother's arrival.

The town contained many families, who, having risen by their industry to extreme opulence, possessed very neat and even elegant residences on its outskirts; and amongst them many very readily proffered theirs for the month required, at a reasonable compensation, so that Mrs. Drayton and her family were easily accommodated; and they had no sooner removed thither, than she wrote to her brother. She informed him of her intended surprise, her daughter's sudden indisposition, and her determination to await his arrival at her present residence.

Caroline's illness was not of a serious nature. Her affectionate mother's care, the sympathetic attentions of her dear Adela, to whom her whole heart was unveiled, the caresses of her child, her own Rosalie, and her little brother, but, above all, a letter from Frederick, conspired to restore her. The studies of Rosalie were continued, and their evenings were again devoted to amusement and pleasure.

Adela wrote to her parents, informing them of the circumstance that had varied Mrs. Drayton's plan, and the necessary protraction of her stay. She entreated them to ease her anxiety during that painful absence, by writing to her as frequently as possible.

"Your Adela is far away from your tender care. She beholds that peaceful, that rustic abode which contains her all of human happiness only in her dreams. But there her spirit lingers, and though her duty bears her thence, her soul is with her parents!"

She wrote to her young friends, Maria and Louisa Arnold, and received their animated and affectionate replies with those of her parents, who informed her that they had the pleasure of Mr. and Mrs. Arnold's society for two days, and expected the girls in the following week. They concluded by imploring the blessing of the Creator on their only treasure.

It was a lovely evening in August, Adela and the girls wandered out, accompanied by Charles, into the neighbouring fields and meadows. Rosalie did not like Warwickshire half so well as the country surrounding their own sweet home; but she continued to run races with her little friend, and receive all the pretty wild flowers he selected for her to copy, until the evening began to close in; when a thin, pale, haggard looking female started forward, and, holding out her hand, implored Adela's charity.

"A few pence, good lady, to save me from starvation."

Adela looked with compassion on the mendicant. Her eye was so wild, and her appearance so pallid and emaciated, that it was evident she was bereft of reason; and this opinion her dress confirmed, for, although torn and disordered, it was of good materials, and made according to the present fashion.

Adela had drawn a shilling from her purse, but she hesitated, lest by proffering it, she should insult the feelings of those to whom she might belong. But it had caught her eye, and she snatched it, hurried it into her pocket, and renewed her solicitations to Caroline, who tremulously shrunk behind her friend, whilst Charles put his arms round Rosalie, who was evidently terror-stricken.

But Adela was unconscious of any such sensation. Her anxiety was increased to know who the unfortunate maniac was, and whence she came, that she might be instrumental in restoring her to her home.

To this inquiry she replied by a hollow laugh ; and, approaching Adela's ear,—

" Some say," said she, " that I am the Duchess of Wellington,—others that I am plain Mrs. Crawley, and that large house in view is mine. But Lord !—I don't believe either the one thing or the other—any more than their flummery about my being very rich, and having everything I can sigh for. Don't you think they're mocking me ? God bless you ! fine riches indeed ! when I've only eaten a dry crust for these three days, and haven't a bed to rest my weary limbs on ! I did dream once that I was married to somebody, and that his extravagance had ruined me,—that he had brought me to my last penny, and sent me wild."

" It must be fancy," said Adela, endeavouring to soothe her ; " return my friend, and compose your agitated mind."

Adela had discerned, through these wild observations, a similarity to the circumstances mentioned by Mr. Arnold, which the name of Crawley placed beyond a doubt.

Was this, then, the favourite of fortune ? the cruel innovation of the rights of others ?—the female who had closed the doors of their dying relative on her beloved father ?—avenging Heaven ! but a fallen foe (and how could humanity fall lower ?)—was a sacred object to this noble-minded girl ; and, endeavouring, in French, to soothe the fears of Caroline, she sought the best means of restoring this unhappy woman to her friends.

The approach of a livery servant, and a female attendant, took this charge off her hands, by approaching and leading her into the gate of the house she had pointed out as supposed to be her own.

She did not oppose them ; but putting her hand through the footman's arm she exclaimed, in a tone of authority,—

" It is well !—I obey the king's mandate. Lead on, my lord, to the palace !"

Wealth, it is said, does not always bring felicity. Here was a terrific example :—Mrs. Crawley had followed her husband to London,—she had witnessed his debaucheries,—been induced, by threats and violence, to pay his debts ; and had returned to see them renewed in the vicinity of his home. Some one had directed her to the village where Susan resided ; and she followed him thither, created a disturbance in the neighbourhood, and got her husband surrounded, and pelted with mud and stones. He with difficulty escaped from an infuriated mob, and she returned to her home, after violently assaulting her already miserable rival.

But peace had deserted her for ever ; and it is thought that this last adventure, united with a calculation her reverend protector had made of the sums expended by her husband, had completed the overthrow of her reason.

This was a singular, and not a very pleasant termination of their walk ; and they returned to relate their adventure. And Adela, in retiring to her pillow, at once breathed her thanks to her Creator for the precepts her loved parents had inculcated ; and implored pardon and restored peace for her fallen enemy.

Well has Milton said, that

" The mind is its own place, and in itself
Can make a heaven of hell—a hell of heaven."

Here was a living proof of the insufficiency of wealth. Robert Crawley had sacrificed, at the gaming table (for that was his ultimate resort), one-third of their yearly income, and from that moment nothing had haunted Sarah but penury, want, and destitution. She was, at that moment, mistress of two thousand pounds per year, with expectations from her mother, and the most splendid ones from her protector. Yet she suffered all the pangs of hunger, terror, and despair. She who had conceived herself above the possibility of a want—who had looked with scorn on the victims of adversity, now, by a singular fatality, endured all their pangs, and partook of all their sufferings. This, under her present bereavement of reason, was not remarkable, when we consider the early associations of ignorant parents, united with prejudices inherited with their wealth. Here, indeed, were the "sins of the fathers visited upon the children;" because the greater portion of that wealth had been obtained in a manner unanswerable to the just or honourable mind.

Such individuals as Mrs. Crawley's ancestors become more opulent yearly, only in proportion to the number of unfortunate beings they can employ in the various ramifications of their manufactures. Their gain thus increasing at so much per head, they become mercenary and selfish in its acquisition,—a feeling which guides all the calculations of the West-India planter, who considers himself possessed of so much per annum, exactly in proportion to the number of unfortunates he is placed in a condition to render desolate and miserable, accumulating the product of their exertions, although unmindful of their sufferings.

CHAPTER XL.

Ne'er peeped the laughing eye of golden morn,
Within these lonely caves. By ages worn,
They seemed amidst a gay luxuriant clime—
Sacred to deeds of tyranny and crime;
And many a captive here has met his doom,
Chained to the horrors of a living tomb.—F. A. KENTISH.

AFTER the departure of Mrs. St. Clair from the home of her ancestors, which occurred on the morning previous to that on which her nuptials with Don Ramella were to have been solemnised, the deepest resentment appeared to have stifled all the tenderness of a mother in the bosom of Donna Angelica, who used every exertion, and ultimately succeeded in alienating her father so completely that he vowed never to behold her more; and this severity was not likely to be softened by the intelligence of her union with St. Clair, whose father they deemed a heretic. Years had elapsed without varying these ungenial impressions. But the alienated heart of Donna Angelica turned, with increased tenderness, to a son, who had ever been her favourite. To his affection she leaned, as the solace of every care, and hoped to receive, in his union with the daughter of a rich and noble family, a consolation for the loss of her own.

But here again were her anticipations defeated, and her hopes overclouded.

The alliance they had so anxiously sought, presented itself in the sister of Don Ramella; and the day was fixed which was to have compensated all other disappointments.

But Heaven had decided otherwise; for the sudden death of Don Luiz crushed the hopes of the parents, and laid the honours of that illustrious house in the dust.

Don Manuel wept over the tomb of his son, whom he fondly loved. He would fain have recalled his daughter to console a mother, whose heart, softened by sorrow, would now relentingly have unfolded to receive her. But all attempts were vain, and the intelligence that they had left Cadiz, whither no one could discover, had so powerful an effect on a mind overwhelmed with regret for her son, and remorse for its former severity, that she only survived him for a few months.

Don Manuel was a most affectionate father. His girl had been his darling; who could now have power to console him under the bereavement occasioned by the death of a wife of a son who had formed the pride of his heart, but his Aurora? He resolved to leave no means untried to discover her retreat.

The solitude of his castle became hateful to him. His memory reverted to the happy days when those three beloved cherubs sported like little loves across his path—

" Or climbed his knee, the envied kiss to share."

These scenes were no longer bearable. He resolved to retire to the mansion of his brother Don Antonio; and the castle remained under the care of an old house-keeper and steward, who had grown grey in the service of the family. He had no sooner arrived at Madrid, than he wrote to all the mercantile houses in Cadiz, and the principal ports in Spain, requesting no English vessel should arrive without an inquiry of the captain, if the family of Edmund St. Clair was known to him, or had ever reached his ear.

Year followed year and brought nothing but disappointment to the hopeless father.

One of the first grandees of Spain, possessed of wealth for which he had neither value nor inclination, envied the lowliest peasant, who shared, amidst his toils and privations, the embrace of his children. The name of father vibrated with a sensation of anguish upon his heart, and he looked forward to an unmourned tomb, as the termination of his afflictions.

But it frequently occurs that when we deem ourselves most desolate, a spring of joy arises in the heart, and hope's cheering smile dispels the gloom. Intelligence was brought him that the captain of an English vessel had heard of a family named St. Clair, in some part of Warwickshire.

Overjoyed, yet scarcely knowing what plan to pursue, he at first thought of writing; but the chance of delay seemed like death to the ardour of his anxiety. All he had loved, excepting his Aurora, were consigned to the tomb, his own life waning fast—should he die unreconciled to his child? No. He would instantly proceed to England; he would himself seek her through all the fatigue and peril such an undertaking might present. He departed from Madrid with one trusty servant, and, having some business of importance in Italy, he seized that occasion as the only one that might again offer.

The intended departure of Don Manuel de Mello was soon whispered at court; and an ambitious rival, who had sought his destruction, seized on the present opportunity to effect his purposes. He therefore laid a plan, that, just as he was entering upon the Italian frontiers, he should be seized by four men selected for that purpose, and instantly despatched.

The first part of the journey was performed without interruption, and the venerable father already enjoyed, in anticipation, the meeting with his daughter after so many painful events, and years of hopeless absence; when, on reaching the appointed spot, he was surrounded and fallen upon in a pass between two mountains.

Being entirely unprepared for such an attack, he would easily have become the prey of the assassins, had not his servant, Pedro, observed them making towards his carriage, along the valley, about fifty paces off.

He hastily gave the alarm—they instantly alighted, and, with concentrated courage, prepared, alone as they were, to offer the utmost resistance; the post-boy being apparently overwhelmed with the utmost terror from the moment of their appearance.

This determined conduct, for a man of Don Manuel's years, and his servant, who was a very few his junior, somewhat disconcerted them, because it was unexpected. It appeared to damp their ardour for the moment, but, after a short consultation, it was agreed that they had advanced too far to retreat, as the conspiracy might ultimately transpire; and, being four to two, they courageously determined on the attack.

Without a moment's further delay they pressed their intended victims closely, and three were directed to secure the nobleman, the fourth to despatch Pedro.

But Don Manuel's pistol was levelled at their leader as he approached, and the aim he took was so deliberate, that he fell from his horse, and instantly expired.

Just at this moment he received the fire of the whole three; but, from that trepidation which usually accompanies a bad cause, neither of the balls struck him. Pedro's aim had also been ineffectual, and before he could draw forth a second pistol, they were closely invested and made prisoners, the postilion having made his escape.

As, however, the chief of these assassins, who was to have received the principal reward, was thus cut off, the second in command bethought him that it might be much more beneficial to treat with Don Manuel for his safety, than to return to Madrid with the account of his death.

A moment determined him, and he gave immediate instructions to his two comrades, that they should not assassinate him, but secure him, unharmed; and on an assurance to Don Manuel, that his life should be in perfect safety on the condition of his making no resistance, he suffered himself to be made captive, because there was no other alternative as a preventative of instant destruction.

It now became a point of debate how the nobleman should be disposed of; and they resolved he should be led to a cavern in the mountains, and there incarcerated, with his servant, in one of those cells which have long been famous amongst the banditti on that part of the continent.

In this uncertain condition, as to what might yet be their fate, they remained, until the chief of his assailants, stealing an interview, informed him that he could not prevail with the other two, to release him on any terms, and that they had determined upon that night for his destruction.

Pedro cast upon his master a glance of unutterable despair; but Don Manuel remained dignified and calm. They were divested of arms, or any other medium of resistance, closely watched, and both declining in years, yet his native pride did not for a moment desert him, and he calmly awaited the moment of destruction, when the fellow returned, and made the following proposal:—

"Don Manuel de Mello, there is a certain sum offered for your life by a minister at the court of Spain. Will you double it in the event of my rescuing you from the danger which threatens you, such an amount being requisite for my future sustenance, since to Madrid I can never return while you exist?"

Pedro turned a supplicating eye on his master, and Don Manuel assented.

But who was this minister? He was unconscious of possessing an enemy!

"That," said the ruffian, "shall be disclosed on my receiving an order for the compensation you promise me. But we must understand each other."

Here a conversation took place in a low tone. And Pedro felt his fears relieved when they were presented each with pistols, he had secretly conveyed beneath his cloak.

"Self preservation," said he, "is the first law of nature! If my comrades will not listen to mercy when even their own interest is at stake, I shall not hesitate about mine. Let each take a deliberate aim at the first that enters, and the report will be a signal for me to despatch the other."

Don Manuel and his servant passed the hours preceding this eventful evening in various suggestions relative to the individual who had thus treacherously sought his life. Pedro spread the repast which the fellow had brought them, accompanied by a flask of excellent wine; and they had but just concluded it when footsteps sounded without.

"And now for life and liberty!" said Don Manuel, as they drew their pistols from their bosoms, and lodged their contents in the heart of the first who entered. He fell, and his comrade shared the same fate; and Pedro would fain have served the third in the same way, but a glance from his master withheld him, and the word *honour*, sternly uttered, induced him to return his second pistol to his bosom.

Their liberator, after congratulating them on their preservation, agreed to accompany them until they had embarked at an Italian port for England, previous to which he was presented with a letter of credit for the sum agreed upon, and Don Manuel received in return the name of his enemy.

This stipulation accomplished, the assassin made the best of his way on board a vessel bound for the United States, whilst Don Manuel embarked for England.

But what had he heard? It must, assuredly, be a dream. Don Francisco! his bosom friend! *He* who had so frequently shared his hospitality—who had condoled with him with so much apparent sympathy,—who had urged him to seek his daughter as the consolation of his declining days? But the individual had been bred in the atmosphere of a court—his heart was corroded by envy, and Don Manuel happened to be the only barrier to his ambition. Alas! it was but too true; the paper was in his hand-writing, which placed it beyond a doubt; and he resolved, on the instant of his arrival, to communicate to his sovereign the plot which had been laid for his destruction.

CHAPTER XLI.

The flying vehicle had now
Proceeded on an hour or so;
It seemed an universal silence
Might be looked for many a mile hence,
 For no one spoke
 In seriousness or joke.—HOB'S MORNING EXCURSION.

THE evening was showery, and unpropitious to Charles's wish for a ramble with his little playfellow. Mrs. Drayton had therefore entreated Adela to read a new publication, whilst she finished a purse she destined for her brother, and Caroline and Rosalie amused themselves with drawing.

The half closed windows opened on a pretty lawn, which was bounded by an iron railing and gate; so that Mrs. Drayton easily recognised her long absent brother, when his chaise drove up.

In the joy of the moment she arose, and Adela arose also, not wishing to be present at the re-union of a family after so long a separation.

But what was her consternation and dismay when she beheld, advancing up the pathway, not the dejected and suffering individual described to her as the brother of her friend, but Captain Grenville, high in health, and apparently in spirits! It was her persecutor, the barbarian who had cost her beloved father so many months of agony, which might have terminated in death.

With indescribable horror she heard him announced, and, scarcely capable of supporting herself, passed unnoticed, amidst their mutual congratulations, to her chamber.

When there she paused not a moment, but putting on her bonnet and cloak, tripped softly down the stairs and passed through the back gate, determined to sleep under the canopy of heaven, rather than beneath the same roof with Captain Grenville.

When she had crossed a spacious field, and a lane that led to the town, she rested on a stile, to reflect for a moment on the best plan she could pursue.

The rain had ceased, but the heavy and louring clouds portended a stormy night; she knew not an individual to whom she could resort for advice or shelter. She feared to seek a bed at the hotel where they had remained on their first arrival for many reasons; Mrs. Drayton would certainly inquire for her the moment the hurry attendant on her brother's arrival had subsided, and when night approached, with maternal anxiety, would search for her in every direction. This must be avoided; she therefore hastened thither, went into a private room, wrote the following note, sealed and despatched it by a waiter.

"MY DEAR MADAM,—I cannot now explain to you the motive of my sudden departure; at a future hour you will acquit me of precipitation or caprice.

"In the meanwhile my esteemed friend, my Caroline, my Rosalie, and Charles, forget not your fugitive, but mingle in your prayers the name of your obliged, your affectionate   "ADELA ST. CLAIR."

Not an instant was now to be lost; she resolved not to sleep in the town, but make the best of her way to the first village on her road homeward, which, from its pleasantness, she had noticed on her arrival, and there to endeavour to procure a bed at a private house for the night.

Unfortunately the coach had passed, so that there was no alternative but to walk thither; although the clouds threatened momentarily to inundate the wayfaring traveller.

The night was obscure, the road lonely, and Adela's light footsteps followed each other in rapid succession over the damp and irregular path—her pace quickened by terror, and her heart palpitating with anxiety.

Observing a female figure at some distance in advance of her, and imagining it might be some one returning late from market, she increased her speed, that she might continue in her vicinity, if she found it impossible absolutely to join company with her; and observing the stranger stop on hearing her approaching footsteps, she inquired how far distant they were from the next village.

"Village!" exclaimed a voice, in which she tremblingly recognised the maniac; "village! fifty thousand miles to be sure! and let me tell you no sinecure you'll find the journey, if this is your first pilgrimage. Why, do you know, we shall have all that way to crawl up a crazy ladder that shakes beneath every step; and then the gulf below! it's beautiful! make haste, make haste, for we've no time to lose, I'll assure you!"

The wild shriek, and wilder antics, that accompanied this invitation excited the terror of a mind already sufficiently perturbed by the previous adventures of the evening; but she soon found it requisite to summon all her presence of mind and self-command, for, seizing her arm with a powerful grasp,—

"Do you hesitate?" said the maniac; "well, then, I'll give you a helping hand, for it's something like the straight road and the narrow path the old boy used to preach about."

Here she would have forced Adela into the ditch that ran beside the road, had she not eluded her grasp, and passed some distance beyond her extended arms, whch were malignantly spread to grasp her.

"Oh—oh! you're not inclined to learn to swim, then," she exclaimed, with a wild and hollow laugh, which ended in a shriek. And fortunate enough it was for Adela that it did so, for it directed her attendants (whose vigilance she had eluded during the early part of the evening) to the spot, and thus relieved the gentle and generous-hearted girl, not only from fears excited by her boundless humanity, but also those her own danger had excited. And she made the best of her way forward to the place of her destination.

The storm, which had hitherto threatened, now poured down with unrestrained violence; and, although she wrapped her cloak closely round her, every article of her clothing was completely drenched.

It was nearly eleven when she reached the village, and very gladly took shelter at a small confectioner's shop, where she requested a glass of whey, being feverish and thirsty.

"Why, my dear lady," said the old woman, who invited her to go through into the parlour, "have you been out in such a night? You're positively wet through—a glass of warm negus will be better than all the whey in the world, and let me beg of you to come in, and dry your clothes, whilst we get it you."

Adela felt anguish and weary: she willingly accepted the proffer of the hospitable stranger, and at the same time mentioning her disappointment of the night coach, inquired if she knew where she could procure a bed, that she might be sufficiently rested to pursue her route by the coach in the morning.

"Why, miss," said the good woman, "there is the inn opposite the coach goes from, but it's not what I like for young ladies to sleep alone at inns. Here's only my daughter and myself, she can sleep with me, and I'll make up her bed for you in a trice, if you please; for although humble, we're very neat and tidy, and the sooner you get off these wet clothes the better, in my humble opinion.

Adela coincided in her opinion, and very gladly accepted her offer; the chamber was prepared in a few minutes, and her clothes hung to the fire. Her last prayer was to be protected from the snares of her persecutor, and safely restored to the seclusion of her beloved home; and she immediately sunk into an entire oblivion of all the apprehension, terror, and fatigue she had so lately encountered.

At half-past six the young woman brought her clothes perfectly dried, and in a few minutes she was ready to follow her to the parlour, where the breakfast was neatly arranged.

Adela felt little inclination, yet the manner of her hostess and her daughter was so attentive and kind, that she sat down and partook of it with them. In a quarter of an hour the coach was ready to depart, and she drew out her purse to shy the expenses she had incurred. But this was positively refused by the widow. "If my poor girl had been so situated," said she, "I should have been glad she could have been so accommodated. We have done nothing more, miss," said she,

No. 25.

'than perform the duties of a very ordinary hospitality, and if our humble attempt to make you comfortable has been acceptable, we shall feel quite satisfied, and hope, whenever chance may bring you this way, you will favour us with a call."

Adela still persisted, but it was in vain; the kindhearted widow would receive nothing, and with the warmest acknowledgments of their politeness, she took her leave, and found an elderly lady, her only companion in the vehicle, which started immediately.

An uninterrupted silence was preserved for the first mile, during which period, not only her countenance, but even her apparel, underwent the strictest scrutiny: at length she ventured to ask how far she was going.

Adela replied, "About ninety miles."

The charm thus broken, one question followed the other, with the utmost volubility, for her curiosity appeared insatiable. But although our heroine's manners were condescending and polite on all occasions, that suavity was mingled with a dignity that, by a glance, threw vulgar importance back into itself; and finding her questions of how old she was, where she lived, who were her parents, and how it had happened that such a genteel young lady was travelling so far alone, either unanswered or replied to with an archness that at once conveyed satire and reproof, she was relapsing into her former silence, when fortunately another subject for investigation appeared in the person of a fashionable-looking young man, who on entering gave his dog with particular charge to the guard.

They had not proceeded far, when, fixing his eyes on Adela, he declared himself happy beyond expression in the chance of passing a few hours in the presence of a divinity; and entreated that she would tell him how far she was going.

The familiarity of the compliment, and its following inquiry, was anything but gratifying. Her reply was such as to convince the beau, he was not addressing a female of ordinary acquirements; and disappointed in the hope of drawing her into an animated conversation, he seemed likely to fall into the elderly lady's taciturnity.

But the questions he had put to her companion had awakened a spirit only momentarily dormant; and she replied that she believed the young lady was only going about ninety miles or so, and was proceeding to catechise the beau in her usual style, when the coach stopped to take up an old gentleman, with a faded camlet cloak over his arm, who had anxiously hailed it.

He ascended the steps with the gravity of Socrates, and sat down with his back to the horses, closed his eyes without the least notice of any one, and remained a considerable time in a profound reverie.

"Quite a caricature!" said the elderly lady in a whisper to the beau, who replied with a smile and a shrug; and all was again silent as though nobody was present.

But this inanity was not permitted to exist long, for the elderly lady, who had seemed very restless under it, espied a paper at the bottom of the coach, which curiosity induced her to take up.

It was a letter, but as the seal was broken she made no hesitation in opening it to ascertain its contents; a natural curiosity enough for an individual who would have trotted miles over the roughest country in Wales, to have obtained anything in the way of a new secret.

Taking out her spectacles, therefore, she read the letter with the greatest attention, looked at the younger gentleman with singular suspicion, and perused it again, with an apparent agitation, sufficiently indicative of the terror with which it had inspired her; at length she exclaimed, with eyes fixed steadfastly upon him,

"This is a most mysterious letter! perhaps sir, it may belong to you? and if it does, I shall instantly desire the coach to stop, for I don't choose to be travelling miles with people of your character, and nature!"

The gentleman looked somewhat astonished at this address, but at length taking the elderly lady for one of those whimsicalities, who make it a point to annoy every individual within their influence — he smiled, and coolly inquired what had occasioned her so much trepidation, assured her he was nothing in but a sportsman, and never did harm to any living being, except now and then killing a hare, or shooting a dozen or two of birds for his amusement.

"Huntsman, sir, did you say? for I'm rather hard of hearing."

"Ay, huntsman, if you please, madam; I've had something to do with foxes and stags too in my time."

"A huntsman! why that comes something near the mark. This letter treats of it. It's evidently addressed to a death hunter—a sort of bodysnatcher, sir!"

"Indeed, madam! perhaps you'll favour us with its contents."

"Contents, why then the contents says,—

"SIR,—I have not been able to procure you all the skeletons you ordered. I have sent you a dozen, which I hope will be delivered in time to go by the coach you are waiting for. They are properly arranged,—you will not find them difficult to put them together, and they will run easily enough."

On hearing the end of the sentence, the old gentleman opened his projecting eyes that glared beneath his eyebrows, and fixed them on the elderly gentlewoman with such an expression of horror and surprise, that she no longer doubted to whom the letter belonged.

Conceiving herself in the society of one who dealt in everything unholy, and, fancying the skeletons already beside her in the coach, her tortured imagination induced a sudden scream. She pulled down the window, and called out to the coachman to "stop and let her out,—to stop instantly for the love of Heaven!" for that she had got into company she would not ride with an hour to save her existence.

The old gentleman had by this time recovered sufficient confidence to inform her the letter was his, and assured her the skeletons were not of a nature to do her any bodily harm.

He then inquired of the coachman if a parcel had been received for him, and was informed it was put into the seat where the elderly lady was sittting.

On hearing this, with a look of consternation, she hurried to open the door, and without waiting for the letting down of steps, or the assistance of the guard, made the best of her way into the middle of the road.

The young gentleman, wishing to investigate this affair, apologised to Adela, hoped this unpleasant occurrence had not flurried her spirits, and proceeded to raise the seat the old lady had left, bringing out a small parcel.

"Here is a something," said he, "addressed to the Reverend Jonathan St. Clair —is it yours, sir?"

"It is, sir! the very parcel that has occasioned so much alarm to the lady who has deserted us so abruptly."

"Upon my soul, sir," said the young gentleman, "your dozen skeletons seem to be packed up in a small compass!"

"Oh, yes, sir, they're not human skeletons."

"Not human skeletons!" exclaimed the elderly gentlewoman, who had approached, on tiptoe, to the coach door, and continued eyeing the parcel with the most impatient earnestness: "then, sir, if they are not human skeletons, they can be nothing but skeleton keys; and, therefore, as I don't choose to travel with housebreakers, hand me down my portmanteau, coachman, and I'll wait here until some other coach passes."

"Impossible," said the coachman, with a grin, "why, madam, we're not within three miles of a pig stye, and no other coach will be likely to pass this spot for upwards of an hour."

"I care not where we are, coachman," replied the elderly lady: "here I'll remain till something comes up, if it's all night, rather than go five paces farther with any such character."

"Why, miss," continued she, addressing Adela, "I no sooner fixed my eyes upon him, than I had a presentiment of what he is. His very appearance betokens it."

Adela, in reply, endeavoured to persuade her to re-ascend the steps, and continue her journey; for she grieved to think a person in years should remain alone in so lonely a spot, with little chance of procuring a conveyance for hours. But she would not listen to reason, and used all her eloquence to persuade her, if she did not wish to be carried to some solitary place, and burked, to alight, and take the chance of another coach.

It appears that this lady, in her younger days, had been terrified by a skeleton, and the impression had worked so powerfully on her mind, that she could scarcely read the word without a shudder.

Adela saw plainly that the foregoing events had terribly disconcerted the old gentleman, whom she recognised by name as well as by Mr. Arnold's description.

He might, in a few minutes, have tranquillised the old lady's fears by a trifling and very simple explanation; but that he was ashamed to undertake; for the fact is, that they were a dozen of skeleton sermons which he had ordered, and that was the last thing on earth a clergyman, possessed of anything like decent intellect, would be likely to acknowledge; so that the relatives continued their journey, the clergyman in ignorance of Adela's vicinity, and Adela equally unprepossessed in favour of the clergyman, and unanxious for his recognition.

The young gentleman paid the most obsequious and respectful attention to his fair companion. The elder remained sulky and silent; but it was not likely that Adela's delicate frame could pass through the fatigues, terrors, and inclemencies of the preceding night with impunity. Her temples throbbed, her head ached, her hands were burning, and every moment increased her apprehensions that she should be unable to pursue her journey.

The old gentleman was set down about five miles on the road, and on his way thither he kept his eyes closed, and his protuberant under lip pursed up, as in a heavy slumber, probably to avoid any farther interrogatories from the young one. But his apprehensions were without foundation, for his attentions were too powerfully attracted by their fair companion, to allow a thought to recur to the mysterious parcel. Her languid eye, and the deepened crimson of her cheek, called forth his anxious inquiries as indicative of indisposition; and so rapidly had these unpleasant symptoms increased, during the last few hours, that it required all her fortitude to support herself until the coach had reached the point of destination, from whence her road homewards would diverge.

The young gentleman descended first, and respectfully offered his arm to assist her; he expressed his regret at being so soon deprived of her presence, and lamented her friends not having arrived to meet her, at a moment when she appeared suffering so severely under indisposition and fatigue.

Adela acknowledged his courtesy, and entered the small inn to await the passing of the stage, which was expected to go by in an hour, from thence to a hamlet in the vicinity of her father's cottage, whilst the coach continued its route towards London.

CHAPTER XLII.

And when all that is said and done,
Perhaps thou'st bought a million who're all gone!
On this what can we justly have to say?
Nothing, but that so many men
Were born, bought, sold, and died again;
And so have rapidly all passed away,
And that in consequence thou'rt rich as Jew!
That's all that we can say of you.—W. A. KENTISH.

GRENVILLE had remained in a state of painful captivity during the period of two months. He had been bought by an individual who speculated upon the purchase of such captives as he was aware would be likely to pay enormously for their liberty.

With this view he had an agent residing in Tunis, whose sole business it was to secure an intimacy with the officers employed in the different pirates, and through their medium to become acquainted, as far as possible, with the circumstances and condition of those who were thus captured, having, at the same time, orders to secure those, at any price, whose connexions were represented to be of consequence.

These were uniformly conveyed to his castle, in the interior, not to be employed in any occupation, but each confined in solitary dungeons, expressly apart, and constructed for the purpose.

In these receptacles their subsistence was wretched and scanty, in order to render their confinement the more insupportable ; and no communication was permitted between the prisoner and any person out of the establishment, until he had been familiar with this kind of torment for some two or three months.

At the expiration of this time, an offer was made to convey any intelligence to Europe that might be desired. But the first terms proposed for relief were generally exorbitant, until it could be ascertained what amount could be exacted from the private fortune or influence of the friends of the captive for his release.

If the sum proposed was not acceded to, it was intimated a fortnight would be taken to determine,—so that any additional period spent in this way added greater impatience to the desire of freedom ; and if there was then the slightest hesitation, fourteen days of accumulated severity and misery were certain to expire before any proposal would be listened to again.

This explanation, of course never deviated from, did not fail to reach the ears of these unfortunate beings, so that when the ransom of a fellow captive enabled Grenville to apprise his friend in England of his wretched condition, together with the amount stipulated for his liberation, which he directed him to receive from the hands of his banker, and forward without delay, little time was lost, and it arrived, accompanied by a letter, mentioning the recovery of St. Clair and his daughter, and their subsequent misfortunes, for he had not failed to inquire respecting them.

He also observed that his friend had nothing to fear from a family in their adverse circumstances, and advised his immediate return.

Grenville's captivity had rendered him another being. He wrote to his friend and to his sister. The latter, in the tenderness of her heart, augmented his described languor and declining health to the extreme of danger. Her reply was replete with sisterly love. (We have related her attempt to meet him at Liverpool, with its failure, in consequence of her daughter's indisposition.) She then wrote to say she should await his arrival in Warwickshire.

She mentioned the acquisition her family had made in the society of a young lady of the name of St. Clair, as governess to her daughter, and dwelt upon their Caroline's improvement in every elegant accomplishment, as an additional inducement to his sharing the intellectual pleasures of their calm and happy seclusion.

This was a startler to Grenville. His hours of solitary confinement had, we have said, induced reflection, ; remorse had visited his hitherto reckless heart, and he had lamented the lovely flower his unrelenting passion had, he feared, crushed in its hour of affliction. Her parent had also fallen by his hand. The retrospect of his past career had brought with it nothing but remorse and despair ; for neither could it be remedied nor restored ; but he fervently vowed, should he regain his liberty, to live a new life, and devote every future hour to some act of benevolence or piety.

In this frame of mind, his friend's letter had surprised him by the intelligence it contained, and whilst his heart awoke to a sentiment of gratitude to which it had long been a stranger, it inspired a gleam of that hope he had deemed for ever extinguished ; and he returned to England anxious to make every reparation in his power.

He was at Liverpool when Mrs. Drayton's letter arrived. An indescribable feeling of regret for the past stole over his heart, as he dwelt upon her description of the angelic qualities and rare endowments of her young friend.

Strange as the coincidence—he could not doubt but it was the same, and his passion, remoddled, awoke in all its ardour.

Oh, that he could, in that moment of contrition, annihilate in her mind the memory of his past transgression ! then might he lay his fortune at her feet, and compensate, by a life of devoted penitence, for its errors and wanderings ! then might his sister plead his cause, and be his recouciling angel !   But how ?—when that virtuous, that unsullied mind should be made acquainted with Adela's story, she would turn from him with mingled anguish and displeasure.   How then claim her as his advocate ?

When the hurry of congratulation had subsided, Mrs. Drayton went to Adela's chamber, in the hopes of participating the satisfaction her brother's arrival had given her, with her young friend, to whom she felt anxious to introduce him, but, to her utmost astonishment, found she was absent.

This being unusual, it occasioned some anxiety on account of the wetness of the evening, and the rain increasing, Charles set out with the footman in the direction she usually took in her rambles with the girls, with her clogs and an umbrella ; but their search was ineffectual, and they returned oniy to bring disappointment.

Mrs. Drayton consoled herself with the idea that she had taken shelter at some cottage, and would return when the shower had subsided. But Grenville too readily judged the cause of her retreat ; and, when eleven o'clock struck, his fears for her safety more than equalled Mrs. Drayton's and Caroline's, whilst Rosalie and Charles set down and wept in their fear lest any evil should have overtaken her.

Mrs. Drayton sent in every direction,—she was in an agony of apprehension. Grenville was ready to rush forward in search of her, although certain she would recoil from his approach : when, just as the clock struck twelve, the waiter arrived with Miss St. Clair's note, which, whilst it tranquillised their present fears, awakened the most melancholy apprehensions by its mystery.

The waiter had met with a friend as he sallied forth on the " pretty young lady's" errand (for such she was termed at the hotel). They had gone together on a stroll, and called at so many public-houses on their way that they became stupified, and it was only after a refreshing nap of about an hour that the note occurred to him ; and, although he had not lost much time after waking, it was not until twelve the note arrived.

Surmise followed surmise at its contents.   Mrs. Drayton mingled her tears with those of the girls, for the departure of one so truly dear to their hearts.

" Whatever may be Miss St. Clair's motive," said she, " I am certain she is guided by delicacy and propriety."

Grenville cast down his eyes. He could have unravelled the mystery ; he resolved to do so on the morrow, and retired to his chamber, overwhelmed with anxiety and apprehension.

CHAPTER XLIII.

"Then cease thy delusions, thy blandishments cease,
    Nor my quiet by useless entreaties annoy ;
In an innocent bosom I'll seek for that peaces
    Which the world cannot give, nor thy falsehood destroy !"

ADELA was conducted to a chamber. But the young person who attended her thither, alarmed at her appearance (for she was extremely ill), hastened to call her sister, who found her burning and shivering, and utterly incapable of proceeding on her journey.

" You had better, madam, lie down, and take a little rest," said she ; " you will, perhaps, feel better able to continue your journey by the evening coach. This room is quiet and retired, and if you require anything, you can just touch the bell which you will find at the head of the bed."

Adela felt the necessity of adopting her advice, and when she had drawn the window-curtain to exclude the light from her half-closed eyes, and left the room, she fastened the door, and rested her weary and aching limbs on the bed.

Her increasing indisposition rendered it impossible for her to proceed onwards that night, and, anxious as she felt to render her parents aware of her situation, her giddy head and dimness of sight prevented her.

She tried to calm the perturbation of her mind, but that was impossible ; for a thousand wild visions floated before her.

First, Theodore was restored to her, uncorrupted, and true as in the first happy hours of their pure and innocent communion. Then he was with her beloved parents—snatched from her for ever ! The angry frown of Sir Edward met her startled view,—the persevering cruelty of Grenville yet pursued her. It was not a dream, for she slept not, but the distracted imagination of bewildered reason.

An hour elapsed, and Mrs. Brown stepped lightly to the chamber to inquire [of the young lady if she was better, and whether she would dine, or take any other refreshment. She found it locked, and at first determined not to disturb her ; but as her breathing seemed uneasy, she feared she might be worse, and passed round through a middle door, which led from her own apartment.

She approached the bed, and observed with extreme concern that her beautiful inmate was in a violent fever, and quite delirious. She lost no time in summoning her sister Ellen, and sending off for medical assistance.

When the doctor arrived, he pronounced her illness o be the effect of cold, fatigue, and agitation of mind, ordered her a composing draught,—requested she might be kept in bed in the most perfect quietude,—that some one should remain constantly with her, and promised to see her again in the evening.

And these directions were strictly fulfilled, for the good landlady unwilling to entrust the invalid to any other person's care, gave her infant to her sister, and having fetched her work, took her station patiently by her bedside

About eight o'clock she awoke, and gazed wildly round her unconscious where she was. She eagerly drank the tea which was prepared for her, and relapsed into a heavy slumber. But she was evidently much worse, and the doctor suggested the necessity of sending for her friends.

" But—where were they ?"

The young lady brought no luggage. Her reticule contained nothing but her cambric handkerchief, a silver pencil case, a vinegarette, and her purse ; all which articles had been carefully consigned to a drawer in her chamber, together with her bracelets and watch.

But no information could thence be gathered ; but she possessed infinitely more property than requisite to answer every expense she would be likely to incur ;—for that would have been the first question with the generality of mankind. But, in this instance, a very different feeling prevailed: neither the landlord nor his pretty little wife were of this cold and worldly-minded class.

The sufferings of the interesting young creature before them, had awakened their warmest sympathy; and had she neither possessed a purse tolerably well lined, nor a valuable gold watch, with a heavy wrought chain, nor any other article to vouch for her respectability, or to ensure them a proper remuneration for their attendance, she would have met with equal care, and been watched over with equal solicitude ; for the wife said it went to her heart to hear her call for her poor dear parents ; and the husband, who had seen her on her arrival, declared he would not for the world anything should happen to such a pretty young creature in his house.

And they were sincere in their professions. The landlord and landlady of the wheatsheaf Inn were the son and daughter of two neighbouring farmers, brought up in the country from infancy: their earliest associations were those of benevolence and integrity, and their association with the more active scenes of their present avocation, had neither chilled the one nor perverted the other. Mrs. Brown's sister, a pretty girl who resided with them, officiated as barmaid; two sweet cherubs had blessed their union; and these, with a man, and woman servant, completed their establishment, where it was fortunate for our heroine fate had let her down, since according to the doctrine of predestination, she was intended by "pale necessity" to be thus thrown upon the mercy of strangers.

In a few days her fever had left her debilitated and low, but tranquil, and her returning reason awakened on strange faces, all however expressive of kindness and sympathy. She reclosed her eyes for a moment to arrange her ideas, and the past events, passed in hurried succession before her; she had however sufficient self-command not to encourage painful retrospections, and anxious only to recover sufficient strength to return to her beloved parents, she fell into a tranquil slumber from which she awoke a few hours after, composed, refreshed, and evidently so much better, that the doctor pronounced her out of danger.

In the evening she expressed a wish to rise; Ellen assisted her, and leaning on her arm, she walked gently about the chamber; the exercise benefited. She retired early, and passed a tranquil night.

The singular coincidence of Captain Grenville's proving to be the long lamented brother of her amiable friend, the "dear uncle Albert" of Caroline and Charles, and even the little Rosalie, whose every feeling was intuitively theirs, at once astounded and afflicted her: the name of Albert had never struck her—how should it? And as Mrs. Drayton generally wrote her letters, whilst she was engaged with the girls in their studies, the name of Grenville had never transpired. Had it done to earlier, how many hours of misery to herself, and anxiety and trouble to others had been spared.

She felt the propriety of writing to Mrs. Drayton an explanatory letter, but deferred it until her arrival at home, when she could calmly recal to mind every circumstance, and clear herself from the imputation of ingratitude or precipitation.

Her beloved parents too! but was she not rapidly recovering? why then awaken their anxieties? It were better to surprise them by her appearance, and breathe not a word of her sufferings or danger, until their roof was her shelter, their encircling arms her protection.

Mrs. Brown brought in the tea, and one of the little ones following her. Adela tenderly caressed it, and requested it might stay with her; this the mother at first refused, lest it should fatigue her, but, as if fascinated by her smile, it clasped her knees, and sat quietly down on a footstool beside her.

Adela requested Mrs. Brown to take tea with her, and as she found herself much revived by the beauty of the evening, she determined upon proceeding homeward by the stage which would pass at seven. She therefore entreated her to procure the doctor's bill, and furnish her own; at the same time expressing her sense of their hospitable care, with that sweetness so peculiarly her own.

It happened that the above mentioned gentleman had just dropped in at the moment, to inquire respecting his fair patient; but he would not hear a word of remuneration, for either attendance or medicine.

He assured her his visits had not not been frequent; and from a traveller suddenly taken ill on the road, and that traveller so young and fair a lady! what compensation could be higher than that of having contributed to her recovery. Adela expostulated in vain, and, with the warmest wishes for her safe restoration to her family, he took his leave.

Adela paid the very moderate amount charged her by Mrs. Brown, and would fain have presented a something additional for their unremitting and hospitable care, but it was decidedly opposed; and taking from her neck a row of coral, she clasped it twice round that of her little visitor, who smiled delightedly as she placed her in Ellen's arms; for it was the little one's accustomed hour of repose, and the ceremony of washing and undressing were yet to be performed.

Mrs. Brown felt flattered and grateful for this attention to her child, and inwardly regretted that a few hours would now remove, from their anxieties, that lovely and mysterious being who had interested all so powerfully.

But Adela was doomed to disappointment! Mrs. Brown heard with delight on inquiry, that every place in the seven o'clock coach was engaged; for she felt assured that another night's comfortable repose was requisite, to enable her to continue her journey.

What could be done? Adela took off her bonnet and cloak, for hers was a heart inured to " hope delayed," and taking a volume of Hammond's Love Elegies from the table, placed herself by the open window, at once to read and enjoy the refreshing breeze that passed over the adjoining meadows.

Wrapped in a dream of enchantment, she followed the youthful and ill-fated

No. 36.

poet, through the varied regions of imagination and passion, at once energetic
and tender.

> " With thee in traceless deserts could I dwell
> Where never human footsteps print the ground
> Thou, light of life, all darkness canst dispel
> And seem a world, with solitude around!"

Led back to scenes of vanished bliss, the lovely enthusiast raised her tearful eyes.
Her ear was attracted by the sound of approaching horsemen; a gentleman,
followed by his servant, rode up to the rustic porch of the inn.

Merciful Heaven! could it be Theodore?

His eyes had glanced on her pale and lovely countenance; trembling and agitated
he threw himself from his horse, and hastened into the parlour, where Ralph
brought him a glass of water, for the cold dew of death was on his brow, and he
was conscious of the surprise that had occasioned it. He walked the room in
doubt what path to pursue.

Could it indeed be the angel of his life, whose colourless cheek and exquisite
features had just blessed his sight, after so many months of despair and desolation?

Sir Theodore was on his return from his visit to his friend Clifford; and as this
was the inn he usually frequented when on this road, on account of the civility of
its landlord, he had resolved to put up there for the night.

Overpowered with the sentiments his vicinity with the idol of his hopes inspired,
yet trembling lest such felicity should prove an illusion, he requested Ralph to
make the requisite inquiries.

He presently returned, happy in the felicity he was about to communicate. It
was from Ellen he had obtained his information, and had the name of their beautiful lodger been a secret, he had become during their casual visits too great a
favourite to admit of its being so to him.

Yes! it was indeed Miss St. Clair, and Sir Theodore listened with impassioned
interest to the tale of her arrival, her sudden illness, the delay of her purposed
journey, and all the affecting circumstances appertaining.

He drew his pencil from his pocket-book, and wrote the following lines :—

" Will Miss St. Clair condescend to listen to the exculpation of one, who is too
wretched to claim any other sentiment than her compassion?

" Hope he has none! yet it would be consolatory to carry the assurance of
her pardon into that exile to which the few brief years of a joyless existence will
be devoted."

Having sealed this note, he gave it to Ellen, who conveyed it to Adela's
chamber, whilst, overwhelmed with conflicting emotions, he awaited the reply on
which all his future hope depended.

On the first glimpse of Sir Theodore's figure, Adela's heart throbbed tumultuously, but no sooner had their eyes met, than tottering to the bed she fell
half fainting upon it, and a gush of tears afforded her a timely relief from the
insensibility into which she would otherwise have fallen.

In those few minutes, a thousand hopes and fears contended in her bosom; had
she then indeed once more beheld the object of those fond, those early dreams!
did they breathe the same air? again partake the shelter of the same roof?

But was not this, her vision of perfection, her *beau ideal* of manly beauty and
matchless worth, now sunk debased and lost to her for ever? Oh no! that countenance was changed by the defacing hand of sorrow only, it could not conceal a
recreant heart. He would seek her, years of anguish and misunderstanding would
be swept away in a moment, and his honour would rise unsullied from his own
vindication. What though they were parted for ever, would it not be sweet to
think he regretted her, that he deserved to be regretted? But whose vindication
was to work these wonders? Whose anxious wish obtain an interview? The
husband of another.

She shuddered, the hand of death seemed on her heart. No, Adela! thy dawn
of life has been o'erclouded by sorrow, but it has not tinged thy parent's cheek

with shame. Thy peace bas been outraged, but thy heart is guiltless," and she sought to arm herself against its most dangerous innovator.

A slight tap at the door roused her from this painful reverie, to receive the lines traced by that well-known hand. How difficult, when she found herself alone, to resist covering them with kisses—but her tears she could not restrain. In the moment of agitation she had unconsciously broken the seal, she read the impassioned contents.

A moment more and her fortitude had abandoned her, but the remembrance that the faith once pledged had been broken, that he was now irrevocably another's, armed her with resolution. Yet how withstand his pleadings? Alas! safety there was none but in flight.

Fortunately she had paid her little account, there was therefore no necessity for mentioning her departure, she should readily procure a shelter at some cottage on the road for the night; for, if Grenville had inspired her with terror, how much more danger would there be in meeting one for whom her heart still too powerfully pleaded! He asked too, only compassion and pardon—a boon which seemed but due to that wretchedness so plainly pourtrayed on his pallid and dejected countenance,—to the voluntary exile to which his remaining days were to be devoted. Would it then be such a crime to bid him an eternal adieu?

Duty, and that sentiment which was enwoven with every fibre of her heart, had here a severe conflict, but one thought of her loved parents, and the triumph was complete; Adela pressed the paper to her lips and to her bosom, she breathed a prayer to her Creator, and having traced a few lines with a trembling hand, which she left on the dressing-table with a present to Ellen, she tied on her bonnet, wrapped her cloak closely round her her, and having descended the stairs, slipped unperceived past the kitcen, crossed the paddock, and escaped by a back gate that led into a bye-road.

Ellen had carried in the tea, and Ralph waited his master's orders, yet he still paced the parlour with eager anxiety painted on every feature. Nine o'clock struck, and no reply from Miss St. Clair. It was very singular.

"Are you certain Ellen delivered it?"

Ralph saw her carry it up; but he would request her to inquire if there was any answer.

Sir Theodore sat down to the table, with trembling hand he poured the cream nto the sugar basin; he filled the tea-pot without once remembering to have recourse to the tea-caddy, and then, suddenly rising, paced the room in feverish and petulant anxiety.

In a few minutes Ralph returned, but his honest face was too true an index of the mind, not to disclose the unwelcome news he had to communicate, even before his lips had severed to give it utterance.

Miss St. Clair had been gone nearly an hour! But she had left a note on the dressing-table, which, as she was in ignorance of his present title, was addressed to

THEODORE VILLARS, Esq.

"Why does Mr. Villars request what it is impossible Miss St. Clair should grant?

"Alas! is it requisite to recal to his memory, that those sacred duties, voluntarily imposed, would render all future communication between them at once reprehensible and unavailing?

"Mr. Villars terms himself wretched!—he demands my pardon, my compassion. The first he has long possessed—and why claim the last? when his own pen has acknowledged him the arbiter of that destiny he seems so deeply to deplore.

"Many and varied events may tend to banish the past. They must have obliterated the recollections of the principles inculcated by the most honoured of parents, or Mr. Villars would be aware that their daughter is incapable of deservedly incurring their censure!

"Adela's future peace will be found in a strict adherence to the duties of that humble sphere to which the vicissitudes of her parents have consigned them; that tranquil and happy home, rendered sacred by their virtues and their misfortunes."

Theodore wept in agony of soul, as he perused and reperused the sentence that consigned his recent reviving hopes to disappointment and despair. He pressed the letter to his lips, he renewed the vows breathed in happier days upon it; for whilst the dignity of an outraged heart cast its exclusive circle around her presence every line breathed the intellectual beauty which had bound him hers—indissolubly and for ever.

Had she but remained, his importunities might yet have ultimately softened her obduracy. Oh! that she might return, but that were inpossible; his supplication had evidently accelerated the confirmation of his misery.

Ralph hastily left the room to make some further inquiries and returned to inform Sir Theodore that Miss St. Clair had proposed remaining there during the night, to proceed by the morning stage to a hamlet about ten miles' distant. That no one had seen her depart, that it was only when Ellen had carried up a light to inquire if there was any answer to the note that they found the room vacant; and as it was impossible she could have proceeded onward without the stage, Mrs. Brown thought she might have walked into the next village, and would, perhaps, yet return.

The heart on the verge of despair is ready to catch at the smallest gleam of hope; and the unhappy youth took his seat at the window, watching every approaching form, and listening to every footstep.

Ten o'clock convinced him of the folly of his expectation. Alas! Adela's mind was not formed to waver in its determinations, and would she venture unprotected to pursue a ramble to such an hour?

Eleven,—twelve o'clock struck, and alas! despair was inevitable!—he called for wine, drank glass after glass with unconscious eagerness, and retired to his pillow determined not to return to the Park, but follow her to the farthest verge of the earth; to convince her he was no longer the husband of another, to remain at her feet until every error had been elucidated, and her pardon and esteem at least, if not her tenderness restored.

But to sleep was impossible. He arose, and paced the room in silent agony. Ah! had he known whose lovely form had pressed that couch on the night preceding!

The moon shone through the curtain, and a folded paper half concealed by the carpet, attracted his eye. He removed the curtain, and saw by its silvery light that the lines it contained were traced by Adela's hand.

But his sight was dimmed by the tears he had shed. Clouds, sombre as his fate, passed over the lustre that had a moment previous illumed the apartment; and as his candle was extinguished, he was obliged to restrain his impatience until day-break.

A thousand terrors, a thousand melancholy presentiments assailed him. His Adela, just risen from a bed of sickness—his Adela, unprotected and far from home, haunted him incessantly. And at the earliest dawn of day Ralph was summoned, the horses brought out, and Sir Theodore on the road in that direction in which he conceived she would have gone, had she departed for the hamlet described.

They had proceeded about two miles when their attention was engaged by a crowd assembled round the ruins of a cottage and barn, yet smoking from the conflagration of the preceding night.

Every eye was in search of some individual who had apparently eluded their anxiety, and the prayers of a young mother were addressed to Heaven for blessings on the angel who had rescued her infant from the jaws of destruction!

Sir Theodore entered the crowd. He inquired of a countryman who stood amidst the throng, if the property of the unfortunate cottager was insured, and listened to the following recital:—

" About a year ago, your honour, my son married the daughter of a neighbour of ours, and he fitted them up as snug a little home as you would wish to see. The little ground around it was well tilled, and its produce, united to my daughter-in-law's industry, brought them in a very comfortable provision. Before the year was out they made me a grandfather to as fine a little blue-eyed wench as you should see on a summer's morning, and we were all as happy as princes."

"Infinitely happier!" said Sir Theodore. "What are the allurements of wealth or ambition to the bliss yielded by the calm enjoyments of domestic life?"

"True, your honour! very true! and yet unexpected sorrow comes and cuts it down in a moment."

Here he drew his hand across his eyes.

"But God forgive me, for, instead of repining, I ought to return my thanks for his mercy in the preservation of our infant. But the story is too surprising to be believed."

"Tell it me, however," said Sir Theodore, "that I may know how far I shall be enabled to assist them."

"Well, your honour," continued the countryman, "last night, or rather this morning, whilst my poor lad and his little wife were sleeping soundly, wearied by the fatigue of the day, a neighbour, who had been sitting up with a sick child, going by chance to the window, saw the cottage in flames. Well, she ran and called the neighbours; they came to me, and we battered and knocked at the door for some time before they awoke. Some lads ran for an engine, but it's a monstrous long way, you understand, sir, and the fire spread alarmingly. Some ran to fetch water from the well, and others helped my son, trying to save the furniture. Poor Ann had taken the baby, but as she was suddenly called on for the key of a closet, where their money was kept, she put it into the hands of a young girl to run out with it; but the fury of the flames increased, and we all stood in consternation. In the midst of our affliction, Ann turned round to take her child. But what was her horror to find another in its stead 'Where is my child,' said the distracted girl.—'where is my child?' said my son. The foolish wench had been called by her mother, who was helping below, just as she was taking the little one; and, intending to run back directly, left it on the bed. The mother had given her little brother into her arms, and, what with the frightful appearance of the flames, and the noise and confusion, she forgot the poor baby altogether."

"Good Heaven! the poor infant, then, was left in the chamber?"

"Ay, and would have been burned with the cottage, but [for the goodness of the Almighty, who sent an angel to save it."

"Well, your honour, poor Ann fainted in her husband's arms: one ran one way, one another—when, suddenly, a beautiful creature rushed through the crowd, she entered the house, and although, to everyone else, death seemed to threaten her, in a few moments, amidst the shouts of the crowd, she re-appeared with our little one in her arms. We could have worshipped her very footsteps, for she could not have been a mortal, but she did not give us time, and, like all spirits, no one saw which way she came, or where she went."

"Is this his honour's handkerchief?" said a lad, "its too foine to belong to anybody here."

Ralph took it, he looked at the corner: "Adela St. Clair" was written by her own lovely hand on the cambric, and, replying in the affirmative, he gave the lad a shilling, then, putting it into his master's hand, with the name perfectly visible, he said, in a low voice,—

"It must have been Miss St. Clair!"

Sir Theodore's heart beat tumultuously as he hurried it into his bosom. It could, indeed, have been no other than the noble-minded girl! But whither had she fled?

He no longer paused over the scene of desolation. He put some gold into the hand of the aged father for the use of his children, and followed by Ralph, was out of sight in a moment.

The golden rays of the sun had chased the mistiness of early morn. The peasant, half awake, passed on to his inheritance of unremitting toil. The smoke began to ascend from a few chimneys, and the birds united their varied notes from their leafy homes.

But Sir Theodore passed unconsciously forward. Adela, the paragon of grace and sentiment, of perfect heroism and feminine softness, is alone before him,

" Fills every sense, and pants in every vein."

And, suffering the reins to rest on the neck of his horse, he continued his melancholy musings, when Ralph, touching his hat, reminded him they were now within a few paces of the valley in the Woodlands.

"I am not astonished," he replied, " my gallant steed has so often trod these paths, that he cannot pass in this vicinity without once more paying them a visit, although a melancholy one. Well," continued he, " be it so."

And they continued their way to the little inn mentioned in the first part of our narrative.

CHAPTER XLIV.

Virtue could see to do what virtue would
By its own radiant light, though sun and stars
Were in the flat sea sunk !—MILTON.

WHEN Adela left the inn she walked on about a couple of miles as rapidly as her yet unrecovered strength would admit; but in her hurry she had mistaken her path.

She recognised her error, but should she, by returning, hazard er countering that dear, fatal being from whom she was hastening? That were indeed imprudent! Could she meet with a safe retreat for the night, it was of little importance where, and in the morning it would be easy to obtain a conveyance home.

The night was indeed delightful, and the moon passed in cloudless beauty from behind her fleecy mantle, as she entered a romantic spot where a few scattered cottages formed a little neighbourhood, although it could not be called a village. But every door seemed closed, and not a light appeared at either of the casements.

She saw no sign of habitation beyond, and resolved on returning, when, seated at the door of the last cottage, without any light but that which the moon yielded, were an old man and woman—the former smoking his pipe, and the latter recounting tales of her youth. Adela paused.

"My friend," said she, " I am going to ask you what you may deem a singular question ; but I am a traveller, disappointed of the coach by which I purposed returning home. It is very late, and I have an aversion to sleeping at an inn. Can you inform me where I can be accommodated for the night ?"

" I really cannot say, young woman," replied the old man rather surlily, "but you might, perhaps, get a lodging in the next village."

" Is it far distant ?" said Adela.

"Only across two fields, and if you pass under the wall of the 'Squire's garden, you'll be there in a jiffy."

Adela looked disappointed. She shuddered at the idea of such an excursion at such an hour, and the old woman looked beseechingly at her surly husband.

" It's monstrous lonely for the young lady at this time of the night, John. If she'd pay us the same as they'd ask at an inn, couldn't I make up Jenny's bed for her?—sheets are aired."

Old John drew four successive whiffs. He regarded Adela from top to toe, as well as the light of the moon would permit, and seeming satisfied with the investigation, inquired,—

" How much can'st pay ?"

Adela was petrified at a manner so entirely new to her. The experiments she had hitherto made of the human heart were favourable, with the exceptions of the Reverend Jonathan, Mrs. Crawley, and Grenville. But she had ever expected to find hospitality the inmate of the cottage; and the Ashtons, the Browns, and the friendly widow might well have authorised the expectation of, if not so disinterested at least as complaisant a reception.

But the aged couple seemed at least decent and respectable for their humble sphere,—the female conciliating and willing to accommodate, although anxious to obtain that remuneration, to which, perhaps, an existence of penury and care had inured them to look in their declining days.

She replied to the question, whatever they might deem a sufficient compensation. "Very well, very well," replied he, "we cannot desire any more!—Light a candle, Peggy, and show Miss in."

On this permission from her lord and master, the good woman took a small piece of candle from the shelf, and having fumbled a long time at the grate, at last succeeded in catching a light. She then dusted a chair, and having taken a pair of sheets, and a counterpane out of the press, began arranging an antiquated piece of furniture, which, according to Goldsmith's description in his 'Deserted Village,' was

> "Contrived a double debt to pay,
> A bed by night—a chest of drawers by day."

She made many apologies, and said her own and her good man's bed-room was up stairs,—and a very neat chamber too; but as he did not like to be put out of his way, she hoped Miss would put up with the bed they kept for their daughter Jane, when she happened to be out of place.

Adela was happy, at any rate, in having obtained a shelter for the night, and assured her loquacious hostess no apologies were necessary. The old man knocked the ashes out of his pipe, which he put up carefully on a shelf, and walked heavily up stairs to bed. The old woman asked her, in a low tone, "if she would like a bit of bread and cheese, and a sup o' milk," which she politely declined; and bidding her good night, with a charge to put out the candle as soon as possible, she followed her husband.

Adela's first care was to fasten the cottage door. She tried the bolt of the window, and having secured that which led to the staircase, she hung up her bonnet and cloak, tied her scarf round her head, and without undressing herself, reclined her weary limbs on the bed, where as sweet a sleep stole over her as if canopied by the couch of luxury or pillowed on down. But this welcome forgetfulness of hopeless affliction, persecution, and the absence of her beloved parents was not doomed to be of long duration.

About three o'clock she was awakened by a violent noise, and a running to and fro without the window. At first she could scarcely collect her ideas sufficiently to call to mind where she was, and the red gleam which shone through the curtains tended only to bewilder. She arose, undrew the curtain, and beheld at some distance a cottage on fire! She listened—and gazed with agony. Alas! some unfortunate family were thus rendered houseless, and perhaps destitute! She went to the staircase, and called to her hostess, but a lengthened snore was the only reply: she called again.

The old woman either did not, or would not hear her. The old man (from the heavy sound above) had stepped out of bed, and having satisfied himself the flames were not likely to reach his domicile, the wind being in an opposite quarter, called out,—

"I never meddles nor makes with nobody's business. It won't disturb me, and you'd better go to sleep again, Miss, for there's no danger."

Adela was too much shocked at his selfish insensibility to make him any reply. He returned to bed, and in a short time was asleep. But Adela's heart was not so easily satisfied:—she threw open the casement—she heard some rustics who conversed as they ran past.

"It's no use staying," said one, "they can't put it out."

" Poor things," said the other, " and what's worse they've missed their baby ;—it's no doubt perishing in the flames, for it was left in the bed-room above."

Adela heard no more,—she unbarred the door, closed it after her ; and, rushing forward, arrived in the midst of the crowd, at the very moment of desperation, when the distracted mother had sunk into insensibility in the arms of her husband.

" Good heavens !" said Adela, " will no reward induce any one to venture a search for the poor infant ?"

The father and grandfather were too distracted to listen to her,—like savages, they lost all presence of mind, and only evinced their anguish by wailings and contortions. No one replied : she did not repeat her question, but darted amidst the spreading flames, heedless of the entreaties of those who considered her as the devoted victim of her humanity. But that all-powerful Creator, whose pervading spirit had animated the bosom of this heroic girl with fortitude beyond the power of so delicate a frame, spread his protecting shield around her.

She was absent but for a few moments ;—a pause of silent agony—the fixed eye, —the clasped hands of the astonished gazers bespoke the excitement of this awful moment. It seemed but an instant when she appeared—her fine hair flowing over her shoulders. her pale countenance animated with an expression which elevated it above mortality. She bore the infant in her arms, to which the occasion had given renewed strength, unmindful of aught but the helpless innocent she was preserving.

The surrounding multitude scarcely dared breathe, from agitation and terror. The stairs tottered beneath her sylphide footsteps, but she passed the door, and had just resigned the precious burden to the arms of its mother, when the whole fabric fell in.

A shout of joy,—a murmur of inexpressible applause followed,—the parents rushed forward to clasp her knees in gratitude. But where was she?"

The cambric handkerchief which Sir Theodore had so fondly sheltered in his bosom, was the only vestige she had left behind her.

Adela, we have said, returned to the cottage, unobserved, amidst the confusion of the impressive scene which had just passed. She had not been missed, and, securing the door, she humbled herself in grateful piety that she had been selected as the instrument of preservation to an innocent babe—of snatching its fond parents from despair. She then arranged her disturbed hair in braids; and, shivering from the chilliness of the early hour, she crept between the blankets, and again reposed sweetly and soundly until seven o'clock, when she was roused by the old woman, who tapped at the door, wanting to make her husband's breakfast. She seemed surprised to find her inmate dressed so early, feared she had passed but a poor night on account of the noise occasioned by the fire, and invited her to stay to breakfast, as it would only be a trifle more than they should charge for the lodging.

This Adela declined; she paid the amount required, the individuals not possessing any other claim on her generosity ; and, although her journey had been far less expensive than under the existing circumstances might have been expected, economy was a duty to those whose future comfort engaged her every care. Adela inquired her nearest way to the hamlet before mentioned, and was told, that six miles off there was an inn from whence the coach started.

" It is a pleasant distance from the valley in the woodlands," said she, " and it would be well worth your while to see so pretty a place."

Adela started—she trembled, and was she, then, so near the vicinity of the home of her infancy ? Oh, could she once more behold ! but her parents—ought she not, even now, to be under their protection? Yet a few hours would make little difference ; she would hasten forward, and having visited that spot, unseen and unrecognised, return and seclude herself at the house from whence the coach started, until evening, when a few hours would restore her to her home. That it was in her way, in a manner strengthened this wandering of the heart. She tried not to think it was the memory of Theodore that led her thither ;—and if it did steal across her, as too fatally true, she resolved it should be the last sacrifice made to hopeless affection.

But a vehicle passed her, it was empty, and she got in, and was set down in the neighbourhood; and Adela fast approached the well-known spot; she met several individuals who did not recognize her beneath her black veil—for her cloak concealed her figure—she was also much paler and thinner than when she reigned the presiding goddess of that rustic scene.

So anxiously had she followed the impression of the moment, (for she dared not trust herself too many minutes reflection) that she had never thought of breakfast, until, looking up, she recollected the Plough Tavern:—she felt faint and tired, and hesitated—for the landlady would be certain to recognize her features. Ap-

preaching, however, she saw a forbidding-looking little old woman in the bar, and seeing the name changed, she was certain she might enter without the smallest apprehension. She was shown into the parlour that looked into the garden, where breakfast was brought her, and she sat down to her solitary repast, pensive and dejected. The waitress was utterly unknown to her, and she ventured to inquire who resided at the farm on the brow of the valley.

The young woman replied, "No one; that she herself was a stranger there, but had heard no one had taken it since a Mr. St. Clair had left it, and as some law-suit had commenced against the purchaser, it had been uninhabited, and shut up ever since."

She inquired for the Ashtons; they had left, and several had followed their example.

No. 27.

When she had finished her breakfast, she began to ruminate on the possibility of secretly visiting the grounds adjoining that now lonely abode; but this could only be effected in the evening. Mrs. Drayton might send to her home, to inquire for her, and her parent's anxieties, and even terrors existed for her safety.

It was now, indeed, she felt the imprudence of listening to the beguilings of her own fancy, and the bitterest self reproaches followed. She questioned her own heart, she hesitated whether she should yield to this inclination. She was anxious for her home, as a bird in absence from its native shades,—she was weary and solicitous for its protection, and gladly would she have fled there to be at rest; and yet there was a sort of feeling that withheld her. She recalled the past, she pictured Theodore in despair, she pictured him hopeless, desolate, sorrowful : and this idea filled every thought with anguish and desperation. All prospect of earthly happiness was fled. He had re-appeared to recal the visions of the past, to impress them on her mind, and to impart their hue of departed peace on every scene that presented itself.

Yet, still—had she not parents—those to whom she owed so much deference, so much respect, so much adoration ;—parents who would sink into their grave, lowly and hopeless, should she make no effort to rouse herself, no attempt to replace herself in that sphere of conscious rectitude from whence she would, with calmness and resignation, look on that felicity it was no longer hers to possess.

Yes—she would be herself again—only one short visit to the scene of her despair, and she would be resigned to all—she would return to the home of her parents, and, concealing the pang in her bosom, which harrassed and distressed her, wear a smile of contentment and peace.

She sat pensively reflecting during the early part of the day, fatigued by the distance, and hurried by the circumstances of the night, and yet more so by the conflicting emotions that contended for ascendancy in her bosom. One o'clock struck, —two, and the waitress entered to inquire what she would take for dinner? She asked for pen, ink and paper, and, with a trembling hand, wrote the following lines :—

"My beloved Parents,

"Singular circumstances (which I will explain when we meet) have induced me to leave Warwickshire rather unexpectedly. I have also met with a trifling delay on the road, but, I trust, not many hours will elapse before we again meet, and unfold our hearts to each other. Dear authors of my existence, once restored to your holy affection, shall I ever more quit your side? Ever more run the risk of losing an hour of that valued society for the intercourse of the world, and all it can boast? Some there are who form an exception—the dear Arnolds will furnish an example, the Draytons, too. But I must conclude, and look anxiously forward for our re-union, when my self-imposed exile will end, and the most beloved of parents be restored to the arms of their

ADELA."

She folded her letter, put it herself into the box, and returned to the parlour, where she remained in quiet seclusion, until evening.

CHAPTER XLV.

There is no fault that so covers a man with shame as to be found false and perfidious, Prosperity doth best discover vice, but adversity doth best discover virtue.—BACON.

Don Manuel de Mello had embarked for England, happy in his escape from so perilous an encounter. His servant Pedro, too, whose courage would not, perhaps, have extended many inches further, breathed more freely when he found himself surrounded by the crew of an English vessel on the bosom of the ocean.

Don Manuel was treated with the greatest possible respect by the captain and all the crew. There was one young man on board, dressed as a sailor, but who, understanding Spanish, was singularly useful to him. His imagination constantly veered towards his Aurora, on his way thither, and he once more embraced her in all her former beauty. Edmund, too, with all his generous fervour—all his enchanting candour—were they still alive, or should he have to mourn them as lost?

Nothing of importance occurred, during their passage to Portsmouth, where, after sojourning a few days, in order to recover the effects of the voyage, he proceeded onward to that part of Warwickshire where he had been informed St. Clair resided; having secured to himself the attentions of the young man before mentioned as interpreter.

A few inquiries were requisite to bring him into the neighbourhood of the Reverend Jonathan's habitation, because as a local magistrate he was pretty extensively known, and therefore, although anxious beyond expression to clasp his daughter and the son of his early adoption to his bosom, he put up at an hotel for the night that he might calm the perturbation of his soul previous to seeing them.

On the following morning he proceeded to the clergyman's residence in a style of as much privacy as the occasion would admit, being only accompanied by his interpreter; and, having obtained admittance, presented his card.

Those who are parents, and have been in absence from a beloved child will form an estimate of the feelings of Don Manuel, whilst he listened to catch the voice of his Aurora, or that of her husband—But all was solemn silence.

Mr. Jonathan was in his study, when Peter delivered the card.

"Don Manuel de Mello! a foreign nobleman, what a pity that Sally had thrown herself away so unadvisedly!" but he banished useless regrets, and gave orders that his lordship should be shown into the best drawing room, and that he would wait upon immediately.

The Reverend gentleman dressed himself, called his man to shake an additional quantity of powder into his hair, and approached the drawing room with an unusual degree of alacrity.

Don Manuel's anxiety increased, as he saw the door open, but no sooner did his eye glance on the burlesque physiognomy of the clergyman, than his disappointment was pretty evident in his features.

Santa Maria! could this be Edmund? what could have so singularly disfigured features beautiful in infancy, elegant in manhood?

Not care or vicissitude—for there was every appearance of prosperity : he had never heard that climate wrought such changes. But it could not be the same, the difference in years was quite sufficient.

The Reverend Jonathan approached, bowing obsequiously; Don Manuel advanced to meet him, and the interpreter, having unfolded the rank, wealth, and importance of the Spaniard, proceeded to state, as his motive for visiting England, the discovery of his daughter, Don Aurora St. Clair, being heiress to all his possessions.

A very few words convinced the nobleman that this was not the St. Clair he sought, but to Jonathan the mention of wealth and title was quite sufficient. He listened with concentrated attention, in doubt by what stratagem he could best turn this affair to his own advantage.

That it was a mistake originating in the name was clear enough, and by what followed equally so, that he was in search of the only relative he himself possessed in the world, although his vicissitudes had induced him to avoid his society.

That wronged and outraged individual was, however, now upon the point of being elevated to his proper station in the scale of society; and his avarice and envy induced him to anticipate that, could he only gain a little time to reflect, he might, with the management of Robert Crawley, secure the splendid inheritance to himself.

He therefore replied that he could not call to mind any other family of the name of St. Clair in England. That he was, indeed, distantly related to a gentleman of name who had lived many years in Spain, but he understood he had died in obscurity; and of one thing he was certain, if that were the case he was the only relative and heir remaining.

A tear now stole down the furrowed cheek of the agonised father, and the young man who acted as interpreter, and was deeply interested in his patron, was scarcely less affected; whilst Mr. Jonathan exulted in the credulity which seemed to presage the completion of all the air-built castles that had already floated in his brain; and another hocus-pocus accumulation to the wealth he had been for the last half century amassing.

He entreated that his lordship would be consoled for a loss that seemed irremediable, and resign himself to the dispensation of an all-wise Creator, and that he would honour his humble roof so far as to accept what accommodation it afforded, instead of returning to an hotel; until he could ascertain the actual fate of the son and daughter, of which, however, he had little doubt.

The unsuspecting bosom is ever ready to listen to the voice of sympathy and kindness, and particularly so in the hour of sorrow. Don Manuel could not doubt that the assertions of a respectable individual (a pillar of the church too) were well founded, and accepted his invitation; under the impression that he would feel an interest in ascertaining its truth, which would be only secondary to his own.

The monotonous uniformity of the establishment now gave way to preparation and bustle. Mrs. Jonathan was informed of the honour that awaited them, and orders were given to entertain their illustrious guest with the utmost magnificence.

A consultation was held with Robert Crawley, who notwithstanding the violent conflicts that had preceded his wife's derangement, always seemed surrounded by a magic circle which precluded even a reproof from her protector, for Mr. Jonathan was under the impression that, as a limb of the law, he might assist him to a plan by which the advantages he had anticipated might ultimately be secured.

Robert, who felt himself perfectly independent, expressed some doubts of the possibility of such a result, and the good man began to doubt whether it would not be more prudent to seek out, and court the friendship of the family he had hitherto so decidedly shunned; for, although according to the common course of nature, they would be likely to survive him, his vanity was deeply interested in the importance which he conceived would result to him, from being so connected with title, even beyond what he had ventured to hope for in the arrangement of his wife's neice.

Robert Crawley was, however, of an opposite opinion, and strongly urged the necessity of throwing every obstacle in the way of tracing any part of the family, "because," said he, "it would argue an immense degree of inconsistency, in a clergyman of your character and importance in the neighbourhood, in the first instance positively to affirm their death, and in the next to unite in a search the result of which must inevitably disprove such an assertion."

The old gentleman appeared convinced of the wisdom of Robert's remarks; but so infatuated was he with the mania, the very idea of being allied with nobility, that he secretly determined to fall upon some plan which might at once withdraw him from this dilemma, and furnish an excuse for the apparent inconsistency.

"I shall not, perhaps, ultimately," thought he, "be enabled to prevent Don Manuel from discovering his daughter; therefore, it would be folly, openly to oppose it. And although, after my assertion, I cannot appear to expect any good effect, from such a search, by seeming benevolently anxious on the occasion, I shall have opportunities of secretly thwarting its success; and thus ultimately secure his rank and fortune to myself in the event of my surviving him."

Several weeks had elapsed, the Reverend Jonathan and his disinterested partner paid their guest the most obsequious attention—invariably lamenting that he had not arrived before Sarah's unpropitious union had been formed.

"Then," said the latter, "he might have been induced to elevate her to his own rank, and instead of the poor thing's fortune being thrown away on a set of vagabonds, and herself mad, we should have secured the grandee's immense wealth, and taken from him all taste for his present search for a runaway daughter."

Not a day elapsed that the anxious and despairing heart-broken father did not anxiously inquire, and offer rewards for the discovery of his daughter; all which commissions the amiable Jonathan not only undertook himself to see executed, but even seemed to devote every hour not employed in clerical or magisterial duties to that effect.

The interpreter had also a powerful attraction back to his native land; he was a very intellectual companion, and therefore received many marks of attention in the house as well as in its vicinity. The story of Don Manuel's arrival, his views and his residence there became gradually known, and frequent inquiries were made of Peter, whether any tidings had arrived of Mr. Edmund St. Clair.

At length it occurred to him, that Mr. Arnold had formerly been intimate with both branches of the family, and that, by gaining his address, they would be likely to come at a certain knowledge as to what had become of them.

The interpreter, willing to give his patron an agreeable surprise, instantly set about the investigation; every particular was obtained with the utmost rapidity and minuteness, and the intelligence conveyed to Don Manuel, who seemed to imbibe a new being from the certainty of still possessing a daughter, he had so bitterly lamented as lost.

The young stranger brought with him an invitation from Mr. Arnold, which he also communicated to Don Manuel in the presence of their hospitable host, who endeavoured to assume the most benign satisfaction at this (as he termed it) blessing granted to his prayers!

But this event came like a thunderbolt upon him; had the earth opened to receive him, it could scarcely have created greater consternation.

Here, then, through the medium of that officious interpreter, were all his plans and hopes of aggrandizement annihilated.

Mr. Arnold he well knew, as a man of honour and integrity, must have the strongest feelings of indignation towards him; from his recent communication the perfidy of his conduct must immediately transpire, and he used every argument to persuade his guest not to accept the invitation offered him. But Don Manuel's anxiety, his eagerness to see his long lost daughter, were not to be repressed, he therefore ordered a travelling chariot, and set off for the residence of Mr. Arnold; having first pressed upon the acceptance of his host a superb brilliant ring, as an acknowledgment of his hospitality.

This the clergyman received with an expression of confusion and trepidation, indicative of a mind in no wise at ease—his countenance betokened evidence of a consciousness, that treachery had no right to the possession of such a present from the individual whose dearest hopes he would have sacrificed; and, he received it with a trembling hand, whilst his tongue faltered his acknowledgments of honour conferred on him.

These peculiarities struck Don Manuel very forcibly at the moment; they had rather the appearance of remorse or apprehension, than of the open hearted friendship he had professed, but it was merely the surmise of a moment, obliterated by the delightful expectations that every mile brought him nearer his beloved Aurora.

CHAPTER XLVI.

Sweet bud of the wilderness emblem of all
    That survives in this desolate heart;
The fabric of bliss to its centre may fall,
    But patience shall never depart.
Though the perils of chance, and the scowl of disdain
    Shall my front be unaltered, my courage elate
Ah! even the name I have worshipped, in vain }
Shall awake not the sigh of remembrance again, }
    To bear is to conquer our fate!—CAMPBELL.

RALPH had secured to his master the apartments he had formerly occupied in those hours of early affection, when the future promised nothing but an uninterrupted sunshine. Adela's handkerchief was his only companion, a thousand kisses were imprinted on the magic name, but he had another luxury in store, in drawing it forth the little paper found on the preceding night fell at his feet, eagerly unclosing it, he read as follows:—

She mourn'd him still—though months and years
    Their circling course had sped,
And sighs unheard, and silent tears,
    Had steeped her lonely bed.

She loved him still, though outraged truth
    Had chased her early bloom,
And in the blossom of her youth
    Had marked her for the tomb.

No fond complaint that maiden breathed
    Her hopeless fate to mourn,
But soon the weeping cypress wreathed
    Its garland o'er her urn.

They whispered, that at midnight's hour
    When sang night's solemn bird,
From that lone, sad, and sacred bower,
    Her song and lute were heard,
And still her gentle spirit moved.
Where first they met, where first they loved.

Oh, how bitter was the feeling, these tender lines conveyed! Yes, he would devote this evening to that spot, her memory had rendered sacred, and then wander through the world until he could reclaim his lost treasure.

It was evening when Sir Theodore once more pursued the winding path that led to the valley. He ascended the litt'e hill, and shrinking from observation, buried himself in the shadow of the Woodlands that surrounded the farm.

The gate at the back stood half open, but he, with difficulty, penetrated the paths, which were overgrown by plants and shrubs that had passed their boundaries, and mingled with the green grass and weeds that interruped his way, the unpruned vine united with the intrusive ivy, and wandered in various directions. The cottage uninhabited, the confiding swallow had built its nest in the recesses of the windows, as if conscious that no one would disturb the solitude of the scene. The crimson hue of departing day tinged the surrounding landscape, the cottage, its garden, and the winding path to the valley.

A solitary rose seemed to droop in pensive beauty alone, on that very bush from whence those were gathered by Adela's hand, that had so unnerved him on the morning of his unpropitious union. There stood the dove cot from whence he took his little envoy when he had left her; and there was the gothic window, from whence she had waved her last adieu, on their agonizing separation.

Agitated, trembling, and overwhelmed with an indescribable emotion, he approached the bower; a female form, closely enveloped, glided from the thicket, and disappeared amongst the exuberant foliage, he followed.   But who was the mourner who came, led by the sympathy of congenial sorrow, to muse amidst these solitudes ?

His heart's wild throbbings had answered the question, even before he caught a glimpse of the colourless cheek and beautiful features that had met his view on the preceding evening.   Yes, it was indeed his own Adela!   Her veil was thrown aside, tears streamed from her eyes, which were fixed with melancholy earnestness on the last rays of the setting sun, reflected on the lake,

"Of joys departed never to return,
How bitter the remembrance !"

sighed the gentle girl, unconscious that her accents vibrated on the ear of one she had imagined at that moment far away, and not likely to interrupt her seclusion. But a slight rustling amongst the bushes startled her—Theodore's presence overpowered her—and he arose from her feet to receive her lifeless form in his arms.

Agonised and bewildered, he knew not what to do ; he pressed that lovely form to his heart—he supplicated her to forgive his impetuosity, and his rashness.

How magical the voice of one beloved!   Adela, whose heroism had, on the preceding night, led her amidst, apparently, certain destruction, to the preservation of a fellow creature, had sunk, overpowered by the presence of one, whose memory, only a few minutes before, she had resolved to consign to oblivion, because she felt it her duty ; but, how little did she know her own heart!   His arms encircled her, his lip was pressed to her's, with the holy fervour of pure affection.   His voice recalled her departing spirit, and she revived.   Terrified and indignant, she endeavoured to extricate herself from his gentle embrace, but her strength failed her, and he supplicated a few moments audience.

"Is this candid, Mr. Villars?" said Adela ; "is it honourable, after my reply to your letter of yesterday evening?   I command, I entreat you to leave me."

"Listen first, my dearest—listen, my beloved—permit me to vindicate my name from the dishonour now unmeritedly attached to it.   A long, mournful history awaits your ear, but it will prove, amidst the deep-laid treacheries that have combined to separate us, that I have never for one moment ceased to adore you—that I am indeed, more wretched than culpable.   But, it is past!—the deception unveiled—the tie imposed by parental authority, severed by death—and my poor deluded father, anxious to expiate his error, has implored blessings on our union with his expiring breath.   Tell me, then, will my Adela permit me to claim this lovely hand, or, by its refusal, doom me to close my joyless existence in exile from my native land?"

Astonishment, joy, the delightful consciousness of yet possessing the only heart which could impart felicity to her's ; of feeling that it was uncorrupted and unblemished as in their happiest hours amidst that enchanting scene, kept him silent Her head reclined on his shoulder, and their tears mingled.   She suffered him to lead her to the rustic seat, and, encircled by his arm, listened to every varied circumstance that had transpired since their last parting on that very spot.   Even Lucy's tragic tale was not forgotten, nor did the gentle girl, amidst her own renovated bliss, refuse a sigh to the attendant of her earlier years, or a tear to her fatal dereliction and melancholy fate.

Every doubt vanished before the eloquence of the impassioned youth.   As Adela listened, the sincerity of his character arose in unsullied beauty, whilst his filial piety and delicacy relative to the part Sir Edward had taken in the transaction, at once elevated him in her esteem, and secured his empire over her heart.   The voice of duty no longer placed a barrier between them ; his future hours were no longer to be devoted to the feelings of any one but his Adela, whose beloved parents would become his also.   Even the last sacred words of a dying father had enjoined their union !—and she again unfolded her fond heart to receive the idol of its early affections.   But Adela had her recital to make also ; and, whilst Theodore eagerly listened to the silvery accents that assured him not a thought of another had sullied the faith of that innocent bosom, he gave past affliction to the winds, and felt a new spirit animate his frame. Adela was too candid to deny his perfect restoration to her esteem, and even her tenderness beyond this confession, which she deemed due to his past sufferings, she forbade him to urge her until her parents had first been consulted.

"Think not for a moment," said he, "I have forgotten those valued friends— for long and unremittingly have I sought them. By my Adela's sanction alone can I plead for the renewal of their favour, or presume to claim my felicity from their hands."

Adela replied not, but the exquisite tinge of innocence crimsoned her hitherto pale cheek, and Theodore received it as the sanction of his wishes. The evening had closed—the nightingale poured her lay of love from the branches that over-shadowed the bower. Adela had never once thought of the coach. The delirium of retrospection in her first visit to this home of her infancy, in the earlier part of the evening; the unexpected events which followed, with the assurance of Theo-dore's unshaken constancy, had rendered her not only forgetful of the flight of time, but of everything sublunary. She must, therefore return to the inn where Sir Theodore earnestly supplicated permission to accompany her, that they might pass an hour in tracing out their arrangements for the morrow; but this she would not allow.

"Has Adela become so inhospitable? She was not wont to exclude me from her tea-table."

But Adela continued inexorable. She, however, conceded to his request to be permitted to breakfast with her in the morning at eight, after which they were to commence their journey to the hamlet. When Adela returned, she requested to be conducted to a chamber where she ordered tea, and sat absorbed in the most delightful reflections until eleven o'clock. What joy would the morrow com-municate to the hearts of her beloved parents, in the assurance that the friend they once honoured by their esteem still merited it. The waitress came to ask if she would require anything more for the night. Adela ordered breakfast in the garden-parlour for eight o'clock in the morning, for herself and a friend, requesting a place might be taken in the earliest stage that was likely to pass to the hamlet, and these directions given she prepared to retire.

She arose to close the curtains, but with vexation and surprise she saw Sir Theodore still on the spot on which they had parted, his eyes wandering from one window, to the other, and not perceiving her, he continued walking to and fro. She threw aside the curtain,—he saw her, and kissed his hand. She waved her hand-kerchief, and dismissed her captive to his repose.

Ralph had been too constantly the participator of his master's sorrows, not to be made the partaker of his felicity. Si Theodore was once more happy, and everything had turned out, by a mere chance, just as though he himself had con-trived it.

Yes, the park would become a scene of hospitality and festivity! Mrs. Stafford and the good steward would live to see their prayers granted, and their honoured master united according to his own inclination;—for who could be worthy of such a heart but Miss St. Clair, who was, he had always said, like enough his departed lady to be her own veritable daughter?

CHAPTER XLVII.

> "Then let me hold thee to my heart,
>   And every care resign—
> And shall we never, never part?
> My life, my life—my all that's thine." GOLDSMITH.

IT will very readily be conceived that neither Adela nor her lover shared an uninterrupted repose, or slept late on the following morning. Sir Theodore's anxious spirit hovered around the spot that contained his treasure. He recalled the dangers which her heroic generosity had exposed her to on the preceding night. He trembled to think, she might have been lost to him for ever!—That, even now, the exertion she had undergone, her want of sleep and above all, the emotions of the mind that animated that exquisitely delicate frame, might occasion a relapse, —or the designing Grenville spread further snares for their mutual destruction.

"It was madness for her to pass the night, unprotected, at a solitary inn," said he, in his restless musings, "and if her too sensitive delicacy forbade my sharing the shelter of the same roof, it was nothing less than a duty to have passed the night where I could have watched over her safety."

Adela had permitted him to be with her at eight o'clock: but at five he arose, dressed with unusual care, indulged himself with a glance at her window, passed onwards to the solitary garden, gathered a sprig of blossomed myrtle as an offering

No. 28.

to his sleeping love, returned, and walked before the house until he had once more the felicity of seeing that pretty hand undraw the curtain.

But eight was the hour appointed—and as yet it was but seven. Did Adela's anxiety, then, almost keep pace with his own?

He was not far from the mark. Half an hour completed her toilette. He cast a supplicating glance towards the window, and at half-past seven she descended, and met him in the parlour, more interesting, more beautiful than he had ever before beheld her.

Again the hue of renovated hope tinged that lovely cheek which was heightened by her lover's ardent gaze;—again he was permitted to place his vernal offering amidst her beautiful tresses, and take his seat, as in other days, by her side.

During breakfast, it was determined that Sir Theodore should remain at the hamlet until Adela had related the circumstances to her parents that had transpired on the preceding evening; and she permitted him to be at the cottage at five or six o'clock. But he would not hear of the coach as the medium of conveyance.

"Dearest girl," said he, "let not a too fastidious severity embitter our felicity. Will not Grenville be again on the watch for you? Believe me, you are only safe under my protection, until once more beneath a parent's roof." Adela's blushing cheek and ingenuous smile, "approved his pleaded reason." And Ralph, who had been ordered early to procure a chaise from the next town, arriving with it, Sir Theodore led her to it, and took his seat beside her. Ralph followed with the horses, and three more happy individuals had scarcely ever, perhaps, passed that road,—for "past sorrow heightens present joy, ever as the desolation of winter endears the jocund smile of spring."

But the hours passed rapidly away. Adela thought the miles singularly short; and Sir Theodore had not uttered half the overflowings of his heart, when they reached the lane, at the end of which was her parent's habitation. He clasped her hand fervently—

"Six, did my Adela say?—not before six?—am I then to pass so many hours in exile?"

Adela assured him she should require at least that period for her explanation; and, permitting him to imprint a kiss on her fair hand, she tripped lightly forward, passed the gate which enclosed her from her lover's ardent gaze, and, was in her parents' arms in a moment.

But she scarcely seemed the Adela that left them! Her eye beamed with the lustre of a heart at ease, her cheek vied in beauty with the rose; and, her parents hung attentively on her gentle accents, as she related the events that had occasioned her sudden departure from Warwickshire,—her visit to the valley,—her recoutre with Sir Theodore, and his candid history of the melancholy, yet exculpatory, events that had succeeded his last visit to the Woodlands. Nothing was omitted but the fire-scene—that tale was left for a more animated speaker,—one whose expultation in the elevated character of their beloved girl, could only be equalled by their own.

They listened with breathless earnestness to the artifice that had for so long a period laid waste their tranquil pleasures. But their young friend was reinstated in their esteem, the sun had chased the mist, and the distant landscape arose again in renovated beauty.

Not a doubt remained on the mind of St. Clair,—"it would be inhospitable to defer the hour of reconciliation until the evening." And he hastened to the hamlet to invite Sir Theodore to partake of the dinner which would be ready by their return, whilst Adela received several letters from the hands of her mother. The first she unclosed, was from Mrs. Drayton;—it ran as follows:—

MY DEAR YOUNG FRIEND,—When your few candid, yet mysterious lines arrived they found me in a state of of agonizing suspense—the girls in tears,—the whole house in consternation!

"Miss St. Clair," said I, to Caroline, "is too reasonable, too correct in her feelings of propriety to have taken so hasty a step without a powerful motive;"

and we retired, consoled by the hope that the Creator would spread his protection around one of the most virtuous, as the fairest of his works.

But the morning arose on fresh anxieties. My brother did not join us at breakfast. I went to his chamber, and found him in a state of agitation approaching to fever. I took a seat by his bed-side, and he related what afflicted me deeply.

Alas, my dear girl, and has all the melancholy which cast its shadow over that young heart, proceeded from the persecution of an individual belonging to a family so deeply indebted to your talents and accomplishments?

Mrs. Drayton here entered into a detail of all the circumstances of her brother's flight, his captivity, his penitence, his restoration to his native land; and, concluded by a supplication, that if she could pardon the past, she would permit him to lay his fortune at her feet, and expiate, by a life of devoted tenderness and contrition, the errors! alas! the fatal derelictions of the past.

"I do not suppose this possible," continued she, "but my dear Adela will, I trust, pardon a sister's anxiety for the restoration to virtue of a repentant mourner who independently of this blemish on his honourable name, has always been the best of brothers. And if, as I have understood, the first tie that bound that gentle heart is alienated for ever;—what felicity should I find, in claiming an elder sister's right to teach you to forget your early affliction, and with your Caroline to scatter the flowers of gratitude and affection over a path that might yet shed the comforts of prosperity over your parents' life."

I listened to his entreaties;—I engaged to be his mediatrex, on condition that he would accompany me back to the Villa, where he still remains with me, the picture of despair; awaiting your permission to supplicate your pardon in the presence of your father, or fix his destination for a distant land, where, alone he says, he can at once expiate his transgression, and forget you.

Need I add how anxious we all are to see you—how earnestly we wish your reply? Yet reflect, I entreat you, before you determine.

And believe me, dearest Adela, your obliged and attached,

ELIZA DRAYTON.

To Miss St. Clair.

Adela's astonishment, could only be equalled by her vexation.

Could Grenville then presume that the heart which was denied him not only by principle but inherent aversion, would be won by outrage and violence? Could he hope, after the injuries reiterated on a parent's health and peace, to win the daughter's hand? or did he deem her so base as to unite her fate to his from the paltry consideration of worldly wealth? No, rather would she, in Fate's most adverse hour, have dared the fury of the most inclement sky, and selected the turf as her pillow.

Mrs. Drayton's disinterested kindness could not, however, be questioned, and she resolved on sending her a candid answer on the morrow.

A letter from Miss Egerton accompanied Mrs. Drayton's, and she pressed to her heart the affectionate communications of those dear girls the Arnolds. But the fond flutterer was not sufficiently calm at that delightful moment to reply to either. She put them into her desk, and went to receive her father and his restored friend, who accompanied his return.

Nor did Sir Theodore, suffer that day of homefelt bliss to fleet away on its fairy pinions, without supplicating an early day for their union.

St. Clair and his Aurora wished their daughter, yet to remain with them some months. Adela's filial tenderness, pleaded some delay, but her lover's impatience was not to be repressed.

Is it requisite, said he, that my honoured friends should resign their treasure, because I am also to possess it? May not one roof cover us, one home be ours?

Yes, our united path shall pass like an unruffled stream, amidst the scene of my earliest recollections. Leave an abode which is indeed unworthy of you, let us instantly set off for the Park; and, from this day, give added comfort to a home where your children's highest anxiety will tend to the casting to oblivion, the vicissitudes of the past.

St. Clair and his Aurora each pressed the hand he extended to them with the fervour of pure affection; whilst Adela's expressive eye spoke the language of her guileless and happy bosom.

The proposal relative to the Park, St. Clair said, would require consideration, but he agreed to resign his daughter to the chosen of her heart at the end of a month; during which interval, he was invited to spend as much time at the cottage, as the arrangements for the approaching nuptials would permit.

The hour of eleven brought Ralph for his master's orders, and the family at the cottage, received him with the most condescending kindness—but they were too happy to heed the flight of time, and Sir Theodore reluctantly departed at half-past twelve; only on condition that Adela would take an early ramble with him, on the following morning—and a delightful ramble it was, amongst scenes glowing with the golden promise of a luxuriant harvest, every prospect was bright as their approaching felicity, even the flowers wore a brighter hue, and the little birds poured a ray of unusual sprightliness and melody.

They returned, glowing with the breeze of the early morning, and partook of a breakfast spread at the cottage door, with an appetite frequently wanted at the banquet of luxury.

But the hour of parting must arrive, a few days must be sacrificed to the preparation for the reception of his affianced bride. He often returned to breathe the impassioned vow to her willing ear, or impress some caution on the minds of her parents; but he must away, and Adela returned to the parlour to reply to her letters, and arrange with her mother the preparations for the approaching union.

Adela's letter to Mrs. Drayton, was affectionate and sincere; it was accompanied by one from her mother, replete with mildness and dignity, she expressed the kindest acknowledgments for her hospitality to her daughter, as well as her flattering preference; assured her that her brother's contrition could not fail to obtain their pardon, when so esteemed a friend became his advocate, for to such a sister what could be denied? and concluded, by mentioning her daughter's approaching nuptials, with the chosen of her earliest affections, as a decided negative to every hope Captain Grenville might yet entertain.

These letters sealed and dispatched, Adela was just sitting down to reply to Miss Egerton's, and answer the letters of her endeared young friends; when Mr. Arnold's chaise drove up to the door. This warm-hearted friend jumped out, and taking St. Clair aside, warmly clasped his hand.

"Don Manuel de Mello," said he, "has arrived! he is in the travelling chariot which approaches. Use what precautions you may, to prevent the surprise from overpowering your good lady, for unexpected joy has produced the same effect as grief; but his lordship approaches, farewell! in a few days we shall meet again."

In vain did the astonished St. Clair insist upon his stay; he got into his chaise and departed, leaving his friend to receive his illustrous father-in-law, whose carriage drove up at the instant.

CHAPTER XLVIII.

"Why was the rustic board so sweet,
    'Twas health and peace that smiled around,
Why did the heart responsive beat,
    To every soft commingling sound?"

St. Clair's majestic figure, the tempered dignity of his countenance, had not changed their influence; although the vicissitudes of a varied fate had shed their silvery tinge over a head which might have served as a model to a statuary.

But from the period at which they parted, less change was discernible in Don Manuel from the customs of his life, the features were then fixed, and the future changes in a manner less conspicuous. In a moment the recognition took place, St. Clair would have clasped the hand of his early protector—of the author of his Aurora's days, to his lips, but he pressed him in a paternal embrace.

In another moment he was in the cottage—his daughter in his arms—his Adela at his feet; how many years of sorrow did this meeting repay? whilst the venerable father gazed on the dark eyes, and still lovely features of his Aurora, and she passed her white hand through the silvery hair, that graced his venerable head.

"Beautiful creature!" said he as he gazed on Adela, "I need not ask, for I feel that she is my grandchild; change but the dark auburn for her mother's jetty ringlets, and the blue eyes for the dark ones, and such was she, at the moment, when an ill-directed severity drove her from the home of her forefathers."

A few more hasty sentences informed them of her mother's and Don Luiz's death, Mrs. St. Clair and her husband dropped a tear to their memory, and Don Manuel, clasping his grandaughter to his heart, entreated to be informed how they had made this lonely dwelling their abode.

St. Clair told him all, he wept at their vicissitudes.

"But how will my grandpapa be accommodated in this humble dwelling," said Adela.

"Where my children have passed months, cannot I spend a few hours," said he, "yes, my little one, such a smile as thine would give a charm to a desert!"

St. Clair now thought of the interpreter.

"Aye," said Don Manuel, "A finer lad never lived, ask him in, and offer him every attention in your power."

But St. Clair was too late—he was gone.

Don Manuel was surprised at his sudden departure, inquired of Pedro whether he had left any message, and learned that he had left a note, which he unclosed and read as follows.

To the Most Noble and Illustrious Senor, Don Manuel de Mello.

My Lord,—In quitting you thus abruptly, I have no other excuse to offer than not having it in my power to render myself any further utility to you.

May you enjoy in your daughter's society, every felicity a good heart can bestow and believe me with the warmest wishes for your welfare.

My lord, your obedient humble servant,

EDWIN MERTON.

"Well," said Don Manuel, "he is a fine youth, I still hope I shall see him again, and recompense his many obligations."

St. Clair, with Don Manuel's permission, dismissed the carriage to the inn, and Pedro to the kitchen, where delighted in once more seeing the dear children he had so often carried in his arms, filled his aged eyes with tears.

"But we must not reside here altogether," said Don Manuel, "we must buy a pretty villa, which will be large enough for us all—for as I shall quit you no more, if you can accommodate me, and if you will not accompany me back, we must live en famille; but say, my sweet girl, shall it be in England or Spain?"

Adella replied with a blush, " in England, if you please, my lord."

"How is it you speak Spanish so fluently, you little rogue? but I see it all very plainly, and that blush whispers a secret which mamma must explain."

Mrs. St. Clair acknowledged that there was a secret, for which she should claim all his parental indulgence at a future hour.

This was indeed a joyous surprise, yet what were they to do—it was a homely reception for Don Manuel, yet he seemed resolved to remain with them, and they determined to accommodate him in the best manner possible, first by fitting up Mrs. St. Clair's chamber for him, she sharing Adela's bed, while St. Clair slept at the next cottage.

The evening was employed in the relation of Adela's and Theodore's little history and the reasons which conspired to bind her so strongly to England. They sat to a late hour; Don Manuel prepared for repose, and enjoyed it as sweetly as if canopied beneath his own gilded drapery. On the followiug morning, the St. Clairs and their lovely daughter awoke early, and they carefully avoided every sound that might disturb his repose; Adela was strenuously employed in antici. pating the requisite arrangements of the day, and, with Pedro's assistance, was preparing the repast.

Nothing was wanting, but the flowers to decorate the table. and fill the vases, and she hastened to gather them. She had nearly filled her basket, and looking to the window of her grandfather, to see if he were yet awake, she sang, and the breezes re-echoed the song,—

"In rapture warbled from Love's breathing lips."

and sweetly did it harmonize on Don Manuel's waking ear, as he rang the bell to summons Pedro's attendance.

———

CHAPTER XLIX.

"It is that witch, adversity, her spell
　Makes beauty ugliness, and wisdom folly,
Change but the scene, and all will yet be well,
　Gold brings back friends and softens melancholy,
High, low, the rich, the poor, the young, the old,
　All how obedient, to that idol gold."

" COME, come, be quick, if you can't pay the small amount of this little apart-ment, you must turn out and leave it for those that can; for my part, when my husband agreeed to let you have it for such a trifle, I was very much against it, for of all the people in the world I hate poor gentry."

These invectives were uttered in a sharp shrill tone by the mistress of the house, in which the unfortunate Mrs. Merton occupied a small back room on the second floor; she had just recovered from a fever produced by the want of sustenance, united with extreme agitation of mind, and she was collecting as rapidly as her debilitated state would permit her, the few habiliments remaining, that she might accede to the harsh and authoritative superiority which fortune in her caprices sometimes gives to the ignorant and worthless over the enlightened and worthy.

With tottering steps she descended the staircase, and was met by the good man of the house at the bottom.

" Let the poor lady go first, my dear," said he, " and see if she can suit herself before you turn her out in this sort of way; remember, she has just got up from a bed of sickness.

" Oh, suit herself,—truly! I think, Mr. Crabtree, a person without a penny to buy a crust may monstrous soon be suited; but I shall be ruler here."

" You are ruler here, my dear, every one knows that," replied the good-natured man, deeply impressed with the truth of his spouse's last remark; you are ruler here, only with all submission, I do think you women are monstrous unmerciful to one another; and if I had my will, I'd let the poor lady stay till she had got some-where to go, that's all."

Mrs. Merton returned her grateful acknowledgments for the well-intentioned proffer, and proceeded to the door, followed by a laugh from Mrs. Crabtree.

" Lady, forsooth! but let her gentility find her a home, and as good a table as we have; and that's all the harm I wish her."

Mrs. Merton walked slowly onward. The evening was closing; the happy villager sung the song of contentment as he passed her, doubtless to his affec-tionate family and home of peace. She, alas! had no home, no resource, no one to receive her: she seemed alone in the world, and her last penny had been expended for the roll on which she had subsisted during that day. Her lips were parched, her knees trembled, and she sat on the step of a stile which led to the neighbouring village.

"Alas! my beloved Edwin," sighed the desolate being, "how would thy filial tenderness weep over this wreck of what thy mother once was! But, *where art thou?* Perhaps the wide ocean now rolls its multitudinous waves over thy lifeless form; and thy pure spirit, united with that of thy lamented father, now watches the moment when this breast shall cease to suffer, and share your joy."

A young lady approached. She turned her eye scornfully on Mrs. Merton, as expecting she would rise and make way for her. Finding, however, that she kept her station, she tripped lightly over and passed on. The next person who passed was a fashionably-dressed female, with her daughter.

"Nonsense, Maria," was the quick reply to an observation, "she is only ill— how do we know what complaint she may have? I desire, miss, that you do not run the risk of carrying home sickness to your little brothers by your ill-timed humanity. If she is in want let her go to the workhouse—we pay poor's-rate, and I think that is all that can be reasonably expected of us."

Mrs. Merton was in too desolate a state, and her native independence of spirit too much depressed by bodily weakness, to reply to those observations, even by reminding the selfish being who uttered them, that as she did not in any way sollicit her bounty, her illiberality might at least have been repressed, and as they continued their path in one direction, she arose to proceed in the other; but her exertion in passing the stile overpowered her, and she was obliged to rest on the other side.

At this moment a gentleman approached, and looked compassionately on her; he hesitated—her appearance was too genteel for that of a mendicant; her countenance, although marked by woe and despair, bore traces of extreme beauty; her manner was that of the severest sorrow, dignified by conscious virtue, and perfectly aware that she was equally deserving in this, as in any other state to receive respect or commiseration—it was perfect integrity and uncomplaining patience. He doubted whether the proffer of assistance might not be deemed intrusive;—"at all events I will risk it," said he, advancing towards her.

"I know not, madam, if your apparent affliction be of a nature to admit of relief; but if this trifle from the hands of a father of a numerous family, not rich himself, will be of any service, I entreat your acceptance of it."

So saying, he put a sovereign into her hand, and departed, without waiting a reply, or to receive the acknowledgments of a grateful heart, that breathed its aspirations to Heaven for this unexpected aid. And she slowly pursued her way towards some cottages that stood in the lane, and in one of which she hoped to obtain shelter until renewed strength might enable her to make those accomplishments she possessed again the medium of a subsistence.

"My dear fellow," said Mr. Seymour to a young man in the habit of a sailor, who crossed his path just as he had reached the end of the lane, "do oblige me by running after that lady; she is extremely ill, and therefore walks slowly—you will easily overtake her. Give her this card—it is my address—tell her, if, as a professional man, I can be of any service to her, or if she should require any assistance within the power of Mrs. Seymour to offer, she may command us. Call on me with her reply, and I shall be most happy to compensate you."

Edwin had inherited a proud heart, but it was that well-directed pride which, although nursed in the lap of adversity, his early education had not lessened; and conscious of the possession of all that truly merits distinction, it was natural enough that he should start at the idea of anything like an innovation of his independence, proceeding from his present very misplaced situation in society, or that he should blush deeply as he paused to listen to the closing part of the stranger's address. But Edwin's youthful heart had already vibrated to the touch of sorrow—a female! in sickness, in distress! what more powerful incentive to his speed—what stronger claim to his forbearance? and although it might be a few minutes longer delay from that maternal bosom to which he longed to be once more pressed, he assured the stranger he required no compensation, and lost not a moment in leaping the stile, and pursuing the object of his search.

Mrs. Merton heard footsteps behind her; she turned her head—"Merciful Heaven! can it be my boy?"

"Mother, beloved mother! is it thus I meet you?"

His protecting arms supported her—his tears fell on her cheek, and it was, indeed, the hand of her beloved, her dutiful son, that wiped the cold dew that hung on her brow.

CHAPTER L.

Montaigne saith prettily, when he inquired the reason why the word of the lie should be such a disgrace and such an odious charge: 'If it be well weighed to say that a man lieth, is as much as to say, that he is brave towards GOD and a coward towards MAN—for a lie faces GOD, and shrinks from MAN.'—BACON.

WHEN the Reverend Jonathan St. Clair saw Don Manuel de Mello depart, not only to the destruction of his golden prospects, but the certainty of his deception being attributed to its proper cause, for he knew Mr. Arnold too well to suppose he would not be perfectly aware of his intention. In vain did the old lady attempt to console him; he waved his hand in silence, and shut himself up in his study, to muse over his past folly and the disappointment of those schemes that had not only led to universal contempt, but the consciousness of meriting it. And what had his injustice to a certain individual brought him?—incessant, uneasy apprehensions; and the necessity of submitting to all the outrages of a vulgar and unprincipled being, whose irregularities he dared not resent. And his protegee, for whose sake he had compromised himself, how had *she* evinced her gratitude, by the most violent invectives, by giving way to those outrageous feelings that could only end in insanity; whilst the injured, the neglected St. Clair would again flourish uninjured; and not only enjoy the opulence of his father, but his importance would secure a most splendid alliance for his daughter.

"Quite a misapprehension—quite a mismanagement," said he, as he wiped the cold persperation from his forehead, "but it can't be recalled—I must try what can be done by conciliating Edmund St. Clair. Mrs. St. Clair shall call on the Lady Aurora—we will invite the daughter to stay a month with us."

He was disturbed in this reverie by a loud knocking at his door, and Mrs. Crawley demanded entrance. He opened the door, and tried to sooth her, She was outrageous, and they found it necessary to confine her in the little dressing room where she had first seen Robert, till the arrival of her medical advisers.

The impossibility of inviting Miss St. Clair was now evident; for, as Robert had insisted on parting with his house, and sending his wife to a receptacle for persons in her situation, Mrs. Jonathan had urged the necessity of having her home, and a couple of apartments allotted to her. Her mother had also arrived to assist in attending to her. These arrangements completed, Robert made the best of his way to London, where he took a handsome lodging; resolved, in his own words, to "carry on the war" in the best style possible.

Nor did Susan any longer detain him, neglected by the being who had betrayed her, terrified by his wife, whose last visit to her had brought on an illness from which she had never recovered; she sunk into the grave of her parents, a lesson to the too-confiding portion of her sex, which may warn them of the recklessness of such individuals.

"Of all the various wretches love has made.
How few have been by men of sense betrayed."

The evening previous to Sir Theodore's return to the cottage, he made every requisite arrangement for the reception of the idol of his soul, and departed, leaving Mrs. Stafford "in the best spirits in the world."

Don Manuel and Edmund St. Clair had set out for a walk in the neighbouring hamlet, and to the smiling faces that welcomed their return, another was added scarce, less interesting, because it was evident he was the elegant youth to whom Adela was engaged.

Sir Theodore did not speak Spanish, but he was sufficiently conversant in Italian, so that they soon understood each other; and, with delight, the youthful pair received the blessing wanting only to their approaching nuptials.

"You are, indeed, welcome," said the delighted girl; "we were just wishing to introduce you to grandpapa, to whom you are indeed no longer a stranger."

No. 29.

But Theodore had brought a selection of love presents, and a beautiful pocket-book, with a magnificent amount for her bridal wardrobe; a miniature, with a medallion of brilliants, and a chain of the same.

'The miniature, my love, like the original, has long been your own." And she fondly pressed it to her lips, as she consigned it to her bosom. But the pocket-book she would not accept. Sir Theodore was obliged to submit, and he urged Mr. St. Clair's attention to the change of residence, and pressed upon him the necessity of removing to the Park.

Mr. St. Clair was just going to apply to him, and they availed themselves so well of the necessities of the moment, that Sir Theodore convinced St. Clair that the Park would be the most desirable residence until the lodge should be in readiness. The mansion was splendid, and would only require a fortnight to put in order. The day succeeding the following one, was determined on for their departure, and with cheerful minds and hearts altogether at ease, they arose to breakfast, which was the last they were to share in that rustic dwelling.

St. Clair, his wife, and the venerable Don Manuel followed in the carriage. Sir Theodore and Adela preceded them in the curricle, and Ralph and Pedro followed —the one happy in the accomplishment of all his prayers, the other well repaid for his former disasters by witnessing his dear lady restored to her family and fortune.

Sir Theodore and Adela felt, really, what it was to be exquisitely happy; they had passed years in absence, they had scarcely been permitted to think of each other, and they now felt restored with all the gifts of the heart, united with all that wealth could bestow.

It was evening when the carriage drove into the Park, and Mrs. Stafford and the old steward received the blooming Adela as the future lady of that ancient abode. Her parents, too, and the venerable Don Manuel were formed to create the respect they excited; and gladly did Sir Theodore welcome them to his native home.

CHAPTER LI.

" Winter's clouds and darksome hours
Frown; but they precede the spring
So do April's passing showers
May's enchanting flowerets bring."

SOMEWHAT revived, Mrs. Merton related the gradations of adversity through which she had passed since his departure; her agonising ignorance of his fate, his hardships, and dangers, so well repaid by the present moment, were also recounted. And Edwin, drawing a purse from his bosom, said,—

" This, dear mother, will provide for you till I can obtain a regular medium of subsistence. I will never more leave you, and even though the education your tenderness bestowed on me should fail, I have strength and health, and the Almighty will nerve my arm to the most laborious occupation when my sacred charge is a mother."

Mrs. Merton clasped him to her bosom, and having found her a seat on a grassy bank, he departed to find a shelter for the night. What emotions of maternal love and gratitude to Heaven warmed her bosom as her eye followed his youthful and elegant form, graceful even in that coarse disguise, as seeming to tread in air, he hastened to provide her an asylum.

Edwin was successful. At the first cottage he obtained a parlour and two small rooms adjoining; and the good woman to whom it belonged, promised to do all in her power to render their residence there comfortable; all was clean and neat; he ordered a fire to be lighted as the evenings began to be chill, and hastened to conduct his beloved parent thither. When Mrs. Merton and her son arrived at the cottage, everything wore the appearance of rustic comfort; the bright tea-kettle stood boiling over a cheering fire, for Edwin remembered every *minutiæ*, where his mother's comfort was concerned, and sincerely did she hail this change from despair to comfort and tranquillity, brought by his return whom she had mourned as lost.

Edwin drew forth from his neck his mother's miniature, there suspended by the same braid of fine hair once worn by his departed father. Never had it been absent from that shrine of filial affection since her hands had secured its golden clasp; through every danger, through every variation that had been sacredly preserved; and this excellent mother, whose once brilliant prospects had all been resigned for the valued being whose pillow of death she would gladly have shared, now formed no higher wish than that of devoting the few remaining years, which yet might sever them, to the comfort of this only remaining pledge of their tenderness. From the home of her father she had long been an exile, and that heart was now cold, which alone could awaken hers to gladness.

The good cottager and her inmates became gradually pleased with each other—where amiable natures meet, and those kind offices are exerted on one hand, which are not to be purchased, and that friendly and mild condescension returned on the other, which is a more welcome recompense than the reluctant gold of the proud and wealthy, years are not necessary to form the bond of such an attachment; and, although the good Elizabeth was unpolished by education, and Mrs. Merton highly accomplished, and possessed of that dignity of manner which threw the common observer at a distance, and would naturally place a distinction between them, yet the heart of the latter acknowledged the inherent worth of the former, and she sighed that those hours of affluence had passed away, which would have enabled her to evince her sense of such unremitting attentions.

The good Elizabeth discovered that it was Edwin's wish to procure documents to copy, and as she had a relative, a solicitor at a town not very far distant, she wrote to him, requesting that if he could influence anything of the sort, she should feel obliged by his giving the preference to the young gentleman the bearer of her note. In the unaffected language of a good heart she mentioned everything that could excite an interest in his behalf, and Edwin, with a quick step, took his way thither on the following morning.

Edwin was successful; the relative of Elizabeth insisted on his dining with him, and promised that on the following week he should be able to furnish him with occupation. He took his leave, but as he had some little commissions to execute for his mother, it was late before he was on his return.

Edwin had just passed a green lane; the overshadowing branches of the trees on either side cast a shade of obscurity even at noonday—that shade was much deepened at the present hour, for evening was far advanced; at the end of the avenue a rude bridge was thrown over a bubbling stream—the scene was lone and solitary.

A sudden exclamation reached his ear, succeeded by imprecations; he followed as the sounds directed, and beheld at the foot of the bridge an elderly gentleman attacked by two robbers. Edwin rushed forward, placed himself beside the devoted victim, and, snatching the dagger from the hand of the ruffian (who had already grasped his neck to execute his cruel purpose), wounded him deeply.

The other, finding the youth was now armed, and prepared for resistance, fired his pistol, which wounded Edwin in the arm; but disappointed that he was not altogether disabled, he dragged his companion through an aperture in the hedge, abandoned the field, and left the venerable stranger expressing his warmest gratitude towards his youthful protector.

"But, my dear young friend, you are wounded."

"Slightly, sir," replied Edwin, twisting his handkerchief round his arm.

"Good Heaven! I fear, indeed, it is not slightly," replied the elderly gentleman, taking his hand; "my house is not far distant; we will send for a surgeon.

Alas! my dear fellow, why did you not leave an aged, solitary man to his fate, since he has nothing left to live for?"

There was a touch of extreme melancholy in the words as well as the air of the stranger. Edwin heeded not his wound, and would have imagined that a bandage, applied by the hand of his beloved mother, would have healed it immediately; yet he felt an unusual interest in the safety of the unknown, and suffered himself to be persuaded by him.

A few minutes brought them to the mansion, which was splendidly furnished, and having entered an elegant drawing-room, and dispatched a servant for a surgeon, with a hand tremulous with age and anxiety assisted to remove the jacket, that his arm might be attended to.

The braid which suspended Mrs. Merton's miniature around the neck of her son became entangled in the sleeve-button of his host; he stooped to take it up—the light of the candle fell strongly on the features—the aged man started.

"Merciful Providence! where did you get this picture?"

"It is my mother's," replied Edwin; "why do you ask, sir?"

The characters of grief and agony that passed over his countenance were terrifying, but what were Edwin's sensations when, suddenly clasping him to his heart, he exclaimed—"Oh, how truly has nature spoken to this, till now, desolate heart! Thy mother, sayest thou, boy? yes, thy countenance, thy features, prove the truth of thy assertion—thou art indeed my grandson."

Edwin fell at his feet, and embraced his knees.

CHAPTER LIII.

And thus as in memory's bark we shall glide,
    To visit the scenes of our boyhood anew,
Tho' oft we may see, looking down on the tide,
    The wreck of full many a hope shining through;
Yet still as in fancy we point to the flowers,
    That once made a garden of all the gay shore;
Deceived for a moment, we'll think them still ours,
    And breathe the fresh air of life's morning once more.—MOORE.

"Oh! tell me, tell me, does my Ella still exist, or has the cruelty of her unforgiving father consigned her to the tomb?"

"She lives, dear sir, my mother lives, to form our united felicity; and an emperor might be proud to acknowledge her. How would that heart throb with transport could she anticipate an hour like this!"

"And thy father?"

Edwin turned aside to hide a falling tear.

"Dear boy, how do those tears reproach me! would to Heaven we could recal him. Alas! years of affliction have not expiated my injustice to that worthy, that lamented being! Why did avarice, why did ambition, blind me to his worth?"

Mr. Seymour, who, in the confusion of his first entrance, and the sensation produced by the account given by the servant, united to so singular a coincidence, did not just at first recognise his young messenger. His fine features, his interesting countenance, however, soon recalled him to his remembrance—his heart sympathised truly, and he urged a moment's tranquillity, that his young friend's wound might be bound up, for the agitation had occasioned it to bleed profusely.

"Oh sir!" said Sir Arthur, for we will now recognise the elderly gentleman by his proper appellation, "you know not what a treasure I have found! But what do I say? Perhaps even now I may see her no more—years have elapsed since I clasped her to my breast, since I scorned, repulsed, drove her from her paternal habitation—and why? Because her pure and virtuous heart had made its own election, which I should have proudly sanctioned if true worth—honour—all that merits distinction and esteem had not been overpowered by that heart-steeling ambition, that savage avarice which, while it made me forget that I was a father, deprived me of a daughter. But it is past—alas! the scenes where she sought my caresses in infancy, became hateful to me, and for years I have been a wanderer on the face of the earth, unsettled and devoid of repose; the morning dew did not refresh, the evening breeze did not revive me; I was desolate and unhappy."

"Be comforted, my dear sir," said Edwin, "my beloved mother will yet form the felicity of your declining years, your Edwin will only exist in your mutual happiness." Then turning to Mr. Seymour, "the lady of whom you sent me in pursuit," continued he, "was my mother, of whom I was actually in search, having recently arrived in England, and found her former dwelling deserted."

Mr. Seymour warmly congratulated both, but as Edwin's flushed cheek excited the anxiety of his grandfather, he was prevailed upon to lie down upon the sofa, while he accompanied Sir Arthur, who had ordered the carriage, according to his grandson's direction, to the cottage.

Mrs. Merton had ordered her frugal repast an hour later than usual; even then she delayed it a little longer, and loitered over it, anxious that her boy should partake it with her. Another, and another hour elapsed, the sunflower began to close, and the bee, humming and heavy, sought its hive—" where could he stay?"

"The young gentleman is safe enough ma'am no doubt," said Elizabeth; "my cousin will give him a hearty welcome I know. Come, let me stir up the fire, it is cold weather for the close of autumn; let me make a cup of tea, your anxiety will make you ill again."

"I am anxious, indeed, Elizabeth: who, possessing one only treasure does not tremble at a shadow, when his safety is concerned? and the way from the town is long. I believe, and lonely."

"Oh no, ma'am, cheer up your heart, Mr. Edwin will be here presently."

Elizabeth vainly sought to calm the fears of her respected inmate—she ran to the end of the lane.

The slightest noise was frequently mistaken for his approach, but he did not appear; and, when nine o'clock arrived, the affectionate mother closed the window, and sat down by the fire to weep. Just at that moment a gentle tap was heard at the door.

"Master Edwin is here ma'am," said Elizabeth, cheerfully opening the door.

But it was not Edwin, and that maternal heart sunk on perceiving a stranger enter. It was Mr. Seymour, the same gentleman whose accents of kindness had once been addressed to her comfortless heart; and who, having accompanied her father within a short distance prevailed with him to remain in the carriage whilst he went to prepare his daughter for his reception.

Mrs. Merton requested her kind visitor would be seated; he took her hand as having casually discovered her habitation, and inquired relative to her health.

Conversation led to former days, her father was mentioned; Mr. Seymour spoke of a gentleman who had purchased an estate about a mile distant, the description was extremely similar, and as a singular coincidence he had frequently heard him mention his anxiety to discover a long lost daughter, whose society his ill-directed severity had for years deprived him.

Tears chased each other down the wan cheek of the patient, the resigned sufferer, and when she had promised to be calm, and not suffer her emotions to overcome her, he related the wondrous tale, assured her of the safety of her boy, and hastened to accompany her long alienated parent to her embraces.

"My dear, my honoured father," was all Mrs. Merton could utter, as she clasped the knees of her venerable parent.

"My Ella, my deserted child, oh, let me restore thee to the home which without thee is devoid of comfort, and let us in the felicity of thy valiant boy (his grandfather's protector) forget the years we have lost; hasten, he now awaits us, let not another moment detain my daughter from her own, her paternal dwelling."

Mrs. Merton, bathed in tears of joy, consented; the good Elizabeth mingled her gratulations, with those of the amiable Seymour.

Sir Arthur put a purse into her hands which she firmly rejected; and Mrs. Merton ascended the carriage, after warmly expressing her gratitude for the continued kindness, evinced by her gentle consoler in adversity.

The joyous welcome Edwin gave his mother may better be imagined than described; her anxiety for his safety united with the proud and happy reflection that he had been the humble instrument in the hands of the Almighty for the preservation of her father.

From that moment Edwin began gradually to recover—in a month he was perfectly reinstated, and he went to the cottage in the hope of meeting with Don Manuel—to his astonishment he found him gone; but, on obtaining the proper direction, determined at a future hour to seek him at the Lodge.

CHAPTER LIV.

Deem not the hopeless outcast's soul
　　With guilt is always mingled,
He haply boasts as fair a fame
　　As Virtue e'er enkindled.
As firm a heart—as pure a mind
As e'er a human form enshrined.
　　　　　　　OUTLAW'S TOMB.

THE next day a letter arrived from Mrs. Drayton to Mrs. St. Clair, and one to Adela, as follows :—

MY DEAREST ADELA,

Your letter I received with infinite pleasure; it assured me of your continued esteem : in your happiness, believe me, I take a real interest—long may it flourish to add to that of your respected parents : with respect to my brother, he seems dispirited, but, I flatter myself, when we set off for our excursion, the variety of incident will divert him; but oh, where will he meet with another Adela?

A circumstance occurred to us which was rather singular; Rosalie had gone on a visit of a month to Miss Egerton, and it was for her return we delayed our excursion. Mrs. Montague, who lives in the next villa, and who occasionally sits with me to attend my brother, had just left me; and Caroline and her daughter Laura had strolled out together. When they reached the gate, they saw an aged man, apparently expiring, and Caroline stopped to inquire.

"Oh, never mind," said Laura, " I dare say we can do nothing for him."

"But, Laura," said Caroline, "he seems expiring, poor old gentleman! want and affliction are painted in his countenance."

"Well, do as you please—I shall return home."

With these words Laura tripped across the lawn, while Caroline approached the stranger, and demanded, in the tenderest accents of sympathy, if she could in anywise alleviate his sufferings.

The voice, the manner of the inquirer struck to his soul, as if a vision of departed felicity had glided before him. The stranger started, he turned his languid eye on the form that hung over him; and, although he did not altogether understand her, that the inquiry was dictated by kindness and pity, he replied in French, that want and irremediable calamity had at length overpowered him, and rendered him incapable to proceed.

"Rest yourself, then, under this tree, sir," said Caroline, " and I will return to you instantly."

Caroline paused not an instant;—it seemed almost impossible that she could have crossed the lawn when she was back and by his side, with one hand supporting his head—with the other presenting the wine she had brought to his parched and pallid lip. But, alas! that eye seemed closing in death; and Caroline, fearing her aid had come too late to restore the venerable being before her, placed him under the care of the servant, who had followed her, and ran again to the house.

I was in the library; agitated, and almost breathless, Caroline threw herself into my arms.

"Dear mamma, an unfortunate stranger is expiring at the gate. Oh, permit me to have him brought to the house : a little care, warmth, and nourishment may yet restore him."

My heart was instantaneously alive to the animated appeal; and, taking her hand, we proceeded without delay to the gate. His appearance, although disguised by his threadbare habiliments and his cheek furrowed by the heavy and defacing hand of adversity, still bore the traces of manly beauty, and the perfect gentleman was discernible in his present state of destitution. His silvery hair seemed more the work of sorrow than time, and could not fail to mingle a sentiment of veneration with that of compassion. A deep moan of internal anguish burst from the lips of the sufferer.

"He shall be removed to the house," said I, "Edward and James shall convey him carefully, and place him on the sofa in the breakfast parlour. Poor gentleman, his present state proceeds, perhaps, from one of those overwhelming vicissitudes from which neither caution nor rectitude of conduct can shield us. Happy, my Caroline, are those to whom Heaven has assigned the power even in the humblest degree, of alleviating his sufferings."

"But where was Laura?"

She looked fearfully on at a distance, now and then cautioning us not to run the risk of catching a fever.

"My aunt would be terrified to death," said she, "to take strangers into the house :—she would always go a distance round rather than pass one of these poor creatures. If he were a gentleman, indeed, who had fallen from his horse, or his carriage had broken down; but look, how shabby his clothes are, and his cravat is darned all over. I think he looks like a foreigner."

"Unfeeling girl," said I, "and if he is a foreigner so much the stronger his claim. To expire in want, in absence from all who may feel an interest in his fate, an exile from the land of his birth—what more affecting picture can be drawn to excite our sympathy? If he were a gentleman—indeed. Now, Laura, what constitutes a gentleman? is it dress?—is it a splendid mansion?—an elegant equipage? No, my child—it is the mind that displays itself in the deportment—it is talent and education alone that can give this distinction, nor can it be otherwise applied unless by the most inferior intellect and most degraded feeling. But, independently of this argument, were he the humblest peasant, do you think my girls or myself would shrink from the duties of kindness and hospitality? Oh, Laura, change these sentiments, and let me not blush to call you the daughter of such a mother!"

Laura was going to reply; but Mr. Marley entered. He took the unfortunate stranger's hand, and perceived his state to be that of entire exhaustion from want and fatigue. A restorative medicine was administered, and after some time Caroline's cares were rewarded by seeing an appearance of returning animation. But —languid, trembling, and weak, how should the stranger pursue his journey.

"Perhaps his home was far distant—if, indeed, he has a home; and where would he find shelter should his terrible indisposition return, and night and darkness overtake him?"

"Would you, then, my dear Caroline, have your mamma keep him here all night I should be terrified to death."

"And why not, Laura?—Caroline judges very justly of a cold-hearted world —there are too many selfish and insensible to the woes and sufferings of their fellow-creatures to render it anything less than a crime, in ourselves, to cast forth this venerable being, in his present weak state, on its mercy."

" Dear mamma, will you then ? "

" Yes, my child," said I, " the request I read in your eyes is granted ; we will have your guest accommodated in the blue chamber." Laura shrugged her pretty white shoulders, and Caroline went to give her requisite orders.

But I must make you acquainted with Laura's mother, for before this time it must have excited your astonishment, and you must have inquired, how it could possibly have occurred, that she should possess feelings so entirely in opposition to an excellent parent.

But a combination of circumstances, as adverse as they were singular, had tended to deprive the little Laura of her mother's care, when the earliest dawn of reason might have done so much, and when a daily example is more than ten thousand precepts.

Nature had, however, at last reassumed her sacred rights ; and although much care had been already exerted to restore a misled, though naturally a good heart, much yet remained to be done.

Laura Wentworth was the only consolation of a widowed mother ; affectionate, intelligent, amiable—her education formed the charm of every hour, her rapid improvement, the purity of her heart and the gentleness of her nature, brought back the sincerest felicity to the maternal bosom.

It was not long before the artless and retiring graces of the lovely Laura, received the homage of many a youthful heart ; and amongst those who visited at Hazlewood, Colonel Montague, at length, obtained a preference in her pure and sincere affections.

The amiable Mrs. Wentworth smiled upon their union, and a few months only had elapsed before her gentle spirit winged its flight to a better world. But an elegant exterior, and manners the most fascinating, are not always security against the approach of sorrow, and it was not long before the fading cheek of the young and lovely Mrs. Montague, bespoke their intrusion.

My heart was ever ready to console her, and to sympathise with her, and to me alone she confided the agonising truth, that Montague was the slave of dissolute companions ; that whole nights were devoted to the gaming-table, that a wealthy aunt (whose eccentricities and fashionable follies had rendered her the object of every reasonable being's reprehension) completely governed their domestic arrangements, and that in reply to every expostulation, he replied " my dear Laura have patience, let her have her way—we must not offend her, consider the extent of her property."

And Laura's patience was indeed exerted to the utmost ; she reasoned, resented, forgave and forgave again, because she loved the delinquent far more than her own existence. What sacrifice would she not have made to recal him to reason and virtue ! but the hope was an illusion—for, although his heart was not yet depraved, he was so completely the creature of circumstance, and so devoid of energy, that all the respectable resolutions formed, in the few moments then devoted to his Laura, were instantly laughed and scoffed away by his licentious associates.

But he was not devoid of sensibility, and on that Mrs. Montague built her hope, that when he should become a father (which event was hourly expected), he would become steady and domestic.

That hour arrived. Montague pressed his lovely infant to his bosom, with all the exquisite emotion of a first awakened parental tenderness ; he kissed its innocent lips, its forehead, its eyes, and seemed to love his Laura still more ardently than ever ; and many delightful evenings were passed in the formation of visions f virtuous felicity for the future ; why were they formed only to be forgotten ?--

" Just this one evening Laurey," said the colonel, " I chanced to meet Sir Henry Danvers, and he drew from me a promise (much against my inclination I assure you) to meet Lord Mervin at his house ; I've been very good lately, you know."

Laura assented with a foreboding sigh—Colonel Montague returned late, or rather early on the following morning ; one evil step preludes another, on the next night he was also absent. He met his Laura, on the following morning, at breakfast, pale and silent; on the next, when he came to apologize for another unavoidable appointment, she expostulated—he replied laughingly—she expressed her fears and wept, while she entreated him to listen to her supplication, and pause ere it was too late. He replied sternly, and they parted in resentment.

On the following morning Montague came affectionately to her.

"My Laura," said he, "must forgive the past—it never shall be repeated. I have in truth been very unfortunate, but my aunt has promised to assist me out of my difficulties, and we must coincide with her whim for the moment; she has always been teazing me to let her have the girl—I never liked to mention it to you because I know you would start at such a proposal; but she will be taken good care of, and go she must."

No. 30.

Mrs. Montague wept bitterly, but her husband assumed a tone of authority, he alternately soothed and threatened her; all these measures the gentle Laura firmly withstood, but when he disclosed the extent of his embarrassments, and promised that no day should elapse without bringing her little daughter to her embraces; in an agony of despair, she resigned her to the arms of the nurse who awaited her decision.

But to see her little treasure daily, to nourish it at least once at her fond bosom, to breathe the supplications of an aching heart to Heaven for its preservation—while, with a miser's avidity, she chid the hasty-footed time, that so rapidly stole away those few dear moments, was not long permitted her. Her husband's military career rendered it impossible for them to remain long in a situation. She could not abandon him, conscious that hers was the only voice capable of warning, hers the only accents capable of saving him from absolute destruction. Meanwhile, she was suffering under the certainty that her infant was nurturing in the midst of folly, by one incapable of inculcating one pure, one estimable feeling.

Unwilling to betray the melancholy that preyed on her heart, she sought by an exterior of cheerfulness, and the most prompt compliance with every reasonable wish, to attract her husband to his home, and embellish it with all those little acts of tenderness, which ought to have rendered it his best delight. But the frequent solitude of her pillow recalled her heart-rending anxieties, and many a bitter hour was devoted to unavailing tears.

It was in the autumn of 1816, that Colonel and Mrs. Montague returned to Vernon Park; and the little Laura, who had just then attained her tenth year, was to go on the morrow to pass a month with her delighted mother, who promised herself, during that period, not only to commence the eradication of many evil impressions, but even perhaps induce her papa not to suffer her to leave them again, at a period when a mother's care was so important to her.

The Colonel had dined from home, and Mrs. Montague with a thousand delightful visions in her delightful imagination, sat until two in the morning awaiting his return. The trampling of a horse roused her from her reverie: she ran to the window, the moon shone clearly on her husband's charger, which stood at the gate. She rung her bell loudly and sent a servant down, imagining he had dismounted, yet wondering his servant was not in attendance; but what was her terror on finding neither Montague nor his servant was there.

Alas! too soon the fatal cavalcade arrived, which bore her expiring husband. The quantity of wine he had taken had rendered him incapable of governing his steed, which had thrown him amidst a heap of stones, that were piled by the road side.

His distracted wife fell from one fainting fit into another, and was only recalled to recollection to learn the impossibility of his recovery, from the medical attendants who had been summoned. What a scene for so affectionate a heart, how soon were his numerous errors forgotten in his sufferings! how earnestly did she implore Heaven to restore him, from whom it seemed worse than death to be severed!

At five in the morning the unfortunate Montague breathed his last, in the arms of his Laura; and the fondly anticipated morning that brought the little girl to her mother's arms found the one a disconsolate widow, the other an orphan.

We will pass over the following months, during which Mrs. Montague, recalled by the maternal duties which yet bound her to life, gained the mastery of that sudden affliction which had threatened to overwhelm her. She arranged her husband's affairs, laid down a plan of economy for the future, and, with a few faithful domestics, retired to the elegant retreat where we have now found her.

But let me return to the stranger: he was conveyed to the chamber prepared for him. Warmth and the medicine he had taken, seemed to have a salutary effect, and a drowsiness stole over his senses. But he had continued insensible to his situation, and we found it requisite to seek some clue to his relations.

In the little pocket book, which was the only thing he possessed, I found a letter and read as follows:

" Dear Sir,

" Mademoiselle is no more! she expired on the evening of your departure at half-past eight; a good gentleman who entered with a neighbour saw my grief, and kindly offered every assistance—but it was too late, and he promised to take charge of the funeral expenses. Mademoiselle spoke of you to the last—her last thought was of you, as the enclosed letter will evince.

" I enclose you a ringlet of her hair—O sir! let me beseech you to be comforted.

" I remain, your afflicted and humble servant,

" MARIANNE."

" To Monsieur the Count de la Roche.

" This letter enclosed the following, which was written in French;—but whither has my anxiety to communicate, led me ?

" I have to apologize for taking up so much of your time, in my next I will enclose you the letter, with the remainder of the poor Frenchman's history.

" Believe me, my Adela, with every wish for your felicity.

" Your sincere friend,

" E. Drayton."

Adela received this letter with heartfelt pleasure ; she flattered herself Grenville would travel, and thus regain his health, which seemed so important to his estimable sister. She felt a strong interest in Mrs. Montague, whose story she had thus been made acquainted with, and felt deeply interested in the fate of the hapless exile, and his unfortunate daughter ; and she looked anxiously forward for the next letter, when the interesting narrative would be concluded.

Sir Theodore led his Adela through every favourite retreat ; he pointed out this verdant shade, that woodland recess, this gently sloping hill, that exquisite retirement; and found with real delight, that they conveyed equal pleasure to her bosom. How could it be otherwise? had they not grown with his growth, and increased with his strength ; had not his mind gathered its tones from their harmonies, and his sentiments their lustre from their tints ? The sunniness of morn gave delight to his heart, for it breathed of Adela, of innocence and love ; the shades of evening charmed her, for all things spoke of Theodore, the beloved, the esteemed, the deservedly happy.

CHAPTER LX.

May no distracting thoughts annoy
The holy calm of sacred love;
May all the hours be winged with joy
Which hover faithful hearts above !

Byron.

An elegant carriage was built for Mr. and Mrs. St. Clair and a chariot for Don Manuel, and, at the end of a fortnight, the Lodge was ready for their reception, and Sir Theodore saw, with regret, the excellent Mr. and Mrs. St. Clair, and the good Don Manuel depart. For Adela, he was aware a few weeks only would separate her from the scenes of his infancy, and he fondly looked forward to that moment as to the consummation of all his earthly felicity.

But Maria and Louisa Arnold arrived, and Sir Theodore received a letter from Clifford, naming the ensuing week for his visit, and accompanied by a manuscript which he had written, as a diversion of those thoughts which still would wander to the grave of Zephyrina.

" Let us hear it," said Adela. " Maria has her netting, Louisa her embroidery, and I my drawing, and you shall (if you please) read to us."

Sir Theodore was always obedient to the orders of so fair a commander; the morning was brilliant, they took their seats in a pavilion, surrounded by the most exquisite scenery, and Theodore, unfolding the manuscript, read as follows :—

KALIX AND ZELINA.—A LAPLAND TALE.

Ask the poor Laplander, rough Nature's child,
For what he'd change his hut and snow-clad wild?
Midst stately cities, still his heart would roam,
And pine in absence from his rugged home.

Kalix was the pride, the hope of his family, and in the hut of his father centred all that he or his sister, the gentle and duteous Ulla, could picture of human felicity. Their unsophisticated imaginations had never wandered beyond the bounds of their own rugged rocks and cloud-tipped mountains, whose summits are covered with everlasting snow, their barren heaths and sandy deserts.

Their long night of winter, it is true, was dark and cold, but the interior of their hut was warm, their fire cheering; and, by the light of their lamps, Ulla assisted her mother in making their garments or in spreading the social repast, while she listened to the tale of truth related by maternal solicitude, or sweetly sung their native ballads.

But their summer! what joy when the period had arrived for raising their tent, furnishing it with clean soft skins as seats and beds, adorning it with all Ulla's fanciful finery, and suspending the gaily embroidered curtain, worked by the hand of her mother when she first became a bride; which was guarded with all the reverence due to a family memento of domestic peace, comfort, and affection.

That period of felicity, when the new-born summer puts on her sunniest smile of beauty, when the snow has given place to the most delightful verdure, and the stranger is pressed to partake of the banquet of hospitality!

The father of Kalix was a herdsman; his rein-deer were numerous, and produced those comforts for which his neighbours accounted him wealthy. Their rein-deer fed, they clothed them, their skins formed their beds, fenced out the rigours of the winter, and formed their summer tents. Their milk the good Christian formed into cheese for their own use, as well as for sale at the neighbouring fairs, or Ulla made it into whey, which constituted their summer beverage.

One of these agile creatures fastened to a sledge, and guided by a cord attached to his horns, at the well-known voice of Kalix bounded over the trackless snows of winter, or carried him to the fair at Finland, where he sold their superabundant produce, and brought home the little luxuries their own village would not afford —the painted apron or handkerchief his mother most approved, or the trinkets with which he delighted to see his sister adorned.

*   *   *   *   *

It was at a festival in the tent of a neighbour that Kalix first beheld Zelina; her youthful loveliness formed a striking contrast with her aged and blind mother, whose side she never for a moment quitted; to whom she presented the best of everything that was offered her, and in whose bosom she placed the finest flowers, that she might enjoy their fragrance, though she could not behold them, while her eye beamed on that wasted form and pale cheek with the most animated tenderness.

"Alas!" said the aged mother to her hostess, "Zelina is my all—her unceasing love in anticipating my wishes, even before they are formed, her industry in supplying every want, her duteous care, stand in place of that sight of which Heaven has deprived me. Our winter hut is cheered by her song, whilst she prepares the nets which procure our subsistence. Where my comfort is concerned no labour tires, no difficulty checks her; for me she cheerfully encounters cold and danger; for me, with her young companions, she guides the skiff, drags the net, and hastens home to bring that comfort to which, without her, I am a stranger."

Zelina's eyes met those of Kalix, earnestly expressive of the interest he felt in her mother's eulogium. They were fixed in silent homage on so estimable a being, but she blushed and turned away. Her mother passed into the inner tent, and

Kalix having long awaited their return, at last heard that they had departed, and after some hours of festivity, in which he vainly attempted to participate, he attended his parents and sister to their tent.

But this image of the duteous Zelina was too deeply impressed to be forgotten and the heart of Kalix felt a new and painful void—when in reply to his inquiries, he could only learn that she was the daughter of a fisherman, who dying, had left only a hut, a skiff, a few nets, and his daughter's dutiful care, exertion and filial love to solace his widow, whose unceasing tears for his loss, had destroyed that sight already on the wane.

She is too interesting, too gentle to bear such occupations—Oh! that I could bring her to our hut, her voice united with my sister's would cheer the winter's night, and give an air of additional comfort to our happy home. But what do I say? would Kalix then take from her venerable parent her only joy, her only support? But she shall also be our inmate, she shall come with my daughter, and make our hut her home. She shall talk with my mother of days gone by, whilst my father sits and listens to them with his smile of benignity and goodness. Zelina shall assist Ulla with her occupations, and they shall mingle their sweet voices in the same song, whilst I will watch over all, wait on all the beloved circle till summer returns, and then we will unite our search for its first blooming offerings, and scatter them in the path that will lead our parents to their tent of joy and festivity.

But, alas! poor visionary, where is Zelina? where is her mother's dwelling? I shall perhaps never see her more! and with a head reclining on his hand, the young and enthusiastic Kalix saw the folly of a dream which had pictured scenes of bliss, raised obstacles to them, obviated those obstacles, formed plans for the future, and then awakened to the reality of disappointment.

* * * * * *

Meanwhile Zelina with her mother had entered their little skiff and returned to their tent, which was formed amidst a scene of luxuriant verdure and delightful solitude, which she had chosen as best suited to her widowed mother's habits and inclinations; and gladly would the good Ulla have devoted every hour of the balmy summer to so sweet a recess.

But Zelina's young companions had spoken in eloquent language of the festivals of their friends in the neighbouring villages. Each family formed some pleasing party; every mother arranged some little excursion that her boys and girls might be repaid for their long winter of labour and seclusion in the gaiety of that joyous season. And should not Zelina's step join in their dances, her voice mingle in their songs; should not her artless attractions excite the admiration of the young, as her virtues deservedly shared the esteem and approbation of their matrons and sires?

Alas! the time would soon arrive when she must return to dust, her spirit pass to the unknown country, and leave her Zelina lonely and unprotected like the desert flower that blossoms and fades unseen and unregarded. It was natural, therefore, that ere this hour, the good mother should wish to see her child the partner of some brave and worthy youth who would cherish her virtues, and make her happiness his care.

Ulla therefore arranged the before-mentioned little excursion, and Zelina reluctantly obeyed, for although hers was the season of youth, when the heart is alive to cheerfulness and joy, yet she feared her mother had sacrificed her own comfort in forming it.

But was Zelina the same happy, tranquil, unruffled being on her return? The glance of the stranger youth had awakened in her heart, a sentiment of inquietude never before experienced. Her duties were performed with the same steadiness, her aged parent equally the object of her tenderest solicitude, her devotion equally fervent; but whose form rushed on her memory amidst her domestic avocations whose glance of tender interest, had called forth her artless sigh—whose safety, whose bliss mingled in her innocent prayers? It was the stranger youth, and with a feeling of self-reprobation she tried to forget him.

* * * * *

The summer had passed away, and the earliest days of winter arrived; Kalix and Ulla had returned, with their parents, to their warmly sheltered hut; and their winter's occupations and duties recommenced.

It was on one of those nights, when the brilliant moon shone on the trackless snow of the plains, and elevated mountains, which Kalix must pass on his return from a neighbouring village; he sang the pains of absence and uncertainty:

> " Midst distant dangers I'd advance,
> To gain one sweet approving glance,
> O'er barren mountains climb my way,
> Through trackless deserts gladly stray—
> O'erpaid Zelina could I prove,
> That all is impossible to love."

Soroe, his young companion who returned with him, led his reindeer laden with the purchases they had made; their path lay along the banks of a river, a skiff bounded forward, and women's voices united their melody with the noise of the wind and waters.

Kalix paused, impelled by an indescribable feeling—one of those voices was that of Zelina, the song was sweetness and pathos itself,—it was Zelina that stood at the helm; he could not be mistaken!

"Take home my sledge, good Soroe," said he, "I will soon follow you," and he bounded forward to the brink of the river at which the skiff had nearly arrived.

The young females, who with Zelina had seized the period, ere the heaviness of winter had set in, to furnish their families with an additional quantity of fish, would have pushed off again, seeing a man on the shore; but he bent on one knee, placed his bow and arrows on the ground, and entreated them not to refuse a poor traveller a passage to the other side, as no other skiff was at hand, and the way by land would be long and dreary. They paused—that voice, that wellknown voice, yes! it was indeed the object of her daily imagination, and nightly dreams; and Zelina, to whom alone he was known, with a sentiment of mingled doubt and pleasure, gave her nod of assent to her companions, who instantly glided the skiff so near the shore, that Kalix could spring on board, and take his seat beside her whose image had long been engraven on his heart.

Nor did Kalix suffer the period, which sufficed to bear them to the opposite shore, to pass unimproved. The frank disclosure of the heart, replete with truth and tenderness was not unwelcome; and his entreaty that she would introduce him to her mother, conceded with all the artless promptitude of an innocent and uncorrupted mind, which needs not the restraint of etiquette, or the outward form of reluctance to veil its pure emotions; and leaving her young companions to secure the skiff and set aside her portion of its cargo, she conducted him to her mother who awaited her return.

Kalix was hospitably received; his own and his father's occupation, his number of reindeer recounted; and the good Ulla's countenance brightened, as he warmly pressed his suit and urged that in the event of its being conceded they should form one family, share one hut, and possess in common all those comforts, their more prosperous fortune had bestowed.

The good mother consented, and the decision now rested with the parents of Kalix, for Ulla would not have permitted her daughter to become an unwelcome inmate in any family however prosperous; nor would Zelina have promised her hand on any other terms than an honourable disclosure of their mutual sentiments; for to her pure and disinterested heart Kalix would have been equally dear, as the humblest fisherman that weathered the wintry tempest and foaming surge for his daily support.

The night devoted to the duties of hospitality on the part of Ulla—tales of tenderness and truth from the happy lover and smiles of innocence and sincerity from Zelina, passed rapidly away. All things bespoke the order, comfort, and neatness which with such a regulator may exist even in the lowliest hut, and he longed for the hour when he should be permitted to conduct her to share the luxuries of his paternal dwelling.

*   *   *   *   *   *   *

The kind-hearted Soroe received his hasty orders from his young friend,—at the first moment he wondered at his sudden abandonment of his sledge, his hailing, the skiff and hasty entrance on board; but he looked into his own heart and the enigma was quickly solved; he therefore took his seat on the sledge, which was followed by his own faithful reindeer, and pursued his solitary way to his neighbour's dwelling.

> Though barren wild, and dreary waste
> To meet my Ulla's smile I haste,
> Suns of my life! her beaming eyes
> Can cheer the gloom of wintry skies.
> Even now she chides my long delay,
> And dreads the storm the trackless way;
> Beloved of my soul! I come,
> Thy truth, my bliss—thy heart, my home.

Thus sang the honest and sincere Soroe, as the reindeer bounded towards his hut—which was situated beside that of his friend, to whose sister his faith had long been plighted.

"It is Kalix," said Ulla, as she sprang forward to unclose the door, in the hope that his friend might be with him, that they might at least exchange their meeting, and parting salutation.

The absence of her brother excited alarm, which only Soroe's soothing accents could lull into security, by the assurance of his speedy return—and this assurance she repeated to her parents, while he hastened to unharness and feed the faithful companions of their journey. Many hours, however, elapsed, the family had reluctantly retired to rest, and had arisen to their morning's repast, before his well-known signal announced his approach, and restored the wanderer to the embrace of his sister, and the blessings of his parents.

But Kalix was another being on his return: his bright eye, his light step, his countenance of contentment bespoke his heart free from the anxiety which had for so long a period oppressed it; and seating himself on the deer-skin beside his sister, he gave a candid relation of all that had occurred during their repast. He dwelt with powerful and natural eloquence upon the charms, the virtues of his Zelina—on her filial piety, and her excellent management in her humble dwelling.

But when he mentioned the name of her departed parent, the memory of earlier years recalled to the mind of his father an esteemed associate, from whom the diversity of their pursuits (the one being a herdsman and the other a fisherman) had at an after period divided them.

All was now hope and felicity, for the approval of his parents sanctioned his choice. Ulla longed to welcome his Zelina as her sister, and it was determined that, on the earliest dawn of summer, the double nuptials of Kalix and Zelina, and Ulla with Soroe, should be celebrated; and that, in the meantime, the aged parent should be invited to pass her winter with them that Ulla and Zelina might together make the requisite preparations. Kalix was the joyful messenger, the bearer of the friendly greetings of the family; and, accompanied by his friend Soroe, hastened to conduct them thither, so that, at this moment, the vision his fancy was at least in part realised.

And closely did Zelina and Ulla ply the needle, to form the garments requisite for the approaching happy occasion, whilst their parents cheered the long evenings with stories of their youth, interspersed by moral and appropriate observations from the good father; and cheerfully they spread the repast and hailed the return of their lovers, who hastened to lay the spoils of the chase at their feet.

All was at length in readiness, and Kalix and Soroe urged their parents to let the anxiously-anticipated nuptials take place immediately.

"Why," said Kalix, "defer our felicity another month? Shall we not hail the season of joy with a yet more ecstatic feeling when they are ours, beyond the danger of separation, and when I can transfer my constant anxiety for my sister on a brave and lawful protector?"

Much was urged in opposition to this entreaty, both by his father and the mother of Zelina. But the good Christian placed herself on the side of her children, and it was conceded, with this reservation on the part of Zelina, that she should be permitted to pass a few days previously with her early companions, that she might conclude some little family arrangements of her mother's, remove all they possessed from the hut, and give her young friends her nets, skiff, and tackle, as a parting present.

This stipulation reluctantly complied with, Kalix accompanied his mistress to the hut where her companions anxiously awaited her return; he clasped her to his heart, and retraced his solitary way, to count the lingering hours that yet delayed their union.

At length the eve of the long-anticipated day arrived. Eve of delight! for the morrow was to restore Zelina to her fondly expecting family.

All within the hut was comfort and order, their fires blazed cheerfully, additional lamps were lighted, and everything that could add to the morrow's festivity in readiness.

Zelina, the charm of every heart, was alone wanting! the fond mother turned her expectant ear to every breeze, and Kalix had prepared his sledge, drawn by his favourite reindeer, to receive her as she landed from the skiff, with a mantle of the finest fur to shield her from the cold; for, as the extreme inclemency of the season had passed, Zelina had determined, perhaps with a little caprice, or a playful exertion of that liberty she was so soon to resign—that Kalix should not fetch her from her native village, but that she would pass the river for the last time.

She, however, permitted him to meet her on its banks, which he now anxiously paced, while his eye awaited the first appearance of her distant skiff—but no skiff appeared, and a thousand melancholy presages thronged on the lover's fertile imagination.

* * * * * * * * *

Zelina wrapped her mantle around her.

"Stay, dearest girl, the night is dreary! clouds pass heavily over the moon, the waters are rough and foaming, the skiff will defy the hand that attempts to guide it! stay yet awhile, a few hours may bring a greater degree of calmness."

"But my beloved mother awaits me—already she has repined at an absence the longest we have ever known. My sister Ulla sings her song of joy, and complains that Zelina's voice does not mingle with its melody. The parents of my Kalix wait to give me their sacred blessing and heartfelt welcome, and Kalix, how will Kalix chide my delay! at this moment he reproaches me, and deems that my absence from the appointed spot arises from a feeling that ill accords with his own. Oh, I must away! yet think not beloved ones that your Zelina can ever forget ye! —our hours of infancy, our combined toil, our united duties, our little festivities shall dwell on her grateful memory through every hour allotted by the great author of all that is good! not shall even the bliss awaiting her, or the beloved one from whom it is to spring, wean her from her dear companions, her earliest friends."

As she ceased, her voice faltered; she clasped each in a warm embrace, and prepared to ascend the skiff which was laden with many a gift of affection, with many a bridal ornament, and where sat a friend of her departed father, to whom her mother had deputed the charge of conducting her child to the place appointed for Kalix to meet her.

"Yet stay, dearest Zelina," said a venerable matron, "at least respect those omens that are sent to warn us! last night a shadow obscured the moon's radiance, in a few minutes it passed away, but a twofold banner of crimson seemed to wave in the air. All the aged and wise who beheld it, deem it an omen of woe, dear child! tempt not the wrath of the Creator."

"Respected beings, thanks for your solicitude, but Zelina, in the performance of the earliest duties impressed on her mind, (duty to her parents, and a strict adherence to truth,) relies firmly on His protection, whose voice can lull the tempest into peace!"

"Oh! look not thus reproachfully! shall I disobey my mother and fail in my word, because a meteor has appeared in the sky?"

"Other eyes as well as ours have beheld it, dear Zelina; be cautioned."

"It must not be! accept the farewell of gratitude and affection."

So saying she lightly ascended the skiff, folded her mantle closely around her, waved her hand, and, taking her seat, offered up her innocent aspirations of piety to the Author of the wild and majestic scene around her.

* * * *

The slight clouds and tempestuous appearances that had awakened the fears of
    No. 31.

the good matrons, settled into a heavy tremendous blackness portending a storm. The winds howled over the heath, and Kalix's brave heart sunk within him, as he strained his eye-sight to discover Zelina's distant bark.

"Why, why," said he, "did I suffer her to come so long a distance without me? How will that fragile skiff live amidst these rough and unruly waters? Oh! she will be lost—we shall meet no more, we shall meet no more."

The thought was madness, he struck his forehead—beat his bosom, and the name of Zelina mingled with the gathering fury of the tempest. At length a momentary gleam of moonshine presented to his view the distant skiff, like a white speck on the foaming waters. It was now visible, now lost in the darkness and violence of the storm. Agonized, despairing—what should he do? Should she be lost in his sight? was he so near her and yet incapable of saving her? The skiff approached—in speechless agony he bent forward, the cold dews of death hung on his forehead, he groaned in anguish of soul. Ill-fated youth! an hour awaits thee beyond the power of human fortitude to support, of human reason to sustain. The darkness which had for a moment rendered his fate doubtful had passed away; the moon shed a melancholy gleam,—merciful Heaven! it disclosed to the distracted lover the skiff upset, and his Zelina lost in the waves. But even in the horrors of death the name of Kalix and that of her mother trembled on her lips, and she stretched her arms to the shore, where she knew he awaited her.

*   *   *   *   *

"'Tis a terrible night," said the anxious mother; "oh that my daughter and Kalix were here!"

Looks of solicitude were interchanged, but expressions of doubt relative to their safety were repressed from respect to the feelings of their guest. Soroe and the father repeatedly looked out into the storm, and Ulla and her mother knelt in fervent supplication. A loud knocking is at length heard at the door.

"Oh! they are here, now all our fears are repaid, our children are restored to us."

The good father and Soroe rush to the door, while Ulla and her mother prepare warm and dry garments, while the meek, patient, sightless parent, extends her arms and listens for the voice of her darling. Hapless mother! her form shall never more be pressed to thy bereaved bosom.

The door is unclosed—awful dispensation! what a sight awaits the father, mother, sister, friend! Dripping from the waters—pale, distracted, lost, their Kalix stands before them—his lip is pale and trembling, his eye red and wild, and in his arms the lifeless form of his bride.

The father groans in agony of soul, the mother and sister shriek and franticly tear their hair. Soroe runs to support the terrified Una, who raves for her child and supplicatingly demands the cause of all this woe.

"Why do you weep, dear mother?" exclaimed the unhappy youth, "she is here, I have brought her—Ulla, Zelina has returned, put on the bridal attire, let the festive board be spread—quick quick! or it will be too late! the demon of the storm thought to have separated us—but even in death we will be united!"

A loud laugh of anguish followed, he laid down the lifeless form of Zelina at the feet of her mother, sunk into a settled, gloomy, uninterrupted state of abstraction, and the night was passed in unavailing lamentations, and continued wailing.

The first emotions of violent grief having subsided, the anxious mother induced her son to change his clothing, but it was done mechanically, and without apparent consciousness; his eye was fixed on vacancy, and no observation could draw from him a reply.

*   *   *   *   *

At length the lifeless form of the departed one, was laid on her bridal couch, attired in her bridal vestments, her long hair braided up beneath the nuptial crown. The chain still hung on her bosom, suspending the little golden heart her lover had placed there on her departure. Alas! how little did he dream of such a re-union.

She was then wrapped closely round in linen, and placed in her coffin; on the following day the hapless Zelina was removed to her last silent habitation. Kalix, supported by his father and his friend, calmly followed. The sledge, which carried her to the river's banks, and which, drawn by his favourite rein-deer, had awaited his return, was now to be reversed over the coffin, in which her lover's bridal gifts were carefully deposited. Kalix had leaned gloomy and silent on his father, he had beheld the coffin arranged in its last resting-place, yet nothing had power to arouse him from his lethargy of woe.

But when the sledge was upturned over the grave, he pressed forward: all the agony of his situation—all the charms, the virtues, he had lost, and the awful manner he had lost her—rushed on his desolate heart. It seemed as though an eternity of calamity had been concentrated in that one gleam of returning memory, and throwing himself on the coffin, he uttered the bitterest self-reproaches, accused himself of having drawn her from her virtuous and peaceful seclusion, to devote her to the horrors of a watery grave, and pathetically called on the ang of death to resign his Zelina!

His heart-broken father did not attempt to console him, there are some sorrows which it is sacrilege to disturb. He at length, with the aid of Soroe, conveyed him to the hut, and placed him on a couch, where he appeared to sleep.

Happy to see him under the influence of repose, the fond mother stole softly to see what aid she could give her afflicted guest, whose dangerous state demanded their attention. She had not long been absent, when returning with Ulla, who had prepared him some refreshment, they found his bed deserted—they called him, they sought him in vain—they found him at his Zelina's grave.

Unhappy father! thy boy, the pride, the support of thy venerable age! his mother's bliss, who first awakened in her heart the sweetness of emotions, his sister's protector, lies cold as the snows that cover his Zelina's last retreat, and which he has chosen for his bridal pillow; yes, even in death we will be united, and too plainly was the assertion verified.

* * * * *

The coffin of Kalix was placed besides that of his bride, from whence the sledge was removed, and a shelter of skins, wood and turf, erected, forming a security against the inclemency of the winter.

It was near this sacred abode of fidelity and death that this heart-broken family erected their summer tent. The earliest flowers were formed into garlands to decorate it, and these disconsolate parents, yet more closely allied in their desolation, sat beside the tomb, and fondly anticipated the hour when it should be rised to receive them.

It was long ere these melancholy circumstances would permit Soroe to resume his prayer for the hand of his Ulla.

"No one can replace the brave, the duteous son you have lost," said he, "but at least allow me to inherit the performance of those duties which the spirit of my lamented friend will demand of me."

Soroe had mourned with them in their affliction—he had performed the last sad duties to the departed, his tears had mingled with those of Ulla over her brother's grave. They were united in love as they had been in woe. In winter no day passes but they together visit the tomb and carry spices, ornaments, and embroidery to deposit there. In summer they suspend the mossy couch of their first-born pledge of affection above it, and Ulla sings the songs her Zelina best loved, blending the sweetest recollections of the cradle with those of the tomb.

Alas! the voice that once mingled with their melody is for ever silent, nor shall the horn again be sounded by the brother of her heart to call his reindeer from the mountains!

Sir Theodore ceased, and the tears of his lovely auditors bespoke the interes the tale had excited in their bosoms. They all gave it the tribute of sincere applause, and expressed their anxiety to be introduced to his friend, who he described as uniting worth with talent to a very impressive degree.

It so happened that Sir Theodore had merely mentioned Clifford as a friend of his, he had not named him, so that Adela and her young friends remained in perfect ignorance of the person who was the subject of discourse. Judge then of their surprise, when, a few evenings after, he made his appearance, and Sir Theodore introduced him to his bride elect.

Here a strange confusion took place, for Adela had not mentioned her rencontre with Clifford, nor he his interview with her, for the reasons we have before stated. There was now no longer a motive for secresy, all was undisguised, and the lustre of Adela's charms shone with greater purity from former mystery.

Another surprise was yet in store for Clifford, when he was presented to the Miss Arnolds, and shook hands heartily with Mr. Arnold, on his and Mrs. A's. arrival, which was the day after, he instantly recognised his hospitable host, and renewed the bond of friendship with the more sincerity when he was informed how true a heart was offered to his acceptance.

But the day drew nigh from whence Sir Theodore was to date his felicity, when in the possession of all that was lovely in person and faultless in mind, he should regard himself as

"Above the vulgar joy divinely raised."

And he delighted in the contemplation of this prospect of bliss. The Arnolds with all the fervour of young hearts, seemed to live only in the sunshine of Adela's felicity, and Clifford's presence gave friendship to the ardour of tried affection.

Sir Theodore presented his Adela with a magnificent set of brilliants, which she gracefully accepted! Don Manuel also had a selection of jewels reset, as a present to his daughter and grand-daughter. Accompanied by Clifford he went at an early hour to the Lodge, where they were received by St. Clair and Don Manuel: Mrs. St. Clair and her lovely daughter appeared shortly afterwards, and Mr. and Mrs. Arnold and their daughters, who were to act as bridesmaids, formed the bridal party.

She came, beautiful, intellectual, unassuming, attired in all the graces of youth and innocence. Her serene bosom seemed to partake the sentiments of the being who adored her, and who regarded this happy moment as the fulfilment of all he had hitherto so fondly anticipated.

St. Clair gave her to the choice of her pure heart, and she chased away the stealing tear, to smile on those who received her with congratulations, fervently and sincerely offered, and returned to the Park, where there was an excellent dinner prepared ; from whence in the evening they set out for Beechwood, amidst the felicitations of this congenial party, where we will leave them to enjoy the autumn in its fullest luxuriance.

Mr. and Mrs. St. Clair persuaded the girls to ermain at the Lodge, but Mr. and Mrs. Arnold set off for their residence late in the ensuing week, the day after Clifford had departed.

"Let us see you, my dear young friend, after our return," said Arnold. Clifford promised he would, and St. Clair and Don Manuel pressed his hand fervently as he departed, for there was a degree of interest in his manner that won the heart, and carried it from its own recesses to find a place in the solitude of his.

The change of circumstance, the change of scene, had not however conspired to banish the remembrance of the interpreter from Don Manuel's bosom ; he felt astonished he should have gone without taking any leave beyond the letter, without any compensation of which he seemed to stand in need, and lastly it was a subject of surmise, how so young a man should possess an inherent independence which seemed to rest on no outward circumstance whatever.

Sir Theodore and Lady Villars returned from Beechwood that day month, they were received with all the affection the warmest hearts are susceptible of, by a mother, father, and grandsire, and the two dear girls who had waited to see them, and they were delighted to witness that the rose of health had resumed its station on her cheek.

Adela, ever ready to transmit her felicity to others, sought for the orphan of Lucy. "Why," said she, "should I carry my resentment to the poor infant; severely she suffered for her error, and her last hour bitterly repaid the past."

Sir Theodore accompanied her; she took the little orphan in her arms, fondly kissed it, and seeing that its grandmother was too much advanced in years to take charge of it, she hired a young nurse to be under her inspection, with directions for it to be taken once a week to the Park.

She was also solicitous to see the little one she had preserved from destruction, on that eventful night when Theodore had ventured forth in search of her: she went thither, the grateful parents knew not how to express their gratitude, the young mother fetched her child, and Adela, pleased with the blue eyes of the innocent, settled upon her an amount, which would prevent her from suffering from the casualties of life—she did not forget any one from whom she had received kindness. Sir Theodore adored his bride, their minds were so perfectly congenial that they appeared to be influenced by one feeling, to be governed by one heart.

CHAPTER LVI.

———— So frequent Death,
Sorrow he more than causes, he confounds;
For human sighs his rival strokes contend,
And makes distress distraction.—YOUNG.

LETTERS arrived at the Park, and Lady Villars looked anxiously for Mrs. Drayton's—she received it, and anxiously breaking it open, read as follows,—

"MY AMIABLE AND ESTEEMED FRIEND,—With sincere pleasure I received your reply to my last; allow me to congratulate you on your union, which has every appearance of felicity, for where love and fortune combine, there must be something extremely unfavourable to prevent it. May years of united happiness be your portion, and health, peace, and prosperity, weave their garlands around your united path!

"I have had a great deal of solicitude for poor La Roche, but I will go back to the time of his daughter's death, and the letter the young woman enclosed, which was as follows,—

"'To MONSIEUR THE COUNT DE LA ROCHE.—Alas, my father! to whom shall thy Heloise devote the last moments of a suffering existence but to thee? Heaven is my witness, how powerfully I have struggled against death on thy account, but it would not be.

"'Already he approaches with cruel rapidity, and in a few hours thy tears, and the few wild flowers that may spring on my grave, will be all that will recal the remembrance of thy Heloise.

"'Alas! my beloved, my venerable father, who will then console thee in thy exile?—who hush the griefs of a widowed heart to soften thy affections? who bid thee be comforted, and point to other scenes where my beloved mother, where Henri smilingly awaits us, and where our union shall be indissoluble.'"

The remaining lines were evidently the wanderings of a wild and distracted imagination, and rendered almost illegible by tears; a ringlet of beautiful hair was enclosed in the first, and while Caroline's tears streamed with mine on the perusal of these afflicting mementos of sacred affection, we refolded and returned them to their enclosure.

But our attention was soon called to our unfortunate guest, whose fever had considerably increased. Sometimes he called on the name of his wife, sometimes he would call on Henri, and then address Caroline as his daughter.

"My girl," he exclaimed, "my only tie to existence, since thy lamented mother was torn from my arms, how wilt thou endure the change from affluence to penury? the luxuries of our splendid home must now be exchanged for the humblest subsistence, and thy hand must fetch the water from the spring for our beverage. Oh! Heloise, how wilt thou repose on that bed of rushes? Sweet seraph, I dare not gaze on that smile of resignation. Sayest thou that for me thou canst endure all without repining? that thy hand shall smooth my pillow, and strew the rugged path of exile with roses?" he uttered a deep groan. "But no!" the convent bell is tolling, its melancholy vibration strikes to my soul. They tell me my child is no more—cold and silent! no vain regret shall ever more wound that motionless bosom. Yes, I will wander a pilgrim to her solitary grave. And Henri, too! brave and generous youth! vainly was thy arm nerved with valour in defence of thy young, thy lovely bride."

"Overpowered by numbers we saw thee fall, and my child, burying her hopeless anguish within her own broken heart, was driven forth an exiled wanderer, with her aged father." Here he wept bitterly. "Scoffed at here, repulsed there, where shall the exiled houseless wanderer find repose?"

"Dear sir," said I, "be composed, you are beneath the sheltering roof of those who are deeply interested in your misfortune. Be comforted! there are afflictions to which it is difficult to be at once resigned—but the hand that has wounded can heal, and the tranquil evening has followed many a day of stormy vicissitude." The stranger listened as I spoke.

"Was that the voice of my wife? it fell like music on my ear—but no, no! it cannot be, those accents spoke of peace, and my sorrows can end but in the grave."

Every hour now rendered his reason the more perturbed; much alarmed, I sent to call Mr. Harley, who found his patient's fever considerably increased, and ordered a composing draught.

"The malady," said he, "is more mental than bodily, the arrow of affliction has entered his soul, but quiet and care may yet restore him."

Although Laura was not sufficiently mistress of the French language to comprehend the whole of the pathetic tale—his affecting exclamations, together with what the letters had unfolded, her tears had fallen several times, and she whispered,—

"Oh Caroline, what would have become of the poor emigrant, if you had been as unfeeling as I was?"

"Dear girl, you feel your error, and I trust will never transgress again; but it is late, and you will require rest." Laura kissed Caroline and set off, and Mrs. Montague presently came to offer her services, which we declined with many acknowledgments.

"Dear mamma," said Caroline, "retire to rest, I will inform you if any change takes place."

"My love, you have not been accustomed to late hours; the morning will find you pale and languid."

Caroline would receive no denial: placid and docile on all other occasions, where virtue or benevolence claims her presence, she is unchangeable in her determinations. In another hour, our inmate became composed, I imprinted my farewell kiss on her forehead, and the following morning found her an unwearied attendant, beside the good housekeeper at the pillow of the stranger.

Many days elapsed without any favourable variation in the malady of the unfortunate La Roche; but Caroline's care, attention and sympathy, knew not a moment's pause. And well was that care repaid the first morning, when she saw him capable of reaching the breakfast parlour; where, in the most courtly language, he expressed his sense of our hospitality and the warm-hearted kindness of his young preserver.

The deportment of La Roche was not that of a being who conceives himself of one atom less importance in the scale of creation in the hour of adversity, than when he was the courted favourite of fortune, and had numbers ready to fly at his command; such a sentiment, as an acknowledgment that those who cherish it, conceive wealth superior to either worth or talent, can only be harboured by the most inferior minds; and La Roche received those many little acts of hospitality with the gentlemanly and graceful ease of one more accustomed to confer favours than to receive them.

Nor did my brother Albert show him less distinction—ill as he was, he felt the deepest commiseration for his sufferings, and every action was dictated by a delicate, generous, and superior mind.

Mrs. Montague paid us frequent visits, many circumstances of her past life were related, as an additional proof to those before stated that the most poignant afflictions may be mellowed by the healing hand of time, and that the Creator will dispense his benign consolations, and perfect peace to the heart, that resigns itself to His all-wise dispensations.

Caroline listened with a tear to his description of the horrors, that brought death and destruction on his family; levelled his spacious and splendid mansion with the dust, and drove him a wanderer from the land of his fathers,—that desolating hour that severed the tie, formed by a mutual and tried affection, and only a few days previously sanctified at the altar, where a fond father gave his lovely innocent child to the arms of his young and valliant friend.

"Can fancy form more finished happiness?"

He painted her fortitude amidst those soul-harrowing afflictions, her patience under the severest deprivations, her philosophical endurance while concealing the hourly consuming anguish that preyed on her soul, she sought to cheer him by the smile of filial tenderness—he described her industry, when, after their arrival in England, and inhabiting a solitary and humble abode, they sought in the mutual exertion of their talents, that had formed the amusement of brighter hours, as a medium of subsistence.

For the first few weeks they had been successful, but months had elapsed, during which a scanty provision was scarcely obtainable. At length the tender frame of his gentle Heloise sunk under the accumulation of want and calamity; and her situation overcoming the pride that had hitherto restrained him, he resolved to apply to an English nobleman, a former friend, who had frequently partaken of his hospitality, that he had not doubted, but that the moment the name of La Roche was announced, an equal hospitality would be extended, and the most prompt and ready assistance yielded them in their misfortunes.

Trembling, however, to leave his daughter (although attended by a young female, whose adversity had rendered her disinterestedly alive to their sorrow), it was decided that a letter should await his arrival at a small inn, at a village through which he must pass to the seat of the Duke of D——.

On his arrival at C——, with much difficulty he induced a servant to take his card; an hour elapsed, during which he was detained in the hall, and subject to a thousand insults from the pampered menials attending; when he received as a reply, that his grace was quite unconscious of ever having heard of such an individual, and at that moment too much engaged to admit of intercourse with strangers.

Chilled to the soul, the unfortunate stranger pursued his way back to the inn. It was too late to return, he had not money to pay for a bed, what should he do? He crept into a door-way, and when others were sharing repose and covering, he counted the weary hours shivering and destitute.

Morning found him unrefreshed and stiff with the cold, he wandered about not knowing whether to proceed homewards, a letter might arrive—it did, and having paid his last little amount, he perused the above-mentioned epistle.

"Scarcely had I read their heart-rending contents," said La Roche, "when my head became giddy, the shadows of death overspread my eyes, and I fell senseless. How long I remained in this situation I know not, but when I awoke to the wretched certainty of existence, I found myself lying on the ground outside the door, and heard a sort of altercation of which I seemed to be the object."

"Turn him out," said the landlady, "yes, surely we have something else to do besides attending to folks what can't pay!"

A person passing said,—"Poor old gentleman, he seems very ill."

"More likely intoxicated," replied his companion, and they passed on.

Faint, weary and desolate, my last tie to existence gone ; sunk into irremediable woe, yet urged on by that affection which clung even to the remains of my departed one ;   I thirsted for the relief of shedding my last tears over her, and following her to her dreamless bed, there to breathe the last sigh of an anguished and hopeless existence.

But it would not be ! my trembling limbs failed me, wild and frantic imaginations passed over my brain, the pangs of hunger united their torture, and I again sunk into a state of insensibility.

But the last vision that floated before my departing reason was the form of my beneficent young friend ; hers were the last accents that vibrated on my ear, and what afterwards occurred you, my kind preservers, best know.

And many an argument was used to reconcile the mourner to his fate ; nor did Caroline forget any one of her little acquirements in the hope of turning him from the melancholy of his reflections. Sometimes she mingled the touching melody of her voice with her harp ; sometimes she read to him the exquisite and affecting morality of Chateaubriand ; or conducting him to the gardens and shrubberies, would point out the autumnal flowers, that even then peeped forth on the declining year.

But the yellow leaf, the thickly-strewn path, were pictures of the desolation of the soul, and it was in vain that even Caroline's silver accents spoke of returning peace to the venerable exile.

The morning at length arrived for the much-regretted departure of the venerable La Roche ; his first point of destination was to the humble grave of his daughter ; and then, we had persuaded him to the prosecution of his former plan of subsistence, by the instruction of music.   Such was my advice ; because I conceived it would steal him from himself—but, in so advising, I had previously secured him a certainty in what I suggested, and furnished him with introductory letters to a circle of friends, with whom I possessed a sufficient degree of interest to secure him a satisfactory income until a favourable variation might occur in his fortune.

And with the most solicitous anxiety for the comfort of her departing guest, Caroline had arranged for him a portmanteau of fine linen ; Mrs. Montague sent him a travelling-cloak which might shield him from the severities of the approaching winter, and I united every other article of clothing proper for a gentleman.   To this, my brother added a fifty-pound note, which we enclosed in a pocket-book, and placed it in such a way that he might not discover it until he reached his destination ; and James carried his portmanteau to the coach, which passed the bottom of the grounds.

But where was Caroline?

Anxious and uneasy, relative to what might have been done for the present subsistence of her friend, yet not wishing to pry into her mamma's arrangements, the weeping Caroline had slipped into his pocket a little green silk purse, of her own netting ; it was adorned with a gold tassel on either end, and contained ten bright sovereigns, which Caroline had laid aside till she could lay it out satisfactorily ; what more interesting opportunity than the present ? and Caroline felt consoled as she stood at the portal, and watched the receding form of the venerable stranger.

So you see, my dear, I have got rid of my visitor ; my dear Rosalie returns to-morrow, and the next we shall set off for France—present my compliments to —Theodore.

CHAPTER LVII.

" Some say his spirit haunted him, some say
His conscience burthened him, both night and day."

DON MANUEL was sitting by the window one morning, when an elegant carriage drove up; a young gentleman got out and sent in his card.

"My young interpreter !" said Don Manuel, "ask him to walk, in." He wa scarcely recognisable, somewhat pale, thin, and differently dressed.

"My dear young friend," said Don Manuel, "I missed you all in a moment before I could offer you my acknowledgments for the numerous benefits you hav conferred upon me." Here Edwin entered into a detail of the various change that had taken place—his discovery of his mother—his recognition of his grand father, and all the singular varyings and windings that had led him to his presen destiny.

No, 32,

Don Manuel was astonished : "see," said he, "the hand of Providence in all things ; when you, my dear young friend, consented to be the medium of a message of kindness, you little expected it was to your mother ; when you stood beside the aged gentleman, you dreamed not it was your grandfather you were defending.   Well, thank Heaven, all has ended happily, and I am restored to an equally estimable family.   Here he introduced him to Mr. and Mrs. St. Clair, Sir Theodore and Lady Villars, and the Misses Arnold.   Edwin spent a most happy day and departed, bearing with him an impression indelible as it was sincere.

Edwin was particularly pleased with Lady Villars, Louisa and Maria Arnold, the latter of whom had won him by her sweetness ; and, when he took leave, he requested to have the honour to pay his respects again to so much worth and loveliness.

The Arnolds stayed and spent their Christmas at the Park, and it was indeed a scene of festivity and amusement.   Sir Theodore took his lady to London in the spring, and she returned into the country more than ever resolved to pass the greater portion of her time there, where she was bound by a correct taste, and an exquisite sensibility.

Don Manuel received letters from Spain, mentioning his brother's death, and his succession to his estates.   Mr. St. Clair went with him to dispose of his lands, castles, and other property, and Mrs. St. Clair spent the time they were absent at the Park.

Clifford was frequently with Sir Theodore.   There he had many opportunities of witnessing Louisa Arnold's amiable nature ; he saw her gentle, mild, intelligent ; he made her an offer of his hand and was accepted ; an union of peace was formed, softening every bitter remembrance and heightening every felicity.

Lady Villars gave her husband a pledge of affection during the ensuing year ; the youthful heir was the darling of every one ; and when the grandfather and great grandfather returned from Spain, the first that hailed their arrival was their grandson.   St. Clair pressed him to his heart with the fervour of parental love, and Don Manuel, kissing his little cheek, declared that he repaid the perils of the voyage.   Nor did Ralph forget the soft smiles and gentle offices of Ellen.   Sir Theodore urged him to bring her to the Park, where he made her his wife.

There was a beautiful farm on the estate, and Sir Theodore urged him to accept it.

"We shall thus be united," said he ; " our children will sport together beneath our native shades, and the union will be the stronger, from the remembrance of the past."

Ralph felt the gratitude the offer demanded ; he united his fate with the gentle Ellen, whose affection for her mistress could only be equalled by Ralph for his master.

Edwin, in his frequent visits at Mr. Arnold's and the Park, had seen so much of Maria, that he became passionately enamoured of her.   His mother and Sir Arthur saw her, approved his choice, and her father's consent being obtained, they were united.   From that moment no sorrow intruded at Heartfield Hall, and had it not been for those vestiges of sadness, when a departed parent would rush on the memory of a wife and son, who mutually mourned that he had not survived to share their comfort and enjoyment, they would have been most happy.

Lady Villars was an excellent mother, she devoted the morning to the nursery, and Sir Theodore thought she never looked so beautiful as when she was nourishing her infant at her bosom—

> "And soft on her ambrosial breast
> Sung the delighted babe to rest."

The cares of the mother for the infant were amply repaid, for he flourished and improved in beauty, and rewarded every anxiety.   Nor did old Jonathan lead a halcyon life ; disease began to creep on him, after an observation that all hope of reconciliation with his formerly despised relative had vanished.   He could no longer bear the sight of Mrs. Crawley, whose adoption he considered the cause of all his misery,   even her ravings had more of method than of madness in them ; for she incessantly   dwelt on subjects he would have wished for ever forgotton.   Several years elapsed, old Mrs. Crawley's death put the dissipated Robert in possession of funds, and not before he required them; for he kept several females in the most expensive style, and was eternally being brought up to the public offices for outrages and assaults in his nightly excursions; he was, in fact, on the very verge of ruin.

About this period, Mrs. Jonathan paid the debt of nature. Her husband had long considered her as the *primum mobile* of all evil, of all the disgrace he had suffered; in the neighbourhood, they considered her a very mischief-making old woman. She was very penurious, so that not many tears were likely to stream to her memory.

The old man parted with his carriage and establishment, and retired with only two servants to a small house. Every one said something weighed on his conscience, and in fact his countenance bespoke it. He suffered his hair to grow, neglected every thing like delicacy in appearance, and remained morning and evening enveloped in his old faded camlet cloak. Sometimes he walked stately and slow, at others, he set off and ran without any evident point in view, and the observation in general was, that he was not far from the state of his protegée.

In a few years Mrs. Crawley died, and left Robert once more at liberty, but not before he had expended his last shilling. He then paid a visit to Mr. Jonathan, and some say that a conversation passed between them, that induced a supply, to continue his routine of expenditure. But a striking difference was now evident in the manner of the old man: his nervous irritability was so great, he was obliged to resign his office as magistrate, he was incapable of attending his clerical duties even though the whole of his sermon was prepared for him, and he retired within a short walk of the Park to a retired cottage, where an old woman acted as servant and housekeeper to him. Sometimes he would watch the carriages of Don Manuel, Mrs. St. Clair, or that of Lady Villars returning to the Park, and take off his hat obsequiously, eager to catch a glance of those who were once his horror and detestation.

"Here," said Don Manuel, "is a striking lesson for the avaricious and unprincipled. My Adela and her mother are ready to compassionate the desolation of reason brought on by this degraded state of moral turpitude. Even St. Clair would fain add to his comforts. Why? that his accumulated wealth, which by the just visitation of Heaven he cannot destroy, should go to the unprincipled and depraved. No, my children, let him suffer in expiation, and wrong not the virtuous and ill-fated victim of adversity of what is justly his due."

St. Clair acknowledged the truth of this assertion, he turned to his own family —he there enjoyed all the felicity virtuous affection and wedded love could bestow. His Adela had given her Theodore another sweet pledge of tenderness, and he then saw all that infant innocence could pourtray to fascinate and charm.

Mrs. Drayton wrote to Lady Villars. She informed her of her brother's death of a lingering consumption. She said they had travelled from place to place in France in hopes of relief; that they had stopped some time in the environs, and no hope presenting itself of any favourable change, they had delayed their journey altogether; that he grew hourly worse, and that, conscious of his danger he was perfectly resigned to his fate. Mrs. Drayton thus continued her account o their return:—

"Three years had now already elapsed—one letter only, at an early period after poor La Roche's departure, had satisfied us as to his increasing tranquillity, and frequently amidst all our grief for my brother, our thoughts reverted to him with extreme interest, and many a prayer for the restoration of his peace.

"In the mean time Laura had gradually improved, and having lost the evil propensities given by her early education, had become the delight of her mother, and the beloved companion of Caroline and Rosalie."

"It was a fine evening, and the girls were returning with me from a walk, when we saw an elegant travelling chariot drive up to the gate, and a gentleman alight from it. I had just entered the hall, when his card was presented, and I approached to welcome the stranger."

"I presume, Madame, I have the honour to address Mrs. Drayton."

" I moved assentingly, and on leading the way to the drawing-room, he presented me with one of the caskets he had taken from the servant, and the other he put into the hands of Caroline."

" Miss Drayton, I believe, Madam. It is impossible to mistake that young lady from the description given of her, and by her departed and venerable friend La Roche."

" Merciful Heaven ! is he then no more ?"

" Caroline burst into tears, and I covered my face with my handkerchief, that I might overcome my emotion. The stranger then presented a second parcel to Caroline.

" I am your visitant, my dear Madam," said he, " on a painful duty, (because it is occasioned by the loss of a faithful friend) but pleasing since it is irremediable. because I am authorised to present Miss Drayton with the whole of these papers, as sole successor to the Count's immense property, restored to him by the re-instatement of the Bourbons on the throne of France.

" My departed friend, Madam, on his death-bed spoke fervently of his grateful remembrances of yourself, and begged me to present you with these jewels ; a brilliant ring of considerable value he intreated me to convey to Captain Grenville ; and another to a lady of the name of Montague."

Here I informed him I would with pleasure introduce him to Mrs. Montague, but my brother was unfortunately no more ! He expressed his regrets.

" As joint trustee with yourself, I shall be permitted to pass some hours with you, on whatever day of the approaching week is most convenient to yourself. Till then, Madam, accept my best wishes and my reluctant adieus !" The stranger arose, and declining to accept any refreshment, departed.

" Does it not seem just like an Arabian Night story ?" said Rosalie, leaning over Caroline's shoulder, whose unclosed casket lay sparkling before her, with emeralds and brilliants of the first water.

But Caroline's thoughts were in another direction, her tearful eyes retraced the characters written by her departed friend. She placed the letter in my hands and I read as follows :—

" To Miss Drayton :—" When the gentle hand of Caroline Drayton shall unclose this letter, her faithful—her *reconnoissant* friend will have sunk into that deep repose, from whence not even the cares of his benign and lovely preserver can ever again awaken him ! Bereaved of all that could give lustre to existence, heart-broken, desolate, of what avail could it be to obtain a restoration of that splendour once possessed, when the idolized beings who then shared it with me, and gave it its dearest, its only charm, are sleepers in the dust ? What do I say ? Ah ! rather inhabitants of the realms of bliss. Alas ! poor solitary ! the inmost recesses of the desert—the hermit's caverned cell were more congenial, and better suited to the few weary steps that yet remain to be traced in finishing thy pilgrimage. But the form of my young and gentle friend was ever present to my imagination, and I resolved to use that exertion for her which for myself I should recoil from.

" Yes ! even at this moment, when the approaching union with my wife—my Heloise, my Henri, fills every sense with ecstasy, and disarms death of his terrors, that hour when thy voice recalled me with cruel kindness, when thy tears fell on my pallid cheek—when thy nightly rest—thy daily pleasures were sacrificed to the aged houseless stranger, is yet strongly—vividly impressed on my memory, and believe me, Caroline, it is one of my sweetest hopes, amidst the state of bliss which I trust I shall share, that my Heloise with myself may be permitted to watch over and guard thy path throughout this chequered scene.

" Innocent and lovely as my departed child, may thine be a happier destiny ! Go as hitherto, form the consolation of the hopeless, cheer the desolate, and every pang thou shalt banish—every tear thy hand shall chase, shall bring down ten thousand blessings on thy head, while the thornless roses of innocence and peace shall spring beneath thy light and fairy footstep.

" Caroline, beloved child, farewell, sometimes give a sigh to the memory of

" La Roche."

"Venerable and lamented being," said Caroline, "can I ever forget thee? Oh that thy days had been prolonged, and returning peace had enabled thee yet through lngthened years to have enjoyed what thy bounty has bestowed."

"But my child," said I, "the broken heart no bonds can bind. Earth had lost its charm for the venerable mourner, and it would be cruelty to wish him back from his native skies.

"Wondrous and mysterious are the ways of Providence, and frequently when wealth and pride in calm security spurn the wretched from their sheltering roof, they dream not that the hand of the Creator is even in their desolation, and thus it shall pass away, for 'whom the Lord loveth, he chasteneth!'

"But the calamities of the excellent La Roche prepared him for a scene more congenial with his pure morality, nor did that sublime Creator, who gives his blessing to the virtuous heart, fail to watch over Caroline. Yes, my honoured young friend, He, who that night sawthe spreading flame—who saw you rush amidst danger and death, to the preservation of a little innocent—sent Theodore to the spot, and designed that by ways the most intricate you should meet and be reconciled. He who heard the sigh breathed in secret over the unfortunate, has rewarded it openly; and little as Caroline dreamed when she watched beside the pillow of sickness and despair, the apparently destitute La Roche would be the patron and bestower of her future fortune.

"Montreville is here, he has been so long put off by my poor brother's illness, his death, and other preventatives, that he will not now leave without his bride. Caroline does not write you now, because next week she intends to share the felicity of your society; and to bring Rosalie with her, who is grown beyond your imagiration. Charles will accompany them.—Adieu, my dear,

"Believe me ever yours,
"ELIZA DRAYTON."

This letter was replete with interest. Lady Villars had followed La Roche through every vicissitude, her tears had streamed for his misfortunes, and she now congratulated Caroline that he was beyond the reach of further evil. She was also pleased with the fortune her young friend had obtained, as it would be a more powerful means than she before possessed of fulfilling her heart's propensities, and she looked forward with delight to the promised visit.

CHAPTER LVIII.

Ah! well may we hope when this short life is gone,
To meet in some world of more permanent bliss,
For a smile or a grasp of the hand hastening on,
Is all we enjoy of each other in this.—MOORE.

AND Ralph was comfortably situated in his farm, and a smiling train of pretty innocents blessed and endeared his union. Don Manuel saw his great grandchildren with pride and pleasure. He recalled the time when his Aurora, Luiz, and Ambrosio sported amidst the gardens of the castle; when they chased butterflies, when they formed garlands with flowers, and enchanted him with their artless smiles. His mind revelled in the past, he transmitted it to the present, and the children of Adela became doubly dear. But this scene of felicity was not to last. One day, when walking with his little ones in the gardens of the Lodge, accompanied by Mr. St. Clair and Sir Theodore, he became suddenly indisposed, he was conveyed to the house, but it was ineffectual, and he expired in an hour after without a groan.

But the grave is the place to which we are all shaping our course, and old Jonathan soon felt himself weary, listless, and incapable of attending to his usual little avocations. He could not walk about, his health hourly declined, and the old servant wrote to tell Robert, who arrived as speedily as possible.   But his cares were ineffectual, he would take no nourishment to support his decaying strength, and he expired a day or two afterwards, unwept and unregretted by a single individual.

Robert superintended the funeral; he said he would have it plain, because the old man's habits were plain, and it was his last wish it might be so, and plain enough it was.

He slept unlamented, and all his possessions were inherited by a being who paid not the tribute of common respect to his memory.

Robert was now at the summit of his wishes; he had, by a system of chicanery, obtained the hand of the possessor of all this wealth; he held a charm over the free will of the old gentleman, and a few words only could at any time obtain his wishes, however reluctant on the part of the giver.

In the exultation he felt for the attainment of so much unexpected felicity, his head became giddy, and he fell into all the extravagancies we have described. Lured by his riches, the worthless and dissipated flocked around him, for his gold was their attraction, and rapidly enough they fleeced him.   Even his wife's awful situation had no check upon him, and when he heard of her death, no tear intruded to speak kindly of her memory.

At this time the letter arrived to warn him of Jonathan's death, and the whole of his property went to Robert.   But at his disposal it was not likely to last for ever. He had associates who would help him to consume, and mistresses who would assist him to destroy; and, as he had not an atom of foresight, this was an event that would in a very few years occur.

Sir Arthur died at an advanced age; in the interchange of the domestic virtues he had lived calm and contented with his daughter, his grandson, and his Maria; and his later years compensated for the affliction of the former.

There could not exist a more perfect picture of felicity than was evident in Sir Edwin and his lady, and they beheld children duteous as themselves, whose conduct reflected credit on their name.   Elizabeth left her cottage, and resided as housekeeper at Heartfield Hall, and the happy mother beheld her days renewed in her children.

Montreville obtained the faith of his lovely Caroline, whose worth had endeared her to his heart.   And a few years afterwards, Charles received his Rosalie's hand at the altar; and, although she was an orphan, totally unallied, she was welcomed with fervour into a family, who knew of no distinction but worth.   Her early beauty had ripened into the lustre of womanhood, and Charles, who had doted on her infant charms, now idolised their maturity.

Egerton frequently visited at the Park.   He had devoted his heart to Adela— passionate, generous, sincere, it was not to be diverted from its object.   He travelled, and returned a different being.   He had communed with his heart—the violence of his emotion was conquered, its petulance subdued, and a gentle feeling of friendship had taken its place.   Miss Egerton resided with her brother, she had devoted her whole life to him—she had travelled with him; and now returned to England, a striking proof that what is generally termed an old maid, may be a very amiable, a very intelligent, and a very happy being.

Mr. and Mrs. St. Clair, happy in each other, and in the restoration of that affluence which enables them to contribute to the wants, and alleviate the distresses of others, share at the Lodge the most perfect peace.   There they witness their Adela's felicity, who, at the Park, enjoys all that an affection the most unfading can bestow.   Boys graceful as their father, girls lovely as their mother, bless and endear their union.

THE END.

www.ingramcontent.com/pod-product-compliance
Lightning Source LLC
Chambersburg PA
CBHW080720290626
47170CB00017B/2805